D1094556

EARTH CALLED

ALSO BY P. C. CAST

P. C. CAST

EARTH CALLED

Tales of a New World

WEDNESDAY BOOKS
NEW YORK

First published in the United States by Wednesday Books, an imprint of St. Martin's Publishing Group

www.wednesdaybooks.com

Library of Congress Cataloging-in-Publication Data

Names: Cast, P. C., author.
Title: Earth Called / P.C. Cast.
Description: First. | New York: Wednesday Books, 2023. | Series: Tales of a New World; 4 | Audience: Ages 12–18.
Identifiers: LCCN 2022058227 | ISBN 9781250879431 (hardcover) | ISBN 9781250290076 (international, sold outside the U.S., subject to rights availability) | ISBN 9781250879448 (ebook)
Subjects: CYAC: Fantasy fiction. | LCGFT: Fantasy fiction. | Novels.
Classification: LCC PZ7.C2685827 Ear 2023 | DDC [Fic]—dc23
LC record available at https://lccn.loc.gov/2022058227

Our books may be purchased in bulk for promotional, educational, or business use. Please contact your local bookseller or the Macmillan Corporate and Premium Sales Department at 1-800-221-7945, extension 5442, or by email at MacmillanSpecialMarkets@macmillan.com.

First Edition: 2023

10   9   8   7   6   5   4   3   2   1

To the many fans of Tales of a New World who patiently waited for this book, encouraging and supporting me as I wrote it. Thank you for your loyalty and love. My fondest hope is that Earth Called *is worth your wait.*

EARTH CALLED

PROLOGUE

On the stallion Tulpar's mighty back, Dove sat straight and tall, awash in the love of her magnificent new Companion whose bond granted her the ability to see through his eyes.

"Oh, Tulpar! That is my pack! Those are my people! They will be your people, too! We just traveled so far. Over water and finally through those mountains and—"

The change came over Dove the moment Tulpar's gaze lifted from the Pack to the mountains from which they had just emerged. The joy slid from her face like tallow from a candle and was replaced by a frozen look of terror. Dove's face blanched almost colorless. Tears cascaded down the stallion's golden cheeks as he shared her feelings. When Dove spoke, her voice took on a familiar singsong tone that had Mari turning cold with fear.

> *"I see it now—they who follow*
> *blue like a wave—dark as the grave.*
> *We must fight Him—we must fight Him—with our last breath.*
> *He brings destruction and blight.*
> *He is Death!"*

CHAPTER 1

Dove collapsed, falling limp against Tulpar's neck. River didn't hesitate. She rushed to catch the eyeless girl as she began to topple from the stallion's back. Tulpar was nickering in distress while he craned his neck around and tried to nuzzle Dove.

"River! What's happening?" On her mare, Deinos, April thundered up, followed by a wide-eyed group of Riders, including a few haggard and sweat-covered stallions and their Riders—though a quick look confirmed to River that neither treacherous Clayton and Bard nor Skye and her Scout were among the group.

"Stop." River held up her hand and her sister and second-in-command of Herd Magenti pulled Deinos to a halt. "Keep the Herd back until I call you."

"Of course." April kneed Deinos around to face the horses galloping up.

"Anjo, steady Gho—I mean, Tulpar," said River.

Instantly, the big golden stallion stopped nickering in distress, though he did continue to nuzzle Dove.

The girl Dove had called Mari ran up. She had a big canine by her side, though he hesitated, remaining respectfully clear of the stallion's hooves, while his eyes never left Mari.

"Does anyone have water?" Mari asked as she dropped to her knees beside Dove.

"Yes, in his saddlebag. I'll get it." River hurried to yank free the water-skin, causing the blanket with Clayton's rolled-up deadly lasso to fall free. Grimly, River crammed it back into the saddlebag. She'd deal with Clayton and his treachery as soon as Dove and her newly bonded Tulpar were settled.

"Thank you," Mari said as she took the waterskin and poured a little on a strip of fabric she ripped from her tunic, dabbing Dove's pale face with the wet cloth. "Dove, can you hear me?"

The girl's body trembled and she sucked in a gasping breath. "Tulpar? Where is my Tulpar?"

The stallion whinnied softly and lipped her hair.

"He's right here." Mari took one of Dove's hands and guided it up to Tulpar's muzzle.

Dove's trembling stopped immediately as she stroked the stallion's muzzle and wide forehead.

"Dove, the vision you had—how immediate is the threat? Is Death here? Now?" Mari asked.

River felt a jolt of fear as she waited for the girl's answer. Were the dark words Dove had spoken before she fainted true and not just a strange, poetic metaphor for the life they left behind? Or did she speak of a literal "death" that followed them?

Dove lifted her head. "No. It is like what I felt about the Saleesh. The horrible thing is in the future, but it *is* there. It *will* happen. *He will come.*"

"He?" River asked.

Mari met her gaze. "Death. He's coming."

"I don't understand."

"I get visions," Dove said. "I believe they are from the Great Goddess of Life. And through Tulpar's eyes She showed me Death descending on the valley."

"But not immediately. Right, Dove?" Mari asked.

"No, not immediately. We have time. Though my intuition tells me not a lot of it," answered Dove.

"I'm going to need you to explain exactly what you mean," said River.

"There is a lot to explain," said Mari. "And we will tell you everything we know."

"That sounds like a good start, but first we have stallions that must be tended. We'll need to—"

"Please do not take Tulpar away from me. Please, oh please . . ." Dove's voice broke on a sob.

River quickly crouched beside Dove. "You do *not* need to worry about that. A Rider is never, ever separated from her Companion horse."

"You-you mean l-like when a puppy Chooses her Companion?" Dove asked shakily. "Once that happens the two are never separated."

River's gaze flicked from the young canine who was waiting several feet from them, staring unblinkingly at Mari, to her own Anjo, who stood just a few feet from River, watching her just as closely.

It is the same bond, Anjo spoke inside River's mind. *The canines are just as connected to their Companions. I can feel it—all the horses can.*

"Yes, it is like the canine and Companion bond," River said.

Dove stopped trembling and nodded, her shoulders collapsing in relief. "Then you understand."

"Of course we do. When a horse Chooses a Rider it is for life. You will never be apart from Tulpar. He would not allow it," River said.

"Exactly like our canine-Companion bond," said Mari.

"I feel better. I can stand now," Dove said.

"Okay, but take it easy." Mari and River helped Dove stand. The girl leaned against Tulpar's damp side, visibly drawing strength from the magnificent stallion. The moment it was clear that Dove was stable again, Mari turned to River.

"This is not how I imagined our first meeting would go, but my people and I are very glad to be here on the Plains of the Wind Riders. You already know her name, but Dove is also our Seer."

River couldn't stop her smile. "I am not surprised that Tulpar Chose a Seer. Did you know that our Herd, the Magenti, are led by Crystal Seers?"

"I know that you are led by women and that you are bonded to the magnificent creatures you ride, but I don't know much more than that—though I am eager to learn. I am Mari, Companion to Rigel, and one of the two Moon Women who lead this group that we call our Pack." Mari bowed her head respectfully as she opened her arms in a greeting that showed she carried no weapon and offered no ill will.

"And I am River, Rider to Anjo, who is Lead Mare of Herd Magenti Central." River, too, bowed her head respectfully, crossing her wrists over her heart in her own traditional greeting. "Welcome to the Plains of the Wind Riders." River gazed over Mari's shoulder to the group of sweaty stallions and concerned-looking Herdmembers gathered several yards off with April. River noticed that her mother was in the center of the group, gazing confidently at her daughter—and she felt a surge of gratitude for Dawn's faith in her ability to lead the Herd, even during an event as bizarre as a rogue stallion Choosing an eyeless stranger as his Rider.

River motioned to her watching Herd and April led them closer.

"I am happy to announce to Herd Magenti that our Herd Stallion, *Tulpar*"—she enunciated his name carefully—"has Chosen his Rider. Her name is Dove, and she is the Seer of this Pack." River nodded to Mari.

The Herd gasped and murmured in shock.

Mari made a slight gesture and her canine padded to her side. As soon as the Herd quieted, she spoke in a strong, clear voice. "I am Mari, one of the two Moon Women who lead our Pack, and this is my Companion, Rigel."

The Pack had reached the floor of the valley by then. They waited in a quiet group, several yards away. From that group another young woman stepped out. She had a thick length of dark hair that was dressed with beads and feathers. River felt a jolt of surprise when she realized that the girl was carrying a bright-eyed puppy in a sling across her chest—as if the pup was an infant.

"I am Sora, Companion to Chloe, and the second Moon Woman who leads our Pack," she said, bowing respectfully to River and then to the watching Herd.

"Mari, Sora, do you seek safe passage through our territory?" River asked. She held her breath waiting for the answer, knowing that whatever the Moon Women said would impact her Herd dramatically.

"No, River. We seek a place to settle—to live peacefully and honestly. We have traveled from far in the west, up the Umbria River, over Lost Lake and through the Rock Mountains, with your plains as our destination. We would like to petition your Herd—your people—to allow us to settle here. We are more than willing to share our talents and experience with you, that we all might be stronger and more prosperous together." Mari raised her voice so that it carried to the raptly listening Herd and Pack.

"Well, then, we have a lot to talk about in addition to Dove and her Tulpar." River met her mother's watchful gaze. Ever so slightly, Dawn nodded to her daughter, conveying confidence and agreement in one small movement. River drew a deep breath and turned to the Moon Women. "Mari, Sora, I would like to invite you and your Pack to be our guests. We were already planning to celebrate our victorious new Herd Stallion, Tulpar, and now we can add to the celebration the joyous fact that he has finally Chosen his Rider."

"My Pack and I gratefully accept your invitation. It has been a very long journey and we, too, would like to celebrate the end of our travels," Mari said.

"Is this all of your people?" River motioned to the waiting Pack.

"Yes, there are forty-two of us—and several canines, including many puppies," Sora added.

"You are welcome to enter our camp. There is plenty of room for your Pack to rest comfortably with us while we discuss the future," said River. "April, I am going to walk back to the campsite with Mari and Sora and their Pack. Please go ahead and begin having quarters in the cavern prepared for our guests."

"Yes, River." April nodded before turning Deinos, and, with the rest of the Herd, she trotted back to the campsite.

"River, will our canines be a disruption to your camp?" Mari asked.

River looked down at the canine at the girl's side. He was large but still had the gangly look of a colt. Her gaze went from him to the small nose and shiny eyes that peered from the pouch slung across Sora's chest. Then she met her mare's intelligent gaze.

These canines are no threat. I sense no danger from them—only curiosity, spoke her mare in River's mind.

"My Anjo doesn't believe your canines pose any threat, so they should not be a disruption, either."

"I assure you that they are no threat." Mari raised her voice. "Nik, Antreas, please join us with Laru and Bast."

Two men broke away from the Pack. One had a huge canine by his side and the other was obviously their guide as a Lynx accompanied him.

"River, this is my mate, Nik, and his Companion, Laru—who is also my Rigel's father." Nik bowed respectfully to River.

River returned the gesture before smiling at the other man. "I recognize you as a Lynx Companion and guide. Nearby Herds will be happy to hear there is a guide who has newly completed a journey. I know of several Riders who will be interested in your services."

"I am Antreas. My Companion is Bast." Antreas crossed his wrists over his heart and bowed in the Wind Rider salute. "Thank you for the kind offer of employment, but I am no longer a Lynx Guide. I have joined this Pack and will remain with them permanently—hopefully here on your beautiful plains."

River's curiosity was sparked. She'd never heard of a Lynx Guide abandoning his solitary profession and joining any group, but there would be time to ask questions later. She was very aware of how badly Tulpar needed to be cooled, as well as how haggard she appeared and felt.

"I'll look forward to getting to know your unusual Pack. This day keeps getting more and more interesting," River said.

"It sure does," said Dove happily. She was still leaning against Tulpar, only now it wasn't because she needed the support, but because she wanted to be close to the stallion.

River had never seen Tulpar look so relaxed. He rested his muzzle on the girl's shoulder, nuzzling her occasionally as Dove stroked his wide forehead.

Tulpar is finally content. He has Chosen his Rider; his loneliness is gone, Anjo told her Rider.

Her mare's words brought River great happiness, which she shared with Anjo.

"Dove, if you remount Tulpar you can ride him as we walk slowly back to camp. He has just been through a long, difficult race, and the walk will help him cool down," River said to the beautiful, eyeless girl.

Dove's smooth brow wrinkled in concentration. "Tulpar says he will need more than walking. Something about bathing him, caring for his muscles, and also he wants to eat a sweet, sticky mash. I—I do not know about any of those things."

"Don't worry. We'll teach you everything you need to know." River rested her hand comfortingly on the girl's shoulder.

At her touch Dove jumped, as if River's hand had been a hot brand.

"I'm sorry. I didn't mean to startle you—only to reassure you that you need not worry," River said.

Cheeks flushed, Dove smiled nervously. "Oh. Um. Thank you. And I wasn't startled. I should remount Tulpar now, though. He says he is getting stiff."

"Of course."

Tulpar dropped to his knees and, once again, River helped the mysterious, eyeless girl mount.

When Dove was astride, she smiled. "It is such a miracle. I see through his eyes. Nik! I used to imagine you with a permanent frown on your face. I am glad to see that was only an imagining."

"You really can see," Nik blurted.

"I can—through my Tulpar's eyes. Bast! You are even more beautiful than I imagined."

The Lynx coughed delicately and purred as she groomed herself.

Deinos calls. The guest quarters are in order, Anjo said. *And Tulpar is stiffening. He needs to be cared for properly.*

"Mari, Sora, if you and your Pack would follow us, we really do need to get back to camp." River tried to sound nonchalant, but it was important that Tulpar begin his reign as Herd Stallion healthy, and not lame from overuse.

"We're ready," Mari said. "And we're eager to meet the rest of your Herd."

River set the pace. Though she didn't mount Anjo, she walked briskly beside her mare as she snuck glances at the Pack, which followed close behind. They didn't look like the ragtag groups that staggered from the mountains asking for sanctuary or safe passage. This Pack appeared to be in excellent health. They wore beautifully woven clothes decorated with intricate patterns. Women far outnumbered men, which made the group especially colorful, as they had dressed their hair in feathers and beads and shells. The people seemed strong, though they also had the look of weary travelers. The litters they dragged were filled with supplies. The plants that were sprouting and practically overflowing the litters, as healthy as the humans who tended them, already intrigued River.

The canines also intrigued her. River thought the big canines were magnificent, but the puppies kept drawing her eye, especially the adorable black ones. Three of them were wrapped in slings, but as they'd begun walking to camp their Companions let them down, and now River counted a total of five pups bounding around, though they stayed carefully away from Anjo's and Tulpar's hooves.

"They're unexpectedly cute, aren't they?"

River pulled her gaze from the frolicking pups to return Mari's knowing smile. "They are."

"Two of them—those two little girls over there by the black Terrier, Fala, who is their mother—haven't Chosen their Companions yet. We're all waiting a little breathlessly to see who they do Choose."

"Do you not have a formal Presentation of Candidates for their Choosing?" River asked.

"No. Pups are allowed to Choose at their own pace, which usually happens between the time they are weaned and when they turn six months old—though there are exceptions," Nik spoke up.

His gaze slid to Sora, who grinned and said, "My Chloe is one of the exceptions. She Chose me before she was weaned. Your horses all Choose together?"

"Yes. They are Presented to their Candidates for Choosing the spring they're yearlings, though we have exceptions, too." River was walking beside Anjo. Tulpar—with Dove on his back—was to her left, and she gave the stallion a pointed look. "Tulpar is three years old. No horse has ever waited that long to Choose a Rider."

"Well, he had to wait for me to get here," Dove said as she leaned forward to hug the golden stallion's neck. Tulpar tossed his head and nickered softly. Dove giggled. "He says that I am worth the wait."

River studied the eyeless girl. "Tulpar is wise. It makes sense that he waited for his Seer, and now the Herd will know exactly why he didn't Choose a Rider as a yearling."

Mari lowered her voice, speaking for River's ears alone. "There really will be no problem with Dove being this stallion's Companion?"

River met Mari's gaze steadily. "I am Lead Mare Rider; I speak for my Herd. I give you my word there will be no problem with Dove being Tulpar's Rider."

Mari's breath left her at her first sight of the full might and beauty of Herd Magenti. Their campsite was spectacular in itself. Set in the middle of a lush valley of green in a circle marked by huge standing stones, it was a marvel of purple tents surrounding an enormous opening in the earth. The Herd was busy. Mari saw people gathering firewood, tending cooking cauldrons that were sending out delectable aromas to spice the air, hanging colorful laundry, repairing traps, and doing so much more that Mari could barely comprehend all the activity, though as the group passed, many people paused to smile and fist their crossed wrists over their hearts and call a welcome.

The Herdmembers did stare at Dove on her Tulpar—a lot. But Mari could hardly hold that against them. She found it difficult not to stare at Dove and her stallion. The happiness the girl and the horse shared was so tangible they almost glowed.

There were so many horses! As they entered camp, Nik captured Mari's hand, squeezing it with excitement.

"They're more fantastic than I imagined—and I've been imagining them since I was a child," Nik said.

River's gaze went to Nik. "Your people have visited us in the past?"

Nik nodded. "My father traveled to your plains many years ago when he was a young man. He brought back stories that intrigued me. My mother was an artist. She used to carve horses for me, but they did not capture the beauty of real horses . . ." Nik paused, cleared his throat, and then asked, "May I touch your Anjo?"

River glanced up at her mare.

Of course. He seems very nice. I would like to meet his canine as well.

"Anjo says yes, you may. And she would like to meet your very large canine," River said.

Nik's eyes widened in happy surprise. "That would be wonderful. Laru, ready to meet your first horse?"

At his side the big Shepherd's ears pricked at he studied the mare, and then his tail wagged enthusiastically.

"That's a yes," Nik said.

"I think I got that. The tail-wagging is a good thing, right?" River asked.

"Right," Nik said.

They'd come to the wide entrance of the cavern, where long lengths of dyed purple curtains waved lazily in the breeze and the swallowtail standard of Herd Magenti flew above it, decorated with white horsehair thread. The Pack halted. Anjo moved from her spot beside River, making her way to stand before Nik.

"Hello, Anjo. You are a great beauty," Nik said as he stroked the mare's smooth neck.

Then Anjo lowered her muzzle to sniff at Laru, who lifted his to her as they greeted each other. At Mari's side Rigel's entire body wriggled with the wagging of his tail.

"Mari, would your Companion like to greet Anjo, too?" River asked.

"Rigel, want to meet Anjo?" Mari had barely spoken the words when Rigel barked and sent her an image of him touching his nose to the big golden stallion's muzzle. "Um, he wants to say hello to Tulpar."

"Tulpar would like that!" Dove exclaimed. "And so would I. Tulpar is going to like the canines. He says they smell interesting."

Mari met River's gaze, and the Lead Mare Rider nodded.

"Well, go ahead. It's okay," Mari told Rigel, who rushed over to the stallion, trailing five black puppies in his wake. "Oh, no. I'm sorry." Mari hurried after the puppies as Jenna and Lily sprinted up.

"Dash, come back here! You're not supposed to be running on that leg!" Lily called.

"Khan! Behave yourself and stay away from those hooves," Jenna said as she jogged after her pup.

"Chloe! Come here, little girl!" Sora called. Her pup turned her head to look at Sora, whining pitifully. "I know the horses are interesting, but you're very little—and they are very big."

Dove giggled. "Oh, let them meet Tulpar. You do not need to worry. Tulpar says he will be careful. He would never harm a baby."

The stallion had lowered his head and was sniffing at the puppies and Rigel, and all the canines were happily huffing and wagging, some even perched on their butts, sitting up so that they could get closer to the horse.

"They look really tiny compared to Tulpar," Mari said.

"You do not need to worry. Tulpar will take care with them," River repeated Dove's assurance.

Mari sighed in relief and decided to simply watch the fun as the pups and the stallion made friends.

"River, everything is ready within for our guests," said April as she returned to the group. "Wow, they're really cute!"

"They are," River agreed. "Mari, Sora, Nik, Antreas—and the rest of the Pack whose names I do not yet know—this is my sister, April, who is also my Second."

Rose rushed up. At her side Fala was whining and shooting concerned looks at her litter. Both human and canine made a wide circle around Tulpar and Anjo as they approached the puppies.

"I am so sorry. I should have collected the pups as we got close to the camp," Rose said.

River smiled at the woman, who was trying to corral the squirming babies. "Young ones are always welcome within the Herd. And these pups are in no danger."

"River and April, this is Rose and her Fala, who is mother to this litter of puppies," said Mari.

"Fala—she is a different kind of canine than your Rigel and Laru, isn't she?" River asked.

"Yes, Fala and the puppies are Terriers. We have another Terrier with us named Cameron, but he'll be back toward the rear of the Pack with his mate and their young litter. Rigel and Laru and the rest of the big canines are Shepherds," Mari explained as the Terrier pups leaped around Tulpar, sniffing at and playing with the stallion.

"I'd like to touch one of the puppies, if that's okay," April said.

"Absolutely," said Rose. "Puppies like to be petted and played with."

April waded into the puppy pile and was instantly bombarded by wriggling bodies vying for her attention.

"They're very enthusiastic," River said, obviously trying not to laugh.

"Puppies are born friendly," said Rose.

"And precocious," added Sora.

"Sounds a lot like foals," said River.

By then there was a large group of Herdmembers gathered in a loose semicircle around the leaders of the Pack and the two horses, their attention riveted on the puppies. Mari took the opportunity to study the Herd and was instantly impressed by how fit everyone looked. Like River and April, they were dressed predominately in purple, but each Herdmember was unique. Some wore long, flowing cloaks over tunics and others—men and women—wore formfitting pants and tight, midriff-baring vests. They were a beautiful people with varying skin and hair colors, though they all held themselves with the same pride. They stood tall and strong, with a sense of open curiosity as well as togetherness that Mari found very appealing.

Their horses were spectacular. Like canines, they seemed to be allowed to roam freely. Their coats were shiny with health, their eyes bright and intelligent. As she stared at them, she understood Nik's excitement. The horses and their Riders were incredible. *Great Earth Mother, please let them see our value and accept us*, Mari prayed silently.

"I think we're causing a scene," Nik said.

"Everyone's just curious. Many of us have never seen a canine before— and I don't think any of us have seen puppies," said River. "I need to touch one, too. They look very fluffy."

"Go ahead. They love the attention," Rose said.

River was heading to the cluster of puppies when April exclaimed, "Ouch! Oooh, their little teeth are really sharp."

"I should have warned you about that," Rose said. "But they know better than to bite, no matter how playfully. Just tell the pup no."

"Oh, well then. No, little puppy. No biting," April scolded the girl pup sitting on her feet.

Suddenly, Mari felt a jolt of shock as April's expression completely changed. She dropped to her knees and took the puppy in her arms. "Oh, Cleo! No, I'm not mad at you. Of course I'm not. Your teeth are just really sharp, so you need to be careful."

A loud neigh suddenly sounded, followed by the pounding of hooves, and a young black horse with a white face rushed up to April and the pup she was clutching in her arms.

Her name is actually Cleopatra, but she says to call her Cleo.

The strange voice echoed in Mari's head. Mari stared at the young horse who was reaching out her muzzle to nuzzle the girl puppy.

Is that you, beautiful girl? Am I hearing you? Mari asked, more to herself than the young horse.

The filly turned her head so that Mari could look into her eye. *You hear me, Moon Woman. How strange . . .*

Mari stifled the urge to laugh hysterically and instead bowed her head slightly to the horse. *I am honored to hear you.*

"Wait, did she just call that pup by name?" Nik asked.

"She absolutely did," said Mari. "That little girl pup just Chose April."

Nik laughed, and then he raised his voice to shout joyfully, "The pup has Chosen!"

"What? Chosen? How—" River began to ask as she made her way to her sister, but before she could continue there was a painful yip at her feet as she accidentally stumbled over another puppy. "Oh! I'm sorry! I didn't even see you down there, little—"

River's eyes widened in shock—a shock that was mirrored in Mari's body as River continued to speak. "Kit? Your name is Kit!" River bent to scoop up the puppy as her gaze found Mari's. "Why did I hear her name in my head? And why am I filled with such incredible love and happiness that I did?"

Because she Chose you as her own, just like little Cleo Chose April. Anjo's response came before Mari could speak—and the Lead Mare's voice also echoed through the Moon Woman's mind.

"River, Kit told you her name because she has Chosen you as her Companion, just as Cleo has Chosen April," Mari explained, feeling dizzy with excitement and surprise.

River's expression mirrored her sister's. They blazed surprise and happiness like a rising summer sun. Anjo trotted to her Rider, lipping the puppy as Kit wriggled happily.

This canine is exceptional. I am going to like her very much.

Anjo's voice drifted through Mari's mind as she heard River say aloud, "I agree. Kit is definitely exceptional."

"The second pup has Chosen!" Nik shouted. And then he strode to River and April. Both girls were clutching and stroking their puppies, cooing to them as their horses sniffed and lipped the pups. "Do the two of you accept their Choice? Do you vow to love and care for these two canines for the rest of their lives?"

"How is this happening?" River asked, her eyes damp with happy tears.

Nik shrugged. "A pup's Choice cannot be influenced or understood—it can only be celebrated—and these two pups have definitely Chosen. Do you accept them?"

"Yes, I do," River said.

We do, Anjo echoed.

"Oh, yes, absolutely!" April said.

Yes! Yes! said Deinos.

Nik turned to face the watching Pack and the gathered Herd. "May the Sun bless them!"

"May the Sun bless them," echoed the pack.

Then each of the Pack canines raised their muzzle to the sky and howled joyfully.

From the Herd a tall, dark-skinned woman stepped forward. Mari instantly saw the resemblance between her, River, and April. At her side was an incredibly beautiful white mare. The woman held herself regally—like a queen or a goddess. Her beauty was timeless, and her gaze was strong and steady as it took in the Herd and then the Pack. Finally, she turned to River. Mari could see that her dark eyes were shining with emotion.

"Daughters, I would like to meet your new Companions."

"This is Kit," said River, holding up the pup so that her mother could stroke Kit's small, fluffy head.

"Hello, little Kit. Welcome to Herd Magenti," said the queenly woman.

"And this is Cleopatra, but she likes to be called Cleo," said April.

The girls' mother turned her attention to the second pup, smiling as she caressed the young one. "I am happy to meet you, Cleo. You made a wise Choice in my daughter. It seems this Pack has immediately become woven within our Herd," she said.

"It sure does," said River as she petted her puppy.

Mari noticed how, even though River was clearly obsessed with her new pup, the girl's gaze kept returning to Dove, still seated contentedly on the big stallion's back.

"'Woven'—that's an interesting choice of words." Mari spoke as she made her way to them. She met the tall, older woman's gaze and felt an instant rush of warmth as something within her eyes reminded Mari of her own beloved mother. "Many of us are from a Clan named Weaver, and we are experts at weaving."

River and April's mother smiled. "I thought I felt the hand of the Great Mother Mare in the events of today, and now I know."

"I feel it, too," River said. "Mari, this is my mother, Dawn, Rider of Echo, and retired Lead Mare Rider of our Herd."

"I'm glad to meet you, Dawn. I am Mari, Companion to Rigel, and Moon Woman to the Pack, along with my co-leader, Sora."

Sora, careful to keep an eye on her Chloe, who was still frolicking between Tulpar's hooves, bowed her head in acknowledgment of the introduction.

River's mother turned to her daughter. "Might you grant me the honor of making the announcement?"

River smiled and nodded. "Of course, Mother."

The woman turned to face the Pack. She spread her arms wide, and in a voice that carried throughout Pack and Herd alike she pronounced, "It is my great pleasure to welcome this Pack to the Plains of the Wind Riders— *your new home!*"

Her words were followed by a shocked silence. Just as Mari thought her heart might explode with happiness, Nik raised his fist in the air and shouted.

"Yes! We're home!"

Like a dam break, Nik's words released the Pack. They cheered and hugged one another, and then the Herdmembers surged forward, greeting them with warmth and welcome.

Rigel trotted to Mari, wagging his tail and grinning a canine smile. Mari bent and took his face in her hands, kissing his nose.

"Since I met you, my life has been filled with surprises."

Nik and Laru joined the two of them. Nik put his arm around Mari's shoulder and Laru pressed against her side. "I hope the surprises have been good."

"They have been magnificent, and I wouldn't have it any other way," she told her mate and their Companions as she wrapped her arms around Nik, Rigel, and Laru, feeling more belonging than she had ever felt before in her life.

And Rigel agreed with her—100 percent.

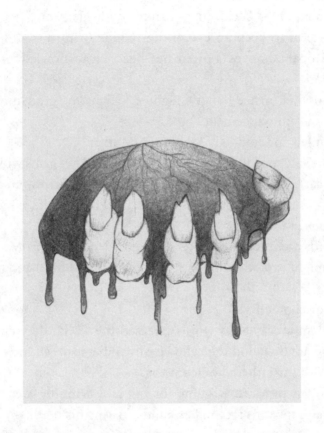

CHAPTER 2

The Goddess of Life, Who was known by many names, which included, but were not limited to, the Great Earth Mother, Yemaja, Sky Mother, Lilith, Buffalo Woman, and even Mother Mare, stirred in Her slumber deep within the womb of the earth. Though sleeping, the Goddess was always connected to the earth and Her people through dreams. She blessed, guided, comforted, created, and loved as She slept, weaving visions and omens and granting gifts as well as breathing the spark of life to the world above. She particularly enjoyed the dreams that came with the change of seasons, and though the Great Goddess delighted in spring when She was always at Her mightiest, there was something particularly satisfying about the close of summer when fields swelled with ripened crops and infants born in the spring began to toddle about and grow as tall as the long days of summer.

She sent blessings for a bountiful harvest through the veins of power within Her living earth, and allowed the gratitude of those who worshiped Her to wrap Her in pleasure—a feeling the Goddess had longed for since Her eternal lover, the God of Death, had awakened and left Her fertile bed. She did not wish to admit it, because it seemed impossible, but the Goddess was lonely. The dreaming Goddess frowned and murmured fretfully. *Surely Death should have slaked His thirst for power—for always wanting more, more, more—and returned to Me by now.*

The Goddess, the Great Earth Mother, reached out with the power of creation She wielded, and in Her dreams She found Him. In the time Death had been absent from Her bed and Her dreams He had taken on a fearful visage—one that was more beast than man—but that did not worry the Goddess. She loved all living things and could find value even in the most hideous of creatures. What did worry the Goddess were those Her lover had chosen with which to ally Himself. Bodies that should have returned to Her fertile earth had been reanimated. Men and women that should be human had been changed, twisted, forced into something that was neither human nor animal, but an abomination of both.

All around Him Death was surrounded by anger and the stench of misery, hatred, and a restless quest for something the awakened God of Death was incapable of providing those still living—peace and contentment.

As the Goddess studied Death more carefully, She began to realize the deep love She felt for Him had tainted Her opinion of His foray to earth. She understood that He was even more committed to creating chaos and destruction than He had been centuries before, when He had last awakened. Then His presence on earth had almost ended humanity. Had the Goddess not acted those many centuries ago, She would have had no more women to breathe fertility to, no more infants to dream into being, no more strong, young men to swell with desire.

Instead of acting rashly, the Great Goddess silently observed the God of Death until She was forced to face the truth. Her lover had forgotten the lesson He should have carried with Him into eternity—without life, death would eventually, inevitably consume itself.

I have turned my dreams from My love too long. Too long has He indulged in His most base nature—so long that He has forgotten the comfort of life and love and the balance Our combined dreams bring the earth.

My love, the Goddess whispered beguilingly through the powerful tendrils of Her dreams. *Hear Me, My love.*

The Goddess felt Death startle as Her voice drifted up through the layers of reality and finally Her spark of creation reached Him. He opened His arms and laughed aloud with such joy that even in Her sleep the familiar sound made the Goddess's lips tilt up.

"Ah, My love. How I have missed You."

As Death spoke, the Goddess watched Him stride away from the sad, somber group He led through a frigid mountain pass.

"Thaddeus, stay back!" Death snarled at a small, twisted man who attempted to follow Him. "I commune with the Goddess of Life, and shall do so in private. Await My next command with the rest of My army."

Death turned dismissively, but the Goddess continued to watch the man called Thaddeus and noted that though he did as Death commanded, the look he sent the God's back was filled with loathing.

Death strode around a bend in the path and stopped. "Where are You, My love? You have not left Me again, have You?"

I have never left You, My darling, My own. It is You Who have left the bed of Your beloved.

Death laughed joyfully again. "Ah, but only for the greater good. My love, look where I am. Look who I lead. When My army and I are through these mountains, we will rule a vast plain and all who flourish there will worship Me. When I have settled, I shall awaken You and the world will begin anew, ruled by Death *and* Life."

My own, You know that cannot be. I create through My dreams, balanced by Death at My side, eternally loving Me—eternally being tempered by life. You know what happened in the before time when You awakened and walked the earth. Death ruled and had You continued Your rule there would have been no mortals left to worship You, no verdant fields to sustain You, no succulent creatures to slake Your hunger.

Death scoffed, "Ah, but I learned from My mistake last time. Then I did not awaken You, My love. Your presence here, dwelling within a body that, like Mine, was mortal but is now so much more, will be a counterweight to death, as life always should be."

Sadness made the Goddess sink more heavily into the womb of Her beloved earth. *It cannot be. Mortals are too delicate, too easily broken. The presence of their Creator among them would be the end of humanity.*

He shrugged. "Then perhaps humanity needs to end! Or at least humanity as We have known it." His voice dropped to a conspiratorial whisper. "I planned to surprise You, but I see that I must reveal Myself now. I have begun to create! Yes, My love, Death is now a creator, too." Death threw His arms wide and bellowed victoriously.

More sadness washed against the smooth, earth-colored skin of the Goddess. She had, indeed, observed the creatures that followed Him. Some were walking abominations reanimated by restless spirits. Others were not new creations, but rather mutations that were not man and were not beast—but something less than either.

"My love? Why are You silent?"

The Goddess chose Her words carefully, only now truly understanding the danger Her love for Him had not allowed Her to see.

My own, return to Me. Rest in My arms. Submerge Yourself in My love. My verdant body aches for You. After You have sated that need We shall meet in our dreams and discuss this new world order You wish to create.

Death's sly gaze narrowed. "And should I visit You and fall back into Your arms, how then shall I return to the living world? Shall I languish for centuries until another mortal accidentally awakens me? No. Not even for You will I leave this world that is so alive, so vibrant, so very much Mine for the taking." His voice softened as He continued. "But rest easily, My love. Trust Me. You will understand when I awaken You. You will never want to sleep again, either."

The sadness that filled the Goddess of Life shifted as She listened to Death's arrogant words and changed to disappointment—and then solidified into resolve. He had learned nothing. Without Her to balance His mercurial desires, there was nothing to stop Death's destructive nature.

The only force stronger than death is life. The Goddess was the only thing that could end the darkness Death was so committed to that He could not see the truth of the destruction He sowed.

I shall rest, My own. And I shall dream of You in My arms.

"And while You slumber I shall continue to create a new world order for Us," Death said.

The Goddess withdrew from Her eternal lover and watched as He strode back to the abominations He called His creations.

Something flashed at the edge of Her vision as Death disappeared around the bend in the path and the Goddess turned Her attention to the glowing being of light that trudged slowly, sadly after the God. The Earth Mother touched the being with a dream tendril and was instantly flooded with misery as the doe's untimely end was revealed to the Goddess.

Sweet doe, Life frees you from the shackles of Death. Enter the Summerlands where you may frolic and forget that Death made you His slave.

The spirit of the doe lifted her head as an arch of light opened before her. With a happy leap and wag of her small white tail, the creature galloped joyously through the arch as it closed behind her.

The Goddess of Life hovered there, unnoticed by Death—Who was far too busy failing to command the doe to Him to sense Her presence.

That will slow Him. And now I shall warn them, My people, My mortals, My creations. They are the only things more beloved to Me than Death, and together we shall force Him back to slumber eternally in My arms where He belongs.

Quickly, easily, the Goddess of Life reached through Her dreams to find Her newest Seer, the blind mortal they called Dove, and sent her a warning that the faithful Seer spoke aloud to the people of the plains.

The Goddess should have been able to rest then, secure in the knowledge that Her people would be prepared for Death when He finally emerged from the mountains, but His blasphemy had been Her forewarning. Death truly believed He could create, could bring forth life, which meant He would think He no longer needed the Goddess of Life. He would walk the earth until He crushed every living thing beneath His cloven hooves.

Death could only be stopped by Life, and as He would no longer listen to Her—no longer be satisfied with resting in Her arms and dreaming balance to the world—She would have to come to Him, and for that the Goddess of Life required the aid of Her mortal children.

It would be tricky. It would not be easy to awaken Her, as to do so went against the ways of the Universe, but She believed in the intelligence, bravery, and tenacity of Her children. They would listen to Her voice. They would understand. They would do the right thing—no matter how difficult.

So, the Great Earth Mother, the Goddess of Life, reached through Her dreams once again and began to stir Her favorite children, those directly in the path of Death, to do Her will. With a resolute smile, the Goddess began by touching Her faithful Seer once again . . .

Dove came instantly awake—as did the magnificent stallion she slept cuddled against. He nickered softly and nuzzled her hair. Dove smiled and stroked his smooth coat.

"All is well, Tulpar, my beautiful boy. The Great Earth Mother whispered to me through my dream, serving notice that She is stirring and that I should prepare Her people to listen to Her signs and omens." The stallion blew gently in her face and she kissed his velvet muzzle. "No, we need not warn the Herd yet. We may rest and wait." Dove yawned mightily and laid her head down against his warm side as she pulled the blanket up more securely around her shoulders. She listened to see if she had awakened Lily and little Dash—her friend and her friend's Terrier Companion who shared the opulent tent Magenti had erected for their Herd Stallion—but except for the sweet puppy snores of Dash, everything was quiet. As Dove drifted contentedly back to sleep, she sent a silent prayer to the Goddess to Whom she had become so attached. *I hear You, Great Earth Mother. I am ready to do Your bidding— now and always.*

Mari slept soundly in Nik's arms with Rigel pressed warmly against her back. Her arm was draped across Nik's chest and her fingers rested on Laru's thick fur. The dream began with an awareness of those fingers, but instead of the big Shepherd's soft pelt, Mari's fingers were playing through water. Her dreaming attention sharpened and focused, and she saw that she was standing before a beautiful well that was in the middle of the Plains of the Wind Riders. It was situated in an area of the plains where the verdant land lifted to a small hillock from which Mari's dreaming self had an excellent view of a massive stone circle and the huge cave that opened into the earth behind it. Purple tents surrounded the cave. Riders and horses went about the business of a prosperous Herd. Over cook fires hung precious iron pots that bubbled and lent fragrance to the warm air. In a wide cleared area a group of Riders performed an intricate dance as they followed an instructor who led them through movements that flowed gracefully like water over river rock. Trees near the cave were filled with apples Wind Riders harvested while their horses grazed peacefully. Others tended large gardens, filling baskets with ripe vegetables. Mari could see that there were several massive skins stretched out in the sunlight to cure. It was a homey, peaceful scene, and even sleeping, Mari was amazed that they had finally made it here—had finally been accepted by the Wind Riders and welcomed to their new home.

The wind caused the water at her fingertips to lap against her skin, pulling her attention back to the well. Mari gazed down at the crystal water and felt a sizzle of surprise as she stared at her reflection. Behind her many Companions gathered: Rigel, Laru, Bast, Tulpar, and Anjo—as well as other animals Mari didn't recognize. As one, they stared at her with eyes filled with hope, as if they waited for her to do something, anything.

She turned, expecting the space behind her to be crowded, but she was completely alone—except for the sweet voice that sounded much like her mama and drifted to her on the perfumed breeze.

Remember, Mari, you are not alone. You are never alone. You will need them and they will be there for you. Remember . . .

River wanted to speak with her mother and her sister about the amazing events of the day—the successful Stallion Run, Clayton's treachery, and then, of course, the Pack. But after River had settled Mari and Sora and their people, learned the rudiments of how to care for their new Terrier Companions, and then ascertained that Clayton—along with half a dozen Stallion and Gelding Riders and two Mare Riders—had disappeared before he could be detained to await the justice of the Mare Council, River's exhaustion was so great that Anjo had been forced to complain *loudly* that her Rider must be left alone to rest and recover. Her mother had nodded in wise agreement with the Lead Mare and retreated from her tent for the night, taking April and little Cleo with her.

River tried to argue with them about leaving, but Anjo's snort and her own exhaustion won out. River was asleep almost as fast as her head touched her soft beaver pelt pillow.

The dream was so vivid River woke suddenly, shivering with cold.

Snow. There was so much snow, Anjo's sleepy voice echoed in River's mind. She yawned and nodded at the mare, who lay on her straw bed across the tent from River's sleeping pallet.

"I know. It was so realistic it made me cold." River shivered again. Kit, the little black Terrier curled warmly against her body, stirred, whimpered, and sent River an image of blinding whiteness that was right out of her dream. "It's okay, sweetie. Go back to sleep. I'll keep you warm." The puppy grunted contentedly as River snuggled her more closely.

River was just falling back to sleep when another image from the dream lifted through her tired mind. In the center of the blizzard there had been an incredibly beautiful quartz crystal. It was huge, easily the size of River's head, and threaded throughout it were tendrils of green—like fronds of ferns had been trapped within it when the earth created the beautiful stone.

It is a powerful water-calling crystal. Anjo's sleepy voice filled her mind.

"Yeah. I think I remember my grandmother using a crystal like that when I was a little girl, but I haven't seen it in decades." She shrugged sleepily. "Not like we've needed it. Spring rains have been plentiful for years, but help me to remember to ask Mother about it if rain is scarce next summer, though it appearing to me in the middle of a blizzard is strange. Like anyone would want to call down a snowstorm?" River yawned. "Good night, my beautiful girl."

Good night, my precious Rider . . .

And the three bonded creatures slept.

The only time Ralina, Storyteller to the extinct Tribe of the Trees, could escape the death-filled hell her life had become was when she slept, though sleep was difficult and uncomfortable as they trudged through the increasingly frigid Rock Mountains. She'd often thought she should just wander away—pretend that she needed to relieve herself and leave the path to never return. Though it would mean the end of her life, it would be a relief to never have to follow the vile God of Death and His army of subhumans and reanimated corpses ever again.

Then her big Shepherd, Bear, would whine and press against her side and Renard would look at her and a rare smile would crease the corners of his expressive green eyes—beside him his faithful Shepherd, Kong, would bark encouragement and Renard's father, Daniel, would say something kind to her. Then Ralina would remember why she must live. Not simply to tell Death's horrid story. Not simply to try to collect the God's terrible secrets until she found something she could use to defeat Him, but because she could not sentence her beloved Companion to die with her, and Renard, Kong, and Daniel to face Death's wrath in her place.

That day the army had stopped even earlier than was their norm. Death had suddenly become excited and had stridden up the narrow trail the spirit of the poor, sacrificed doe had been leading them, ordering the army to stay back—stay away. Usually, He would have commanded Ralina attend Him so she could add more to what He believed to be the magnificent ballad she was creating to chronicle His victorious journey to the Plains of the Wind Riders, but that day He hadn't called her to Him and she had allowed herself to savor that small reprieve.

When He'd returned from whatever had called Him away from them, Death had seemed as baffled as He was angry. The spirit of the innocent doe He'd called to Him and then slaughtered and enslaved as their guide through the mountain passages had disappeared. The little creature had been tied to the God of Death, miserably doing His bidding for unending day after day, but suddenly she would not answer His call.

Silently, Ralina cheered the doe, *Good for you, little one. You figured out how to escape Him.*

While the army awaited the next command from their temperamental god, Renard had surprised Ralina with a small cave-like shelter just off the trail he'd packed with thick blue Saleesh blankets.

"Rest until He forces us to continue again." Renard spoke kindly as Bear lay down on their makeshift pallet and looked expectantly at his Companion to join him.

"No, I'll help you and Kong and your dad forage for hare and anything green we can stuff them with," she said, though she looked longingly at the little refuge of blankets and warmth.

"Father and I will hunt. You must rest. You never know when He is going to command you entertain Him with more stories, and your ability to recall those stories is all that keeps us from being Death's target. Rest," her lover repeated.

"Okay, yes. You're right. I-I've had so little sleep since we left Lost Lake that my mind is foggy." She reached out and squeezed his hand. "Thank you for your kindness."

Renard raised her hand to his lips. "It is my pleasure to be kind to you."

Wearily, Ralina allowed herself to lie beside Bear, using his shoulder as a warm, furry pillow. Renard covered both canine and Companion with another blanket, touched her hair gently, and then left, calling

Kong to him as he and his father picked up their crossbows and a brace of arrows.

Ralina's eyelids became heavy as she watched her young lover, his Shepherd, and his father head off the trail to hunt. "It's strange, but somehow in the middle of this horror, I think I have fallen in love with him."

Bear's tail thumped and he filled her with warmth and happiness.

"I'm glad you like him, too," Ralina muttered sleepily. Her eyelids fluttered and then closed as the Storyteller of the Tribe of the Trees fell deeply asleep.

The dream began immediately. It was white. Everything was white. Snow was everywhere. The flakes weren't like the delicate carvings the most talented of the Tribe's artists used to decorate their city in the trees with. Instead, the flakes were tiny, but there were so many of them that they seemed to crowd the very air around her making it as difficult to breathe as to see.

Come . . .

The sweet voice was filled with compassion and in her dream Ralina turned in a tight circle, trying to find who was speaking.

Then a brighter flicker of white caught her attention and before her was a doe. She looked much like the spirit of the poor beast Death had used as His guide through the treacherous Rock Mountains, but this deer was alive, and even a purer white than the snow. Her eyes were ebony, exquisitely beautiful, and filled with intelligence. She nodded her magnificent head at Ralina and then turned her back and trotted away—off the trail. Before she was enveloped in the blinding snow, the doe looked back at Ralina and the sweet voice rang between them.

When you see her, follow her. You have done well, and your time with Death has come to an end.

Even sleeping, Ralina's heart felt as if it would explode from her chest at the anticipation the gentle words caused.

"Leave?" she asked the doe who still stared at her. "But I can't without Renard and his father. I can't leave them here to face Death. Plus, He'll just come after me. I can't get away from Him."

When the snow comes and the doe calls to you, follow her. Bring your loved ones. Your time with Death has come to an end, Storyteller. Your future is not here. You have many more stories yet to tell . . .

Then the white doe disappeared into the blizzard.

"Storyteller, to Me!" Death bellowed.

Ralina jolted awake at the terrible sound of His voice. "I hear You, my Lord, and I come!" Ralina called through cupped hands as she struggled to unwrap herself from the blankets she'd burrowed within, sharing Bear's warmth. When Bear automatically got up to follow her, Ralina went to her knees and kissed his muzzle. "Stay here. I don't like the way He looks at you." With a grumble that clearly said he'd rather be with her, Bear lay reluctantly back within their nest of blankets.

Ralina kept one blanket wrapped around her shoulders. Shivering, she hurried to the head of the long line of Milks, the corpses Death had reanimated, which clustered in strange little groups staring listlessly at nothing, and the Warriors, both Skin Stealers and those that used to be part of the magnificent Tribe of the Trees, who daily became more beast than human.

She found Death warming Himself before a massive campfire. He sat on a huge boulder that had been draped with blankets dyed the beautiful blue that marked them as belonging to the slaughtered Saleesh people. Four young women He called His Handmaids waited on Him. One fed Him strips of venison she cut from a haunch rotating over a more sedate cook fire. Two of them rubbed His broad, furred shoulders. The fourth young woman, barely past puberty, sat on His lap and kissed His thick neck as she rocked rhythmically against Him. Ralina noted, not for the first time, that these women were also becoming more animalistic—though the creature Death had flayed and packed into their skin-sloughing wounds had been a small, beautiful hare He'd captured alive. So, while Death's Warriors morphed into nightmarish, bestial beings, His Handmaids grew softer, rounder, more timid and biddable.

Ralina pitied them, those poor girls whose wills Death had subverted, but they also sickened and terrified her because the Storyteller knew that it was only her wits and the mercurial whim of a terrible god that kept her from becoming one of them—or worse.

"Ah, Storyteller. There you are. I find that My guide is suddenly absent, and I would like you to come with Me as I claim another—a better, stronger guide. It should add depth to the ballad you're creating."

Ralina bowed her head. "Of course, my Lord."

"Excellent. Now, let us begin." Death stood, absently knocking the girl from His lap and roughly brushing the others aside. He flung back the lush cloak He wore—more of the spoils that came from the destruction of the Saleesh—threw back His massive, antlered head, and bellowed so loudly that the pines around them quivered in response.

He drew a deep breath, which expanded His enormous, fur-covered chest, and then bellowed again.

The sound was like nothing Ralina had heard from Him before. The God of Death usually bellowed like a rutting stag, but this noise was more guttural, deeper, more dangerous.

Ralina's stomach heaved. What was Death calling?

"Come, Storyteller." His cloven hooves bit the dirt of the path and rang against the old iron rails He trod on as the God paced away from His raptly watching army.

Thaddeus, the disgusting little man who had betrayed the Tribe of the Trees for power and greed, hurried after Death, almost knocking Ralina over as he surged past her with a sneer.

Death turned and frowned. "Tell me, *Thaddeus*, when did I change your name to Storyteller?"

Thaddeus's back had begun to hunch, as if he might do better walking on his hands and knees than his feet, so he had to twist his head oddly to look up at the God. As he spoke, his newly elongated canine teeth gleamed with spittle and malice. "You did not change my name, my Lord."

"Exactly. So you shall wait here, tending My cook fire and My succulent venison haunch until I return." Death turned His back to Thaddeus and continued away from the army. "Storyteller, come."

As Ralina moved around Thaddeus, she resisted the urge to knock him aside. Death might find it amusing, but the God also might be offended that she took it upon herself to lash out at Thaddeus.

Your time with Death has come to an end, Storyteller.

The words spoken so sweetly, so kindly, in her dream lifted from Ralina's memory. Though she did not truly believe them, they did lighten her mood as she left Thaddeus and the army behind—following the hoofprints of Death.

Death finally stopped after Ralina had trudged after Him long enough that even in the bone-chilling cold she'd begun to sweat. The narrow rusted rail path the spirit of the doe had been leading them along had widened into a valley, which surprised Ralina. There had been no breaks from the sheer rocks that had flanked their trail for many days, but here the grass still showed green-and-yellow-leafed aspen trees surrounded the area.

"It's lovely here." Ralina hadn't realized she'd spoken the thought aloud until Death responded.

"It will be even more lovely in the plains away from these mountains where land will stretch around us, fertile and ready to be ruled by a living god."

Ralina opened her mouth to ask Death a question but thought better of it and pressed her lips into a line. However, the god was observant when He wished to be.

"If you have a question, ask it of Me, but first I shall repeat My call. We will have plenty of time to speak while we wait for him." Then Death threw back His antlered head and bellowed again and again, the horrible, dark cry that was a clarion call for something Ralina absolutely did not want to meet.

"That should bring him to Me." Death wiped saliva from His mouth and smiled at Ralina. "Now, what is it you wish to ask your god?"

Ralina hesitated only long enough to order her thoughts. From experience she knew that Death's moods were mercurial. One wrong word could change Him from amiable to deadly.

"Well? What is it?" He stomped a hoof impatiently and then His annoyed expression changed to slyness. "Ask your question, Storyteller—any question—and I shall answer it, but then I will ask you a question in return."

Ralina blinked in surprise at the god. "My Lord, You may always ask me anything."

"Of course, of course." He waved away her words. "But today I feel like playing this game with you. So, ask—I shall answer. Then it will be your turn to answer Me."

Ralina's stomach turned with anxiety. *What could He possibly want to ask me?* But she really had no choice but to play the god's game. "Yes, my Lord. I will be happy to answer any question You have.

"I was wondering—for Your ballad I am creating, of course—how do You plan to defeat the Wind Riders? What I know about them is only from stories, but there are thousands of Rider/Companion teams that fill five Great Herds. Your army is mighty, but will we not be badly outnumbered?" Ralina held her breath as she waited to see if Death would take offense to her question, but He only nodded thoughtfully and scratched His bearded chin contemplatively as He answered her.

"I have heard the same from Thaddeus. He has spoken at length about the power of the Wind Riders—though he believes we will have no problem defeating them. And we will not, but only because I have planned to drastically reduce their numbers, *before* we battle them."

Ralina's stomach lurched as she realized what His plan must be. "You're going to infect the plains with the sloughing disease."

"Oh, not the plains. Just the Herds. I learned from my defeat of the Tribe of the Trees that I must not make the mistake of infecting the land I wish to rule."

"Then, what will you do?"

His smile was feral. "Play close attention to this plan, Storyteller. It will, indeed, make an excellent verse in your ballad. I will send out our men— just one or two at a time. They will track Riders and then stealthily infect them by slipping tainted meat into their supplies. I will even tell them not to allow the Riders to see them, so it will seem as if the infection has no source." Death chuckled. "That is, of course, unless we happen upon a group of Wind Riders. Then I shall capture them, infect them, and then offer them the cure, which they will take if they want to live. Then I will control them and their horses."

Ralina stared at Him, unable to speak as she remembered the horrors of her beloved Tribe being poisoned in much this same manner, but the god wasn't watching her. He was speaking animatedly as if she was an applauding audience.

"Yes, the more I think on it the more I believe that we will get lucky and come upon a group of Wind Riders. I will pretend as if My people and I are journeying through their lands and even ask for directions, invite them to sup with us, and serve them tainted meat. Then when the Herds are ill— dying and desperate—I will graciously offer My cure." Death laughed again. "I may defeat the powerful Wind Riders without so much as one battle." His gaze snapped to hers. "What do you think of My plan, Storyteller?"

Ralina told the absolute truth. "I think You will very likely be successful."

"Indeed, indeed." Death threw back His head again and bellowed. "I am somewhat surprised that it takes so long for my new guide to come to Me. It is good that you are with Me. I do enjoy talking with you, My Storyteller, but now it is my turn to ask you a question. Think back to the day I first arrived at the Tribe of the Trees."

Death was watching her expectantly, so Ralina hid her horror at remembering that terrible day. "Yes, my Lord. I remember."

"Excellent. There was a young woman who called down fire from the sky before she escaped with others to the river. Who was that woman?"

Ralina blinked in surprise but answered Death's question, "Her name is Mari. She is a healer for people called Earth Walkers, or scratchers."

"Do you know her well?" Death asked.

Ralina shook her head. "No. I only met her that one time."

Death frowned. "She was with your Tribe. You must know something about her."

Ralina blew out a long breath. "I only know that she is of mixed blood. Her mother was an Earth Walker and her father was one of our Tribesmen, which is why she could call down sunfire."

"Ah, that was the fire she called from the sky."

"Yes. It's a rare skill."

Death nodded as if that pleased Him. "So, she is a Warrior and a Healer. Excellent . . . excellent." Then He clapped His hands together and smiled. "You have answered My question well. Are there more questions you would like to ask? It is important to Me that your ballad is accurate."

Death was watching her expectantly and by now she understood all too well how easily angered He was when He became frustrated. Ralina forced herself to return the god's smile. "My Lord, I do have another question."

The God of Death nodded. "Good, good—ask and your god shall answer."

"I do not understand why You must call a new guide. What happened to the spirit of the little doe?"

Death made a dismissive gesture with a thick hand. "Blame the Goddess of Life. She has eternally been too softhearted."

"Oh, you spoke with the goddess today?" Ralina held her breath. Even when Death was in an amiable mood, it was almost impossible to anticipate what would anger Him.

"Yes, Storyteller. I am pleased you asked. I had forgotten to inform you. My Goddess called to Me earlier today."

Ralina didn't need to feign interest. Any mention of the Goddess of Life commanded all of her attention. "You mean when You walked away from the army You went to speak with the Goddess?"

"Exactly. My lover awakened enough to call to Me." Death chuckled softly, a sound that made Ralina's skin crawl with disgust. "She is so predictable. Such a worrier."

Ralina forced herself to laugh with the God. "What could a goddess possibly have to worry about?" She asked the question as if speaking almost to herself as she grinned at Death, hoping she hadn't pushed Him too far.

Thankfully, Death shrugged His massive shoulders and looked amused. "My Goddess misses Me. She tried to coax Me to return to Her, but I am not interested in eternal sleep. I am interested in ruling the mortal world—awake."

The God was unusually chatty, so Ralina nodded and asked another question. "And that worries Her?"

Death scoffed. "Needlessly, of course. You see, Storyteller, though My Goddess is a life bringer, She has not walked the earth for so many eons that She has forgotten how delightful it is to be truly awake—truly alive."

"Is the goddess not excited about awakening and ruling the world with You?"

"As I said, My lover is a worrier. She remembers what happened when last I awakened. She worries worse will happen this time, so She resists— though I have explained to Her that with Life awake and vibrant beside Me, everything shall be different." Death threw wide His arms and bellowed the strange, guttural cry again.

When He was silent once more, Ralina asked one last question. "My Lord, when did You last awaken?"

Death met her gaze. "When the ancients were destroyed and the world shifted from what it once was, to what it has now become." His huge head tilted to the side and Death bellowed again. Then from across the clearing came an answering call—deep, guttural, and angry.

"Yes, come to Me, mighty one." Death laughed and then roared another call, and then another. "Storyteller, behold what I now do. Remember it,

34

as I shall do something very like this to force My fretful Goddess awake."
He bared His teeth in a feral grin at her. "Once I have found My perfect
vessel on the Plains of the Wind Riders, of course."

Something huge began to crash its way toward them and Death glanced
at Ralina. "Climb up on that boulder there." He pointed. "I will, of course,
best this beast, though he wields great power. I would not want you to get
caught between us."

"Y-yes, my Lord." Fear skittered through her, causing flesh to rise on
her forearms as she hurriedly climbed the rugged boulder to perch above
Death.

From her vantage point she had a perfect view of the creature as he
entered the clearing. Her breath caught and she shook her head in disbelief.
Ralina had never seen such a beast in person, though the Tribe's now-dead
artists often traveled to distant lands to return and create spectacular draw-
ings and carvings of strange creatures—including this one that she remembered one artist had named bison, a massive beast that was usually found
on the Plains of the Wind Riders.

This bison was an enormous bull. The shaggy, earth-colored fur that
covered his head and cascaded down his shoulders was thick and slightly
darker than the pelt on the rest of his heavily muscled body. His ebony
horns were thick and upturned, ending in deadly points.

The creature seemed confused at first. He stopped just inside the clearing and stared at the God of Death.

"Yes, you will do nicely," the God murmured. Then He bent at the
waist, tore the earth with His cloven hooves, and roared a challenge at the
mighty bull.

The bull's response was instantaneous. He bellowed in return, strands
of saliva flying from his mouth, and he, too, tore the winter grass with
ebony hooves. The bison dropped his head and charged the God.

Death roared an acceptance of the challenge and raced to meet the
beast. As He did, the God drew a long, razor-tipped knife from the sheath
belted around His thick waist and gripped its handle between His teeth.

The God didn't meet the bull antlers to horns. Instead, He spun to the
side at the last moment and as the bison hurtled past Death sank His
fist into the thick fur of the beast's neck and the God leaped and landed
astride the creature.

The bison roared in rage and spun around. He attempted to gore Death's thigh, but the God grabbed one of the dangerous horns with His left hand. With His right He took the knife from between His teeth, and as the bull bellowed in impotent anger Death pulled his head so far back that Ralina thought He would surely break the animal's neck. While the beast's neck was thus exposed, the God sliced the knife across it, causing scarlet to spurt in rivulets onto the beaten grass.

The powerful bison fell to his knees and still he tried to gore Him, but Death's strength was superhuman—a god melded with a stag—and while the beast panted and struggled Death leaped from his back and flipped the bison so that his underbelly was exposed. Then, using the knife that still dripped scarlet, He plunged the blade into the sternum of the beast, disemboweling the living creature.

Ralina wanted to look away, but she couldn't. She had to know exactly what He was doing so she could try to stop Him from awakening the Goddess.

As the poor bison grunted with pain and began to slide into unconsciousness, Death plunged His hands inside the beast, felt around, and then, with a thunderous shout of victory, the god pulled the still-beating heart of the creature from his body, and took an enormous bite from the steaming organ.

Ralina's mouth flooded with bile-tinged saliva. She swallowed several times, commanding her gorge to stay down. *I cannot get sick. I must gather information and remember—always remember—everything He has told me and every vile thing I have witnessed Him doing.*

So, the Tribe of the Trees' Storyteller watched as the God of Death ate the bison's steaming heart. When there was nothing left of it, He licked the blood from His fingers before going to the bison's great, still head and resting His hand on it.

"Now, come to Me once more. Serve Me," Death commanded.

From the bison a thread of light began to glisten inside his dead eyes and then the light lifted, swirled, and glowed to form a glistening, spirit version of the great, slain beast.

"I am Death. You are bound to Me. Lead Me through the mountains to the grassy plains on the other side. I command you shall remain in My sight until I release you."

The spirit of the bison snorted and pawed the earth, but then he bowed his massive head in acknowledgment of the god.

"Excellent!" Death turned from the body of the beast and his spirit to look up at Ralina. Blood was smeared down His neck and His chest that was bare except for the fur of a stag. Rusty gore spattered His legs and His hooves were slick with intestines and blood. He motioned to her with a crimson hand. "You may climb down now, My little Storyteller."

Ralina focused on making her limbs obey her. When she reached the grassy ground, Death was already talking as if what had just happened was an everyday occurrence.

"We shall feast on bison steak tonight. Even you shall eat with Me, Storyteller, as this beast's meat is not tainted by sickness."

Ralina tried to form words. Tried to get past the horror of what stood before her—the gore-covered God of Death, the eviscerated body of the bison, and his glowing spirit who stood, head lowered in somber submission, just behind the god.

"What is it?" Death asked, but didn't wait for her response and instead answered His own question. "Ah, you have never tasted bison. Let Me assure you—it is even more delicious than venison." When Ralina still didn't speak, Death frowned. "Do you not believe Me?"

"Oh, I believe You, my Lord." The words burst past the dam of her revulsion. "I was, um, just pondering a question, but I am not sure that it is one You would find appropriate."

Death's thick brow lifted. "Now I am intrigued. I give you leave to ask Me one question that might be inappropriate with no repercussion."

Ralina swallowed several times before asking, "To awaken Your goddess you must kill a beast, like this bison, and then She must eat its beating heart raw? Forgive me, my Lord, but perhaps that is what worries Her."

Death's laughter boomed around them. "Storyteller, you do amuse Me. No, My Goddess need not eat the creature's heart, and I would not choose a bison to awaken Her. That beast would be too crude. No, a lovely young doe, much like the one She freed from My service, will suffice. And She need not eat of its heart. All I need do is infect the vessel I choose with the skin-sloughing sickness and then flay the doe's living flesh into her wounds as I bleed into the earth the human body to the point of death.

Then I shall call My Goddess and She will have no choice but to do as I command—awaken and walk the earth beside Me."

"Oh, I see." Ralina made herself smile at Death.

"You find that more palatable than consuming a beating heart?" He asked as if He was genuinely curious.

"Well, yes. Though the skin-sloughing sickness is unpleasant . . . ," said Ralina honestly. She paused then, wanting to ask Him more, but unable to tell how long the God would continue to indulge her.

"Go on. I can see you have even more questions," Death said as He began to retrace their path back to where the army awaited them.

Ralina fell into stride beside Him—and behind them the spirit of the bison reluctantly followed. "Why did You eat the bison's heart?"

"It is a simple way for Me to absorb the mighty creature's power. Watch and learn, watching and learning. You shall see, Storyteller." Death lifted His arms and flexed His thick muscles. He threw back His head and bellowed the call of a charging bison. "It is good to be alive!"

Ralina couldn't agree with Him, so she remained silent as she pondered what she had just learned, as well as her dream. *If there is any chance it was a vision from the Goddess of Life, I will listen. I will obey. If a white doe appears to me in a snowstorm, I will follow her. I will finally, finally leave.*

That night, after they'd feasted on bison, Ralina whispered to Renard that it was time—they must be ready to leave if Life beckoned.

CHAPTER 3

Eyes blazing with anger, Morgana, the oldest member of the Mare Council and Rider of the ancient mare Ramoth, shouted, "Repeat what you just said, Lead Mare Rider of Herd Magenti!"

River cleared her throat. She stood in the center of the Choosing Theater Field. Members of the wise Mare Council had formed a semicircle around her. The tiered grandstand was crowded with Riders and their Companions, as well as the new Pack members who River had insisted attend the unusual gathering. *I need you to understand our laws and the penalties for those who break them*, River had explained to Mari and Sora when she requested they join the Herd.

Somberly Mari and Sora had agreed—and just as somberly River complied with Morgana's request and repeated the terrible things she had just said while her Herd stared in horror at the lasso wrapped with knife-sharp goathead thistles she'd placed on the ground before Morgana and the Council. "Clayton used this during the Stallion Run yesterday. Gho—" River hesitated and glanced at the golden horse who stood quietly beside Anjo with his newly Chosen Rider, Dove, astride, listening attentively. "Forgive me. *Tulpar*"—she enunciated his new name carefully—"was at a full gallop. Had the Mare Rider, Skye, not forewarned me of Clayton's treacherous plans, the stallion and I would be dead and unable to speak the truth. Clayton used the goathead-wrapped lasso because we had just avoided a thicket of the deadly thistles but were still near enough that he could make it appear like an accident when we were found." River looked from one Council Member to another, glad so many of them had been present to watch the Stallion Run. Her gaze met her mother's and lingered as she finished, "Had the fall not done his work for him, I believe Clayton would have killed Tulpar and me to silence us."

"Mare Rider Skye, from Herd Magenti, come forth!" The strength in Morgana's voice belied her age as it rang with righteous indignation throughout the theater.

There was a shuffling at the edge of the crowd and then Skye, with her dapple-gray mare, Scout, at her side, came forward. Pale and trembling, she stopped and bowed first to Morgana and the Council, and then to River. "I am Skye, of Herd Magenti Central, Mare Rider to Scout."

The ancient Council Member didn't prevaricate. "What exactly were Clayton's plans for the Stallion Run?"

"H-he did not . . ." Skye paused, sobbed softly, and wiped at the tears that leaked down her cheeks before she continued. "He did not tell me specifics."

"He told you enough that you felt the need to sneak to my tent before dawn and warn me." River's voice was firm and emotionless. She was utterly done being patient with Clayton and his enablers, which included his lover, Skye.

Skye's gaze darted to River, but she couldn't meet the Lead Mare Rider's eyes. She drew a deep, haggard breath. "I warned you because what Clayton did say, over and over, was that he was determined to win the Stallion Run, that he *deserved* to win it more than any of the other stallions, especially Ghost."

"His name is Tulpar." Dove's pleasing voice had taken on a razor edge.

Skye turned to look at Dove astride the golden stallion. For a moment her eyes narrowed angrily, but her mare, Scout, leaned into her Rider, who instantly deflated. Skye nodded wearily. "I'm sorry. You're right. Clayton holds a great hatred for Tulpar and told me that under no circumstances would he allow that stallion to be his leader."

"An interesting choice of words," River said. "Stallions do not lead our Herd or *any* of the five Great Herds."

Skye swallowed audibly before she responded, "Clayton planned on changing that, too. He believes stallions and their Riders should have at least an equal voice in Herd leadership, as well as be accepted to the Mare Council."

The Herd erupted into shouts of outrage, which Morgana allowed to continue for a few breaths, and then her lifted hand silenced the assembly.

"It is outrageous that one Rider thought he had the ability to change a tradition and a set of laws that has served us, and served us well, for hundreds of years, which leads me to believe there are more Stallion Riders in Herd Magenti who likewise have traitorous thoughts," said the Councilwoman.

River turned in a slow circle as she spoke, being careful to meet the gaze of every Stallion Rider within her sight. "Is this truth, Riders?" Anjo punctuated River's question with an angry squeal, which was echoed by Tulpar.

When no Rider stepped forward to speak, Dove's voice cut through the tension. "Forgive me. I do not yet know your rules or traditions, but Tulpar has asked me to be his voice. Might I have permission to speak for him?"

"Yes, absolutely," said River. "It is our tradition that the Herd Stallion represents the other stallions, geldings, and their Riders. He is their voice, so it is proper that you are his voice, and that the Herd hears his words."

Herd Magenti Central went silent as Tulpar trotted with Dove astride to the center of the theater to join River, Skye, and the Council. Dove's eyeless face was serene and she sat with confidence on her golden stallion. Her head turned with Tulpar's as she viewed the Herd through his dark, expressive eyes.

"Tulpar tells me that the Rider Clayton had whispered lies about the unfairness of your traditions and laws since before the Mare Test, and that those whispers changed to shouts after Anjo and River were named Lead Mare and Rider of Magenti Central and River rejected him as a potential mate."

River's tawny cheeks flushed—not with embarrassment but with anger. *What Clayton desires is not my responsibility nor my shame*, River reminded herself, and held her head high while Dove continued to speak her stallion's wise words.

"As Herd Stallion Tulpar wants to be clear—he will follow Anjo and

River, and will fight to protect Magenti against anyone who would rule with ego instead of wisdom." Tulpar and Dove concluded by facing River and Anjo and bowing respectfully. "Tulpar and I together add, may the blessings of the Great Earth Mother, in the form of the Mother Mare, guide our Herd through our Lead Mare and her Rider, as well as the wise Mare Council."

River bowed in return, grateful for the Herd Stallion's vocal support.

Morgana spoke solemnly. "Young Dove, I would like to know from your Tulpar how many Riders and their Companions followed this outlaw in his sedition."

Dove cocked her head as she listened to Tulpar's voice in her mind before she replied. "A total of ten stallions and geldings, and their Riders from Herd Magenti Central, and three young Riders and their mares, though each horse counseled their Riders not to leave the Herd—not to follow Clayton."

"And yet the Riders ignored the sage advice of their Companions." Morgana shook her head, her lined face twisted with disgust. "Every one of those Riders are traitors—to their Companions and to their Herd."

From the edge of the crowd there was movement as Jasper, who had been Herd Stallion Rider until the day before when Tulpar had won the title, and his big bay stallion, Blaze, stepped onto the field. "Dove, would Tulpar allow me to speak?"

"Yes, of course. Tulpar acknowledges your wisdom," Dove said with a warm smile.

"As do Anjo and I," agreed River.

Jasper bowed his head respectfully and then spoke directly to the Mare Council, though he pitched his voice so that it carried throughout the theater. "Blaze and I believe Clayton's treachery is even more advanced than the violence he attempted yesterday. We have heard rumors that Clayton has followers in the other four Great Herds as well—young Stallion and Gelding Riders and the Mare Riders who care for them, or have become their mates. We think he began inciting such sedition during the six months of Warrior training he spent with Herd Cinnabar three years ago."

"Why did I not hear of this sooner?" River snapped.

"Or I?" Dawn, on her beautiful mare, Echo, moved from the crowd to join them. "I was Lead Mare Rider when Clayton returned from Cinnabar."

Jasper sighed heavily. "Forgive me for being silent. I thought Clayton would mature, and with maturity he would stop his blathering. Had I come to you, Dawn, or you, River, it would have been with nothing but rumor and speculation. I see now that I should not have excused his behavior as youthful foolishness."

River spoke quickly. "This is not your fault alone, Jasper. I heard the whispers and the rumors. I knew they were becoming more serious, but I hoped being defeated in the Stallion Run would check Clayton's ego—and those of his followers. Or at least I hoped that until yesterday." She turned to face Skye. "What do you know about the involvement of the other Herds?"

The sharpness in River's voice worked like a goad on the young Mare Rider and words spilled from her pale lips. "Clayton has followers in all of the other Herds."

"How many of these traitors are there among the other Herds?" Morgana shot the question at Skye.

Skye dropped her gaze to the grassy ground. "About as many as from our Herd."

"We must send Riders immediately and warn the Lead Mare Riders of the other Herds," said River.

"It is too late." Skye's voice was barely audible.

"Speak up!" River's command was punctuated by an angry squeal from Anjo, which almost dislodged little Kit from where she lay on the mare's wide back.

"It is too late," Skye repeated, her voice filled with tears. "They were all here to watch Clayton win and declare himself leader. As soon as Clayton was beaten, they fled with him."

River fisted her hands on her waist. "Why are you still here? Why aren't you with your lover and the other traitors?"

Skye wiped at her face again. "Because I didn't think he'd actually do it! And when he did, I—I couldn't bear it. I couldn't support him."

"Bear what?" River asked sardonically. "The fact that he tried to kill Tulpar and me or the fact that he encouraged Riders to be traitors to their Herds?"

"Kill you!" Skye was unable to hide her own anger. "I warned you, but I—I didn't believe he'd really do it, and then the race was over. You beat him and—"

"It wasn't just Tulpar who beat him!" From the audience Regis, Rider of the stallion Hobbs, shouted angrily. He and his blond stallion wore the green of Herd Virides. "Hobbs passed him easily."

"My Red beat him as well!" shouted Jonathan, one of Magenti's most respected Stallion Riders. "For all of his blustering, even had he committed the atrocity and murdered Tulpar and our River he still would not have won the Stallion Run. He and his stallion are unfit to protect any Herd. They are not the strongest or fastest—"

"Or wisest," one of the senior Mare Riders added loudly. "Clayton and his Bard are mediocre, at best. They are unfit to be the protectors of any Herd, and my mare would *never* agree to mate with him."

Angry shouts of agreement from scores of Mare Riders had Skye dropping her head again. River raised her hand for silence. "Continue, Skye. After Clayton was well and truly beaten by *three* better Riders and their stallions, what happened?"

"He told me he was going to start his own Herd, called Herd Ebony, where stallions and their Riders would rule." Her gaze finally met River's. "But had he been allowed to start a new branch of Herd Magenti—"

Again, enraged shouts cut off her words, but one squeal from Anjo silenced the crowd.

"Continue, Skye," commanded River.

"Had Clayton been allowed to start a new branch of Herd Magenti I would have gone with him," River said in a rush. "But only if his leaving had been approved by the Mare Council. I explained that to him and that is when he told me we *must* leave because he knew you would report to the Mare Council what he'd tried to do." She swiped at the tears that continued to flow down her cheeks. "He told me then that he'd tried and failed to kill you and Tulpar. He said the Riders from Magenti and the other four Herds who feel as he does left as soon as Tulpar won the race." She shook her head sadly. "I couldn't go with him then, no matter how much I love him."

"May the Great Mother Mare save me from that kind of *love*," River said with disgust. "Where are they, Skye?"

"I do not know."

Anjo laid back her ears and reached her long neck forward to bite Scout squarely on her rump. Scout snorted with shock and pain and moved quickly out of the Lead Mare's range.

"Stop! I *am* telling the truth!" Skye's voice was shrill. "Every time I asked Clayton, he said he was going to surprise me, and his friends always quit talking about it when Scout or I were around. What about the rest of you Stallion Riders? Didn't your horses talk with theirs? Don't *you* know?"

Morgana's sharp gaze skewered Skye. "Check your attitude, Mare Rider. It is *you* and *your lover* who are at fault here, not our faithful Stallion Riders."

"I–I know," Skye said with a sob. "I really am sorry. I just didn't believe Clayton would do it." Her gaze beseeched River. "You can understand that, can't you? You've known him since you were children. You know he's not actually a bad man. Tell them. Please, River."

River sighed. "Skye, the boy I used to play with no longer exists. He is not a child. He is a man. The sedition he has been spreading throughout *all five Herds* and his actions yesterday have proven Clayton has grown into a man fueled by arrogance, unearned pride, pettiness, and a greed for power that has already cost him his home and his integrity. He isn't simply a bad man. He is a dangerously deluded man who is leading others into shame and banishment." River spoke slowly and clearly as Skye's face flushed and sobs caused her shoulders to shake.

Then River went to Anjo and took the sleepy puppy from her precarious perch on the mare's broad back. She cradled Kit in her arms as she spoke aloud to ensure the Herd would understand what came next. "Anjo, question Scout about Clayton's whereabouts."

The lead mare turned dragon-like. Ears pressed flat against her head and teeth bared, she approached Scout as the smaller mare attempted to stand her ground, though her head was lowered in submission and her flanks trembled.

"No! Stop!" Skye cried. "The stallions didn't tell Scout anything, but I did overhear Clayton talking about Iron Springs and how outdated it was that the Mare Council forbids the Herds to migrate there."

"Outdated," Morgana scoffed. "Only if remaining free of the poison from the ruins from a toxic city of the ancients is outdated."

"Might I speak? I grew up in the ruins of a toxic city," said Dove.

"You may speak," River said.

"Port City is so poisonous that it diseased any of our people who ate of the animals trapped and killed in or near it. That poison is so lethal that it is the root cause behind the destruction of the Tribe of the Trees as well as

Mari and Sora's Weaver Clan. If an ancient city is toxic, it must be avoided. Always. That is a truth that I know, not simply from living it, but from the Great Earth Mother."

River nodded in agreement. "Skye, you know the decrees that forbid migration to certain ruins were not made frivolously. You should have come to me the instant you heard such talk."

"I would have, but I didn't—"

"Let me finish for you," Morgana interrupted. "You didn't believe he'd actually go there. Young Skye, if you are to be an effective Mare Rider you are going to have to expand your belief system and stop being so naïve and easily led astray." The ancient woman's head bowed wearily. The Herd watched Morgana carefully, waiting for her to continue. Then she straightened. Morgana reached into the voluminous pocket of the tunic she wore embroidered with the colors of all five Great Herds, and lifted a faceted clear quartz crystal the size of her hand. As she raised it, the crystal began to glow with a pure white light. The senior Mare Council Member's voice was amplified by the crystal so that it carried throughout the crowded arena.

"Most here know this story, but we have new Herd members who have not heard it—and, sadly, some of our own people appear to have forgotten it." Her gaze paused on Skye before she continued. "So, hear me all and hear me well as I speak the truth. There is a reason Mare Riders make up our ruling Council as well as lead our Herds. We learned from the time of the great fires and quakes that changed the face of our earth. Until then men were the leaders—and their desire for war and control and violence led their world into destruction. As we rebuilt all those centuries ago we were determined to form a better society—one led by those who create life, who will stop and think before sending their children to war—a society led by compassion and wisdom instead of greed and insatiable lust for more power, more land, more riches. *That is why we are a matriarchy and why we shall always be a matriarchy.* We follow the path of wild equine herds. We value our males, be they stallion, gelding, or human, but we will never again be ruled by their volatile natures.

"This history lesson is over. The Council has heard enough. River, you are Lead Mare Rider here. It is you who must pass judgment on Clayton and his Bard. The Mare Council shall support that judgment." Morgana offered the crystal to River.

River didn't hesitate. She took the crystal, warm and glowing from Morgana's touch, and held it high. She'd been considering what she should do since the moment Skye had snuck into her tent the night before the Stallion Run and confided that he meant Tulpar harm. "My judgment is that Clayton and his Bard will be found and banished from the Plains of the Wind Riders. If after they have been advised of their sentence they refuse to adhere to the banishment, they will be put to death. Any Rider from our Herd, Magenti Central, who has followed Clayton's traitorous actions will be banished with him—and should they refuse they, too, will be put to death. Those Riders who are not part of our Herd must be judged by their Lead Mare Riders."

"We have Council Members here from each of the other Herds who may speak on behalf of them." Morgana turned to face the women of the Council who sat on their mares in a semicircle behind her. "Cinnabar, what say you?"

A dark-skinned woman whose hair was streaked with silver nudged her sorrel mare forward. "The Warriors of Herd Cinnabar do not abide treason. We agree with River's judgment."

"Virides, what say you?"

Another mature Mare Rider urged her Companion forward to join Morgana. "Fleet Virides is in agreement with River."

"Indigo, what say you?"

A woman whose hair was dyed brilliant blue came forward on a white mare whose mane was dyed the same blue. "The healers of Herd Indigo honor life. And because of that we understand the import of this judgment. There can be no honor in life if Herdmembers behave with arrogant selfishness that puts us all at risk. Indigo agrees with River."

"And Jonquil, what say you?"

The last Rider who came forward had hair so blond it appeared to glisten like precious silver. Her mare was solid black, except for gray around her muzzle and eyes. "The expert Hunters of Jonquil do not tolerate sedition. We agree with River."

"The Council concurs with the Lead Mare Rider of Herd Magenti," said

Morgana after she and her mare faced the crowded theater again. "Judgment is passed on Stallion Rider Clayton, his Bard, and all those who follow them. It has been said!"

"It has been said!" echoed the Mare Council.

Morgana bowed to River. "Continue, Lead Mare Rider."

The Choosing Theater was utterly silent as River, holding the glowing crystal aloft in one hand and cradling little Kit with her other, went to stand directly in front of Skye and Scout—Anjo at her side. "Make your decision now, Skye. Do you follow Clayton or do you follow your Herd?"

Skye's face lost all color. "I—I made that decision when I didn't go with Clayton."

"I'm not so sure you did, but know I will never ask you again. Choose!"

"I choose Herd Magenti," said Skye softly.

"Louder for the Herd to hear. We will never again tolerate whispers."

Skye raised her voice. "I choose my Herd!"

"It has been said!" River shouted. She turned her back on Skye and reverently returned the still-glowing crystal to Morgana before announcing, "The judgment is complete. You may depart. Hunters and Stallion Riders, please remain. We have much to—"

A commotion at the mouth of the Choosing Theater interrupted River's words. The crowd's attention shifted to the entrance to the field where a huge male Lynx limped into view with his Companion staggering behind him.

"I—I must speak with the Mare Council!" the man shouted before he fell to his knees, where he gasped for breath as his Lynx circled him, staggering and mewing with concern.

CHAPTER 4

D ax! Bloody beetle balls, I think that's Dax and his Lynx, Mihos."
From their place in the viewing stands Nik stood to stare at the
Lynx and his exhausted Companion.

"You know him?" Mari asked.

"Wilkes, that's Dax, isn't it?" Nik asked the tall Shepherd Companion
sitting behind him who had led the Warriors of Tribe of the Trees for
more than a decade.

"Yes, I believe that is Dax," said Wilkes.

"Where's Antreas?" Mari asked.

"Here—here." Antreas, with Bast and Danita, his mate, beside him hurried down from their seats higher in the grand stadium. "That's Dax and
his Mihos. Something's gravely wrong. I've never seen a Lynx allow his or
her Companion to become so exhausted."

"Let's get down there." Mari grabbed Nik's hand. "Come on. We need
to help." Mari, Antreas, and Nik, with their Companions closely following, made their way quickly through the crowd and down to the field,
where Mari pushed past the circle of concerned Herdmembers. "Excuse
me, please. Sorry. Excuse me. Please let us through," she murmured as
she shouldered her way to the fallen Lynx Companion.

They broke through the circle of people to see River trying to calm Mihos
while the injured Lynx stood over his Companion, hissing and snarling at

53

her. There was blood everywhere the big feline stepped and Dax was absolutely still.

"This looks really bad," said Mari.

The moment Antreas got inside the circle, he told Mari, "I can try to help, but everyone needs to back off before Mihos hurts someone."

"River!" Mari called for the Lead Mare Rider's attention. "Antreas knows this Companion. If you allow it, he can attempt to help."

River nodded with relief and backed slowly to the circumference of the circle of silently watching people. "Yes, please."

"Bast, speak with Mihos right away. Tell him we only want to help Dax." Antreas spoke quickly to his Lynx before he made any move to approach the fallen Companion.

Bast padded into the circle. The angry Lynx even turned on her, hissing a warning. Bast held her ground and made soft, soothing sounds that were a mixture of meows and chirps.

"Yes." Antreas nodded. "I hear you, Bast. I know Mihos is injured, too, and not in his right mind. I will not go to Dax until Mihos gives me permission."

"Our healers will gladly care for both Companion and Lynx if Mihos will allow," said River.

The big male Lynx hissed at Antreas, though he lurched slightly to the side of his still Companion.

"Mihos, listen to Bast. We are a bonded Lynx pair. Scent me. You know us. I would never harm you or your Companion. I need to check your Dax. I need to help him." Antreas spoke calmly to the Lynx, who growled low in his massive chest as he alternated holding one paw and then another off the ground.

"The Lynx's paws are all bloody. They're bleeding badly, and I don't like how still Dax is. I need to do something *now*," Mari said.

"Careful." Nik spoke quietly to her. "As long as Dax is unconscious his Companion could be very dangerous; Mihos is clearly not in his right mind."

Mari squeezed Nik's hand. "I can communicate with him. It'll be fine." She stepped into the cleared circle around Dax and his Mihos. Closer to the pair Mari could see that it was as she suspected. The Lynx's bloody paws soaked the grassy ground around Dax. Mari drew a deep breath and concentrated on the big feline. First she sent him waves of love and comfort.

Mihos had been watching Antreas, yellow eyes narrowed menacingly, as he moved slowly toward Dax, but as Mari touched his mind the big Lynx's head snapped around and he stared at her.

That's right. It's me. I'm Mari. I'm a healer. I can help you, and I can help your Dax. Will you let me, please? With her words Mari sketched a picture in her mind that showed her putting salve on the feline's wounded paws and a second sketch of her gently examining Dax.

At the same time Bast padded closer to Mihos while she continued to chirp and mew calmly.

Dax hurt! Paws hurt! Must get to Council!

Mari almost staggered back at the force with which Mihos responded to her.

"I understand, and you have made it. The Mare Council is here." Mari spoke aloud calmly as she kept sketching pictures of help, adding the Mare Council to the frames as she sent them to the Lynx. "But you have to let me—let *us*—close to both of you." Mari gestured at Antreas, River, and the rest of the silently watching crowd. "Will you?"

Help Dax first. Mihos flooded Mari's mind with his answer as he finally groaned with exhaustion and lay down beside Dax.

"Thank you, beautiful boy," said Mari. "Sora!"

"Right behind you. Jenna ran for our medicine baskets as soon as she saw the Companion fall to his knees." She shoved a basket loaded with salves and bandages into Mari's hand and then scooped her Terrier pup, Chloe, from her baby sling and handed her to Jenna, who was panting beside her. "Chloe, stay with Jenna."

"Mihos, this is Sora. She is another healer. Will you let her tend to Dax?" Mari asked the Lynx as she sent him a visual image of Sora examining the Companion.

Dax first, Mihos blasted into her mind.

Mari glanced at River as she and Sora entered the cleared circle. "Mihos will let us help them, but Sora must see to Dax first. Could someone bring fresh water?"

"Right away." River nodded to April, who sprinted away. "We can take them to our infirmary inside the cave—if Mihos will allow."

Sora went quickly to Dax while Mari approached the wounded Lynx. She knelt slowly beside him. "May I touch you?"

The feline's gaze was locked on Dax, but he responded, *Yes.*

Mari gently stroked the big feline's head. She could feel that his body was trembling. "It's going to be okay. Everything is going to be okay." The Lynx chirped pitifully and fretfully licked at one of his paws as he sent Mari waves of pain and fear for his Companion.

"I'm going to touch your paws, but I will be very careful and try not to hurt you." Mari spoke softly to the Lynx.

Paws hurt, he told Mari as he slid a huge, bloody pad toward her and then leaned on his side so that she had access to all four—though he never took his gaze from Dax.

Quickly, efficiently, Mari examined the feline's paws. They were in horrible shape, torn and seeping blood—worse even than Rigel's paws had been after he'd fought a Swarm to find and Choose her. Mihos must be in terrible pain. It would take weeks for him to heal, even after she called down the moon and used its power to soothe him.

"May we move you, sweet boy?" Mari asked.

Help best moved? The Lynx's question filled her mind.

Mari ignored the headache the Lynx's loud psychic voice built in her temples. "Yes, Mihos. It will be a great help if we can move both of you."

Me with Dax!

Mari cringed slightly but nodded. "Yes, of course. You will always be with Dax."

Move. Help. The Lynx began to struggle to his feet again but yowled in pain as he put weight on his bleeding paws.

"Oh, no." Mari wrapped her arms around the Lynx and pulled him onto her lap to ease the pressure from his paws. "Let us carry you. Please, Mihos."

You carry, Mihos told her.

"I will definitely carry you," said Mari. Then, as she guessed the full-grown male feline probably weighed almost as much as Laru, she added, "May my mate, Nik, help me lift you?" Mari motioned for Nik to join her.

"Hey there, Mihos." Nik spoke softly to the Lynx as he joined Mari. "Remember me? Remember Laru?" Behind Nik, Laru huffed a greeting.

Mihos sniffed the air as he looked from Nik to Laru. *Sol's Laru?*

"He asks if that's Sol's Laru," said Mari.

Nik crouched before Mihos. "Yes, Laru was Sol's, but when my father died I was greatly blessed when he Chose me as his Companion. I will be very careful if you allow me to carry you. I give you my word."

Laru's Nik can carry, Mihos told Mari.

"Thank you, Mihos." Mari spoke quickly. "Mihos will allow Nik to carry him to the infirmary, but he must remain close to Dax."

"I—I'll be fine." Dax's voice was weak, and when he struggled to sit Mihos mewed pitifully.

Antreas, who had joined Sora as she examined Dax, gently pressed the Companion's shoulder down. "Old friend, I do not believe you are fine, but with Sora and Mari caring for you, both you and your Mihos will be."

Dax lay back, but he reached out and touched Mihos's shoulder. "My boy . . . I—I tried to get him to rest, to wait and let me finish the trek here, but he refused. His paws . . ." The Companion's voice broke as he continued. "N-nettles—goatheads—he tried to find a shortcut here and ran into a thicket be-before I could stop him."

Mihos mewed pitifully and licked Dax's hand.

"I can heal Mihos. I promise you," Mari said to Dax.

"And I can heal you," said Sora firmly. "But you'll need rest, hydration, and food. You and your Lynx are practically skeletons."

Mari felt a jolt of shock as she realized she'd been so focused on Mihos's shredded paws that she hadn't noticed that the Lynx was all bone under his thick pelt.

"Dax, we're going to carry both of you to the infirmary. You and your Lynx are in shock," Mari said.

"Yes. Whatever is best, but I must speak with the Mare Council and whoever is Lead Mare Rider of Herd Magenti—I am in Magenti territory, correct?" Dax said.

"I am River, Lead Mare Rider of Herd Magenti." River stepped closer to them. "A majority of the Mare Council are here as well," she told Dax.

Dax ignored Antreas's hand on his shoulder and sat up as he said, "You must know"—but his voice broke off as his eyes rolled to show their whites and he sank back down to the bloodstained grass.

Mihos yowled and began to struggle in Mari's arms.

"Sssh, be still," Mari soothed.

Sora raised her voice over the Lynx's protestations. "Where's that water? We need to stop the talking and transport these two *now*—and we need warm blankets and water boiled."

"Here! Here!" The crowd around them opened to allow April through. She carried a skin full of water and was followed by two men with a stretcher between them. Dax had regained consciousness again, though his face was the color of old milk.

"Here, carefully, just drink a little right now," said Sora as she held the water to Dax's lips.

He took two long pulls from the skin before he wiped his mouth with a trembling hand and said, "Mihos. Give Mihos some, too."

Sora passed the skin to Mari, who poured the water into Nik's cupped hands, and the Lynx lapped thirstily.

"Ready to carry him?" Mari asked Nik.

"Yes, absolutely."

Nik lifted Mihos as Mari helped take care with his bloody paws. At the same time Dax was placed on the stretcher. The crowd parted and River led them from the Choosing Theater, calling over her shoulder, "Dove, Tulpar, Morgana, and Mother, please stand by to join us. April! Gather our Stallion Riders and Hunters, as well as any Rider team from the other Herds who are still here. I will speak with them shortly."

Side by side, they transported the Lynx and his Companion through the heart of Herd Magenti and to the enormous cave. Just inside the entrance River turned to the right and led them to a large circular room that was filled with comfortable pallets—some equine sized and some human sized—a briskly burning hearth fire, and crystals everywhere that glowed like they were ensouled.

They placed Dax and Mihos on pallets beside each other as River made quick introductions. "This is Griffin, our Lead Healer." She gestured to an attractive woman with kind brown eyes and a compassionate smile. "She is Mare Rider to Minka, and this is her assistant, Mikayla, Gelding Rider to Avalon. Ladies, please support Mari and Sora in any way you can."

"Of course," said Griffin. "How may we help?"

Sora took a sachet of herbs from her basket. "Please steep this in a large mug until the water turns dark brown. He'll drink that right away. Then I need muddled goldenseal root in warm water for his hands. I must clean them before I can tell if they need to be sewn, and he must have water to drink and broth as well, right away."

"I will get these things for you immediately." Mikayla accepted the herb sachet and hurried through a curtained doorway in the rear of the room.

Sora turned to her patient. "Dax, other than the lacerations on your hands, are you injured anywhere else?"

Weakly, Dax shook his head. "No. I don't think so." He looked down at his bloody hands. "I got these freeing Mihos from the nettles. We haven't eaten or slept for days. We had to get here. We had to warn you." Dax began to struggle to sit up again.

Sora easily pressed him back to his pallet. "River's here. She'll listen to you, but you have to be conscious to warn her about anything."

Dax nodded and sank back into the pelt. "Mihos, his paws. Please help him."

"I will help him," Mari continued to assure the Lynx Companion.

The Lead Healer of Tribe Magenti spoke before Mari could continue. "You will need goldenseal root to clean his paws, as well, correct? You will have to tell me what else as I have never treated a Lynx."

"Neither have I," Mari muttered as she studied the deep puncture wounds and lacerations on Mihos's bleeding paws.

"Y-you may ask me," Dax said. He'd begun to shiver with shock and Sora was covering him with a thick, soft blanket. "Mihos and I have been together for more than a decade. These are not our first injuries."

Mari felt a surge of relief and quickly asked, "May I use a poultice of honey, witch hazel, sage, and calendula flowers on Mihos without harming him?"

"Yes. You may use poppy juice to help him with the pain, and basically the same medicines you would use on your canines, except any type of lily is highly toxic to felines. Also he cannot ingest flower bulbs," Dax said.

Mikayla rushed back into the room clutching two wooden bowls full of cloudy warm water. "Water with goldenseal root for disinfecting," said Mikayla.

"Is there something I can give Mihos to numb his paws? I may need to sew some of the deepest cuts," asked Mari as Mikayla passed her one of the bowls of goldenseal-muddled water for the Lynx.

Griffin spoke up. "We have a numbing salve that is basically lard mixed with ground crystals our Seers have infused with the ability to mask pain. Could your Lynx tolerate that?"

Dax opened his eyes. "I believe so."

"Then Sora and I need plenty of that salve, along with a strong lavender and poppy or cannabis tea—if you have those things."

Griffin's smile was kind. "Of course we do. We also have the ingredients for the poultice ready for your use. Mikayla can mix them while you disinfect and numb Mihos's paws and his Dax's hands."

"That would be wonderful. Thank you."

The teas were brought to the two patients. Mihos lapped his up gratefully, but Dax asked, "Will it make me sleep?"

"Absolutely. You'll want to sleep through my cleaning of your hands," said Sora. "Even with the numbing salve."

"I will only take the water and broth. Either the cleaning will wait or I will deal with the pain. I must speak with the Lead Mare Rider and the Council." Dax lifted a bloody hand when Sora began to speak. "No. My Lynx and I almost killed ourselves to get here."

Mari and Sora shared a look and then Mari said, "Do you have news of the God of Death?"

Dax's gaze went to Mari. "You know He has followed you?"

"River," Mari said. "I think you should bring Dove in."

"Agreed," River said. "I'll get her, Tulpar, Morgana, and Mother."

"I can go for you, if you wish," said Nik.

"Thank you. Yes."

While Nik jogged from the infirmary, Mari began gently submerging the Lynx's gory paws while the feline held very still and appeared to be asleep but panted with stress and pain. While Mari tended to Mihos, Sora held a mug of steaming broth to Dax's lips as he drank greedily—and almost immediately color began to return to his sallow cheeks. When Morgana, Dawn, Dove, and Tulpar joined them in the large room, Dax had been propped up by pelts to a half-sitting position and his hands were submerged in bowls of warm goldenseal water.

River nodded to Dax. "Speak, brave Lynx Companion. We shall listen."

CHAPTER 5

Dax cleared his throat and began his terrible story as the small group listened attentively.

"I was summoned to the Tribe of the Trees several months ago, in the middle of spring. What I found there was not the Tribe as I had known it for many years." Dax met Nik's gaze. "I am sorry about Sol. He was a very good man."

"Thank you," said Nik somberly.

"I was not prepared for what I discovered when I reached the Tribe," continued Dax. "That they had been devastated by fire was bad enough, but they had also been taken over by Skin Stealers and their god, the God of Death, and infected by His sickness." Dax shuddered. "The stench was so bad that I believed the Tribe had started tanning hides in the trees."

"Why did the Tribe summon you?" asked River.

"They wanted me to guide them here, to the Plains of the Wind Riders. I accepted the job not knowing the truth about them—that they were an invading army. Death wisely kept hidden the twisted things His people were becoming, but the Tribe's Storyteller, Ralina, came to me and told me the truth."

"Ralina lives!" Nik exclaimed.

"Or at least she did several months ago," said Mari.

"She lives still," Dax said somberly. "She was alive seven days ago, but I get ahead of myself. Let me go back to the beginning, please."

Wise Morgana moved closer to the pallet on which Dax reclined and sat on the wooden chair Mikayla placed there for her. "Tell the story in your own time, brave Companion. You are here now. All will be well."

"This is Morgana, Leader of the Mare Council," said River.

Dax's eyes were shadowed with misery. "No, Council Leader. I'm afraid after what I have witnessed no one will ever be well again." He drew a deep breath and then continued. "Ralina warned me about the intentions of the Death God—that He meant to invade, not immigrate. That He had poisoned their forest. That He was creating an army of men mutated to be more beast than man." Dax shook his head. "Though then I did not fully believe her, nor comprehend the extent of the god's power. I was a fool."

"No, you are a rational man who wasn't prepared for the horrors the God of Death is unleashing." Dove spoke in a clear voice. She stood beside her golden stallion, one hand resting on his shoulder.

"This is Dove," said Mari. "She is a Seer of the Great Earth Goddess and was just Chosen by Magenti's Herd Stallion, Tulpar."

"But before that I was one of the People, or, as you rightly call them, a Skin Stealer, and I intimately know what it is like to underestimate the God of Death," said Dove.

Dax shook his head again. "You don't understand. It is my fault that they're dead."

"Who is dead?" asked Dawn.

River finished the introductions with, "This is my mother, Dawn."

Dax's lips lifted at the corners briefly. "Yes, I recognize the longtime Lead Mare Rider of Herd Magenti."

Dawn's smile was sweet. "Retired now, and grateful the Herd is in my daughter's capable hands. Who is dead, Lynx Companion?"

"The Saleesh," Dax said. "Ralina told me Death was an invader—a murderer—that I must warn all Lynx Guides not to answer any call from the Tribe of the Trees, that we must disappear into our dens, and that I must warn the Saleesh, as well as the Wind Riders, of Death's intentions." Dax's gaze swept the room. "I should have done what Ralina instructed immediately. Instead, I thought I had time. I did make the emergency call so that all Lynx Guide pairs retreated to our northern Gathering Place in the mountains. I reported to them what Ralina had said, and what I had seen for myself—that there is, indeed, a creature Who appears to be a god amassing a mutant army where once the mighty Tribe of the Trees thrived. I informed them of the poison the God had purposely spread to the forest and warned them not to eat of any meat from animals acting oddly or smelling foul. Then I waited. I assumed that the Tribe would put out another call for a guide. At that time I planned to begin the trek to warn the Saleesh and then cross the Rock Mountains to your plains and warn you."

"Death did not call for another guide," Dove said.

"No." Dax spoke the word as if it left a bitter taste in his mouth. "And finally, with the approval of the Lynx Chain, my friend Tobin and his Companion, Prospero, joined Mihos and me to journey to the Saleesh and warn them of what might happen." His expression twisted in pain as he remembered. "I waited too long. We were too late. Death had already been up the Umbria River. The Saleesh are no more."

"So the Goddess foretold. So the Goddess warned." Dove leaned against Tulpar, who blew softly on her smooth cheek.

"Dax," Sora explained, "we tried to warn the Saleesh. Dove had a vision when we were in the first of their villages. We reported the vision to their priest—that the Goddess told Dove the Saleesh must leave their homes for a full turn of the seasons, or they would not survive. They did not listen. Again we tried to warn them when we left their territory, and again they refused to believe."

"They would not have believed you, Dax," said Dove. "Or had they believed you, they would have simply armed themselves and tried to fight. But they would not have defeated Death. That is why the Great Goddess wanted them to leave, and warned them through me."

"You aren't responsible for what happened to them," Mari added. "Their priest is—as is the God of Death."

"No matter," said Dax darkly. "It gets worse from there."

"Explain *worse*," said Morgana.

Dax's gaze found a spot on the smooth wall of the cave. He stared at it as he continued. "Tobin and I crossed Lost Lake. We knew once we were in the Rock Mountains we could travel much faster than an army. We meant to catch up with Death and witness the demise of His army as they became lost in the mountains. As Death had no guide, He should not have been able to find and follow the path through the passes, but I was wrong again. He had a guide—the spirit of a dead doe."

River jolted as if someone had struck her. "What? A spirit is leading this monster to us?"

"I know it sounds mad, but I saw her. Tobin and I traveled the more difficult, but shorter, path Lynx Guides use to traverse the Rock Mountains when we are alone. We move from tree to tree—impossible without the abilities our Companions share with us when they Choose us. We traveled that way until we caught up with Death and His army. Then we observed them. It is how I know that at least a week ago Ralina still lived. She and her Companion are with Death."

"The Storyteller has joined Death's army?" Nik blurted the question.

"No, no—not at all. Ralina had already explained to me that she believed she had to remain with Death. He has tasked her with telling His story, and she told me that because of the god's vanity, He tells her many things about Himself. She is determined to discover how to send Him back to His place within the earth where He sleeps in the arms of the Goddess of Life."

"Death's ultimate desire is to awaken the Goddess of Life," Dove said.

"I know nothing about that," said Dax. "But Ralina mentioned that Death awakened before and then He almost destroyed the world."

"What else did you observe?" Morgana asked.

"We saw their *guide*, the poor enslaved spirit of a little doe. She leads Death along the path guides use to take groups through the Rock Mountains. But the doe isn't the worst of it. His army—" Dax shuddered. "They are ghastly. The men have mutated. They are grotesque mixtures of human and animal." Dax met Nik's gaze then. "The Tribesmen who are with Him—Thaddeus and his ilk—are becoming something twisted, something *not* human, because they flayed the flesh of their Companions and somehow their bodies absorbed that flesh. It has changed them— horribly—and in more than just their physical appearances. They are cruel, arrogant, heartless, and their canines seem to be avoiding them."

Nik's face drained of color. "We know. Mari and I saw it happening when we escaped the Tribe."

"There's more," Dax said. "The Saleesh are also with them. The dead

66

Saleesh. The god somehow reanimated their bodies. Their eyes are completely white. They walk. They carry weapons. We even got close enough to hear that they speak, though their language is odd and difficult to understand."

"How many?" River asked. "How many are in this invading army of mutants and dead things?"

"There are almost three hundred of the mutated men. We counted more than a thousand more of the Saleesh walking dead."

"The Herds outnumber them," said River. "By many. With our Companions we are a formidable force—more powerful than an army of twisted men and the dead."

Dove's soft voice was filled with sadness. "Unless Death poisons the Wind Rider Plains and then convinces Riders to take His *cure*. The poison will decimate the plains—and forever change its Riders."

"No Rider would fillet the flesh from their beloved Companion," said Dawn firmly. "No Rider would do such a terrible thing."

"Forgive me, Mare Rider," Dove said. Then she turned her eyeless face toward Nik. "Nik, son of Sol, before everything changed with the Tribe of the Trees, would you not have spoken the words Dawn just said about your people?"

"Absolutely." He sent Dawn an apologetic look. "I know too well how you feel—how the belief in the goodness of your people can be blinding. The Tribe thrived—so much so we were greatly expanding our city in the trees. Harvests were plentiful. Pups were born often. Artists were revered. We were greatly blessed. So it was easy to overlook what festered just beneath the surface . . ." Nik paused and continued hesitantly. "Forgive me. I apologize if I overstep with my words. The Sun Priest of our Tribe was my father. Much like Dax, I will always wish I had done more, believed the signs, acted sooner."

"Apologies detract from facts," said River flatly. "Speak plainly. What happened? How did Death infiltrate such a powerful, prosperous Tribe?"

"A Companion named Thaddeus used to be our Lead Hunter," Nik said grimly. "He had long been an irritant. He always wanted more than he had earned. More respect. More power. More status. Even though Thaddeus is several years older, I used to think of him as a petulant child. I thought he needed discipline, and his position taken from him, but I did not think he was a serious threat to our Tribe. I couldn't have been more mistaken. Somehow Death knew Thaddeus's true nature, got to him, infected him with the Skin Stealer disease, and then offered him their *cure*."

Dove said, "I was there when Thaddeus was brought to the city. It was clear then that his selfishness was greater than his dedication to your Tribe. It was through his selfish lust for more that Death was able to use him." Beside her Tulpar pawed the floor and blew angrily. "Tulpar says Clayton is our Thaddeus. He wants me to ask the wise Mare Riders in this room whether they believe Clayton would turn down the offer of power and status to protect our Herd."

"He would not," said River.

"Agreed," said Morgana.

"Yes, I can see that. I agree as well," added Dawn.

"Clayton and his followers must be found, captured, and held," said River. "After we are free of the threat Death and His army pose we will banish them. Dax, how far behind you are they?"

"If they keep up the pace they have, which has been ridiculously slow, they will be here in seven days—perhaps a few more." Dax shook his head in disgust. "The God acts as if He plays a game. Tobin and I watched Him make camp early and break camp late. The Hunters with Him provide plenty of game, and He feasts daily and spends half the daylight being fondled and fed by His women. It is only blind luck there has not been heavy snow in the mountains yet, or they would all be trapped," said Dax.

"So we only have seven days to prepare," said River.

"Yes. When Tobin and I realized Death's army did have a guide, and they would truly make it through the mountain passes, we raced for your plains." Dax's expression fell. "We were traveling fast, with little regard to our safety because we knew what was at risk—the extinction of every Wind Rider Herd. Tobin and his Prospero were several years older than Mihos and me. They—they tired. I tried to get Tobin to let me go ahead—tried to get him to return to our Chain. He refused. Three days ago Tobin missed a toehold on a tree and fell. He was swallowed into the depths of a crevasse. Prospero did not hesitate. He followed his Companion to his death. Mihos and I have not rested since. Forgive me for not arriving sooner."

Morgana leaned forward and placed her age-lined hand on Dax's leg.

"There is nothing to forgive. Tobin and Prospero's sacrifice shall never be forgotten. We will sing of them for generations—as we will sing of the bravery of you and your Mihos, too."

"If you live. If we all live," said Dax grimly.

"We will live," said River.

"How do we prepare for an invading army of mutants and walking dead in seven days?" Dawn sounded uncharacteristically shaken.

As the silence stretched into despair, Mari said, "We need more time."

Sora smeared numbing salve on Dax's disinfected wounds and muttered, "By the tits of the Goddess we need a mountain snowstorm. That'd slow them down and buy us some time."

River's chin jerked up. "My dream!"

"What dream, Mare Rider? You must speak it," Dove said urgently. "The Goddess came to me last night and served notice that She is stirring and that I should prepare Her people to listen to and watch for Her signs and omens; She often speaks through dreams."

River's smile was fierce. "She spoke through my dream last night! Now it makes sense! The Great Mother Mare sent me a dream that was filled with snow—and showed me the crystal needed to bring about such a storm." She turned to her mother. "Didn't Grandmother have a rain crystal? A huge one that was threaded with green, like fingers of moss?"

Dawn's eyes widened. "She did. We haven't needed to use it for many years."

"Well, we need to use it now," said Morgana.

Confused, Mari asked, "You're going to make it rain?"

"In a way," River said. "In the hands of a powerful crystal Seer the stone will call down rain, which means if it is used in the mountains it will call down—"

"Snow!" Sora said excitedly.

"I've thought of something else that would slow them down," said Nik. "Dax, you know the long suspension bridge that crosses the gorge?"

"I do."

"Can Antreas and Bast reach it before Death does?"

Dax shook his head. "No. Even moving as slowly as they are, Death's army will reach the bridge in a couple days or so. It would take twice that time for Antreas to get there."

"We should have known that Death would follow us," Nik said. "We should have destroyed that bridge after we crossed it."

"I am so sorry, River," Mari said. "I can't bear that we have led Death to your plains."

River shook her head. "You didn't set evil loose. You're no more responsible for Death's actions than I am responsible for Clayton's lust for power."

"We shall do everything we can to help you—to fight and rid the world of Death and His army," Dove said. "And I believe we have a powerful ally in the Goddess. While I was being used by Death, I began to believe the Goddess did not want to awaken, then when She made me Her Seer I hoped it, and now I truly believe it. So, consider your dreams as you look for omens and signs."

"And you believe this goddess Who speaks through you, Who you call Goddess of Life, is also our Great Mother Mare?" Morgana asked.

"I absolutely do," said Dove.

"I'm counting on it," said River. "Now, Mari and Sora, while you finish tending to Dax and Mihos I will gather the Herd. Join us in the Choosing Theater as soon as possible. We have much to do, and little time to do it."

CHAPTER 6

How are the Lynx and his Companion?" Danita asked quietly as Mari and Sora joined the rest of the Pack in the Choosing Theater stadium.

"Dax's hands just needed to be treated and bandaged," said Sora. "He wasn't hurt badly—just exhausted and dehydrated."

"Mihos didn't fare so well," said Mari as she greeted Rigel by kissing his nose and hugging Nik, who scooted over to let her sit beside him and Laru. "That poor feline's paws were shredded. I cannot imagine the pain he must have endured as he walked on them. I had to sew lacerations and deep punctures on all four paws. Tonight is Third Night and when we draw down the moon I'll be sure to channel healing to him. Still, I wouldn't be surprised if he is unable to bear weight on them for weeks. It was a very brave thing the two of them did."

"It has given the Herds time to prepare," said Antreas from his spot beside Danita.

"I think it's saved all of our lives," said Sora. "But I hate that we led Death to these beautiful plains and these amazing people." Her shoulders slumped as she brushed her hair from her face.

"We don't actually know what made Death come here," said O'Bryan, who touched Sora gently on her shoulder. "We might never know."

"Though I also hate that it seems Death is following us here to these plains, I agree with O'Bryan. Logic says we cannot be responsible for the decisions of a god, but we're going to do everything we can to help the Herds defeat Death and His army," said Mari. "I can already tell River is an excellent leader, and the Mare Council, especially Morgana, seem wise."

Sora nodded. "From what we've heard about that Rider named Clayton, I believe Mari and I would have passed a similar judgment had he been one of the Clan."

Antreas said, "Wind Riders are known for their excellent governance—their fairness and honesty. Their strong matriarchy has prospered for centuries. I just don't understand men like Clayton—or Thaddeus."

"I think any decent person has a hard time understanding men like them," said O'Bryan.

"Here comes River now." Mari pointed to the entrance to the Choosing Theater. River rode Anjo, the brilliant silver-white mare. Mari smiled to see that she'd already fashioned a type of basket strapped to the mare's broad back. Inside it Kit's little dark head and bright eyes were just visible as she peered out at the world from atop the mare like a puppy queen.

Mari leaned forward so she could catch Rose's attention. "How are the pups who Chose the Wind Riders doing?"

Rose's smile punctuated her answer. "They're settling in happily. Both are completely taken with their Companions' mares. I worried at first they'd get trampled under their huge hooves, but the horses are incredibly careful and very gentle with them. It's impressive." Rose pointed to the field. "Look, April and River have fashioned those little baskets on their mares so the pups can stay with them."

Everyone's attention turned to the field as River's Second, April, entered the field on her black mare, whose face had a pretty white blaze. Following on their aging mares were Morgana and the half-dozen older women who Mari knew represented the Mare Council because, as River had explained, they wore the colors of all five Herds.

Protectively bringing up the rear was the spectacular golden stallion, Tulpar, with Dove astride.

"Dove looks so proud," Lily said from her seat behind Mari as she cuddled little Dash in her arms. "I would be afraid to ride that huge horse."

"I'd love to ride one. I think the horses are magnificent," said O'Bryan.

"Hey, Cuz, I finally get why you've been obsessed with them since we were kids."

Nik grinned over his shoulder at his cousin. "Where's your wolverine?"

"Cubby's nursing with the rest of the pups. Mariah is an excellent mother," said O'Bryan.

"How is the baby wolverine doing?" Sora asked.

O'Bryan's eyes sparkled. "Cubby's growing fast but is still too little to be away from Mariah for long—though I make sure to spend time with him every day."

"Cubby? Is that what you've decided to call him?" Sora asked.

O'Bryan shrugged. "Well, yeah, unless he can figure out how to tell me his name."

"Don't hold your breath," said Nik. "A wolverine is *not* a canine."

"Or a Lynx," said Antreas from the other side of Danita as he scratched Bast's tufted ears.

"I think Cubby's going to show all of you someday just how magnificent he is," said O'Bryan.

Mari opened her mouth to agree with O'Bryan—she was all for giving the fuzzy little creature a chance—when River's voice rang throughout the theater.

"Would the leaders of our newly accepted Pack please join me on the field?"

"That's us." Sora stood and rearranged the carrier her Terrier pup, Chloe, rested within, close to her heart.

"Wish us luck," said Mari, kissing Nik quickly. "Come on, Rigel. They might as well get used to seeing you with me."

"A mare's luck to you," said Nik with a glint in his eyes.

When Mari and Sora reached River, they joined April and the Mare Council, who stood in a semicircle behind the Lead Mare Rider. Mari was, again, impressed by the confidence with which this young woman held herself. Like Mari, River couldn't have seen much more than eighteen winters, but there was an authority that radiated from her and induced trust. *Mama would have liked her—a lot.*

As if reading her mind, Sora whispered, "River reminds me of a Moon Woman."

River remained astride Anjo, and from the basket in which little Kit sat she took a blue crystal the size of a man's fist and held it at the base of her neck. The Herd was attentive but silent as their Lead Mare Rider drew several deep breaths, and then Mari had to stifle a gasp as the blue crystal began to glow. Still holding it, River spoke—and her voice was amplified so that it carried easily throughout the theater.

"Not long ago when I was named Lead Mare Rider I vowed to myself and to my Herd that I would be honest with you. Because of my vow, and because I trust that you will not panic, I am going to be honest with you about the news the courageous guide Dax and his Lynx Companion, Mihos, risked their lives to bring us.

"There is an invading army approaching our plains. They are led by the God of Death. The God's army is made up of mutated men and reanimated dead. Their god adds to His army by spreading disease. *We must stop Him. We will stop Him.* But to do that we must ready the Herds for battle and siege. Dax has reported that the army is seven days away in the Rock Mountains passage. The Great Mother Mare has shown me how to slow their approach, but that will not stop them. Death's army will reach our plains—and Magenti must be secure and ready for Him. I have already ordered the signal fires to be lit. All of Magenti will immediately retreat to our stronghold in the Valley of Vapors."

River motioned for Dove and Tulpar to join her and then continued. "Tulpar, choose the four swiftest Rider/Companion pairs. They will each race to the other four Great Herds. The Herds will be warned about Death and His army and understand that they must immediately break camp and go to their strongholds—The Buttes, The Caves, The Great Southern Forest, and The Tex Islands. Let me make that warning clear so that the Riders can be accurate in their retellings. Our new Herdmembers, the Pack, know of this god and how He spreads His poison. All Herds must be advised that they cannot eat of any meat from an animal that acts odd, or whose meat smells foul. The animals must be destroyed and their bodies burned. If anyone, human or animal, eats of their flesh, they will be infected with a skin-sloughing disease that can only be cured by a worse fate—one that happens when a Rider fillets the living flesh from their Companion and packs it into their skin."

River had to pause to allow the Herd to shout their outrage. Her raised hand quieted them, but before she could continue Mari stepped forward.

"River, may I speak?"

"Yes, Mari." River kneed Anjo to Mari's side and passed her the glowing blue crystal.

Mari was surprised at the warmth of the crystal and the pleasant sense of serenity she felt as soon as she touched it. She drew a deep breath and faced the crowded theater. "As some of you already know, Sora and I are Moon Women, which means we can call down the healing power of the moon. With that power we can cure the skin-sloughing sickness, though it is a serious disease. It isn't difficult to avoid eating tainted meat, but we have learned from the destruction of the Tribe of the Trees that the God of Death targets people who are discontented within their Tribe—or in this case it would be Herd. That is how He destroys—from within. You must all understand that, and you must make that part of your warnings to the other Herds." Mari passed the crystal back to River.

"And that is why Clayton and his followers will be found, captured, and held until we have dealt with Death and His army," said River. "It is sad that we must waste time on tracking and imprisoning Clayton when we should be preparing to battle Death and His army, but I believe the Pack and the Lynx Guides. Clayton is our weakest link. We cannot afford to ignore him and his followers and leave them to Death—not when Death can use them to enslave the rest of us."

Before River could continue, a dapple-gray mare carrying her Rider trotted into the field. Mari was shocked to recognize Skye—the Rider who had been Clayton's lover. Surprise crossed River's face and was replaced quickly by irritation.

"I can find Clayton. I will tell him whatever you want me to tell him. I can say the threats against all of us outweigh his deeds and he has been forgiven because we need every Rider to help protect the Herd. He would never believe I would lie to him. I can convince him to take his followers to the Valley of Vapors, where you can imprison him. I can do this for our Herd so that our Warriors do not waste valuable time."

Even though Skye's voice didn't carry into the stadium, the people closest to the field spread her words like fall leaves rustling to those behind them.

River's crystal-enhanced voice silenced everyone. "Skye, I have no reason to trust you."

From the edge of the stadium River's mother, Dawn, on her magnificent mare, trotted into the field. She bowed respectfully to her daughter. "Might I speak, Lead Mare Rider?" she asked formally.

"Of course." River passed her mother the glowing crystal. Dawn did not turn to face the crowd but instead spoke directly to her daughter, though her voice lifted throughout the theater.

"Will you allow Skye to go to Clayton if I accompany her?"

River waited for the surprised gasps of the Herd to subside before she responded, "Why would you do that, Mother?"

Dawn's response was swift and clear. "What Clayton did was inexcusable. His followers have made the mistaken, irrevocable choice to join him in his sedition. They will—they *must* pay the consequences of their choice. But they are still our sons and daughters, brothers and sisters— our friends. I ask that we hold them accountable for what they have done and attempted to do, but that we do it with compassion."

River drew a deep breath and let it out slowly. "What is it you suggest?"

"I do not believe even Clayton and his Riders will disrespect me. I choose to be honest with them. They will listen when I explain the danger we are all in. Perhaps when they understand the threat to our Herd we will not have to imprison them. Perhaps they will willingly join us at the Valley of Vapors. We know that Clayton's followers are mostly Stallion Riders. It is in their blood, their hearts, their very souls, to protect their Herd. I do not believe they are so far gone that they will not listen to and heed their instincts."

"And if they do not listen? They did not heed their instincts when they followed Clayton's sedition." Enhanced by anger, River's voice lifted to the raptly watching Herd. "If they refuse and remain on the path Clayton has chosen for them, what then?"

"Then Skye and I will leave them and report back to the Herd that they are beyond hope," Dawn said. "And I will recommend to you and the Mare Council that we waste no more time on them—that they be executed quickly and as humanely as possible before they cause the destruction of us all."

River turned to face the Mare Council. "Morgana, what says the Council? I will follow your advice. Do we send Warriors to capture the traitors, or do we send Dawn and Skye to attempt to reason with them?"

Morgana nodded respectfully to River before the ancient mares huddled in a tight circle as their Riders spoke quietly to one another. It took only a few minutes, and then Morgana rode to River's side.

"The Council agrees that Dawn and Skye should seek out Clayton and his followers and give them the opportunity for redemption—though we are also in agreement that the banishment must stand."

"And should they reject our proposal?" River asked.

Morgana responded with no hesitation, "Should that happen, Lead Mare Rider, the Council prays their deaths be fast and merciful."

"Then I agree. Dawn and Skye, leave today for Iron Springs immediately. Inform Clayton and his followers they will be allowed to do their duty to their Herd and regain their honor before they are banished from our plains. If they refuse, leave their camp immediately and meet us in the Valley of Vapors and our Warriors shall deal with them. Their end will come swiftly—before Death can use them against us. It has been said!"

"*It has been said!*" the Herd roared their agreement.

"Now Anjo and I will journey a short way into the Rock Mountains, where I will call a snowstorm to close the pass to our plains. We must not count on that to stop Death and His army, but it will grant us time to warn the Great Herds and to escape to our strongholds so that we may prepare for battle and plan how we will defeat the God of Death."

From the middle of the theater stadium a man stood. Beside him his Lynx was silhouetted against the morning sun.

"Bast and I would be honored to guide you into the mountains!" shouted Antreas.

River grinned and nodded. "Good, I was going to ask if you would."

Antreas saluted her, which caused the Herdmembers around him to smile.

The golden stallion pranced to Anjo. Dove's serene, sightless face was turned to River. "Tulpar asks that we accompany you as well, Lead Mare Rider."

River bowed her head respectfully to Dove and Tulpar. "I welcome the company and the protection of our new Herd Stallion and his Rider."

Dove's cheeks flushed pink, but she held herself regally and nodded in return. "Tulpar and I will be ready to leave whenever you are, Mare Rider."

"That will be soon. The storm must begin today. Herd Magenti, pack only essentials. Understand we may well be preparing for a long siege. Herdmembers who usually remain here year round and tend to our Choosing Theater and the surrounding fields, it is not safe for you to stay here. *All* of Herd Magenti departs at dawn for the Valley of Vapors." River turned to speak directly to the Mare Council Members. "Morgana, I ask that you and the Council aid me in sealing the cave in the morning."

"That is wise of you, Mare Rider. We shall certainly aid you," said Morgana.

River faced the theater once more. "Herd Magenti, we must move quickly. Keep in mind that with all of Magenti in the Valley of Vapors there is only room for us to bring necessities. Move the priceless things you cannot carry into the bowels of our cave. Tomorrow at dawn we will seal the entrance, which will keep everything within safe until our return." Anjo trotted forward, closer to the stadium seats that were filled with Herdmembers. River spoke earnestly and clearly—and the Herd barely breathed as they listened. "I know the thought of the God of Death leading an invading army to our plains is frightening, but look around—gaze at the might of our Herd. We will be safe in our stronghold. We will defeat Death's army—and we will defeat Death. And how do I know this with such certainty? Because I know you. I believe in you. I believe in *us*. The strongest force in the world is not death or disease or lust for power. The strongest force in the world is evidenced right here—between us and our Companions, between our families, between our mighty Herdmembers. Our love and devotion to each other is the strongest force in the world. Death cannot break it; Death will not break us!"

From behind River, April raised her arm and shouted, "It has been said!"

As one, the Herd responded, "*It has been said!*"

And even though Mari's stomach felt sick with worry, her spirit lifted as she shouted with the Herd, *her* Herd—and she smiled fiercely as the Pack shouted with her.

CHAPTER 7

"Watch Skye closely." River spoke quietly to her mother as Dawn finished strapping a saddlebag with her bedroll and supplies onto Echo's strong back. "If she tries to speak privately with Clayton, do not allow it. Remember, Mother, he tried to kill Tulpar and me."

Dawn turned and smiled serenely at her daughter. "You must not spend energy worrying about me, Daughter. Focus on one thing at a time. First coaxing snow into the passes, and then moving the Herd to the Valley of Vapors. In my decade as Lead Mare Rider I dealt with many difficulties. Remember that group of Riders who decided they wanted to circumvent my authority and choose for themselves with whom their stallions mated? I put a swift end to that. I am used to handling men who wish for more than they deserve."

"Yeah, but none of them tried to kill you." River frowned as she stroked Echo's smooth neck.

Dawn touched her daughter's smooth, umber cheek. "I will never forget how close I came to losing you, and that Clayton is responsible for breaking our most sacred law—*no Herdmember shall ever harm another Companion or Rider*. He will pay for his arrogance and for his crime, but I intend to treat him and his followers with compassion, whether that means offering him the opportunity to redeem himself before he is forever banished from our homelands or helping the Herd give him a swift and merciful death. Remember, Lead Mare Rider, showing compassion and kindness does not mean you are weak. It means you are merciful, and mercy is never weakness."

River hugged her mother tightly and whispered, "I will remember all the lessons I have learned at your side."

Dawn stepped back and mounted Echo as Skye and Scout trotted up. "Skye and I will join you in the valley. Until then, may a mare's luck be with you, my daughter."

"And you as well, Mother," said River. She met Skye's gaze. "Don't make me regret that I agreed to let you go."

"I won't, Lead Mare Rider," Skye said formally.

"Daughter, do not overthink using your grandmother's rain crystal," Dawn said. "Ground yourself. Set your intention. Speak that intention to the crystal and free its power. It is as simple as that."

River nodded. "I will do so. I love you, Mother."

"And I you, River." Echo stretched her muzzle forward and lipped River's hair, which caused mother and daughter to laugh softly. "Echo loves you as well."

River kissed the velvet muzzle of her mother's spectacular mare. "Love you, too, gorgeous. Take care of our Dawn."

Echo spun neatly around and pranced away, tail up, looking a decade younger than her years.

Followed by her mare, Deinos, and Anjo, April hurried up to River. The two pups Kit and Cleo gamboled in the grass around the mares; both horses watched the babies, careful where they put their hooves. In her arms April cradled a magnificent crystal that was the size of a human head. It was brilliantly clear, except for fingers of green that looked like frozen moss tendrils that threaded through its sparkling depths.

"This crystal is amazing," April said breathlessly. "I don't remember Grandmother or Mother using it. Actually, I don't think I've ever seen it before, though it was right where Mother said it would be—wrapped in purple cloth in the bottom of that big wooden chest that used to be Grandmother's."

Carefully, River took the crystal from her sister, and it immediately began to warm against her hands. "Rain has been plentiful on the plains for at least a decade, so we haven't needed it. I remember seeing it once, though, when we were little girls. Grandmother used it one night when there was a dry lightning storm. It was late summer and lightning strikes had started a fire in the grasslands. I was so young that I couldn't make myself stay awake to watch Grandma call down the rain, but I do remember that I was shocked by the size of the crystal. Oh, and it definitely worked. Rain followed the lightning and quenched the fire."

April sighed. "I was too young. I don't remember at all."

"Well, you're not too young now." River's eyes sparkled as she smiled at her sister.

"Wait, you're going to let me go with you?"

River nodded. "Of course. The Herd knows what to do. We're experts at moving our camp and our people. There's no need for you to supervise, especially with the Mare Council here. They'll keep the Herd focused. That is, unless you *want* to stay in camp."

"No, no, absolutely not." April bounced up and down on the balls of her feet. "I want to go with you and have a story to tell my grandchildren."

River's dark brows went up. "Are you and Brax getting serious?"

April's fawn cheeks flushed. "No. He's too . . ." She shrugged and then whispered, "He's too *boring*."

River cocked her head and studied her sister, who was growing into a beautiful young woman. "Well, good for you not wasting your time with someone who isn't interesting."

"Yeah." April's gaze found Skye's disappearing back. "I do want someone to love, but not just anyone."

"Wise and beautiful," said River, mimicking their mother's voice perfectly, making both of them giggle, which is when Tulpar joined them with Dove astride. Mari, her Shepherd Companion, Antreas, and his Lynx walked beside the golden stallion.

Antreas whistled long and low. "Stormshaker! That is some crystal."

"I've never seen anything like it," said Mari. "May I touch it?"

"Sure." River turned so that Mari could reach the crystal.

Mari touched it with her forefinger first. "It's warm, like that smaller blue crystal you used in the Choosing Theater to make our voices louder." Then she stroked it with her hand—gently, as if petting a nervous puppy.

River watched the Moon Woman closely. "You feel the warmth of the crystals?"

Mari reluctantly took her hand from the crystal. "Well, yes, but this one is different than the blue crystal."

"Go on," River coaxed. "What do you mean by 'different'?"

"Both crystals felt warm when I touched them, but the blue crystal also felt soothing. I was nervous about speaking to the Herd today—worried that the Pack would be blamed for Death's invasion—but the moment I held the blue crystal I stopped worrying."

"We do not blame your Pack. You are not responsible for the choices of a god," River said. "After poisoning your lands it isn't surprising that the God of Death decided to move on."

"Thank you, River. Thank you for understanding that," said Mari.

"But tell me more, Mari. You said this crystal felt different than the aquamarine I used earlier. How so?"

Mari rested her hand on the skin of the crystal once more. "This one isn't soothing. It's cooler. Which doesn't really make sense because it's warm to the touch, but it makes me think of springtime and green and growing things." Mari smiled. "Our women would be fascinated by this crystal. You haven't had time to learn much about us yet, but all Earth Walker women are attuned to growing things."

"And do you use crystals to aid your growing?" April asked.

"No, we have no knowledge about how to connect with crystals." Mari smiled. "But won't it be fun to see what happens when a Crystal Seer and a Moon Woman combine their talents?"

"It absolutely will," said River. "Mari, would you like to come with us and observe how I use this crystal to draw down the snowstorm?"

Mari's face lit with excitement. "Yes, I would love that." Then her expression fell. "But I have a feeling you'll be moving too quickly for me. Rigel could keep up with you, but I don't think I could."

Tulpar snorted and took a step closer to Mari, and as he did her eyes widened and she grinned up at the big golden stallion. "Really? You'd really let me?"

From astride Tulpar's back, Dove laughed musically. "Yes, Mari, Tulpar will happily carry you as well as me into the mountains."

River felt a jolt of shock. "Mari, did you just hear Tulpar?"

Mari's gaze met hers. "Well, yes. I can hear all Companions, but I don't eavesdrop. For instance, I cannot hear what Anjo says to you unless Anjo wishes me to," she added quickly.

"That's fascinating, and something we'll have to discuss later. Can all of your Pack communicate with other Companions?" River asked.

"No," Mari said. "I asked Nik about it when I first realized that I could communicate with his Companion, Laru, and he said he's never known anyone who could hear other Companions." She shrugged. "I don't know why I can." Then her gaze lifted to Dove. "That reminds me, Dove. You asked us to pay attention to our dreams. Last night I had a strangely vivid dream. It even woke me. Lots of our Companions—along with animals I don't even know—surrounded me, and I could hear all of them. They were supporting me, grounding me, comforting and holding me. It was strange and beautiful."

Dove nodded contemplatively. "Thank you for telling me, Mari. Try to remember all aspects of your dream. The Goddess of Life stirs. She sends signs and omens. Like River's dream about snow—it might make no sense at that moment but be very important in the future."

"I'll remember," said Mari.

"Hey, we'd better get going," said Antreas. "It's Third Night, and I know Mari needs to be back by moonrise."

"Yes, absolutely," said River. "April, would you help Antreas boost Mari up behind Dove?" Then she whistled sharply and called, "Kit, come here, little girl. Time to ride Anjo!" Immediately the fat pup waddled from under Deinos's hooves to River, yapping excitedly as she was scooped up and deposited in the basket strapped behind River's saddle. "I'm putting this next to you, little girl. I know you'll protect it." River kissed her little black nose before she secured the large crystal beside the pup in the basket.

"Antreas, make a step with me by grabbing my wrists." April held out her hands, showing Antreas what she meant. "Okay, good. Now Mari, just put your foot on our linked hands and on three we'll boost you up onto Tulpar's back."

As Rigel watched intently and Tulpar held very still, Mari did as April instructed and she found herself astride the golden stallion.

"Oh, Goddess! We're so high up." Mari stroked the stallion's glossy coat. "Thank you, Tulpar, you are as kind as you are handsome." She grinned down at Rigel. "Just like my Companion." Rigel's whole body wiggled as he wagged his tail and barked.

"What did Tulpar say?" asked River.

"That he will be gentle with me so that I won't fall," explained Mari.

"My beautiful Tulpar will be very careful with us," said Dove as she patted the stallion's neck affectionately. "But be sure you squeeze tightly with your legs and sit deeply. You will find your balance."

"It won't hurt him?" Mari asked.

River, April, and Dove laughed softly, a sound that was echoed in the amused snorts of the three horses.

"Let me guess." River spoke over her shoulder as Anjo led them through the camp at a smooth trot. "Tulpar just spoke to you again."

Mari grinned as she gripped the stallion's flanks. "He just told me that such a small thing—and by 'small thing' I'm pretty sure he means me—could not possibly hurt him."

Tulpar was careful. His gaits were so smooth that it didn't take long for Dove and Mari to become comfortable with his rolling canter. The three horses followed Antreas and Bast as they seemed to fly among the trees, heading back into the Rock Mountains. Rigel, tongue lolling, kept pace with them.

After they entered the Rock Mountains pass, they had to slow to a ground-eating trot—a pace the horses had no problem keeping up as the sun traveled up the sky above them and the air around them got colder and colder, until the horses appeared to be breathing smoke. Mari was grateful for the warmth of Tulpar and Dove, and surprised herself by feeling more nostalgic than she expected as the trail she and her Pack had so recently traversed seemed to blur past.

"Our journey through these mountains would've been a lot faster and more comfortable if we'd been riding your magnificent horses." Mari spoke to River as Anjo trotted beside Tulpar, with April on her Deinos directly behind them.

River snorted a laugh. "Horses can't travel very far through the pass. Much of it is too steep and too narrow, but they are a lot swifter than being on foot."

"Unless by 'being on foot' you mean a Lynx Companion," April added, gesturing at Antreas, who moved almost as fast as his stealthy Lynx.

"Danita says Antreas can fly," said Mari. "But she's never ridden a horse." She stroked Tulpar's flank again. "Before we got up here into the pass, when we were able to . . . what was the word. Oh, yes, *canter*, it really did feel like Tulpar was riding the wind." Mari grinned at River. "And now I understand why you're called Wind Riders."

River returned her grin. "You've found your seat well. Perhaps on the way back Tulpar will show you what it's like to really move."

"I would love that." Mari grinned, and Rigel barked as punctuation.

Antreas leaped from a tall pine to land a few yards in front of them in the middle of the trail. The beard he'd grown on their trek through the mountains had frost on it and his breath hung in a cloud around him. As the horses halted, Bast seemed to materialize at his side.

"It is almost midday," said Antreas without preamble. "Just ahead is where the trail takes a steep upward turn. I'm not sure if the horses will be able to go much farther."

"They don't need to," said River. "We've traveled far enough into the mountains, and if I take a position ahead where, as you say, the trail turns up, that should work perfectly. All I need do is reach the clouds above the mountains. The crystal is powerful enough that the storm will brew here and then spread throughout the pass."

"Tulpar says we must be ready to leave quickly," said Dove. "He is concerned that we, too, will be trapped here."

"He's right to be concerned." Antreas nodded. "To stop Death and His army you need to call a real blizzard—to create whiteout conditions that are so vast that He is forced to halt and hunker down, instead of just speeding up to make it through the storm."

"I understand," said River. "And don't worry. We won't need to stay. We can leave as soon as it begins to snow."

"Good, that puts my mind at ease," said Antreas. "Come, the area is just around the next bend in the trail."

Antreas, with Bast and Rigel flanking him, jogged ahead as the horses trotted after. The frigid trail bent to the left and then, just as their Lynx Guide said—and Mari remembered—it narrowed and shot up, disappearing among pines that got smaller and smaller as the pass went higher and higher.

River kneed Anjo to a stop. "Yes, this will be perfect, and give us time to get back before dusk." Her gaze found Mari. "I'm looking forward to your drawing down of the moon." She spoke the words carefully, as if tasting their strangeness.

"Me too," said April.

"I think you will enjoy it," said Mari, who was surprised to realize she was a little nervous about this particular—and very important—Third Night.

"It's okay." River met her gaze. "Remember, you're one of us now. You don't have to prove anything."

"Thank you," said Mari.

"Watching Mari and Sora draw down the power of the moon is pure magick," said Antreas. Bast chirruped her agreement as she settled to groom herself.

"I'm quite sure it is. My little Kit has been sending me some incredible images," said River as she took the pup from the basket. "Though I don't actually expect you to glow. I think my sweet girl has a tendency to ex-aggerate." She kissed the pup on her little black nose before putting her down.

Antreas and Mari shared an amused look but said nothing.

"Now, if you'll excuse me I'm going to prepare to awaken the crystal." With the large, sparkling rock cradled in her arms River walked several paces from them up the path that lifted into the mountains.

"Hey, Mari, don't worry. We're not judging. We're just excited," added April as she dismounted, took her pup from the basket attached to her saddle so Cleo could play with her sister, and then began untying odd-looking bag-like contraptions filled with grain from across her saddlebags.

"Is that part of the spell to call snow?" Mari asked April.

"Oh, no, River only needs the crystal and the power in her blood to do that. These are feed bags for the horses. Grain has already been scooped into them. I tie them onto the horses' heads so they can feed and have plenty of energy to return us to the Herd."

Mari watched closely as April fed the horses. "Huh. That's a really good idea."

April smiled. "Well, we are nomadic. Over the centuries we've learned tricks about how to be efficient as we travel."

Rigel barked twice and wagged his tail, tongue lolling in a doggy grin at Mari.

Mari laughed. "No, I do not think we need to weave something like that for Shepherds."

April laughed. "I never thought about canines having a sense of humor, but even my little Cleo makes me laugh."

"Puppies are pure joy," said Dove.

"They sure are," agreed April. "Here, let me help you and Dove down." She offered a hand to stabilize Mari as she slid from Tulpar's wide back.

"Thanks," Mari said. "He really is big." She stroked Tulpar. "Thank you for carrying me."

"Dove?" April offered the same hand to her.

"Oh, that is kind of you, but I prefer to remain astride my Tulpar. He is my eyes, and I would very much like to see River awaken the crystal."

"We can move closer," April said.

"I would not want to weaken River's concentration," said Dove.

"Oh, you won't. Well, not if you are quiet and don't ask her a bunch of questions," said April.

"Oh, I would not do that," said Dove firmly.

"Nor would I," said Mari.

"I'd like to watch as well. I have visited Herd Magenti before but have never witnessed anything like what River is attempting. I promise I won't ask any—" Antreas broke off abruptly when Bast made a strange yowling sound as she stared back down the path they'd just traversed and then abruptly padded away from them.

"Is something wrong?" April asked.

"I don't think so. Bast just caught a scent she can't identify and is going to check it out."

"Should you go with her? If Cleo took off, I'd definitely go after her. We can easily follow the path back," said April.

Antreas shook his head and his long, shaggy, lynx-colored hair moved around his shoulders. "No. If she needs me, I'll know it. Bast is a lot more independent than canines—not that I mean that as a slight toward little Cleo." Rigel yipped, which caused Antreas to grin and ruffle the big Shepherd's ears. "Or you."

"April, is she starting?" Dove's soft voice returned the group's attention to River, who, even though she stood several paces away with her back turned to them, they could clearly see a bright light had begun to glow around.

"Yes, let's join her," April said.

As the mares chewed their grain peacefully and the puppies played around their hooves, the humans, Rigel, and Tulpar moved silently to stand close behind River.

She faced the mountain pass. Her head was bowed over the huge crystal she held firmly in both hands. River was whispering something to the crystal when Anjo suddenly trotted past them straight to her Rider.

Without speaking, April went quickly to Anjo, untied her feed bag, and patted the white mare affectionately before she stepped back to join Mari and Antreas. Then Anjo knelt and River mounted her. Mare and Rider faced the mountain. River raised the large crystal so that she held it against her forehead. To Mari it seemed Anjo had become a marble statue, glistening white and still in the cold midday, as the glow that had only touched the crystal and River engulfed the mare as well.

> *"My intent is to release from the clouds a flood.*
> *My crystal is aglow.*
> *Now, enhanced by the power of my blood,*
> *make it snow, make it snow, make it snow!"*

River raised the shining crystal and held it over her head, and as she did so the light that radiated from it shot straight up. Mari held her hand over her eyes to shield them from its brilliance as, arrow-like, it pierced the lazy, puffy clouds far above them that hung like the beard of an ancient giant on the mountainside.

There was a sharp, tearing sound and the pretty clouds began to roil and expand, changing color from pristine white to the gray of slate. They continued to billow and blow as the first fat snowflakes drifted down to coat River's dark hair. She turned in her saddle, holding the now-dark crystal close to her breast. Her smile was fierce.

"The storm comes. We should get out of here."

CHAPTER 8

The snow started gently when the sun was midway in the sky just a day after Ralina dreamed about the doe. One moment the weather was as it had been for weeks—clear and cold with just a few fluffy clouds drifting around the mountaintops—and the next the sky went from blue to gray, the clouds expanded to cover the sun, and thick, filigreed flakes drifted down on Death's army of mutants and the walking dead.

Ralina's heartbeat sped as she gazed upward at the snow-pregnant clouds and wondered . . .

"Keep moving! Why are you standing around staring as if you have never seen snow before?" Death's voice bellowed. "We knew it would come eventually. Now we must get through these mountains. *Move. Move. Move,*" the god's voice echoed from the front of the army. He strode down the path, and with each word "move" He knocked aside who- or whatever was within reach. *"Storyteller, where are you?"*

"The God calls for you." Renard and his Companion, Kong, hurried toward her with his father, Daniel, close beside them. Between them they carried three newly skinned rabbits, and their supplies rolled neatly and strapped to their backs.

"It's snowing." Ralina spoke quickly and quietly. "I don't know if my dream was sent by the Goddess of Life, or if it was just a figment of my hopeful imagination, but . . ." She moved her shoulders.

"But we are ready to follow you out of here should your white doe appear," said Daniel firmly.

"Yes, absolutely. All morning Father and I have been secreting extra supplies into all three of our packs. We even managed to take a fire starter tin without being seen," added Renard. "But we cannot follow you out of here if Death insists you travel at His side."

"I'm going to make sure He doesn't." Ralina hefted her own pack to her back, bowing under its weight. "Stay together and keep me within your sight."

"We shall." Daniel touched her shoulder fondly. "Do not worry for us. We're used to keeping you in sight."

Ralina put her hand over Daniel's. "The two of you, Bear and Kong, are all that have kept me going."

"And you us," said Renard. He hugged her tightly and whispered, "You have saved our lives many times over."

"STORYTELLER."

She disentangled herself from the young man who had become family—whom she had fallen in love with—and smiled briefly. "I hope the dream was sent by the Goddess, but if it wasn't—"

"If it wasn't then we continue on until you say it is time to rid ourselves of Death," said Renard.

Ralina nodded and then she turned and jogged up the path toward the sound of Death, with Bear at her side. She rushed to the god as the fat, lazy flakes began to change to smaller, harder, icier droplets that had already intensified and shortened visibility.

"Ah, there you are. Storyteller, you know I do not like you to be far from Me." The god gave her a dark look. "And now it is snowing. I will *not* lose you in this storm."

Ralina fixed her expression into a smile before she answered him, "My Lord, You need not fear You will lose me. Even if I cannot see You, Bear's nose can easily track You. Should we get separated he will lead me to You."

The god's face relaxed. "Noble Bear. I tend to forget the Shepherds can track as well as the Terriers." Through thick brows Death peered down at the canine. "He would truly lead you to Me should you get lost?"

"Of course, my Lord."

"That eases My mind. Though do try to stay close to the front of the army, where I shall be as soon as I get them moving. Their laziness is My burden to bear—but do not speak of it in your epic story chronicling our magnificent journey. I would rather that particular aspect of My victorious army not be known."

Ralina nodded somberly. "I agree, my Lord." She glanced behind Him at the spirit of the bison who was never far from His side. This spectral guide was much different from the sad little doe who had led Death through the pass until she'd unexpectedly disappeared the day before—only to be replaced by the bull bison, who had been bound to the God, but whose eyes blazed hatred at Death. Ralina's gaze went from the spirit to the God and she felt a flutter of shock. The God of Death had eaten the creature's still-warm heart only the day before, but already Ralina could see that Death had begun to change—again. His antlers were thickening and darkening, His facial features were becoming more animalistic, His nose flatter, more snoutlike, and His hair was also darkening. *He's rejecting the stag and becoming more bison-like.*

"Do you approve of what you see, Storyteller?" Death's voice was sly.

"Forgive me, my Lord. I did not mean to stare." Ralina hastily cast her eyes down, noting as she did that the ground around them was already carpeted with snow.

"Oh, you may look. You *must* look. How else will you be able to fully describe My magnificence? I only wonder what you think of the changes happening within Me."

Ralina lifted her gaze to meet Death's. As always when speaking with the God, she chose to stay as close to the truth as possible. "I think You look even more powerful than before You ate the bison's heart."

He threw back His head and bellowed a bizarre laugh that was more roar than levity. "You are correct!" Then He shook Himself, and snow flew from His immense body. "It is a shame we cannot chat as we normally would, but I must move this army before we are trapped in the pass. Have a care, Storyteller. Keep your Bear close so that he can return you to Me should you become lost." Then Death strode past her, cloven hooves biting the snow-covered ground as He shouted, "Thaddeus, Iron Fist, to Me!"

Ralina glanced over her shoulder to see Renard, Kong, and Daniel watching her from a distance. She motioned surreptitiously for them to follow her. Renard nodded, and then Ralina, with Bear by her side, walked along the path toward the front of the army. When Death stomped past her again, He hardly spared her a glance but was busy berating Thaddeus and His Blade—and insisting they force the army to *move, move, move.*

Ralina looked away to hide her disgust. The ridiculously slow pace that had them meandering through this frigid pass as if they were on a picnic outing was Death's fault. He set the pace—and that pace had been plodding and self-indulgent. *Everything about the God of Death is self-indulgent,* Ralina thought.

She kept walking forward, purposefully lagging behind the suddenly swiftly moving mutant men and reanimated dead as the snow changed again. It now fell in tiny, icy flakes so thick that it felt as if the air had become a net of white that had trapped them all.

The army trudged forward as swiftly as possible into the blinding white. Heads bowed against the wind and snow. No one—not even the traitorous Companions who followed Thaddeus and who seemed to always be watching her—took any notice of Ralina as it was so difficult to distinguish individuals in the storm. All they could do was plod after whoever was directly in front of them. Death did not reappear. He did not march up and down His line of soldiers shouting encouragement or threats. Ralina imagined Him at the head of the army, unbothered by the storm, following the spirit of the beast shackled to Him. When she realized Death would probably not reappear, she motioned for Renard and his father to join her, and together they sloughed along with the army.

Then, through the pelting snow, Ralina's attention was caught by a flash of ebony amidst the suffocating wall of white. She blinked, rubbed snow from her lashes, and peered off the path to her left and up into the tall pines and boulders that lined this part of the pass.

Ralina's heartbeat increased so quickly it felt as if it would burst from her chest. Standing under a clump of snow-covered pines was a doe, so white she would've been impossible to see against the snow were it not for the bottomless black of her eyes, which were staring directly at Ralina. The doe tossed her delicate head and, still staring at Ralina, took several steps back into the surrounding forest. There she tossed her head again and waited, her dark gaze never leaving the Storyteller.

Ralina reached out and grabbed Renard's hand, pulling him close to her. She whispered urgently, "Look! Do you see her, too?" and cut her eyes to the doe.

Renard blinked several times, clearing his vision. Through their joined hands Ralina felt him jerk in surprise. "Yes! Is that your doe?" He spoke low, though even Daniel, who walked on the other side of him, could not hear what they were saying over the whine of the wind.

"She looks exactly like the doe that came to me in my dream."

Renard squeezed her hand. "Are we finally going to leave?"

"We are. Now. Tell your father. Follow me. If anyone tries to stop us, say that I need the privacy of one of the boulders. You and your father are going to stand guard for me."

While Renard whispered urgently to his father, Ralina and Bear left the path and began to climb up rocks and between boulders, heading for the doe who had stepped back into the cover of the trees and was so camouflaged by the snow that had her dark eyes not shined like a still mountain lake at night Ralina would have completely lost sight of her.

After months of traveling with Death and fantasizing about escape Ralina was shocked at how ridiculously easy it was to leave the army. The Milks and mutant Companions were too busy trudging against the wall of white to notice three people and two canines leaving the path—and as soon as they were within the forest it was as if a curtain of white closed behind them. The snow swallowed everything—the three of them, their two canines, and even the sounds of the marching army.

Under the pines Ralina approached the doe, who offered her muzzle for the Storyteller to stroke.

"Thank you. I believe the Goddess of Life sent you. I will forever worship Her for leading me away from Death." Ralina spoke to the doe as she marveled at the softness of her flawless coat. "I choose to believe in and serve the Goddess."

"As do I," said Renard from beside her.

"And I," echoed his father.

The doe tossed her head and then allowed the men to touch her sleek neck reverently.

"Where you lead we will follow," said Ralina. The doe blew gently against Ralina's cheek before she turned and trotted farther into the forest with the three humans and two canines close behind.

They traveled up the side of the mountain, picking their way between trees, around boulders, and through snow-covered underbrush for so long that even though her body had been thoroughly conditioned by weeks of hiking the pass, Ralina's legs began to ache with the strain of the constant uphill climb through increasingly deep snow. The pace the doe set was grueling, but Ralina understood it. They must put as much distance between themselves and Death as possible.

It was difficult to tell how much time had passed. The sun had been absent since midday. The world had turned gray and white. The wind was never-ending and the biting snow narrowed visibility to just a few yards around them.

The three humans tied scarves about their faces and bowed their heads against the snow-driven wind and kept moving.

The day had begun to shift to the deeper gray that signaled twilight when the doe made an abrupt turn to the right and Ralina was relieved to discover that she'd led them to a threadlike path, so slim that they had to walk it single file. It was much too narrow for a bulky army to traverse. It still wound up the mountains, but they were now also heading east. By this time the snow had become so deep that the doe was pulling away from them. When Ralina fell and struggled to get back to her feet, the deer returned to her immediately, encouraging her as Renard helped her up.

"We should stop! You must rest!" Renard shouted over the wind.

"We can't." Ralina wiped sweat from her face with her scarf. "This is it for us, Renard. If Death catches us He will kill the two of you—or worse—and I will be His prisoner. I cannot even think about what He would do to Bear and Kong. I would rather die out here in the snow than face Him."

"We must keep going," Daniel said bravely, though the older man looked as exhausted as Ralina felt.

"The snow is making it impossible to keep up with the doe," Renard said as his gaze went to the magnificent deer who stood beside Ralina.

The doe tossed her beautiful head, nuzzled Ralina briefly, and then turned and, once more, led them into the east. Ralina stared wearily at her and then drew a deep breath and staggered after the doe—only to gasp in happy surprise. *The snow parted for the doe!* It was as if the deer radiated an energy that only the snow could feel. As she walked the slim path the wall of white fled from her. It swirled away in miniature tornados that exposed the dirt and rock under their feet.

"By the Sun, she's clearing a path for us!" Renard said.

"Yes, hurry! We have to stay close to her, though." Ralina pointed to a few feet behind Daniel, who brought up the rear of their group, where the funnels of white dissipated and snow once again covered the path, thick and wet.

With renewed energy, the three humans and two canines followed the doe until the last of the light drained away around them. Ralina was trying to decide whether she should call to the doe or just eternally follow her when the deer stopped, turned to meet Ralina's gaze, and then led them off the path just a few paces to the maw of a snowy cave. The deer got close enough to the cave for the snow to be blown from the entrance; then she backed out and looked expectantly at Ralina.

"Get the tinderbox!" she called to Renard. With a groan he took off his backpack and then reached into it and brought out a priceless, ancient tin. Renard moved just far enough inside the mouth of the cave that there was a chance the wind would pull out the campfire smoke. His father and Ralina huddled around him as he crouched and took out the flint strikers, a handful of pine needles, and pine bark that had been smeared with highly flammable resin.

"I have some wood in my pack," said Daniel, quickly taking his backpack off and laying out a thick blanket in which he'd rolled dry pine boughs. "I worried about what we'd do for fire if we were caught in the snow."

"That was wise of you." Ralina smiled wearily at him.

Just a few strikes of the flint and a spark easily lit the resin—and the resin in turn lit the boughs.

"I don't think I've ever seen anything so beautiful," said Ralina as she warmed her hands over the fire.

"Look behind you." Daniel pointed to the rear of the cave. "Your deer has thought of everything."

"She's not mine. She's the Goddess of—" Her words broke off with a happy gasp. The cave wasn't large—she guessed only about twenty paces long and a little less wide—but piled in the rear of it was a big nest of dried grasses, branches, and a lot of long pine needles. Some animal had definitely made a cozy den of the cave, but there was no sign of scat and no scent of urine marking its territory, which meant it had been abandoned at least for a full turn of the seasons. Ralina went to the doe, who stood at the entrance to the cave watching them. "Oh, Goddess, thank You." Impulsively, the Storyteller wrapped her arms around the neck of the deer and sobbed into her sleek coat. "I-I'm sorry," she told the doe. "I'm u-usually n-not like this." When Ralina managed to pull herself together, she stepped back and wiped her face as she gazed into the magickal creature's dark, intelligent eyes. "We've escaped Him. If we die tonight, here in this cave, or tomorrow out there, or any day after, please know that we'll die content because we're away from Him."

The doe stretched her neck to nuzzle Ralina's cheek gently.

As Renard and Daniel made a cooking skewer for the rabbits they'd caught earlier, Bear, Kong, and the beautiful silver-white doe lay beside the fire, watching the flames. From the nest-like pile of dried foliage in the rear of the cave Ralina found a pile of birch bark and grasses, which she placed before the doe—who immediately began to delicately nibble the bark. The smoke from the fire was carried out of the cave by a strange little wind, and soon the cave was filled with warmth, flickering firelight, and the delicious scent of cooking rabbit. Daniel took their one precious pot and collected enough snow to melt for drinking. As they filled their bellies with rabbit and their water bladders with water, Ralina felt herself truly relax for the first time since the deadly forest fire had burned through her beloved Tribe of the Trees, heralding the end of her world.

"I feel like I can finally take a deep breath," said Ralina.

Renard nodded. "It is as you said to the doe." He smiled fondly at the ethereal creature. "Even if we don't make it to the Plains of the Wind Riders, we will be content with our fate."

"Because it is finally *our* fate, and not something orchestrated by that monster," said Daniel.

"I do not believe we're going to die out here." Ralina spoke while she stared into the campfire. "The Goddess of Life is guiding us, and it's not an accident She sent me the dream immediately before Death lost His own guide and then slaughtered the bison to take her place." Her gaze lifted and went to the doe. "I think I finally learned enough."

"Enough to for you to stop Death?" Renard asked.

Ralina shook her head. "Not me. I don't have that kind of power, but maybe there's someone on the Plains of the Wind Riders who does."

"I'm going to believe that," said Renard.

"I believe it," said Daniel firmly. "After all we've seen—all we've suffered—there must be a reason for it. I am going to believe that reason involves sending Death back to whence He came."

"The arms of the Goddess," said Ralina softly. Then she spoke with more surety. "Death must return to sleeping within the embrace of the Goddess of Life or our world will end."

"You won't let that happen, Storyteller," said her young lover.

"I will do everything in my power to prevent it," said Ralina.

Daniel smiled across the fire at her. "Sleep first. Save the world after you have rested."

"I'll do my best." Ralina returned his smile. She'd come to think of Daniel as her own father and loved that she could always count on his kindness and optimism.

"That is all that the Goddess could ask of any of us," said Renard.

A very short time later Ralina could not keep her eyes open, and she curled up between Bear and Renard and fell quickly into the deepest, most restful sleep she'd had in months.

CHAPTER 9

M ari returned to Herd Magenti thoroughly soaked but invigorated by the trip from the pass. The snow that was already blanketing the foreboding mountains changed to rain as soon as they reached a lower elevation—and that rain continued almost all the way to the Herd.

Not that Mari minded. Tulpar had galloped for part of the return trip, and just thinking about the power and grace with which the stallion moved sent a little thrill through Mari. They had only slowed because Rigel had fallen behind. Antreas and Bast had joined them near the end of the pass, and even they had trouble keeping up with the horses.

"They really are glorious." Mari sighed happily.

Sora's deft hands stilled on her hair. "By 'they' you mean the horses?"

"The horses, their Riders, River—all of them. Sora, it already feels so right that we're here. I only wish we weren't being shadowed by Death."

"It doesn't seem the Herd blames us for that." Sora continued to braid feathers into Mari's hair as they spoke.

"River said as much to me," said Mari. "But I feel guilty. It's us He's following."

"Actually, it's more likely Death's following Dove. She was supposed to be the vessel for His awakened goddess. So, do you blame Dove for what the God of Death does to try to capture her?" Sora asked.

"No, Dove escaped Him. I'm glad she did—and it seems the Great Earth

Mother is glad as well. If it wasn't for Dove being Tulpar's Choice, which also led to Kit and Cleo Choosing River and April, we might not have been so readily accepted by Herd Magenti." She turned to meet Sora's knowing gaze. "And that's the point you're making, isn't it? We're not responsible for the actions of a god."

Sora shrugged her round shoulders. "Well, we aren't. What we are responsible for is calling down the moon and caring for our people." She stepped back and studied Mari. "And now we're ready. Or at least we *look* ready. I'm nervous."

Sora's pup, Chloe, yapped up at her Companion, which made Sora and Mari smile. Sora scooped Chloe up and kissed her little black nose, and tucked her neatly inside the carrier that held the pup close to her heart. "I hear you, and I know *you* aren't nervous."

"Chloe makes an excellent point. You shouldn't be nervous, either." Mari scratched the pup behind her ears before bending to kiss Rigel on the muzzle.

"Why aren't you nervous?" Sora asked her friend.

"Well, I was earlier, but then I realized that drawing down the moon and Washing our Pack—and whoever else needs it—is one of the few things I'm truly confident about. We can do this, Sora. We have done this—over and over again together for the past many months. Remember, you won't be alone out there. I'll be with you every moment. We're stronger together," said Mari.

Sora's furrowed brow relaxed and she smiled. "You sound like your mother."

"That is a very nice compliment. I feel her sometimes—here with me. Sora, I think she knows we made it to the Wind Rider Plains."

"I'm *sure* Leda knows."

"Hey, are you two ready yet?" Jenna's head appeared inside the curtain that served as door to Sora's little room within the Herd's enormous cave system. "Everyone is already in the Choosing Theater. They're all waiting for you!"

"We're ready." Mari took Sora's hand in hers. "Right, Moon Woman?"

"Yes. Absolutely. Let's tend to our people."

"Oooh, good! I'll let them know you're coming. And by the way, you two look beautiful. The Pack is so proud of you." Jenna sprinted from the doorway.

"I love this cloak." Mari smoothed a hand down the exquisitely embroidered material that would always remind her of her beloved mother. Then she touched her hair. "Thanks for doing my hair."

"I enjoy it, and it soothes my nerves. Well, it usually soothes them." Sora, too, wore an embroidered cloak—one she'd finished for herself on the long trip over Lost Lake. Sora glanced down from her bare, sun-kissed legs to Mari's. "You're sure about not covering our legs?"

"Have you looked at the Wind Riders? They wear almost nothing. It helps us fit in. Plus, from the first night you bared your legs to call down the moon I thought how powerful and sensual you looked. A little like one of our Great Earth Mother idols come to life."

"Really?"

"Really," said Mari firmly.

"Well, Goddess-like is a good look for us." Sora tossed back her thick, elaborately dressed hair. "Let's go show them what Moon Women can do."

Together Mari, with Rigel beside her, and Sora, carrying little Chloe in her pouch-like sling, walked from the huge cave through the neat, colorful tents to the Choosing Theater. They paused at the gated entrance to take in the sight. It was fully dark. The crescent moon hung low in a cloudy sky. The mighty Herd Magenti filled the viewing stands. All around those stands torches burned brightly. Flames caught the crystals the Herd adorned themselves with, so that the Riders sparkled like living jewels. The Pack waited on the field with Dax and his Lynx, Mihos. The injured Companion pair reclined on a large stretcher around which gathered River, April, and the members of the Mare Council who had decided to remain and retreat with Magenti to the Valley of Vapors in the morning. Mari felt a flutter of nerves as she recognized the wise Mare Council Riders. *They will judge us by what we do—and do not do—tonight.*

"Moon Women! Our Moon Women are here!" Jenna's sweet voice lifted into the night.

"Moon Women! Mari! Sora! Blessing to you! Our Moon Women are here!" As the Pack's voices welcomed them, joy replaced Mari's sudden trepidation.

"Blessed Third Night to our people!" Mari called, and the Pack—and even some of the Riders—smiled and waved.

"You were right," Sora whispered as she waved at the waiting crowd. "We know what we're doing. We have nothing to be nervous about."

Side by side the Pack's Moon Women and their Companions entered the theater. River, with Anjo beside her, greeted them. "Welcome." She smiled at Mari. "I'm glad to see you're not too waterlogged after our rainy journey today."

Mari returned her grin. "Getting to ride Tulpar and watch you use crystal power was worth every bit of the rain."

"And now I'm eager to watch you call down moon power. Do you need anything from us?" River asked.

"The only thing we need is for you to announce that anyone who is not feeling well should come down here to the field. When Sora and I draw down the moon and release its power, it heals."

River nodded. "That's what Sora explained while we were in the mountains today. So, we moved Dax and Mihos out here. There was no one else in the infirmary today."

"It doesn't have to be a wound as serious as Dax and Mihos's injuries," Sora explained. "Should anyone feel a little off—or have an old injury that pains them—Washing in moon magick will help as well."

River's smile blazed. "The Herd will love to know that, but I think the invitation should come from you." She lifted her hand and opened it to reveal the beautiful blue crystal she'd used earlier to amplify her voice. "Mari, I already know you have an affinity for crystals. Please, use this one tonight to speak to the Herd."

"Thank you, River." Mari took the crystal, loving the warmth and calm it exuded, and then she and Sora faced the crowded viewing stands. "Herd Magenti! Sora and I are going to call down the power of the moon and then Wash our Pack with it. For those of you who don't know, every Third Night Sora and I Wash our Pack. We must. Earth Walkers not bonded to a canine Companion become sick if they are not Washed, but there is more to moon magick than the necessity of Washing melancholy and madness from us. In the hands of a Moon Woman, the power of the moon heals and makes whole. So, Sora and I would like to invite any Herdmember—

Rider or horse—who might not feel completely well to join us on the field. It would be our great pleasure to share with you our moon magick."

For a moment no one moved, and then Morgana trotted to them on her ancient mare.

"I have a question," said the old woman.

Mari bowed respectfully to her.

"Will your moon magick work on, say, an old woman's bones that ache because of the rainstorm today?" Morgana's clear eyes sparkled with good humor. "I ask for a friend, of course."

"Oh, of course." Mari grinned before turning to the attentively watching Herd. Using the crystal to amplify her voice again, she explained, "Herd, Morgana asks if moon magick works to Wash aches from a Rider's bones. Our answer is absolutely."

"Ah, good. Then *my friend* and I shall remain on the field for the Washing." Those close enough to Morgana to hear her response chuckled as the old woman kneed her mare around and trotted back to the other members of the Mare Council.

Morgana's acceptance rippled through the Herd as a dozen or so Riders and horses made their way down to the field—and every member of the Mare Council remained on the field.

"I didn't expect that." Sora spoke softly to Mari. "But I am glad of it."

"As am I. Let's Wash them, Moon Woman," Mari said.

"Indeed."

Mari returned the amplifying crystal to River with a grateful smile.

"You may keep it for the duration of the ritual," River said. "And if Sora would also like a crystal I can quickly send for one for her."

"That is kind of you," said Mari. "But the moon is all the amplification we need."

River's brows rose, but she nodded and she and Anjo moved back to stand with the rest of the waiting Pack and Herdmembers.

Mari and Sora took position in front of the group gathered in the middle of the field. Mari caught Nik's gaze. He smiled at her and Laru barked encouragement. Then the Moon Women drew several deep breaths together, easily falling in sync as they grounded themselves. Once grounded, they raised their hands and gazed up at the crescent above them. As they'd discussed before, Mari began, speaking the ancient conjuring as the power of the moon magnified her voice and carried it throughout the Choosing Theater.

"Moon Woman I proclaim myself to be."

Sora continued in a voice likewise amplified:

"Greatly gifted, I bare myself to Thee.
Earth Mother, aid me with Your magick sight.
Lend me strength on this Third Night."

It was Mari's turn again, and as she spoke she felt the cool light of the moon cascade into her body.

"Come, silver light—fill us to overflow
so those in our care your healing touch will know."

Together, Mari and Sora completed the ritual.

"By right of blood and birth channel through me
the Goddess gift that is my destiny!"

Mari gritted her teeth as frigid moon magick filled her to overflowing. As always, there was a moment when she was afraid she couldn't contain the power—that she would lose the connection and vomit sickness and failure into the grass—but beside her she felt Sora's steadying presence. Mari turned her head and met her friend's gaze. Sora's gray eyes glowed the same silver that settled over her skin. Sora's thick ebony hair lifted around her, just as Mari felt her own shorter, lighter locks play around her shoulders as if they were caught in wind made of moonbeams. *This Goddess gift is our destiny.*

Before them their Pack went to their knees, and Mari and Sora moved forward to their people. As Sora began working her way through the Earth Walkers, starting with Jaxom's younger brother, Mason, Mari went to Dax and Mihos. She placed her hands, which radiated moonbeams, gently on each of their heads and recited, "Brave Dax and faithful Mihos, I Wash you free of pain and gift you with the love of the Great Earth Mother." Mari concentrated and imagined that she sketched a picture where healing moonlight flowed from above her into her body and, like a waterfall, cascaded through her into Dax and Mihos. She kept the icy stream going until Dax gasped and looked up at her. His face was flushed, and he stared at her incredulously.

"I—I don't believe it. My hands!" Dax opened and closed his hands. "They feel so much better!" His gaze flew from Mari to Mihos, who was purring loudly as he licked his paws. Dax laughed—a sound filled with relief. "Mihos's paws aren't so painful. It's such a relief for him! Oh, thank you, Moon Woman."

Mari smiled down at him and then moved to the next person, who happened to be her Nik. He bowed his head and she placed her hand lovingly on it. "Nikolas, I Wash you free of pain and sadness and gift you with the love of the Great Earth Mother."

He lifted his head. "Thank you, my beautiful Moon Woman."

Mari went to Morgana next. The old woman had dismounted and was standing beside her ancient mare. As Mari approached, she began to drop painfully to her knees, but Mari caught her arm.

"You need not kneel. I can see it causes you pain."

Morgana straightened with relief, and said quietly, "I would ask a favor of you, Moon Woman."

"If it is in my power to grant it, I gladly will," said Mari, curious about the Lead Council Member's request.

Morgana rested a well-aged hand on her mare's slick gray neck. "If possible, I ask that you Wash Ramoth as well. Her joints pain her, especially when it is damp."

Mari realized that Morgana hadn't been kidding when she'd said she asked *for a friend* about the power of the moon. She'd been thinking of her mare first.

"Yes, of course." Mari placed one hand on Morgana's shoulder and the other on Ramoth. The mare snorted at Mari's cool touch but held very still as she stared at the glowing Moon Woman. "Morgana and Ramoth, I Wash you free of pain and gift you with the love of the Great Earth Mother." She concentrated, shifting her focus to the pair and guiding the healing light of the moon through herself and into them.

Morgana sighed in relief. "May you be blessed with a mare's luck for your kindness, Moon Woman."

Your touch has given me great relief, Moon Woman, Ramoth's voice echoed in Mari's mind. *I sincerely thank you.*

Mari bowed her head. "It is my pleasure and my honor."

Like human torches alight with moonbeams, Sora and Mari wove their way through the people, touching each with moon magick, leaving sighs of relief and pleasure in their wake. When they had tended to each person and Companion who needed their touch, the two Moon Women returned to where they'd begun in front of the crowd. As they'd prepared for this unusual Third Night, Mari and Sora had talked about the very real possibility that they would channel all of the power of the moon into the people and end up being drained and sick and too exhausted to be of any use the next day when everyone was expected to begin the trek to the Valley of Vapors. In order to save themselves from this, Mari came up with a simple plan—one that was only possible because they had broken with tradition by having more than one Moon Woman.

Mari and Sora faced each other and clasped hands. Together they spoke softly.

"Sora, I Wash you free of weariness and gift you with the love of the Great Earth Mother."

"Mari, I Wash you free of weariness and gift you with the love of the Great Earth Mother."

Invigorated, they faced the crowd once more. On an impulse, Mari grinned and shouted, "And may a mare's luck be with us all!"

"It has been said!" the Herd roared enthusiastically back to her.

Smiling, River and Anjo joined them. River lifted the blue crystal and the gathering fell silent. "Mari explained to me today that it is customary that there is feasting, music, and dancing after the Washing on a Third Night, and I very much wish we could follow that tradition. But at dawn we must seal the mouth of the cavern and then begin our journey to the Valley of Vapors.

"It will be a journey unlike any of us have made in our lifetimes. As you know, it usually takes Magenti at least four weeks to move from our Choosing Grounds to our winter home. This time we do not have the luxury of an easy trip. We travel with the entire Herd. We will leave no one behind. We will travel light and ride hard. Because of Dax's warning we know Death and His army are only seven days behind us. Today I have ensured that those seven days will be stretched, but we have no way of knowing by how much. We must get to our stronghold and prepare for war—all in a very short span of time.

"So we cannot feast and celebrate tonight, but know that when we defeat Death, Herd Magenti will have such a celebration that our bards will sing of it for generations!"

The Herd cheered in response. When they quieted again, River concluded with, "Sleep well tonight. At dawn we move. And may the blessings of the Great Mother Mare—as well as a mare's luck—go with us."

"It has been said!" shouted April.

"It has been said!" echoed the gathering.

CHAPTER 10

"Have you noticed that Bast is acting strange?" Danita asked.

Antreas's gaze went from Danita, who was combing out her long dark hair, to the curtained door to the snug cave room he and Bast shared with her. Bast was absent, which was decidedly odd because it was time for them to sleep and the Lynx always curled beside Danita, lending her warmth and a sense of safety the young woman counted on.

Antreas blew out a long breath. "I have. I suspect it has something to do with Mihos."

Danita moved to their thick pallet of furs and sat next to Antreas, who took the brush from her and began to slowly stroke her hair. She sighed contentedly before asking, "Mihos? What do you mean?"

"Well, Mihos is an adult male Lynx. Bast is definitely of the age to mate and have kittens. His presence could definitely cause her to go into estrus."

Danita turned so she could meet his gaze. "You mean she'd mate with Mihos and then have babies?"

"Yes. We call them kittens." Antreas smiled. "It may not be the best time for Bast to be pregnant, but I would definitely be excited about a litter."

Danita's brow furrowed. "I heard Dax tell you that he and Mihos are staying with the Herd until their wounds are fully healed, but if Bast and Mihos mate doesn't that mean they'll want to stay longer? Or want us to leave with them?"

"Oh, no. Don't worry about that. Lynxes mate solely to reproduce. The males and females don't stay together. Usually the kittens only stay with the mother for about one year. Then they leave and take another year to mature alone before Choosing a Companion, but remember, Bast and I are different. I don't think she'll want her kittens to leave so soon. One of the reasons she and I decided to become members of the Pack is because we choose not to be solitary." He smiled and touched her cheek gently. "You are the other reason."

"I'm glad you and Bast are different. I'm different, too. That's why the three of us make such a good team. And I would love it if Bast had kittens. The more the better."

Danita went into his arms and nestled her head against his shoulder. Antreas held her loosely, always aware that because she had been beaten, raped, and left for dead just before they'd met a little over six months ago, Danita controlled the physical part of their relationship. Antreas had spent months gaining her trust and proving to her that she would always be safe with him. They had eventually been able to make love. Antreas was happy that Danita had healed so well that she could accept his physical love, but what brought him the greatest joy was what she was doing at that moment—resting contentedly in his arms because she trusted him completely.

"That would be nice, though she hasn't said anything to me about wanting to mate with Mihos."

Danita lifted her head so she could look at him. "She'd tell you that?"

"She pretty much tells me everything—but only when she wants to. You know how she is."

Danita grinned and nodded. "Independent and bossy."

"Exactly."

"And completely wonderful," Danita added.

"Absolutely."

Danita cocked her head and studied him. "So, what is it like for you when Bast mates? Claudia told me sex with Davis was *especially delicious* when Cammy and Mariah were mating."

"You and Claudia talk about sex?"

"Of course. We're friends. I used to talk about it a lot with Sora and Mari, too, but that was before you and I were able to have sex. It helped to talk with them." Danita spoke matter-of-factly, like she and the Moon Women had been discussing which plants heal wounds the best.

"Oh, of course. That—that was a good idea. I mean, to talk with them. Moon Women are very wise." Antreas realized he was rambling, but even after being part of the Pack for months he was not quite used to how open Earth Walkers—and even the members of the Tribe of the Trees—were about mating and sex in general. He didn't dislike it. It was just so different from the solitary Lynx mind-set that it was still a little surprising.

Danita's smile was knowing. "Are you going to answer my question?"

"Oh, yeah. Yes. I will know when she mates, but how much she shares with me is, as always, up to Bast." He added softly, "Out of her love for you I expect she won't share much. You know you do *not* need to worry about me . . . well . . . um . . ."

"Becoming filled with uncontrollable lust for me?" she finished for him.

He couldn't tell by her expression whether she was kidding or not, so he answered her seriously. "I will never be filled with uncontrollable lust. I promise you I will always be in control, which means *you* will always be in control of that part of our relationship."

"Thank you," she said. Then her lips turned up in the beginnings of a smile. "Only *that* part?"

He tugged playfully on a lock of her thick, curly hair. "Bast is in charge of everything else, remember?"

She laughed then. "Of course I remember. I wish she'd come back. I miss her. Can you call her?"

"Sure, but whether she comes or not—"

"Is up to Bast. I know, but would you tell her I'm asking for her?" Danita sighed and her gaze went to their curtained doorway.

"Absolutely. She'll be much more likely to return if she knows you need her."

"Don't make her worry, though. I don't *need* her. I just miss her. It's bedtime and I sleep a lot better when she's near." Danita rested her head back on his shoulder.

Antreas stroked her hair. "Sleep, love. I'll stand in for Bast until she returns."

Danita yawned and relaxed against him. "Well, you are very furry."

He snorted a laugh and kept stroking her hair as he called his Companion. *Bast, Danita misses you. So do I. Will you come back soon?*

Bast sent him reassurance that she was on her way to the cave, but Antreas was surprised at the sense of distance that came with her response. He knew Mihos and Dax were still in the infirmary, and that even though Mari had speeded their healing with moon power, Mihos was in no shape to pad around the plains with Bast. Antreas wondered what his Lynx was up to . . .

"By the tits of the Goddess you scared me!" Sora clutched her hand over her heart as she sent O'Bryan a hard look. At her feet little Chloe barked her irritation at her Companion being startled.

"Sorry, that's totally my fault. I didn't realize anyone else was still awake." O'Bryan sent her an apologetic smile as he patted the back of the bulge inside the front of his shirt.

"Chloe had to potty before we went to sleep. She gets restless before bed, especially when we're turning in early like tonight, so I let her wander around a little. What are you doing out here anyway?" Sora glanced around them. They were atop the entrance to the cave where the grass was lush and the moon illuminated the distant rain clouds in the sky above them. The camp was unusually quiet as the Herd had bedded down as soon as the Washing was done.

"Oh, I was a little restless, too, so Cubby and I decided to wander." His gaze lifted to the moon. "I like it up here. I miss living close to the sky." As he spoke, he kept patting the front of his shirt.

"O'Bryan, are you nervous?" Sora asked.

"Nervous? No. I mean, I'm concerned—worried even—about Death and His army, but I wouldn't say I'm nervous. Why?"

Sora pointed to his chest. "You're patting yourself like you need comforting."

"Oh." He grinned and pulled down the neck of his shirt so that a white furry face with shiny ebony eyes was revealed. "I'm patting Cubby, not myself."

"Well, that makes a lot more sense." Sora lifted her hand but paused before she touched the infant wolverine. "May I pet him?"

"Absolutely. I want people to handle him often, but watch his paws.

Those little claws are surprisingly sharp. Mariah and I have discovered that wolverines don't retract their claws."

"Really? Ever?" With a finger Sora petted the little kit's head. The baby made contented little snuffling sounds and closed her eyes. "I've watched Bast groom her paws, and her claws definitely retract—so do Antreas's for that matter."

"Well, Cubby's don't. Claudia and I talked about it. We think it's normal for wolverines." He smiled fondly at the baby, and his thumb stroked her side. "Though Cubby is more and more careful not to scratch me with them."

"So, you've definitely decided on calling him Cubby?"

He shrugged. "He's started responding to his name. I guess that means he likes it. I can only hope that one day our bond will develop enough that he can tell me if he chooses another name."

Sora met his gaze. "You think he'll make you his Companion? Do wolverines even do that?"

"Not that I know of, but once upon a time canines and Lynxes and horses didn't have Companions, either. Maybe Cubby and I will be the first wolverine-Companion pair." His gaze went back to the baby nestled against his chest. "I know most of the Pack, and the Herd as well, think he's going to become dangerous as he grows up, but I don't believe it. I trust him already. He's my boy, and I won't give up on him." When Sora said nothing, O'Bryan looked up from the kit and added, "Yeah, I'm sure I sound foolish."

"I don't think you sound foolish at all. I think you sound like a Companion. I'm pretty new to this whole bonding-with-animals thing, but my Chloe Chose me far too soon. That didn't matter to me—or to her. Stay faithful to your Cubby. Faith and love and trust are good foundations for any relationship." Sora bent and picked up Chloe so that the pup could sniff at the sleepy wolverine kit, which she did with enthusiastic tail wags and licks that had the baby mewing in irritation as he burrowed into O'Bryan's shirt. "Let him sleep, Chloe." Sora laughed and put the pup back on the grass. "And finish doing your business. We need to get a full night's rest." As Chloe waddled a few steps away to crouch, Sora turned her smile on O'Bryan. "Chloe likes your Cubby. Be sure you let him play with the other Terrier pups—not just with his adopted siblings—and bring him around the horses a lot as well. He may just grow up thinking he's a canine."

O'Bryan grinned back at her. "With unretractable claws."

"That could come in handy someday," said Sora.

"I hope so. That's a good idea—to be sure Cubby mixes with all the other Companions. I've hesitated to do so because I know so many people are prejudiced against him." O'Bryan stroked the kit again, and the baby made more contented sounds as he fell quickly back to sleep against him. "I've, um, been sleeping with him."

Sora snorted softly. "Really? But he's so young. Can he be away from Mariah all night?"

"No. Absolutely not." His grin was crooked and endearing. "Cubby can sleep about half of the night away from Mariah. Then he starts to knead against my chest—"

"With those unretractable claws?" Sora interrupted.

"Yes." His grin widened. "Which very effectively wakes me. I take him to Mariah. He feeds while I wait, and then I scoop him up and take him back to my pallet."

"How long have you been doing that?"

"Oh, from the first day I found him. Only then he was so little he couldn't stay away from Mariah's milk for more than just a fraction of the night, so I made sure I camped close to Claudia and Davis. It's really only been the past few nights that Cubby has started sleeping so long."

"Half a night isn't really very long," said Sora.

"It is when you compare it to one fourth of a night." He moved both of his shoulders. "But you would've done the same if Chloe had Chosen you when she was this young."

"Yes. You're right I would have." Sora studied O'Bryan with new eyes. She'd known he was a nice guy from the moment they'd met. He'd been singed from rushing into a blazing forest fire to save Fala's pups—which included her precious Chloe—but she hadn't realized the extent of his compassion. She'd thought he was nice for a Tribesman and also kind of funny and cute, though freakishly tall like the rest of the Goddess-forsaken Tribe of the Trees; then she'd not thought much more about him. That night she began to realize that perhaps O'Bryan deserved more thought.

"Sora?"

"Oh, sorry. What did you say?"

"I was just worrying aloud. I watched Mari return today on Tulpar with Dove and River and April. Those horses pounded over the plains. Antreas and Bast and Rigel could barely keep up with them. River said it will take us two weeks of hard travel to make it to the Valley of Vapors. I'm worried about how we're going to keep up with the Herd tomorrow—well, actually, not just tomorrow but for the two weeks it'll take us to get to the Valley of Vapors."

"I spoke with Morgana about that today." She dimpled at his surprised expression. "Apparently the Leader of the Mare Council is rather taken with Terrier pups. She described them as *exceedingly adorable.*"

O'Bryan laughed. "They are."

"I agree." Sora made kiss noises at Chloe, who crawled onto her feet and began chewing on one of her leather shoe ties. "Destructive, but adorable." She scooped the pup up and put her in the pouch-like sling that had been her carrier for months. "Anyway, I wondered the same thing as you about how we'd keep up with the horses—and not just us, but the dozens of Herdmembers who have never been Chosen and who usually remain here at this magnificent cave year round."

"What did Morgana say?" O'Bryan went back to patting the lump in his shirt that was Cubby's fat rump.

"That I needn't worry. Their horses can do a lot more than just be ridden. They can pull carts, which people and supplies ride in. They can also pull the litters we dragged across the mountains—apparently with very little effort. So, it seems we'll be riding horse carts to the Valley of Vapors and we won't be dragging those horrid litters again."

"Huh. I did not expect that."

"I'm beginning to believe that our new life on the Plains of the Wind Riders is going to be full of things we didn't expect," said Sora, watching O'Bryan closely.

"I'm glad," O'Bryan said. "I like surprises."

"I don't usually. Well, unless the surprise has to do with gifts of jewels or feathers or perhaps lovely woven cloth, but I'm learning to look at some things with new eyes." Sora met O'Bryan's gaze, and she thought his cheeks might have flushed a little pink. Chloe yawned and then yapped sleepily. "Yes, yes, I hear you. *Now* you're suddenly ready for bed."

"May I walk with you to the cave?" O'Bryan asked.

"Well, we are going to the same place—all four of us."

"We absolutely are," said O'Bryan.

Sora walked beside O'Bryan as they made their way down from the grassy ridge that was the roof of the enormous cave. With one hand he kept patting his kit's round rump, and with the other he offered to steady Sora during the steepest parts of their reverse climb.

Sora appreciated O'Bryan's kindness more than she actually needed his help. His hand was large and strong and warm, dwarfing her much smaller one. When they came to the curtained door to Sora's little room, O'Bryan stepped forward and she thought for a moment that he was going to try to kiss her—the unexpected rudeness of such a presumptuous action shocked her into momentary silence, though she sucked in air, intending to let him know clearly and firmly that Earth Walker women decide when they want to be kissed and by whom! And then she was glad she'd been temporarily mute when, instead of demanding a kiss, he'd simply bent to lightly pet Chloe and murmur a sweet good night first to the pup and then to Sora before he turned to go to his own room, still patting the rump of his kit.

That night Sora fell asleep thinking that she might decide to like surprises that weren't strictly jewels or feathers or beautifully woven materials . . .

CHAPTER 11

River stood on the incline above Weanling Creek and continued to towel dry her hair as she leaned against Anjo's warm side and gazed down at her Herd. In the west behind her the sky was dark and bruised, so that even before sunrise River was assured that it was still snowing heavily in the mountains. In front of her it was predawn, and the light was like a dove's wing—gray and opal and just touched with the palest pink. The Herd would normally have been sleeping—*she* would normally have been sleeping—but not today. Today River had awoken well before dawn so she could bathe in the cool, crystal waters of her favorite creek, just as she had done more than three years ago on that magickal day Anjo Chose her.

River looked up at her magnificent mare. "It's hard to believe it's been three years. It feels like yesterday *and* a lifetime ago you Chose me."

You have always been mine. Anjo snorted and then snuffled River's damp hair. *The Herd has been busy.*

"Yeah, they're almost ready to leave the site. I'm proud of the Herd already, Anjo. No panic. No whining. No complaints. It's only been a day, but we'll be ready to leave with the rise of the sun."

It is because they trust us. Her mare's voice was familiar within her mind.

River sighed. "I wonder if they realize what a difficult trip it's going to be—nothing like our usual migration."

They know, and they are ready. Do not worry so, my River.

"Have you heard any discontented rumblings from the Herd about the Pack?" River asked her mare.

No. The opposite. They like the canines, especially the puppies, and they appreciated the Moon Women's magick last night.

Yip! Yip!

River and Anjo turned their attention to the little black pup who had been asleep on River's feet, but who was now staring up at horse and Rider sternly and flooding both with waves of anxiety.

River grinned and picked up the pup. "Hey, we said the Herd appreciates the Pack, *especially* the puppies. They're part of us now, and that's not going to change. Don't fret, little girl. All will be well." She kissed the pup's nose before placing her in the basket rigged behind Anjo's trail saddle.

"I am glad to hear it."

Her voice should've startled River, but instead it was like she was just another part of the dawn. Anjo turned her head and rumbled a low greeting to Tulpar as he and his new Rider joined them on the incline.

"Good morning, Dove—Tulpar," River said, and Chloe yapped her own hello from her basket.

Dove's laugh was soft and sweet. She leaned slightly so she could ruffle the curly black fur atop the pup's head. "It's good to see you, Chloe." Then she straightened and her face turned toward River. "And good morning, River and Anjo. Tulpar said we would find you near the creek. I hope we are not intruding."

"Not at all. I was just taking a last look at the Rendezvous Site before heading back to close the mouth of the cave and begin our journey."

"It is quite beautiful—and impressive. Herd Magenti is strong. I will always be so grateful that by Tulpar Choosing me I gained the ability to see through his eyes. It would be difficult for me to comprehend the size and might of the Herd were I still in the dark."

River studied Dove's beautiful, eyeless face. "Is it difficult for you to get used to having sight?"

"Difficult? In what way?" Dove asked.

"Well, I remember when I was a girl a young boy was brought to my mother from Herd Cinnabar."

"The Warrior Herd?" Dove asked quickly.

River smiled and nodded. "Yes, Cinnabar is where many of our War-riors train."

"Morgana has been helping me learn about the Herds. But, please, go on. What about this young Warrior?"

"He was brought to my mother because he was deaf—he had been since birth—but his mother was Lead Mare Rider and she and my mother had been friends since they were girls. She hoped Dawn would be able to use the power of crystals to grant him hearing, something the healers of Herd Indigo had been unable to do. Miraculously, Dawn was able to break the blockage within the boy, which was mental and not physical, and he was able to hear."

"That's wonderful!"

"One would think so, but the boy was miserable. He said everything was too loud—too abrasive—just too much. It took him years to accli-mate. He never seemed truly content after that. I wondered if you were having similar difficulties."

Her lips tilted up. "Do I seem to be having difficulties?"

"No, not at all, but women are much better than men at covering our pain. So, if it is not too presumptuous of me, I thought I would ask."

Dove considered for a moment before responding, "I understand the boy. It is an assault—to suddenly be granted a sense I've never had—but it is different for me because of my Tulpar." She ran her fingers through the stallion's long white mane. "He helps me understand what I see. And I know he is with me here—" She touched her forehead. "And here." Dove touched her chest over her heart. "He soothes me when it all seems too much, and explains to me things I see and have a hard time comprehending."

"Huh. That makes sense. I'm glad for both of you." River grinned at the beautiful stallion and then asked, "What is the most surprising thing about being able to see?"

"The colors!" Dove's voice filled with excitement. "Dead Eye and Mari tried to explain colors to me before, and I thought I understood—but I had no idea. The world is so filled with colors. So many greens and blues, browns and whites and yellows and reds, but I think my favorite is gold." Her hand stroked her stallion's sleek golden neck. "My second favorite is purple."

"Well, that's lucky," River said. "As we are the purple Herd." Then she added, "Dead Eye? I don't think I've met that Pack member yet."

Dove's expression fell, and River was instantly sorry she'd asked.

"He wasn't a member of the Pack. He was the vessel the God of Death now inhabits. He is no more."

"Oh, I am sorry." River felt a strange twinge deep in her gut. *What is that feeling? It couldn't be jealousy. That's absurd.*

"Yes. I am sorry as well. Thank you."

They stood there together in silence watching the sky lighten and the Herd buzz busily as they loaded wagons and saddlebags. River was just going to suggest they head back to camp when she remembered something Dove had said earlier.

"You said Tulpar told you I'd be here. Did you need my help with something?" she asked Dove.

"Oh. Well. No. We just—" Tulpar snorted, which had Dove correcting herself. "*I* just thought to check on you. So much has happened in such a short time. The Pack, Tulpar Choosing me, Kit Choosing you, Clayton's betrayal, and discovering the God of Death is leading an invading army against your homelands. I thought you might need someone to talk with, and Tulpar explained his, *our*, role in the Herd—that we are tasked with protecting the Herd and supporting the Lead Mare and Rider—so it seemed to me that it would not be presumptuous to check on you and let you know that Tulpar and I are here for you." Dove's fingers combed through Tulpar's perfectly groomed mane as she spoke, as if she was having a difficult time holding still.

"That's kind of you," said River. "And Tulpar is absolutely correct. Often the Rider of the Herd Stallion and the Rider of the Lead Mare form a close relationship. My father and April's was a Lead Stallion Rider." River hurried on as she felt her cheeks warm. "I do hope we'll be good friends and I appreciate that you sought me out." River meant to leave it at that, but there was something about Dove's listening silence and Tulpar's protective presence that had her continuing. "Anjo and I were just discussing the Herd. I worry about how difficult this migration will be. Usually we make our way to the Valley of Vapors laden with newly harvested crops, slowly, with much feasting and merrymaking on the way."

Dove nodded. "Yes, and Tulpar says you do not usually have to migrate from this far of a distance from the valley—that you're only here and not at your fall campsite because of the Stallion Run."

"That's right. We're usually at our harvest grounds, which are much closer to the Valley of Vapors," said River. "Could we migrate at our usual leisurely pace from here it would take us at least one full month, but we have to cut that time in half if we are to get to our stronghold to prepare for Death's army."

"Your Herd is in excellent health. Tulpar and I have moved among them. He has observed them closely, and he reports to me that the horses are well and in good condition—many in extraordinary condition because of this year's Mare Test and Stallion Run. Tulpar says we will make it to the valley in time," said Dove.

River patted her mare's shoulder. "That's pretty much what Anjo was just reminding me. I know the three of you are right." She smiled at the golden stallion. "Thank you for the reassurance, Tulpar. If my Herd Stallion says we are ready then I know it to be truth."

"Do you still look so worried because of Death, or is it the Pack that troubles you? You can tell me. I will not hear it as a slight against them."

"Oh, no. Your Pack just journeyed much farther than we'll need to go, and you are all fit and sound," River said.

Tell Dove. Share your worries. She is Rider of your Herd Stallion. It is her place to support you.

River's finger found one of the long purple ribbons she'd hastily braided into her hair in the dark of predawn. She twirled it around and around as she finally admitted, "It's my mother. I wonder if I did the right thing in letting her and Skye go after Clayton and the other traitors."

"Do you fear they will harm her?"

"Yes. No. Yes." River sighed. "That's part of the problem. I simply do not know. Normally, I'd say there is no chance any Herdmember would harm another Herdmember, especially not a beloved Lead Mare Rider."

"But Clayton tried to kill you and my Tulpar."

"Exactly. Mother means to show them compassion. While I agree in theory, in practice I question her choice."

"Dawn and her Echo are wise. You have said so. Tulpar says so. The Herd loves them and respects them—that is obvious. I understand your worry, but your decision has been made. Your Mother and Skye are already well on their journey. Perhaps you must trust them and give your worries to the Great Mother Mare. Morgana explained that all Lead Mare Riders are blessed with a mare's luck. Would it help you to be reminded of that?"

River opened her mouth to quip that no, that doesn't really help—but her Companion's gentle voice closed her mouth. *A mare's luck is with them, my River—as is the Great Mother Mare. It is good to be reminded of that.*

River looked from Anjo to Dove, who was serene and confident astride Tulpar. "I did need to be reminded of that."

Dove's face blazed with happiness as she smiled. "I am so pleased I could help! Tulpar said we could, but I am very new to this, so I was concerned about intruding."

"Dove, you and Tulpar are never an intrusion." River closed the few feet between herself and the stallion. "Thank you, Herd Stallion Rider," she said formally, and then she impulsively reached up to put her hand over Dove's.

Dove drew in a sharp breath at River's touch, though she didn't pull away from her. Instead, slowly, she turned her hand so that their palms rested against each other, and threaded her fingers through River's.

"You are most welcome, Lead Mare Rider," Dove said.

River gazed up at Dove. She knew the girl couldn't actually see her through her own eyes—she had none—and she felt Tulpar's gaze on her. The gaze he shared with his Rider. River felt something else—something more than their shared gaze. Through Dove's warm palm she felt a tingle that spread into her own body and nestled deep within her, stirring feelings that made her suddenly pull her hand away, clear her throat, and say, "We should get back. The sun will be rising, and the Herd must move out."

"Yes, of course," Dove said. Then with a cheeky smile she added, "And you won't want to miss the Pack greeting the sun. Tulpar says it's something the Herd will enjoy."

Anjo knelt so that River could mount her. "The Moon Women also use sun magick? I think I still have a lot to learn about your people."

Dove's smile widened, but she said nothing more as Tulpar kicked into a smooth canter beside Anjo.

The Herd was packed and ready to begin their hasty journey as the sun lifted from the eastern horizon and bathed the Rendezvous Site and the massive stone monoliths with bright canary light. The combined Herd and Pack waited expectantly just outside the circular ring of stones that stood, sentinel-like, before the opening of the huge cave that had been filled with household goods, clothes, and all the extra supplies deemed not necessary to take with them to the Valley of Vapors.

"Look at that," Mari said to Nik as she pointed. "I didn't notice it before, but those giant stones and the mouth of the cave are sparkling. It's like there are tiny crystals embedded in all of it."

"There are. Gotcha." April scooped up her pup with an exasperated sigh, though she kissed Cleo on the nose and snuggled her close. "Hundreds of years ago Herd Magenti chose the sites for our permanent camps because of the presence of crystals. These are a little difficult to see unless the sun shines directly on them, like at dawn, but wait till we get to the valley. The crystals there are magnificent."

"I'm looking forward to seeing them," said Mari. Then she added, "April, our Pack would like to greet the sun before we leave. Should we do that now, or—"

"Oh, sorry," April interrupted. "Chasing this little girl wasn't the only thing that brought me to you. River said Dove mentioned that your people greet the sun at dawn. She sent me to your group to ask if you'd like to do so in the middle of the monoliths, where the sun's rays are concentrated this early in the morning. Then we'll seal the cave and be on our way."

"Is that okay with you, Nik?" Mari asked him.

Nik looked surprised, but he nodded enthusiastically. "Yes, that would be powerful."

Mari turned to April and explained, "Nik is our Sun Priest. He leads the sunrise greeting."

"That's interesting. River and I assumed it would be you and Sora leading your people in greeting the sun. Well, we're ready now if Nik is," said April.

"Pack!" Nik called to the people behind them. "Follow me to greet the sun!"

There was a stirring in the crowd, and then Mari was delighted to see that every single member of the Pack—even those who had no Companion and did not used to be members of the Tribe of the Trees—moved forward with her as Nik led them to the center of the circle of giant crystal-embedded boulders.

Nik stood in front of his people facing the eastern horizon. He glanced behind him and smiled at the Pack before lifting his arms as if to embrace the newly risen sun. Mari and the rest of the Pack mimicked his movements. Their canine Companions took position beside each of their Chosen people. As Nik spoke, he and the Pack, including the canines, tilted their heads so that their faces were bathed in sunlight.

"Behold the wonder of our Pack and the Herd we have newly joined. Behold the first beams of our lifeline—our strength—our sun!"

Mari didn't have to look at Nik or the rest of the Pack to know that their eyes—hers included—changed color to reflect the golden light of the sun. And as they absorbed the powerful morning light, filigreed patterns of the fronds of the Mother Plant began to be visible just under the skin on their arms.

Mari heard Nik and Wilkes, Claudia, Davis, O'Bryan, and several of the other ex-members of the Tribe of the Trees laugh joyfully as they and their Companions absorbed the sunlight. She glanced at Rigel, who stood beside her. His eyes were glowing with light and his tail was wagging so vigorously his whole butt wiggled.

And then there was an enthusiastic yipping and two black pups dashed to the Pack with River and April jogging after them.

"Kit, wait!" River called.

"Cleo, come here, baby girl," April coaxed.

But the pups didn't pause until they'd reached Nik, where they stopped to stare up at the rising sun as their Companions rushed to them.

"I am so sorry we interrupted," River said. "I don't know what's wrong with Kit. She usually listens much better than this."

Nik, his face blazing with sunlight, smiled joyously at River. "You aren't interrupting at all! The pups are simply joining us, as usual. You are more than welcome, and as their Companions the power of the sun is yours to absorb. Look at your pups' eyes."

River and her sister looked down at their pups, whose body language perfectly mimicked the adult canines. They stood, except for their wagging tails, holding their bodies very still as they gazed up at the rising sun with eyes that glowed gold.

"That's incredible! What do we do?" asked April.

"Simply stand beside your Companion, lift your arms, and welcome the power of the sun," said Nik.

"Will images of ferns rise from beneath our skin, too?" River asked as she lifted her arms.

"I have not known that to happen to anyone who was not swaddled in the Mother Plant," explained Nik.

"But even without being swaddled by the Mother Plant it's possible to absorb the power of the sun," said Sora from her place beside Mari. She held Chloe in her arms as she and the pup gazed up at the sun. "I know because I was not swaddled by the plant, but my bond with Chloe allows me to soak in sunlight. Try it. It feels wonderful!"

River gasped. "I can feel it! Warmth is filling me like I just awakened a crystal."

"Me too! My Cleo and I feel it, too!" shouted April.

From outside the circle of stones Anjo and April's mare, Deinos, trotted to join their Riders, and then neighed in excitement as their eyes also began to glow and the power of the sun flowed from two small Terrier pups, through their Riders and into both horses.

"Anjo feels it!" River laughed with joy.

"So does Deinos!" echoed April.

The Herd gasped in surprise, which was reflected in Nik's shocked expression. He met Mari's gaze, grinned, and said, "Our new world is full of wonders."

"It sure is," said Mari as Rigel, Laru, and the rest of the canines barked in agreement.

"Let us show you another wonder," said River. "Unless there is more to greeting the sun—then we will happily do that first."

"No," Nik said. "We simply welcome the sunrise, drawing it within ourselves and our Companions—and give thanks for its power and warmth."

"We would definitely like to see more wonders," added Mari.

"Then get ready to observe the might of Herd Magenti." River's voice was filled with power as she raised her hand and called to her Herd, "Crystal Seers! Join me within the stone circle!"

April touched Mari's arm. "If you and the Pack come with me, we can watch from outside the stone circle with the rest of the Herd."

Mari motioned for the Pack to follow her and they quickly moved outside the stone monoliths as women of the Herd joined River and Anjo. April remained with them, which Mari appreciated as she had question after question after question she wanted to ask the young woman, though she didn't want to bombard April, so she wanted silently as Herdswomen formed a circle within the circle of stones.

"River is doing an excellent job directing all those women," said Sora.

April grinned and nodded as she leaned against Deinos and watched with the Pack. "You'd never know how nervous she is, would you?"

"Absolutely not. She hides it well," said Sora, who shared a look with Mari. "But Mari and I understand that a leader must be good at hiding such things."

"We sure do," added Mari.

"River wouldn't be so nervous if our mother was here. The last time the cave was closed—almost a decade ago—Dawn and Echo led the ceremony. But I know my sister will do well. Though we all miss Mother," said April.

"Of course you do," said Sora. "The plan is for Dawn and Skye to join us somewhere on our trip to the valley, right?"

"That's right. Or perhaps at the valley, but they should be able to travel faster than we will." April's look darkened. "With or without Clayton and the rest of his traitors."

Nik's voice was kind when he said, "I know what it's like to have traitors in your Tribe or, in this case, Herd. Dawn is doing the right thing in confronting them. Ignoring them is dangerous for everyone."

"Hey, are those stones glowing?" Sora pointed at the monoliths.

The bright smile returned to April's face. "They are. Keep watching. It has only just begun."

As the Herdswomen formed a circle within the circle of stones, Mari couldn't hold her questions. "April, why aren't you inside the stones with River and the rest of them?"

"I'm not a Crystal Seer yet." April shrugged. "I may never be."

From beside Mari, Nik asked, "I thought all of Herd Magenti were connected to crystals?"

"Oh, most of us are, but being connected to a crystal and being a Crystal Seer are very different things. To be considered a Seer one must be able to do more than just awaken a crystal. A Seer has the ability to project the power of the crystal, or its properties, outside herself, as River did yesterday when she created that snowstorm," said April.

"You said *herself*," said Nik. "Does that mean only women are Crystal Seers?"

"It isn't unheard of for a man to become a Seer, though it is rare. Only men who have been Chosen by a mare have attained that level of expertise with crystals, and mares rarely choose men," said April. Then she grinned. "But with the Pack joining us it will be very interesting to see what happens in the future, especially when it is Choosing time for yearlings in the spring."

Nik's brows shot up. "You will allow the Pack to be presented to the yearlings for Choosing?"

"I can't speak for River, but it wouldn't surprise me, though there is an age limit for Rider Candidates." April's gaze went from Nik to the stone circle. "They are beginning."

Nik clearly wanted to question April further on the rules for Rider Candidates, but he politely turned his attention to the stone monoliths and the women within them. Mari understood exactly how he felt, as her own questions for April swirled around in her mind, but the last thing she wanted to do was make April uncomfortable or be impolite, so she, too, turned her attention to the stone circle.

Each woman standing directly in front of the huge, glistening stones pressed one hand against the boulders. The other hand was held by the woman beside her—and so it went around the great circle until each woman was connected to the others and to the stones in a living chain. River took a position that faced the open mouth of the cave. She stood between two stones. To her right was Morgana. To her left was another member of the Mare Council, though the only way Mari knew that was because, like Morgana, she wore ribbons the colors of each Herd braided into her long gray hair. *So at least two members of the Mare Council, including their leader, are from Herd Magenti and are Crystal Seers. It seems this Herd is as powerful as it is wise.* The thought warmed Mari like the touch of the sun.

The center of the circle was filled with mares—old, young, in so many different colors that it made Mari's head a little dizzy. Each mare stood behind her Rider, as if lending them strength.

"Do the mares help the Seers?" Sora asked April.

"Absolutely," said April. "A Seer can always awaken and transmit the properties of a crystal, but that ability is amplified by the presence of her mare." She glanced at Nik and smiled. "It's a little like how our canines amplify the power of sunlight for us."

Nik nodded. "That makes sense. The human-Companion bond is strong on many levels."

"Speaking of humans and their Companions, Dove didn't greet the sun with us today." Mari looked over her shoulder at the Pack and easily found Lily where she stood holding little Dash beside Rose and her Fala. Before they'd reached the Wind Rider Plains, Dove was rarely far from her friend, but today Dove was nowhere to be seen.

"That's because Dove has taken on her new responsibilities as Rider of our Herd Stallion. Look there, where the land is higher." April pointed to the west, and Mari followed her finger to see golden Tulpar and Dove, along with at least a dozen other stallions and their Riders spread out overlooking the Herd.

"What are they doing?" Sora asked.

"Watching over us so that River and the Seers can concentrate on closing the cave," said April. "It is our stallions and their Riders' duty, led by Tulpar and Dove, to be sure that the Herd is always safe."

"Dove will do a good job at that," said Nik.

Mari sent him a surprised look, and he laughed. "What? You know when I'm wrong I own my mistakes and try to do better. I was wrong when I didn't trust Dove. I realized that during her run-in with the Saleesh. Since then, I've come to understand that what is most important to Dove is to be loved and accepted by her people. In return she is fiercely loyal and protective."

"Then you're saying Tulpar made a good choice in Riders," said April.

"Yes!" Mari, Nik, and Sora responded together.

River's voice, filled with power and confidence, pulled everyone's attention to the stone circle. She began with a rhythm that seemed driven by the combined heartbeat of the watching, waiting Herd.

"In this place of power
my sisters do stand."

The women inside the circle responded together with, "*Seers all—Seers true.*"

River continued, her voice gaining unnatural strength so that it was as if the enormous silent stones amplified her words.

"At this very hour
together we band"

The women responded, "*Seers all—Seers true.*"

River said, "*Through right of blood*
Bonded by horse and stone."

"*Seers all—Seers true,*" the women echoed.

"*Hear my call.*
Seal the maw," concluded River.

Then all the women joined River in shouting:

"Let no one through,
let none get through,
until Magenti's Crystal Seers reopen you!"

As River and the Herdswomen spoke the words of the spell, the stone monoliths' glow intensified. It appeared to Mari that the small specks of crystals that dotted the skin of the boulders were lit from within, until they shined so brightly that it was difficult to look at them, and then Mari's gaze was pulled away from the stones to the enormous opening of the cave. Slowly, carefully, so that almost no rocks or even dirt around it were disturbed, the top of the cave began to close.

"It's like the Great Earth Mother is closing Her eye and going peacefully to sleep." Sora spoke reverently. "I've—I've rarely seen anything so magickal."

April turned to look at Sora. "Exactly. You understand it exactly. We say that the openings of our caves are the eyes of our Great Mother Mare and when our Seers close the caves it is as if the Mother Mare sleeps."

"I think Dove is right," said Mari—and as she spoke she felt the veracity of her words deep within her. "The goddess we call the Great Earth Mother is just another face of your Mother Mare and, ultimately, they are all just different versions of the Goddess of Life."

"Then let us hope She stands with us against Death," said April.

"From your lips to the Goddess's ears," murmured Sora.

CHAPTER 12

"STORYTELLER!"

Death bellowed the bitch's title again, and Thaddeus sneered in disgust—though only because the God could not see his expression through the relentlessly falling snow. *She's gone, isn't she, Odysseus?* In his dark and twisted mind Thaddeus often talked with his Terrier. It helped him believe the canine was still alive—still with him. *I hope to all the hells she is gone. No, more than that. I hope the bitch didn't get lost or fall from the path to her death. I hope she escaped and Death discovers that she left him.*

"STORYTELLER."

Thaddeus could just make out the outline of the God's horned head as He paced down the long line of the army looking for Ralina. It had to be some time in the early morning, or at least Thaddeus assumed it was morning. The wall of white that surrounded them and kept falling from the sky had lightened somewhat as Death had bellowed for them to *GET UP—GET MOVING.* Then He'd ordered Iron Fist to bring His Storyteller to Him, and when the Blade couldn't find her—or her Shepherd, her lover, his Shepherd, *or* her lover's father—that's when Death started searching the narrow, snow-covered path for her Himself. It is also when Thaddeus began to feel certain the scheming woman had used the cover of the storm to finally escape Death. *Little good it will do her. She won't survive on this mountain in this weather.* Thaddeus stopped himself from taking that thought further to the truth waiting just beyond—that none of them would survive much longer if the snow didn't stop and they didn't get off this mountain.

The day before they'd sloughed through snow as it changed from soft flakes to smaller, harder pieces of ice, and finally became an unending wall of white that fell and fell and fell from the sky so thick and so dense that it was difficult to tell which way was up and which way was down. When a whole group of Milks took a wrong turn and tumbled, screaming eerily, from the side of the mountain to what Thaddeus could only assume was their real death the God finally called a halt. The army had huddled, miserable and cold and wet, against the overhanging mountainside above them, pressed next to one another—which Thaddeus hated—covering themselves with the thick, luxurious blankets they'd taken as spoils of war from the newly extinct Saleesh, and tried to sleep.

"STORYTELLER!"

Thaddeus had to choke down laughter. Death sounded so pitiful. He actually thought the bitch wanted to tell His story? Thaddeus knew better. Ralina had wanted to survive. Period. Unlike Thaddeus. He planned on doing more than simply surviving. He was determined to thrive. He'd already been elevated from Leader of Hunters to Leader of Tribesmen—or at least the ones smart enough to accept him and the cure that changed them from mere men to more. So, so much more.

But he had no intention of being Death's lackey forever. Once they conquered the Wind Riders and took possession of their land he'd manipulate Death into letting him rule his own Tribe. Again, Thaddeus had to stifle laughter. Death was ridiculously easy to manipulate. Flatter Him. Lie to Him. Tell Him what He wanted to hear and Thaddeus would get his way. Wasn't that what Ralina had done? Only she was too stupid to play the long game.

Thaddeus wasn't stupid.

Thaddeus knew Wind Riders claimed an enormous amount of land. Death led the conquering army, but it would be impossible for Him to rule so much land by Himself. The God would need leaders—those who could take charge of men. Thaddeus would be one of those leaders. He would wait until Death chose the settlement from which He would rule, and then Thaddeus would discover where his own settlement should be—as far from the God's site as possible. Thaddeus would flatter and cajole, manipulate and lie—whatever he needed to do to get Death's permission to take charge of that settlement.

Then, Odysseus, I will no longer be the pawn of a god.

"Thaddeus. Good. We found you." Several Tribesmen trudged through the snow to him. They were Hunters with their Terriers following reluctantly behind them through the knee-deep snow, miserable and shivering.

Thaddeus felt a little jolt of shock as he studied his men—the strongest of his surviving Hunters. *When was the last time I really looked at them?* The five Hunters walked hunched. They were covered with blankets from head to toe, but Thaddeus could see that their hair was unusually shaggy and it mixed with their beards, which looked much like the snow-covered fur of their Terriers. Though their hands were gloved, it was obvious that their fingernails had lengthened to such a degree that they strained, and even tore, the tips of those gloves. Their eyes had also changed color from the green that used to mark all members of the Tribe of the Trees to the brown of Terrier eyes.

Thaddeus glanced down at his own hands. Yes, they, too, were more claw-like than before he'd taken the cure from his loyal Odysseus. His vision had recently begun to change, too. Colors weren't as vibrant, but he didn't mind that because his ability to see in dim light, or even no light, had drastically increased. And his sense of smell was incredible. Daily, Thaddeus was amazed at the nuances in scents that he'd never before noticed. Yes, he knew that his body seemed to hunch more and more as time went on, but that hadn't bothered him. Thaddeus had actually been glad of it as it was easier to scramble, Terrier-like, up the steeper, narrower sections of the trail than walk upright like the Milks. Thaddeus hadn't been bothered about any of the changes happening to him. He thought of them as tribute to his Odysseus—but a small part of him was disturbed at actually seeing the same changes in his men. Even their voices were different. Deeper, rougher, almost inhuman.

"Thaddeus?"

He mentally shook himself and faced his men. "What is it?"

"Death sent us to you." Wilson, whose Companion, Spud, was a blond

Terrier and an excellent tracker, spoke first. "He cannot find Ralina, Renard, Daniel, or their Companions."

Thaddeus snorted. "That doesn't surprise me."

"Would it surprise you to know He commands that we—the five of us and you—are to track her in this blizzard?" James, whose Companion was a feisty Terrier named Garth, ground the words at him so that the sentence ended in a growl.

"We can't track anything in the storm," said Thaddeus. "To think otherwise is madness."

"Death is commanding such madness. Thaddeus, we will perish if we leave this path on a fool's chase," said Stephen. Behind him his black brindle Terrier, Rocker, punctuated his words with an irritated bark.

Thaddeus squinted through the biting snow. He could only see a few yards ahead before white swallowed everything. The line of men were moving forward, but slowly, with their heads bent against the snow. When he looked up the mountainside above them, he could only see different shades of white and gray—and blobs that were either snow-covered trees or snow-covered boulders.

"We can't track anything in the storm," Thaddeus repeated.

"Bloody beetle balls, here He comes," said Wilson.

Thaddeus looked up the trail. The God's shape striding toward them was only visible because His mass and strength were so great that He plowed the snow away from Him as He moved through it. And, of course, there was also the eerie light that came from the spirit of the bison bull who now led Death through the pass. The spirit was never far from Him and Thaddeus could see his glow behind the God.

"Go over there. Quickly." Thaddeus pointed at the dismal line of men who were trudging forward, single file, through the never-ending snow. "Join the others. I'll take care of this."

His men nodded and then hurried to do as he directed. Thaddeus prepared to face the God.

"Thaddeus!"

"I am here, my Lord!" Thaddeus shouted his reply, and waved.

The God of Death stomped to him. As He reached Thaddeus, the God's huge body blocked some of the falling snow. Thaddeus looked up at Death and was amazed anew at the physical changes happening to the

God. He had been stag-like, until the day before the snow began to fall and the spirit of the doe who had been leading them disappeared. The God had returned to camp with the Storyteller—dragging the body of an enormous bison bull. Now Death seemed to be rejecting the stag and taking on the physical traits of a bison.

"Thaddeus, My Storyteller is missing." The God shook His massive head, displacing chunks of snow.

"Yes, my Lord, so I have heard. Is it true that her lover, his father, and their canines are gone as well?" Thaddeus kept his expression open—his voice concerned.

"It is. I need the skills of your Hunters. They must backtrack down the pass until they pick up her scent or tracks. Then they must find her and return her to Me," said Death.

Thaddeus blew out a long breath. "My Lord, I would gladly recapture the Storyteller for You, but—"

"Recapture?" Death narrowed His eyes and His voice took on a dangerous edge that Thaddeus recognized all too well.

"Forgive me, my Lord. I assumed that because the Storyteller's whole group is missing—even their canines—she must have escaped."

"What have you heard? And why did you not tell Me the Storyteller was discontented?"

"I heard nothing, my Lord. Had I heard such a thing I would have immediately come to You with such information," Thaddeus said hastily.

"Then why assume she ran from Me?"

"I cannot say, my Lord. Forgive me. I misspoke." Thaddeus made himself bow submissively.

"No, no. There is more to this than what you are saying. Out with it. Speak the truth," Death commanded as He stomped a cloven hoof.

"I do not wish to upset You, my Lord," Thaddeus simpered.

"I am a god! I do not become upset. I become righteously angry. I command you to tell Me what you know."

Thaddeus had to hide his smile. Death really was too easy to manipulate. "It's about the canines—Bear and Kong. Were Ralina, Renard, and Daniel lost or injured they would send their canines for help. Though they are only Shepherds and not Terriers, they do have the ability to backtrack and find the pass, which they would follow to rejoin us. Then they could lead You to Your Storyteller to rescue her . . ." Thaddeus paused and moved his shoulders restlessly.

"Go on," Death prodded.

"So that means that either all five of them fell from the pass to their deaths or Ralina used the snowstorm to escape into the mountains."

The God was silent, considering. Then He closed His eyes and seemed to withdraw. The air around Him changed. Thaddeus found it difficult to breathe—and the cold suddenly intensified so that he had to wrap his scarf over his nose to keep his breath from freezing in his lungs.

Then the God opened His eyes and the world changed from a frozen nightmare to a much more mundane blizzard. "She is not dead," He said. "Were she dead I would know it."

"Ah. Well. I am sorry, my Lord," said Thaddeus. "It is unforgivable for her to repay Your kindness and generosity with such disloyalty."

When the God's eyes narrowed again in anger, His wrath was not directed at Thaddeus.

"I want you to track her. Find her, and return her to Me. Alive. But kill the rest of them. Not her canine, though. I have other plans for him," said Death.

"My Lord, it would bring me great pleasure to complete this task for You." At least that much of what Thaddeus said was absolutely the truth. "But it is impossible for me, or any of my Hunters, to track in this blizzard."

"Explain why." Those two words were laced with vitriol.

"Gladly, my Lord. Canines find their prey two ways. One is through smelling the scent that all things shed as they move. The other is catching the scent of the prey in the air. The Terriers can do neither in this storm because the ground scent is being covered and obliterated by the constantly falling snow and the air scent is being dissipated by the strength of the winds." He lifted his hands and let them fall helplessly. "I cannot track the Storyteller as long as the weather remains like this."

"Then tell me what you *can* do, Thaddeus, for I am sick of being told what you cannot," said Death grimly.

"I can find her body for You after the storm passes and the snow melts. Forgive me, my Lord, but if You sent me or my Hunters back there"—Thaddeus pointed down the pass—"we would surely perish, and then You still would have no word of Your Storyteller. Let us get through this pass, defeat the Wind Riders, and at first thaw, I give You my word that I will lead my best Hunters back into these mountains. We will find her. We will return her to Your side where she belongs." He bowed his head and waited.

There was a long silence through which Thaddeus remained speechless, with his head bowed before the God.

"I can find no fault in the logic you speak," the god finally said. "I will hold you to your word, Thaddeus. When spring thaws the snow, you will find My Storyteller—or what remains of her—and return her to Me." Death sighed deeply and spoke quietly, as if he'd forgotten Thaddeus was there. "I will know when she dies. I will mourn her then, for even though she broke faith with Me—" His words ended abruptly. When He spoke again, excitement filled His voice. "Thaddeus, perhaps it was not My Storyteller who broke faith with Me. Perhaps it was her lover."

Thaddeus looked up at the God. "My Lord, Renard was years younger than Ralina—and though she and I were never friends, I can admit that she is one of the wisest, most independent women I have ever known. It is hard to believe Renard was able to talk her into leaving if she did not truly want to go." It was difficult to keep the sneer from his voice, but he managed it—though Death was so distracted by His newest fantasy that He probably wouldn't have noticed.

The God rounded on Thaddeus. "So it is easier for you to believe My Storyteller has betrayed Me than to believe her young lover manipulated her?"

Thaddeus knew he'd pushed too far. "No, no, You are obviously right, my Lord. I was just reasoning aloud. Now that You mention it, I am not surprised that her young lover manipulated Your Storyteller. We all know young men can easily sway women of a certain age. That is clearly what happened to Ralina. I just hope she does not pay for her mistake with her life." And that wasn't a lie. Thaddeus hoped the bitch would somehow survive the winter in the mountains so that he could track her, capture her, and drag her back to the God of Death so that He could see—once and for all—that Ralina, Storyteller to the Tribe of the Trees, had indeed betrayed Him.

"Yes. Good. Yes. That is what happened. I will look forward to the spring when you return My Storyteller to Me. Ah, and do not kill her lover. Bring him to Me as well. I shall cut off his manhood in front of her. That should be enough to keep her from being so easily manipulated again," said the God.

"Excellent idea, my Lord," said Thaddeus.

"Now, I must see to My army. Can you believe they are hesitant to move today?" Death didn't wait for Thaddeus to respond. "They think snow can stop Death. *Nothing* can stop Death." The God began to turn away, but He paused and motioned for Thaddeus to join Him. "Come with Me. Stay close. I would have you describe My actions to My Storyteller when she returns to Me."

Thaddeus stumbled through the snow after the God until they reached the head of the line of men that made up Death's army. They were barely moving forward as the snow relentlessly pelted their faces. It blew across the narrow pass, blinding them. Mostly it was knee deep, but in some places it drifted almost to their waists. As Thaddeus stared at the world covered in deadly white a shiver of fear fingered its way down his spine.

I will not die out here, Odysseus. I will not.

A blast of air, even colder than the gale that raged against them, had Thaddeus cringing into the side of the rocky pass as the glowing spirit of the bison bull passed him and took position in front of Death.

The God faced His army. When He spoke, His voice was a clarion reverberating down their line.

"Snow cannot defeat Death! Follow Me into the east—to the plains that await us—and the spoils that will be ours. *To the east!*" Death bellowed.

Then He turned His back to the long line of exhausted men. He nodded His great, horned head to the bison, who also turned to the east and began walking forward. Death strode up the pass, plowing through the snow as if it was dust. Thaddeus quickly fell into line behind the God, finding that it was easier to walk in Death's footsteps. The army followed, trudging slowly as they blindly fought the wind.

No, Odysseus, I will not die here. I will follow Death, flatter Death, use Death—and then be rewarded for my wits.

The doe woke them at dawn—or rather Ralina believed it must be dawn. The snowstorm covered the sun so much so that it made it impossible to tell the time according to light, but the doe stood and shook the snow from her pristine coat—which woke the two canines, and the canines woke their Companions. They'd taken turns keeping the fire going during the night, so it didn't take long to heat enough snow to boil leftover rabbit so they could break their fast. Then they melted more snow to top off their water bladders, carefully repacked their precious tinderbox, and then humans and canines faced the doe who stood at the snow-covered entrance to their little cave.

"I hate to say it, but I almost wish we could stay here," said Ralina wistfully. "It's such a relief to have peace and warmth. It makes me wonder if we could ride out the winter here and then when the spring thaw comes try to return to the Tribe of the Trees."

Daniel shook his head. "There is no Tribe of the Trees left to return to, and our beautiful, lush forest has been poisoned. Even if we returned, we couldn't trust that any animal we hunted would be safe to eat."

"We could trap live rabbits on the way back," Ralina insisted. "And raise our own warren of healthy rabbits, and then only eat them and vegetables while we culled the poisoned beasts from the forest."

Renard took her hand. "If that is what you truly want Father and I will remain here with you. We'll work to survive this winter and retrace our path come spring. But, my love, could you live with yourself?" When Ralina began to argue with him, Renard shook his head, stopping her words as he continued. He pointed at the white doe who stood by the entrance to their little cave and observed them closely. "You know the Goddess of Life sent the doe to you to help you escape Death. You remained with that monstrous god for all this time because you were determined to find His weakness, and I believe you have."

"All I know is a bunch of arrogant musings He forced me to listen to— and the horrors He made me observe. Renard, the truth is *I don't know what I actually know.* So, why not return home? I doubt if I can help the Wind Riders, or any other people Death decides to conquer," Ralina finished pitifully.

Daniel pointed at the watching doe. "She is your proof, Storyteller. The Goddess sent her to you, which means what you know must be important. Very important."

Ralina's gaze met Daniel's. "I-I'm afraid you're right." She looked from him to the beautiful doe. "Why speak to me through my dream and then send this doe to guide us if I'm just supposed to return home?' She sighed heavily. "So, I'll keep moving forward, though I long for home."

"As do I," said Renard. "But, perhaps, we will discover another home in our future—one not tainted by death and disease."

"We have to go on," Ralina said.

"We must," said Daniel.

"I agree," said Renard.

Bear leaned against Ralina's leg and wagged his tail as he stared out past the doe into the snow-covered day and he flooded her with encouragement. Then Renard's Kong pressed against her other side and barked as he, too, looked out at the white day.

"Okay, I get it." Ralina smiled and stroked both Shepherds' heads. Then she lifted her gaze to meet the compassionate brown eyes of the doe. "I'm done second-guessing. We're ready to follow wherever you lead."

The doe dipped her head slightly in acknowledgment before she turned and plowed through the snowdrift that had almost sealed the entrance to their cave.

The frigid air that rushed into their cozy cave made Ralina gasp and hastily lift her hood and tie her scarf around her face before she hurried after the doe. Like the day before, the doe magically cleared a path as the snow fled from her delicate hooves, though that clearing only lasted for just a few yards behind the deer—after that snow again swirled over the small path, completely obscuring it.

Ralina and Bear followed so closely behind the doe that she could've reached out and pulled on her tail—though she would never do something so disrespectful. Daniel came next, with Renard and Kong bringing up the rear. Their world became a tunnel carved from white. Ralina's burning leg muscles told her that the doe led them on a serpentine path that snaked its way up and up and up as they continued to head east. She knew they were heading east only because occasionally the never-ending wind would blow the snow and clouds so hard that for a moment she could glimpse the distant outline of the sallow sun as it lifted from the east—the direction they were headed. And then Ralina gave up attempting to decipher direction, bowed her head against the wind, and sloughed after the doe.

Ralina had no idea about how long they'd been trudging behind the doe when Daniel tapped her on the shoulder and handed her a hunk of the hard, unleavened bread that had become their staple. Thankfully, the three of them had been hoarding wild onions and the small, tart strawberries that had been easily foraged during most of their journey through the mountains. The onions they'd used to season rabbit and the strawberries had been cooked into the hard, flat bread that filled a good portion of Renard's backpack. Ralina chewed the bread slowly, savoring every bite. *How long will it last? And we only have one fully cooked rabbit left. That will give us each a bite or two for dinner tonight. After that we have nothing but the bread. What do we do then? Starve out here?*

As if reading her thoughts, the doe suddenly stopped and craned her neck around so that she could look into the Storyteller's eyes. And then something truly unbelievable happened. *Several rabbits rushed past the doe and ran straight into Bear and Kong!* The canines made short work of the hares; a bite on the back of the neck and a quick shake and Daniel collected four—*four*—fat hares. They paused long enough for them to be gutted, skinned, and stuffed with snow, wrapped, and stowed in their backpacks. Then the doe continued moving forward—and Ralina, this time much less worried, followed.

They walked and walked and walked. Time lost all meaning. The world was white and cold—and the only bit of warmth and sanity was the doe they followed.

Finally, as white began to fade to shades of gray the doe led them from the thread of a path to a grove where the moss-draped arms of the squatty evergreens formed a kind of a shelter. The doe's presence caused the snow to swirl away from under the protective boughs so that the loam of the forest floor was exposed and they were able to build a fire. While Ralina cooked the onions and rabbits, Renard and Daniel gathered as much firewood as possible. All the while the doe reclined at the edge of the shelter—a magickal barrier to wind and snow and the kind of cold that kills quickly and silently.

"Thank you," Ralina told her. "After the last months with Death I never thought to find safety again, but I'm safe with you—*we're* safe with you. I don't know how long this will last, but whatever happens—however this ends—I want you to know that I will be eternally grateful for the kindness you've shown us."

The doe reached forward and nuzzled Ralina gently, and the two of them remained like that—touching, appreciating, loving. Slowly, ever so slowly, Ralina began to heal.

CHAPTER 13

It wasn't until almost dusk the second wet, cold day that Dawn saw signs of Clayton's settlement. They were subtle. Threads of paths that had hoofprints even the rain couldn't obscure. Broken tree branches. The distinct scent of campfires and of cooking venison.

"They aren't hiding." Dawn spoke aloud, but more to herself and Echo than to Skye.

"No. Clayton would not hide," Skye said softly, hesitantly.

Dawn signaled Echo to slow so that they trotted beside Skye and Scout, rather than leading them as had been the norm for the past two days. "Did he tell you he would not hide?"

Skye shook her head. "Not in those exact words. After the Mare Test Clayton stopped sharing specifics with me, but I know him. Clayton believes he's right, and that means he shouldn't have to hide . . ." She paused and added, "Or I thought I knew him until he tried to kill Ghost and River."

"Tulpar," Dawn corrected her automatically.

"Yes. I keep forgetting," said Skye.

Dawn turned so that she could meet the young woman's gaze. "My dear, it seems you tend to forget a lot. That is a weakness you should work on correcting. Connecting with and carrying opal next to your skin can help.

It strengthens memory, and also heightens faithfulness, loyalty, and good judgment." She studied Skye, who had a difficult time meeting her gaze.

"I—I just wanted him to love me like I loved him. I never meant for anything bad to happen. Clayton can be so sweet, so charming. I really thought we had a future together *with* our Herd. And he was River's friend a long time before he even noticed me. I didn't think he'd actually hurt her."

"Stop lying." Dawn spoke firmly, but not unkindly. "If you'd truly believed Clayton wouldn't harm River or Tulpar, you wouldn't have felt the need to warn my daughter. Face the truth, Skye. You owe it to your Herd, yourself, and your mare."

"I'm sorry," Skye said.

"Apologies mean nothing if your behavior doesn't change. Just do better. That is apology enough." Then within her mind Echo's words pulled Dawn's attention from Skye to the narrow path they'd been following. *I hear a horse ahead. Not far. Coming this way.*

"We're close now," Dawn said. "What will you say to him?"

"I do not know," said Skye.

Dawn pulled Echo to a halt. "If you have chosen to remain with Clayton no matter what happens, you need to tell me that now."

Scout stopped without Skye pulling her up. Skye shook her head. "No. I have chosen our Herd and not Clayton."

"This is something you must hear. How you deal with the guilt that is rightfully yours for following Clayton as long as you did will determine the woman you will become and set the course for the rest of your life. Know this, Skye, Rider of Scout: Had you chosen your Herd sooner it might have been possible for us to save Clayton from his ill-considered fate. He is not much older than a child. Before he broke our most sacred law and attacked a horse and Rider he might have been persuaded to reconsider his path. Now it is too late for him. I hope it is also not too late for you."

Tears leaked down Skye's pale cheeks. She quickly brushed them away. "I wish I had gone to River—or to you—about Clayton, but I don't think he would have reconsidered. Clayton may be young, but he is set in his ways. He believes it is time for a change of leadership in our Herds—that stallions and their Riders should rule and mares with their Riders should step aside. Talk of tradition and reason would not have shifted his beliefs."

Dawn nodded contemplatively. "Thank you for that honesty. It helps a great deal in my understanding of Clayton."

"If you really want to understand me, you should ask Clayton about Clayton, and not get your information secondhand from an ex-lover, Mare Rider!" The deep male voice boomed from above them.

He and Bard are on top of the incline to our left, Echo told her Rider. *Bard is not happy. Neither are the other stallions. But their Riders refuse to listen. They are dangerous, my Dawn. Have a care. I shall be ready to carry us from here. There are still few stallions who can best me in a race, and none of them are followers of Clayton.*

Dawn patted her mare's smooth shoulder. *Steady, my love. We are a Lead Mare and Rider pair. No matter the enmity the Riders have fabricated against us, no stallion will allow us to come to harm.*

Just remember, I am ready to run . . .

Dawn drew a deep breath and tossed back her long silver-streaked mane of dark curls. "Stallion Rider, that is not a proper greeting for a Lead Mare and her Rider."

"Well, I am unaccustomed to Lead Mares and Riders sneaking into my camp!" Clayton shouted from above them.

Dawn didn't have a chance to answer him. Instead, Echo's voice shot through her mind. *Hold tight!* Then the mare responded by rearing and trumpeting an angry challenge that had the leaves on the trees quivering around them.

Instantly, Bard responded. Dawn was pleased to observe the shocked expression on Clayton's suddenly flushed face as his stallion rushed down the incline to slide to a halt before Echo. Bard nickered a soft greeting as he bowed his head before the mare and touched his muzzle to the ground in front of her.

Echo neighed another challenge and blew through her muzzle like a bull bison before she arched her neck and allowed Bard to lift his head to touch muzzles with her.

"Lead Mare Riders do not sneak." Dawn's voice sliced through the air between them. "We made no attempt to hide or to be still. Which is more than obvious by the fact that you easily heard us coming. Now, will you greet me properly, or Clayton, Rider of Bard, have you lost all sense of propriety?"

Clayton's jaw tensed, but he bowed his head and fisted his hand over his heart. "I greet you, Dawn, *retired* Lead Mare Rider, and your Echo."

Dawn looked down her nose at him. "I will be considered a Lead Mare Rider until the day I die. You know that very well, Little Clay." Purposefully, Dawn used the nickname of his childhood to address him. Her smile was motherly and indulgent. "But I shall let the slight pass as I often changed your soiled swaddling clothes, so I still fondly remember your innocence and childhood."

When Clayton said nothing, Skye spoke into the uncomfortable silence. "Hello, Clayton. Hello, Bard. It's good to see you."

Bard nickered softly to Scout, who touched muzzles with the stallion, but Clayton barely glanced at her. "You greet me and say it is good to see me, yet you lead an outsider to us."

"No." Dawn's voice was ice. "That is not how this will go. Skye has not led me. River allowed her to accompany me. Echo and I found you. Now, will you continue your rudeness or will you welcome me—and my friend, Skye—to your camp? Or shall I speak the words you must hear now and then we will be on our way?"

Clayton's lips turned up in a half smile. "Indeed I will welcome you to my Herd, Lead Mare Rider. Come this way and prepare to be amazed."

As Clayton spun Bard around and began to climb the ridge Dawn's voice lifted to him. "Oh, Little Clay, I have been amazed at your behavior for some time now."

The mares followed Clayton and Bard up the ridge. No one spoke as they trotted slowly single file along a narrow seam of a deer path that wove around several stands of ash trees whose leaves had already begun to change color. It didn't take long for the little path to open up to a lush valley. In the center of the emerald clearing was a wide, clear pool. It was shallow and dotted with boulders—and steam lifted from it in misty waves. The acrid scent of minerals drifted from the pool, distinct but not so strong as to be unpleasant. Surrounding the steaming water were neat tents. Dawn quickly counted at least two dozen of them. They represented all five colors of the Wind Rider Herds, but each flew a black flag where individual Herd pennants would normally be displayed. As they entered the clearing, Riders came out of their tents. Those tending the many pots that hung over campfires stopped stirring and stared. Horses trotted into view—and each bowed respectfully to Echo, who snorted, tossed her head, and pranced like she was a decade younger than her years. Dawn didn't realize Clayton had turned in his saddle and was studying her until he spoke.

"Yes, Lead Mare Rider, I have followers from all five Herds."

Dawn's gaze met his. "More's the pity for the five Herds."

"There is nothing to pity here. We have created our own Herd—Herd Ebony. We just haven't dyed our tents yet. We've been too busy adding to our wealth." Then Clayton raised his voice and called, "Come, greet our esteemed visitor. Show Dawn and Echo the solidarity of Herd Ebony!"

There was a rush of whispers and soon the clearing was filled with men and their stallions—as well as a few women and their mares. Each horse bowed to Echo respectfully while each Rider fisted hand over heart, though with visibly less respect than their Companions.

"Dinner is almost ready," Clayton said—his voice still raised. "I ask that you join us. It has been cold and wet for the past two days. A hot meal and a warm tent will be yours for the night should you wish."

Dawn noticed that Clayton spoke only to her—looked only at her. It was as if Skye and Scout didn't exist. She very badly wanted to turn to the foolish young woman at her side, shake her, and say, *You see. He used you and has tossed you aside. Choose more wisely in the future!* But now was not the time for such admonishment. Dawn sincerely hoped Skye was seeing Clayton and his inconsiderate behavior for what it was—the actions of an immature, arrogant young man who was not worth her time. But when Dawn glanced at the girl she saw that her pale, thin face was shadowed by sadness and loss.

Dawn nodded briefly at Clayton. "We will sup with you and shelter here tonight, but we leave at first light. We must rejoin Herd Magenti quickly." Dawn slid from Echo's strong back and faced the gathered Herd. "I come with dire news that you all need to hear, and I would like to share this news first, before we join you for dinner. As we eat you may ask me questions. I will share all of the knowledge I have with you—openly and truthfully."

"We would expect no less from you, Lead Mare Rider."

Dawn nodded with recognition at the Stallion Rider who had spoken. "Thank you, Rand." He was a young man who had been Chosen by Herd Cinnabar's largest yearling four years before. The rumor she'd heard from

Cinnabar's Lead Mare Rider when last they'd spoken was that Rand and his Merlin were contenders for Herd Stallion and Rider next year when their current Stallion and Rider pair retired. *I wonder how Clayton was able to poison him away from his Herd.* Dawn held the young Rider's gaze as she added, "I would say it is good to see you—were the circumstances different."

Clayton spoke before Rand could. "We do not need your judgment or your pitying looks, Mare Rider. Herd Ebony holds several surprises for you. Come." Clayton cued Bard so that the stallion cantered to the largest of the tents, which was positioned in the center of the others. Before it a campfire burned tongues of high, yellow flames from a pit lined with what appeared to be bricks. Clayton slid from his stallion and strode confidently past the bright fire to the tent. With a flourish he flipped back the front flaps to expose a collection of marvels within.

Dawn and Echo walked to the entrance of the tent. Inside candlelight and firelight joined to glisten off dozens of shiny surfaces that Dawn realized were mirrors of different shapes and sizes—and the one thing they had in common was that they were large, intact, and unblemished. There was a trestle table in the center of the tent, laden with precious iron pots of all sizes. Piled along the sides of the tent were tools and weapons—knives, bows that were not made of wood but looked deadly beside heaps of sharply pointed arrows, also not made of wood. There were heaps of rusted chains, metal poles, and other ancient items Dawn had trouble identifying. In the rear of the tent she saw heaps of thick pelts—obviously not foraged from ruins, but trapped and tanned recently.

"I can see your shock." Smug self-satisfaction coated Clayton's words. "This is what can be harvested when we stop being held hostage by the frightened whisperings of old women and actually go out and explore our lands fully."

Dawn met Clayton's gaze. "Where did you find these things?"

"We didn't *find* all of this. We trapped the animals for the pelts, though beaver, yoties, bison, and deer are so plentiful here that they practically fall into our laps. The rest we discovered in the ruins not far from here. The ruins the Mare Council forbade us from exploring for hundreds of years."

Dawn felt a shiver of fear. "The Mare Council didn't forbid us from exploring the ruins because they are fearful or cruel or ignorant. They did so because ruins like the ones you have pilfered have proven toxic to horses and their Riders."

Clayton crossed his arms over his chest. "Well, my people and I have been *pilfering* these ruins for more than one full turn of the four seasons. None of us have gotten ill—none of us have been poisoned."

Dawn's brows lifted and she smiled beatifically. "That is glorious news! All you needed to do was come to the Mare Council—or your Lead Mare Rider—with this information, which would have been joyously received."

Clayton snorted. "Don't you mean I would've been berated for breaking the rules?"

"No, Stallion Rider." Dawn's smile extinguished like a snuffed candle. "I mean exactly what I said. Your Lead Mare Rider and the Mare Council are just and reasonable. Had you provided them the proof you have shown me that these ruins are no longer toxic, they would have rejoiced and granted you leadership of Rider teams that, under your supervision, would fully investigate and harvest items of use from them."

"Clayton, you would have been a hero to the Herd! I didn't even know you had been exploring the ruins. You told me you stayed on the outskirts of them." Skye had joined Dawn at the entrance of the tent and was staring wide-eyed at the riches before them.

Clayton snorted and barely glanced at Skye. "I lied to you because I know you have no loyalty."

Dawn felt Skye shrink back at Clayton's cruel words. She reached behind her and snagged Skye's hand to keep the girl beside her. "Then you know nothing, Little Clay. Skye has so much loyalty that she chose duty over a crush—Herd over flirtation and childish infatuation. You could learn a lot from Herd Magenti's Skye, Rider of Scout."

Clayton scowled, but before he could respond Dawn continued. "I would like to speak to the Riders now; then I will accept your offer of food and a dry place to sleep before Skye and I depart at sunrise."

"Of course, Mare Rider." Clayton walked past Dawn and Skye to exit the tent as he continued to speak. "Herd Ebony is gathered, and unlike Herd Magenti, we will always allow Riders to speak their minds."

Dawn let his inaccurate slight go and instead focused on the Riders who had congregated outside the tent. They stood around the campfire that burned with out-of-place cheerfulness—their horses beside them.

Except for Merlin and his Rand, all stallions and Riders here are unimpressive—none could ever come close to being Herd Stallion. The three mares and their Riders with them are young, weak, foolish things. Echo's voice in Dawn's mind was disdainful.

That is no surprise, Dawn told her mare. *The foolish and unimpressive are easily manipulated.*

Easily manipulated can also mean dangerous. Have a care, my Dawn.

Always, my beautiful girl.

"And now, to show that we are not barbarians—that we do honor mares and their Riders, especially those who have been Lead Mares—I will allow Dawn to address Herd Ebony." Clayton nodded to Dawn, who stepped quickly past him.

Dawn sent Clayton a hard look and said, "Lead Mare Riders do not need permission to address any true Herd." Then she turned her back to him and faced the Riders. "An army is converging upon our Wind Rider Plains. The God of Death leads the army. He means to conquer all five Herds and rule in our place."

Shocked silence met Dawn's proclamation and then the group began to speak at once. Dawn raised her hand, and from habit engrained in them since they were old enough to remember, the Riders went silent.

"This army led by the Death God is not made up of humans. They are the reanimated dead."

"The reanimated dead?" Clayton shook his head. "How is that even possible?"

"I have not spoken to Him, but my guess, Stallion Rider, is that the God of Death can manipulate corpses." Dawn was pleased that her tenure as Lead Mare Rider enabled her to sound calm, even when she spoke of un-imaginable horrors. "But that is not the worst of it. We know that this god has the ability to spread a terrible disease among Companions. First they are infected with a skin-sloughing sickness that will eventually be fatal. Then the God offers the sick a *cure.*" Dawn spoke the word as if its taste was bitter. "Which means He flays the flesh from a diseased human's living Companion, packs it into their sloughing skin, and that brings about a change in the human."

"What?" a Rider blurted.

"How can this be true?" said another Rider.

"It is an abomination!" shouted Rand.

Dawn waited until there was silence again before she continued. "We know it is truth because Herd Magenti has granted sanctuary to Companions who have escaped the God of Death. Several of them are from what was once the Tribe of the Trees, which fell to Death many months ago."

Clayton spoke up then. "But the Tribe of the Trees is powerful and prosperous."

"*Was*," Dawn corrected firmly. "Discontented members of the Tribe were taken in by the Death God's promises of power, and now those Companions have been altered irrevocably." Dawn looked from Clayton to the rest of his small Herd. "The Death God's disease and His *cure* have turned the men into creatures of nightmare—not human, not canine, something that is a twisted version of both.

"And now the God has targeted our plains and our people. Two days ago our Lead Mare Rider, River, called down a snowstorm into the Rock Mountains to buy the five Great Herds time to retreat to our strongholds and prepare for war before Death's army arrives on our plains, but Death will not be stopped so easily. He and His army will enter our plains in a week, perhaps a little more."

Dawn walked slowly back and forth before the gathered Herd as she continued speaking, letting her gaze pick out individuals so that it seemed she spoke directly to each of them.

"Death will poison our plains by tainting the animals we depend upon for food. Once He has spread disease He will offer us His *cure*. Death will have you flay your beloved stallions and mares so that you will be changed into His creatures."

"No!" several Riders shouted. "Never!"

Dawn's voice was ice. "I am quite sure that is what the Tribe of the Trees shouted as well, but they are no more."

"We will fight!" yelled a young Stallion Rider. Several others cheered.

"You will fight? What are there—barely two dozen of you? And none strong or swift or wise enough to be Lead Mare or Herd Stallion Riders." Dawn shook her head. "No, you will not defeat an army of more than one thousand. You will be captured, poisoned, and *cured* if you attempt to stand alone against the God of Death."

"Then we will join with Herd Magenti," said Clayton. "You saw the weapons we have discovered. Our bows are strong. Our arrows are made of a substance that does not crack and break. They are tipped with metal that will kill even mutated humans."

Dawn turned to Clayton. "Herd Magenti will gladly have you fight by our side, but you and your Herd must know the whole truth. Clayton, Stallion Rider of Bard, for your attempt on the lives of Tulpar, who you knew as Ghost, and Magenti's Lead Mare Rider, River, who rode him in the Stallion Run before he Chose his Companion, you have been sentenced to banishment."

Dawn turned from Clayton to confront the Herd again, and into the ominous silence she finished proclaiming their sentence. "Because you have willingly followed a Rider who broke the most sacred of our laws, each of you shares Clayton's sentence. You also have been banished."

"Then why are you here?" Clayton's voice was filled with anger—his face splotched crimson. "To taunt us with our sentence?"

"Of course not." Dawn spoke kindly. "I am here so that you may redeem yourselves by fighting honorably to save our plains. Afterwards—after the Death God and His army have been defeated—we will wish you well and send you on your way to form your Herd, with whatever rules and leadership you desire, outside the Plains of the Wind Riders. But when you leave it will be with honor and the respect of your people."

"These are my people! They already honor and respect me!" roared Clayton.

"I only came to bring you this news and give you and your people this choice, Stallion Rider," Dawn said formally. "Should you decide not to join Herd Magenti then you must leave the Wind Rider Plains immediately, for if you do not as soon as we have defeated Death and His army the Warriors of Herd Magenti will hunt you down and kill you, each and every one." Clayton's face blazed scarlet as he opened his mouth to shout again, but Dawn cut him off. "No! I will not argue with you. I will not allow you to bluster and bully and berate me for something that is solely *your* responsibility." The Lead Mare Rider's voice rang throughout the clearing with righteous anger. "*You attempted to murder my daughter. I have shown you all the compassion of which I am capable. Be a true leader. Think before you speak and again act foolishly and needlessly sentence all of these Riders and their Companions to death.*"

Silence.

The only the sounds were Clayton's heavy breathing and the crackle of the campfire.

Dawn could have insisted Clayton give his answer that moment, but she was too wise and compassionate to do that. Instead, as the silence lengthened, she met the gazes of the gathered Herd.

"What are you doing?" Clayton's voice shook. "Why are you just staring and not speaking?"

Dawn turned to him. "I am putting to memory each Rider's face—and that of his or her Companion."

"So you can tell the Magenti Warriors who they need to kill!" Clayton shouted.

Dawn continued to meet his heated gaze. She responded slowly, in a voice that was kind and motherly, "No, Little Clay. That is not who I am. That is never who I have been, as you well know. I put each face to memory so that I may recount to their families and loved ones that I found them well and whole. Whether they remain that way or not depends upon their leader, as each Herd depends upon its leader's wisdom. Will you keep them safe, Stallion Rider, or will you continue to lead them to doom?"

"No one here is doomed!" Clayton snarled the words.

"That makes me exceedingly happy." Dawn smiled. "Now Echo and Scout need hot mash and hay—and to be wiped down. We have neglected our mares for too long. Then we will gladly join you for dinner."

Rand stepped from the gathered group and fisted his hand over his heart respectfully, bowing to Dawn and Skye. "Mare Riders, if you allow I will see to your Companions."

"Yes, do that," Clayton clipped.

Dawn smiled slowly when Rand did not move to obey Clayton. Instead, he continued to meet Dawn's gaze. "Thank you, Stallion Rider. Skye and I appreciate your hospitality. Echo has a fondness for your Merlin."

Just behind Rand, Merlin snorted and tossed his head happily, which caused Dawn to laugh. Then she turned to Echo and kissed her muzzle. "Rand and Merlin will care for you, my beautiful girl."

And I shall remain ready to ride hard and fast, my Dawn.

CHAPTER 14

Dinner was a mostly silent affair, though that didn't surprise Dawn. As thick venison steaks and hearty braised greens were doled out Dawn reiterated that she would honestly and truthfully answer any questions, but as the wise Lead Mare Rider had already ascertained, few members of Clayton's Herd Ebony had the confidence to speak out in front of him.

Dawn finished the last bite of venison and spoke with a lightness she did not feel. "That was delicious and much needed. Scout and I thank you, but now we must retire. We leave at first light."

"You may sleep in the main tent." Clayton seemed to have recovered his composure and managed to speak to her with close to the respect a guest deserved. "We've piled our extra pelts in the rear. They make comfortable sleeping pallets."

"The hunting here seems excellent," Dawn said.

"Yes, that is something Herd Magenti would know if they hadn't made these ruins off-limits," Clayton said.

Dawn shook her head. "It seems you lack the ability to learn, Little Clay. I already said we would have welcomed the news that these ruins were no longer toxic, but to have that discussion now is pointless. I was simply making polite conversation with my host. You do remember politeness and conversation, do you not?"

"I remember talk talk talk is about all the Mare Council is good for." Clayton spit into the ground beside him.

Dawn narrowed her eyes and her voice hardened. "We will agree to disagree on that, Stallion Rider." Dawn stood and Skye shot to her feet beside her. The Lead Mare Rider let her gaze travel around the campfire at the Riders who were staring at her over plates of food that were mostly uneaten. *Good*, she thought. *They understand the gravity of their choice to leave their Herds. Perhaps it is not too late for them to redeem their honor. Oh, Mother Mare, please give them wisdom.* When she spoke, Dawn filled her voice with the honest care and love she had always felt for her people. "Riders, I know my words have shocked and upset you. It is not pleasant for me to bring you such news. It is not pleasant for me to pass along to you what my daughter and the Mare Council decided is the consequence of your decision to follow Clayton."

"Herd Ebony does not need your pity," said Clayton.

Dawn didn't bother to look at him but spoke to the Riders who stared at her instead. "Does it not? You call yourself a Herd, yet you have no Lead Mare and Rider and except for Rand you have not shown me the respect I have earned through a lifetime of service to Herd Magenti. You call yourself a Herd, yet you hide away here when you are needed by your true Herds. *You call yourself a Herd, yet you follow a Rider who broke our most sacred law.*" Dawn sighed and brushed a hand across her face. "But what is done cannot be undone. You have lost standing in your Herds, but you may still regain your honor. When I leave at first light, I will not ask for your answer. I will simply give you three days after I arrive at the Valley of Vapors to join us there. If none of you do, that will be my answer. Magenti Warriors will take it from there. I thank you for this warm meal and a dry place to rest my head tonight. May the Great Mother Mare bless those of you who are honest and true. Good night."

Without so much as a glance in Clayton's direction, Dawn walked into the large, treasure-filled tent with Skye close behind her. She closed the flaps, though she did not tie them as Dawn knew Echo and Scout would join them when they were finished with their meal.

Dawn was already moving to the rear of the tent to unroll the thick pelts Clayton had bragged about when she heard muffled sobs and turned to see that Skye had crumpled to the ground, buried her face in her hands, and was crying so hard that her shoulders shook.

Scout is worried about her Skye. Echo's voice was inside her mind. *She knows something about her Rider she will not share with me.*

Do you think it's that Skye intends to remain here with Clayton?

No, my Dawn. Scout has told me that Skye will not remain here with Clayton.

Well, then all I can hope is that Skye trusts me enough to take me into her confidence. Tell Scout I will comfort her Rider. Finish your meal and let Rand groom you, my beautiful girl. Then join us in the large tent with the mirrors. We leave at first light.

Except for Rand and his Merlin, they have not shown us proper respect. I will be glad to see the last of this place and these Riders, said Echo.

As will I.

Dawn smoothed out two pelts and placed their bedrolls on top of them before she went to Skye. The girl looked up and the Lead Mare Rider felt a tug of sympathy for this child whose heart was so clearly shattered.

"I will be right back," Dawn said. She stepped outside the tent and the whispers that filled the clearing abruptly stopped. "Might I have some water?"

"Water?" Clayton barked a sarcastic laugh. "We can do better than that. Bring the Lead Mare Rider a flagon of summer beer and our best chalice."

"Two of your best chalices," Dawn corrected. "You may have forgotten Skye, but I have not."

Clayton shrugged. "Two, then. And of course you have not forgotten her. Skye gave you her loyalty. I would remember her, too, had she been loyal to me."

A Rider Dawn recognized as Cali, a young friend of Skye's and Mare Rider of Vixen, hurried to her with a chipped pitcher filled with fragrant beer and two battered, but intact, mugs.

"Thank you, Cali," Dawn said.

Cali dipped her head and did not meet her gaze.

Then Dawn turned to Clayton. "Skye was loyal to you—to her detriment. She remained your lover and your supporter until you broke our laws and her heart. It is a true shame that you, Clayton, Rider of Bard, have proven unworthy of such loyalty." She didn't wait for his response. There was very little Clayton could say that was of interest to Dawn. Instead, she ducked back through the tent flap.

Skye stared up at her with wide, tear-filled eyes. "T-thank you for saying that."

"I spoke only the truth. Come. Have a drink with me." Dawn moved to the table in the center of the room, where she sat and filled both of the mugs with what was very good beer. As Skye sat across from her Dawn said, "This is delicious. For a group that has made many very poor choices they certainly have an excellent supply network."

"The Stallion Riders that joined Clayton from Herd Jonquil are amazing Hunters, and they also brew beer." Skye took a long drink of the amber liquid, sighed, and wiped her face with the back of her sleeve. "It is really good."

"Are you better now?" Dawn asked as they drank and examined the pile of precious pots and pans on the table.

"Yes. No." Skye hiccupped a little sob before she shook herself and wiped her face again. "Dawn, I have loved Clayton since we were children and he did nothing but stare after River. When he finally understood River would never love him the way he wanted her to and he turned his attention to me, I thought we would be mated for life. I gave myself completely to him, and now he hates me. I—I have made so many bad choices." She wiped more tears from her cheeks.

"Skye, I ask that you listen to me closely, as I will not repeat myself. Your feelings for Clayton were honest. You loved him openly and completely, but he used you. He preyed on your emotions and naïveté. Clayton is a prime example of why our Herds must remain matriarchal. He is driven by his need for status, power, and greed. I look here at these riches and think how such things could benefit our Herd, but Clayton only sees them as a way to increase his status and prove that he is worthy to command the loyalty of others. Just look at what he has done. He has withheld these much-needed, precious things under the guise of pretending he would be admonished for their discovery." Dawn shook her head as her hand traced the lip of an iron skillet. "We would have welcomed the knowledge that these ruins were no longer poisoned. Think of the good just this cookware alone could do for the Herd. Yet Clayton hoarded all of this *for an entire year* and then bragged and blustered about it to me.

"He has done the same with your love. He hoarded it and cared only for how it could serve him. Skye, Clayton is a user. He is filled with anger for no reason other than the fact that he believes he is entitled to a status he has not and will never earn. Child, he is not simply unworthy of your love—he is unable to reciprocate it. If you do not let him go and learn from this experience, he will taint the rest of your life with sadness and disappointment."

Skye had been staring into her beer, but she raised her gaze to meet Dawn's. "He said no one would ever love me like he does. What if he is right?"

Dawn laughed softly. "Oh, Skye, pray to the Great Mother Mare that he *is* right. Why would you want more of the empty, hurtful love he has shown you?"

Skye blinked several times and sat up a little straighter. "You mean, it's him, not me?"

"Oh, not fully. You were foolish enough to continue to be his lover even after you knew he was cruel and arrogant."

"But I didn't—"

"Stop that lie now," Dawn cut her off. "Think, Mare Rider! Except for very early in your relationship, when did he treat you with respect and kindness and care?"

Skye's gaze fell again. "But when it was good, it was *so good*."

"If you think an instant of kindness and lust is *so good*, you will be delighted when you discover what it is like to take a lover who truly respects and cares for you. Look at me."

Skye raised her gaze to Dawn's.

"I do not believe Clayton will advise his Herd to join us against Death. So, if there are words you need to say to him you must speak now—or you will probably never have the chance again."

"But River told you not to allow me to be alone with Clayton."

"I will keep my word to Herd Magenti's Lead Mare Rider. I will be close by, but I will give you privacy," said Dawn.

"You don't trust me, either," Skye said miserably.

"Trusting *you* is not the issue. River's trust in me is. I gave her my word and I will not break it," explained Dawn.

"Oh. I—I didn't think of it that way." Skye took a long drink from her mug and then wiped her mouth. "There is something I need to say to

Clayton. It is the reason I asked to come with you. Will you help me talk to him tonight? I don't want to wait until morning. When the sun rises, I just want to leave."

"Yes, of course I will help you." Dawn stood and went to her saddle pack. She returned with a wooden comb, with which she gently began to work through the travel tangles that snarled Skye's long hair. As she combed through her tresses Skye's shoulders relaxed and her eyes stopped leaking tears. When Dawn began to speak, her voice was as calming as the long, gentle strokes of the comb. "You are Skye, Mare Rider of Scout, a member of the mighty Herd Magenti. In your veins runs the blood of countless generations of powerful Crystal Seers. Our Mare Matriarch has ruled in peace and prosperity for centuries. We choose our lovers; men do not claim us—we have autonomy over ourselves. We do not tolerate disrespect. We are wise and strong and constant. We bring forth life. Remember that when you speak to Clayton."

Skye turned and grasped Dawn's hand. "Thank you. I will remember. Always."

"Good. This is what we will do." Dawn quickly explained her plan to Skye. The girl stood and brushed at her travel-stained tunic and pants. Dawn smiled. "You are perfect as you are. You look like a Mare Rider who has traveled far on an important mission for her Herd. Every wrinkle, every smudge of dirt and sweat, has been earned. Wear them with pride."

Skye's spine straightened and her chin lifted. "I am Skye, Mare Rider of Scout, daughter of the mighty Herd Magenti."

Dawn nodded. "You absolutely are. Now go say what you must to him and may a mare's luck be with you."

Skye left the tent with a stride that was confident and firm. Dawn went to the tent flap and peeked carefully out. Clayton's back was to the tent. He still sat on the large stump he'd claimed at dinner. Stallion Riders surrounded him. They sat on the ground, nodding as Clayton talked quietly to them. Dawn could see that they were so deep in their discussion that none of the Riders noticed Skye until she spoke.

"Clayton, I would speak with you," Skye said.

Clayton glanced over his shoulder at her and scoffed, "I'm busy."

"Stallion Rider! I did not ask!" Skye's voice crackled with anger.

Dawn smiled as she watched Clayton turn all the way around in surprise. He stood. "Fine. Then speak."

"Thank you. Follow me." Skye walked away from the men and around to the shadowy side of the large, treasure-filled tent.

Dawn was pleased to see that the girl didn't once look back at Clayton, who said something under his breath to his men. They chuckled as he shrugged and sauntered after Skye. Dawn mirrored his path on the inside of the tent. She walked slowly around, picking her way between mounds of weapons and other unimaginable treasures, until she came to the spot where she could easily hear Skye's muffled voice.

"I won't take much of your time. You'll be able to return to your men in a moment," Skye said.

"Well, it's never taken long with us." Clayton's voice had deepened, become charming and intimate.

Dawn wanted nothing more than to grab one of the many knives at her feet, slit the tanned skin of the tent, and press the weapon against the boy's throat, but she remained still and silent. This was a battle Skye must fight if she was to spend the rest of her life free of this arrogant Rider.

"No." The side of the tent rustled as Skye stepped away from Clayton. "I said I need to speak with you, and that is all I need from you—just a moment of your attention."

The charm drained from his voice like sand through a sieve. "Then speak. As I said, I'm busy."

"I carry your child."

Dawn felt a jolt of shock at Skye's words.

Without giving Clayton a chance to respond, Skye continued. "*That* is why I asked River to allow me to join Dawn on this trip. It wasn't because I wanted to be with you. That has been impossible since the moment you tried to kill Tulpar and River. I came because I wanted you to know— thought you had a right to know."

"I'm not sure what to say." Clayton's voice had lost its arrogance and he sounded young and sad.

"You don't need to say anything," said Skye. "There is only one thing I ask of you." Again, she didn't wait for his response. "I want you to choose life for yourself and your Herd. Accept Dawn's offer. Fight with us. Redeem your honor. If you won't do it for Herd Ebony, then do it for your child, so that I can tell her or him stories of their father's bravery and decency."

There was a long silence and then Clayton asked, "And if I do not? If I choose not to join Herd Magenti and simply ride away from the only homelands I have ever known?"

"Clayton, you chose to leave your homelands the moment you raised your hand against a stallion and his Rider. If you do not join Herd Magenti against Death's army, I will tell our child nothing of you—nothing at all except that you are dead."

"You wouldn't really do that," Clayton said.

"I will do what is best for my child and for me—and that is *not* to be shackled to the memory of a Rider who betrayed his Herd." Skye's voice shook, but her words were as sharp as arrows. "I—I haven't been strong. I've behaved foolishly. I would say I forgot who I was, a Mare Rider and daughter of Crystal Seers, but I don't believe until now I truly thought of myself as anything but a girl who has been in love with the same boy for as long as she could remember.

"That has changed now. Here. Tonight. I see you for who you are—a boy unworthy of my love. What you do next will decide whether your child knows your name and that you redeemed your honor, or knows nothing about you except that you died young and meant so little to me that I refuse to speak your name. Because, Clayton, Rider of Bard, if you choose dishonor I will never acknowledge that you are my child's father. *That* is what's best for the baby and for me. Good night, Clayton. And goodbye." The side of the tent moved as Skye began walking away.

"Wait! Let's talk about—"

Skye continued to walk away. "No. I said I've changed. You will never manipulate me again. I also said goodbye. I meant it."

Skye ducked under the door flaps and into the tent just as Dawn was hurrying to the entrance to meet her. She looked up at the Lead Mare Rider and burst into tears. Dawn pulled the girl into her arms.

"You did well. You did so, so well. I am proud of you, Mare Rider," Dawn murmured as she stroked Skye's back. "And congratulations. A child is a blessing."

Skye pulled away from her and met her gaze. "Even a child with a father who is a traitor and a mother who is weak and foolish?"

Dawn used the hem of her tunic to wipe Skye's face. "What you just said to Clayton was neither weak nor foolish."

"But he's still a traitor."

"He is, and that is out of your control. But your child will take after you—and the other strong, wise, powerful women of Herd Magenti who will help you raise her or him. Do not fear, Mare Rider; your Herd will always be there for you." Just then Echo's muzzle moved the flap aside and she entered the tent, followed by Scout, who went to her Rider and nuzzled her, nickering softly. Dawn smiled at Echo. "My beauty, I am proud to announce that no matter what Little Clay and his Herd decide to do, we return to Magenti with joyous news. Skye, Mare Rider of Scout, is with child!"

Echo tossed her head and then went to Skye. She touched the girl's cheek with her muzzle and then blew gently on her still-flat stomach before nickering happily.

"You see, Skye. Mares know the importance of new life. It is to be celebrated and cherished," Dawn said.

"It will be okay?" Skye smiled through tears at the Lead Mare Rider.

"Yes, child. It will be okay."

CHAPTER 15

T he new day was cold and wet, and Dawn shivered when she and Skye emerged from the tent just before the sun lifted from the horizon. Rand was there with a smile and two mugs.

"I brewed strong tea for you, Mare Riders. A day such as this calls for it," said Rand as he handed them each a steaming mug. "There are eggs and venison cooking. If you take a moment to sit and eat, I will gladly saddle your mares and load your packs."

Dawn smiled gratefully and accepted the mug. "I thank you for your hospitality, Stallion Rider. Echo and Scout are still within. They resist awakening, but I am quite sure they are hungry."

He fisted his hand over his chest and bowed low to Dawn. "It has been my great pleasure to serve you, and I know exactly how to win a mare's heart." Rand grinned at Dawn and then picked up two large wooden bowls filled with fragrant sweet mash before he entered the tent to care for the sleepy mares.

"Echo does love her sweet mash," said Dawn as she headed to the fire to spoon eggs and venison into the waiting plates.

"So does Scout." Skye looked eagerly at the eggs. "I'm ravenous."

"Of course you are." Dawn smiled warmly at her. "Eat your fill. The sun has not cleared the horizon. We have time to break our fast without rush."

They sat on the stumps that had been placed around the main campfire and ate silently, but Dawn's mind was anything but quiet. She kept glancing at the tents, waiting for the Riders to emerge, but the only Rider to join them was Rand, followed by both mares—tacked up, muzzles sticky from their breakfast.

"That was delicious," Dawn said to Rand. "A hearty meal like that will help us with the day of travel we have ahead of us—and that means we must say goodbye and be on our way." She glanced around again before adding, "I would like to speak with Clayton before we leave."

Rand shifted his weight from foot to foot before he responded, "Clayton and the Herd are hunting. He asked me to bid you farewell."

Dawn's gaze was piercing. "Do not lie for him, Rand."

The Stallion Rider sighed and ran a hand through his hair. "Forgive me. I wanted to show you more respect than Clayton and the Herd have since you arrived. He isn't here. It is not unlike him to leave before sunrise and head into the ruins to bring back more treasure. He and several Riders left camp just before you woke."

"Several of them left, but not all?" Dawn raised a brow at the silent tents that surrounded them.

"Several but not all," Rand answered quietly.

"He did not ask you to bid us farewell and none of the remaining Riders intend to speak with us this morning." Dawn did not state it as a question, but Rand answered anyway.

"I do not believe any other Rider intends to speak with you. All Clayton said was to be sure you are gone before he returns."

Dawn laughed humorlessly. "I already made it clear to Clayton and to the rest of the Herd that Skye and I can spare no more time to try to convince them to do the right thing. We leave at first light. There is no reason for Clayton's slight or the inhospitable disrespect the Riders hiding in their tents show us this morning."

Rand sighed heavily. "I know. His behavior and that of the rest of Herd Ebony saddens me." Then he straightened his back and met Dawn's gaze. "But it would be my honor to escort you and Skye from our camp to the path that will take you back to the main Wind Rider trails."

Though Dawn could easily find her way back to the well-traveled trails, she smiled at Rand. "Thank you, Stallion Rider. Your hospitality is much appreciated."

"Dawn, would you like to take some of the treasure with you?" Rand gestured at the tent of riches behind them.

"Are you making that offer, or did Clayton tell you to gift us with something from the tent?" Dawn asked.

Skye spoke up, her voice filled with disdain. "Clayton didn't make the offer. He gives nothing away that he doesn't think will benefit him in some way, and he has probably decided not to rejoin Herd Magenti, so there is no benefit to gifting us with any of his treasure."

Rand shrugged uncomfortably. "You are right, Skye. It is my offer. There is so much within that Clayton would not notice the absence of a few things."

"Thank you, Rand, but we have no desire to take what has not been offered to us," said Dawn. "Your escort is gift enough."

Rand called to Merlin and the three of them mounted. Rand led them from the pretty little clearing, choosing a different path than the one they'd arrived on. They rode silently, weaving their way around the beginnings of the ruins of a large city that had once been filled with thriving people but was now covered with vines and grasses and trees. The sun had fully risen and begun its climb to the western sky when they came to a cross-timbers stretch that marked the edge of what had been considered for centuries a poison zone.

Rand pulled up Merlin and pointed. "There is a small creek within the cross timbers. Echo and Scout won't even need to swim it. The water is cold and clear; it comes directly from the mountains. It's a good place to refill your waterskins." He glanced up at the sky. "At least you are headed into better weather. Looks like it will be cold and wet here again all day."

"That is a very good thing." Dawn's gaze found the snow-shrouded mountains lurking behind them. "The longer it snows the more time we have to prepare for the coming war." Her gaze went from the mountains to the Stallion Rider. "Tell me true, Rand, has Clayton made his decision about what he and Herd Ebony will do?"

"Late last night he asked for the Herd's vote. Well, more precisely he asked each Stallion Rider for his vote."

"What of the Mare Riders?" Dawn asked.

"He gives them one vote in total. He says it's the same as Stallion Riders have had for centuries," Rand said.

"You know that is a lie!" Dawn snapped. "Any Rider can petition a Lead Mare to be heard. The Herd Stallion does place his vote for his Riders, but that is only after he carefully and wisely considers the concerns of each Rider." Dawn shook her head angrily. "I should not need to give you a lesson on Herd traditions, but it seems the lot of you have forgotten yourselves."

"It does, indeed, seem that way," Rand said. "The vote was split three ways. One group argued to do as you said—join Herd Magenti, fight, and redeem our honor before we are banished. Another group wanted to leave our plains now and begin our banishment far away from the Death God's army."

When Rand said nothing more, Dawn prodded him. "And what of the third group?"

"That is the group Clayton leads. He wants to fight Death's army on his own terms—not ruled by any other Herd."

"You have two dozen Riders. Death has *an army*. Clayton's choice is suicide," said Dawn.

"Yes, I agree with you." He ran his hand through his hair again. "I was wrong to follow Clayton. It was a mistake."

"Then why did you?" Skye asked, though her voice was gentle and she spoke kindly.

"Why did *you*?" Rand shot back the question.

Skye answered without hesitation or guile, "Because I thought I loved him."

Rand nodded slowly. "That is a better reason than I had. I wanted *more*. More riches, more say in how Herd Cinnabar is governed, more authority—*more*."

"Last spring your Lead Mare Rider told me she thought you and your Merlin had an excellent chance at winning the Stallion Run next summer when Samson and his Blaze retire." Dawn shook her head. "Did you not think of that when you followed Clayton on a fool's quest?"

"My Merlin did." Rand stroked the neck of the powerful young stallion he rode. "But I let Clayton's words shout out my Companion's common sense, and that is something I will regret for the rest of my life."

"Come with us," Dawn said. "Now. We will share our supplies with you—you need not even return to camp. Though I cannot speak for my daughter or the Mare Council, I believe if you fight beside us and admit your mistake to the Council as you have admitted it to Skye and me, there is an excellent chance they will pardon you."

"I wish I could go with you, but if I do who will talk reason to Clayton? He and I became friends during the months he trained with Herd Cinnabar. He respects me more than the other Riders. Sometimes he even listens to me. If I leave now, without trying again to get him to alter the path it seems he has chosen, then I will feel as if I sentenced each of those Riders and their Companions to death—or worse." He blew out a long breath. "No. I must stay and attempt to get Clayton to lead the Herd to the Valley of Vapors. But thank you, Mare Rider. I will always remember your kindness." He fisted his hand over his heart. "Ride swiftly and easily, and may you always find the way back to your Herd."

Dawn returned the salute. "And may a mare's luck be with you, Rand, Rider of Merlin."

Rand's gaze went to Skye. "Goodbye, Skye, and congratulations on the news that you are with child."

Skye's cheeks pinkened, but she also returned his salute. "Thank you. May a mare's luck be with you, Rand and Merlin."

Merlin whirled around and galloped away. Dawn was watching him fade into the fog-shrouded trees when Skye spoke.

"Look. There, on that little ridge to the south." Skye pointed her chin in a southerly direction.

Dawn looked to see the distant outline of a Rider and stallion silhouetted against gray snow clouds. "So, he watches from a distance. Oh, Little Clay, you had such potential as a child, and now I will have to deliver the sad news to your mother that all of that potential has been squandered."

"I would like to ask a favor of you," Skye said.

"Ask. If I can grant it, I will."

"Do not tell anyone I am with child."

Dawn met the girl's gaze and was pleased to see strength growing there. "Your Herd will not judge your child by the actions of her or his father."

"Maybe not, but if Clayton does not change his mind—if he does not join us at the Valley of Vapors—I will not risk my child's future being tainted by Clayton's mistakes."

"I can understand that. I will not share your news with anyone except our Lead Mare Rider. You have my word," Dawn said.

"River won't tell anyone else?"

Dawn sighed. "River will keep your secret, but unless you choose not to give birth to this child—which is your right—everyone will soon know that you are pregnant."

"It is not the child's fault that her or his father is a traitor. I will keep my baby," Skye said quickly.

"I agree. No child is responsible for the mistakes of her or his parent. Now, we must ride and ride hard. Herd Magenti will be frantic if we do not rejoin them soon," said Dawn.

"Scout and I are ready. Lead on, Mare Rider. We will follow," said Skye.

As the two mares raced away to the east, the silhouetted stallion and his Rider remained motionless, watching them until they disappeared into the horizon.

Ralina's world had become snow and ice and exhaustion. Because of the unending gray-white it was difficult to judge the passage of time, so they relied completely on the doe. When she halted, they stopped for the night; when she awoke, they ate what was left from their meal the night before and then trudged after her.

Ralina tried not to think about how long they'd been following the doe—how long she'd been shifting the snow momentarily from their path. Sometimes Ralina would turn her head and watch the snow re-form behind their little group and it appeared as if they'd never passed that way.

"He can't possibly follow us," Renard said after one of the times Ralina stared behind them.

"I know it doesn't seem possible," Ralina agreed. "But He is a god . . ."

"If He was going to leave the army and come after you, I think we would know it by now," said Renard. His gaze shifted from Ralina's face to the white doe walking in front of them. "And I believe she would know."

"You don't think that's why she's pushing us so hard and taking us along this strange path that is more like a ribbon than an actual trail?" Ralina brushed snow from her eyes with the back of her hand. The scarves they'd tied around their mouths and noses muffled their voices, but the only sounds that competed with them were the wind and the panting of their two Shepherds.

From behind Renard, Daniel spoke up. "I believe the doe is setting this pace because you must reach the Wind Riders before Death does."

Ralina's shoulders drooped. "I don't know how much good I can do. He destroys everything and everyone in his path."

"He hasn't destroyed us," said Daniel.

"Father is right," said Renard. "And never forget—the only person, the only being, who knows as much as you do about the God of Death is the Goddess of Life, Who is helping us. We will make it to the Wind Rider Plains ahead of Death and His army, and you will tell them everything you know. And that, I truly believe, will be key to stopping Death."

Ralina met her lover's gaze. "Thank you."

His smile showed in the crinkles at the corners of his green eyes. "For what?"

"For believing, even when I haven't been able to."

"We must continue to believe good will eventually vanquish evil," said Daniel. "That belief, and acting on it, makes life worth living."

"Please remind me of that whenever I forget it," said Ralina.

Renard paused only long enough to take Ralina into his arms and hold her close for a moment—and then the doe was pulling away from them and the snow began to pile over their feet, and they hurried after the magickal creature who kept going forward. Always forward.

CHAPTER 16

"I had no idea that riding in a cart could be so exhausting." Danita wiped the sweat from her face with her sleeve and grimaced as the cart she sat in bounced crazily over the rough dirt road. "I'd rather be crossing Lost Lake again."

"I know what you mean, but it's a good thing Nik's riding double on one of the stallions and he didn't hear you say that," Mari said.

"Nik hates water more than anyone I've ever known," said Sora.

"That's definitely true," Mari agreed. The cart bumped over another of the endless ruts in the road and she flinched. "My rear end has never been so sore. I was almost jealous that Nik's riding a horse."

"Then you remembered how sore you are?" Danita asked.

"Yes, and decided I'd let Nik and Laru and Rigel have their adventure today and I would just try to find something softer than a horse's back to sit on." Mari patted the pelt she'd taken from her bedroll. "I'll let you know if this helps."

Sora snorted. "Please do. Who would've guessed that I'd look forward to the breaks we give the horses when we walk beside the carts."

Danita sighed and tried to find a more comfortable spot to sit on. "I think my rear end is bruised, and I mean that literally." She looked from one Moon Woman to the other. "Is it inappropriate for me to ask you to heal my butt during Third Night ceremony tonight?"

"Danita!" Antreas's brow furrowed as his gaze went to her. "I don't think Moon Woman powers are something to jest about."

Danita frowned and looked down as she picked at her thumbnail, but she shook off the hurt her lover's unusually harsh words caused, raised her eyes, and said, "I wasn't jesting, and in case you've been too wrapped up in yourself lately to remember—our Moon Women are my friends and they have a sense of humor."

"She's right," Mari said. "Plus, Danita's in training to be a Moon Woman. If she wants her butt healed, she could do it herself."

Sora grinned at Danita. "Though Mari and I will be happy to oblige tonight." Then her gaze went from Danita to Antreas and her smile faded. "When did you lose your sense of humor, Lynx Guide?"

Antreas blinked in surprise and then wiped a hand across his sweaty face. "I haven't."

Sora snorted. "Yeah, you definitely have."

"Forgive me. I-I'm not myself."

"Don't tell me. Tell Danita," said Sora.

"I am sor—"

"Stop apologizing," Danita cut him off. "Just return to being yourself. That's apology enough for me." She shifted in the cart so that her back was to Antreas. Automatically, her hand began to reach out to stroke Bast, who was usually close by, especially when Danita was upset, but the Lynx wasn't in the cart with them. As had been her pattern for the five days they'd been traveling, the Lynx only rode in the cart with Antreas and Danita early in the day. When the midmorning break came and everyone dismounted their horses or exited the many carts that carried Herdmembers who had no equine Companion, the Pack, and supplies that were necessities—Bast disappeared into the tall grasses. She rarely returned before they stopped when the light was too dim for the horses to continue and they were forced to make camp.

Danita knew Bast's absence was taking a toll on Antreas. The first couple days he'd tried to go with his Lynx but had returned sweaty and frustrated when Bast—for the first time since she'd Chosen him years before—set a pace that even Antreas couldn't keep up. Add that to the fact that Bast refused to explain why she was acting so strange and, as Antreas had told

Danita days before, he was finding it difficult to be himself as he tried to reason through his Companion's troubling behavior.

"What's wrong with you?" Sora's voice cut into Danita's inner musings.

Sora was staring at Antreas, and when he didn't respond she continued. "You've lost weight. You have dark circles under your eyes, and I've never heard you speak gruffly to Danita before now. So, what's wrong with you?"

"He's—" Danita began, but Mari's raised hand hushed her.

"No," Mari said. "Let Antreas answer for himself. I, too, have noticed that he isn't himself, and as the Moon Women and leaders of his Pack, we have a right to know what's wrong."

Antreas nodded slowly. "You are correct, and I apologize for how I've been acting."

"Like Danita, we don't need apologies," Sora said. "We need to understand."

"And we need you to return to the kind, witty, intelligent man we know you to be," said Mari.

"There's something wrong with Bast," Antreas blurted.

Mari sat up straighter. "Why didn't you tell me last Third Night? Sora and I would have healed her."

"Of course we would have. What's wrong with her?" Sora asked.

Antreas moved his shoulders restlessly. He started to speak—glanced at Danita—and closed his mouth. "I don't think it's something you can heal."

Sora scoffed, "Of course it's something we can heal."

Danita sighed loudly, then turned so that she faced Antreas again. "I really wish you would stop acting as if I will shatter into pieces if you talk about it! It will *help* if you talk about it."

"What it?" Sora asked.

"Just say it," Danita prodded.

"Bast is in estrus," Antreas said.

"Oh. Well, that's a good thing, right?" Sora said.

"Yeah, Mihos is here and even though his paws aren't fully healed yet, he should definitely be able to perform his mating duties," Mari said.

Danita shook her head. "Bast doesn't want Mihos."

Antreas's gaze instantly went to hers. "How do you know that?"

"How do you not?" she shot back. "Bast won't go near the cart that carries

Dax and Mihos. She doesn't hang around the campfire at night with him. I even heard her hiss at him yesterday when he limped over to greet her before we loaded up the carts. She doesn't like him."

Antreas lifted his hands and the let them fall by his sides. "I wondered what was going on between them. She's definitely in estrus, but I've also noticed she seems to want nothing to do with the only male Lynx within months and months journey of us." He shook his head and scratched the back of his neck where Lynx fur made a soft trail down his spine. "It's so strange."

"Can Lynx females control when they go into estrus?" Mari asked.

"Yes and no," Antreas said. "They need the presence of a male Lynx, but then the female decides if he's a worthy mate. If he is, she goes into estrus, they mate, and then when she is sure she is pregnant the two go their separate ways."

"But Danita is saying Bast doesn't like Mihos," said Sora. "So, doesn't that mean she shouldn't be in estrus?"

"That's exactly what it means," said Antreas.

"And you're sure she's in estrus?" Mari asked.

"Absolutely," said Antreas. "And she won't tell me anything. I ask what's wrong with Mihos and all I get from her is, *Mihos is not my mate.* Then she shuts down and won't say more about it. I think, well, I think . . ." His words trailed away as he glanced at Danita.

Without looking at him, Danita finished his sentence. "Antreas thinks Bast isn't allowing him to fully understand what is happening with her because she's worried that it will affect Antreas—sexually—which means it will affect me."

"Oh!" said Sora.

"Huh." Mari nodded. "That does make sense."

"No it doesn't!" Danita's words exploded around them so that the young driver of their cart, Christina, who was Companion to Dozer, the heavily muscled gelding who pulled it, looked over her shoulder in concern at her. Danita shook her head. "Sorry, Christina. I didn't mean to be so loud." When Danita spoke again, she'd regained control of her voice. "I am not a delicate, fainting woman who needs to be coddled and protected. Antreas and I have been having sex for months. I'm not worried about the addition of some Lynx lust." She took Antreas's hand in hers. "Nor am I afraid of it. Please stop thinking I'm going to fall apart over this."

Antreas lifted her hand and kissed it. "Bast and I would never want to do anything that would hurt you."

"I know that, my own true love. Please trust that I know that."

"Maybe it's not Antreas who needs to know it," said Mari. "Danita, have you told Bast what you just told Antreas?"

"Well, no."

"You should," said Sora. "That Lynx is smart, and she loves you very much. She's probably just trying to protect you. Maybe if you talked to her and told her you're not afraid she would feel free to mate with Mihos."

"And then we'd have Lynx babies," Mari said happily. "What do we call Lynx babies?"

"Kittens," said Antreas, his face softening as he spoke about them. "Bast will have anywhere from two to eight kittens. Normally, the kittens only stay with their mother for one full turn of the seasons. Then they go off to find their own Companions and make their own dens—usually far away from the mother so that their territories aren't overhunted."

"But our Bast is different," said Danita as she smiled at Antreas. "Just like our Antreas is different."

"Well, I've certainly bumbled this whole my-Lynx-needs-a-mate thing," said Antreas wryly.

"Oh, that's fixable," said Sora.

"Definitely," said Danita.

"Different how?" called Christina from her bench seat at the front of the cart. The group's attention turned to their driver and she shrugged. "What? I've been listening to you talk all day. I want to know the rest of it."

Antreas laughed softly. "Well, it's not a secret. Bast and I are different first because it is extremely rare for a Lynx to Choose a Companion who is not of the same sex. The second difference is that most Lynxes—actually, *all* Lynx-Companion pairs I've ever known—are solitary. Meaning the females do not want their kittens to stay close to them; male or female, they prefer to live in isolation. Bast and I do not. It's one of the reasons we joined the Pack. We like to be around people. We like living with others."

Danita finished for him. "And Bast will want her kittens to stay close and to Choose Companions who also want to live as a part of a group instead of as solitary den mates."

"Thank you for explaining that," said Christina. "It is interesting. It also makes sense now why a Lynx Guide pair has become part of our Herd. Oh, wait. Dozer needs to speak with me." Christina turned her attention back to her gelding and then she nodded and smiled over her shoulder to her passengers again. "River has decided we are to camp at the Pawhuska Cross Timbers for the night. You will be happy to hear the cross timbers are not far ahead."

"You mean we're going to stop before it's fully dark?" Mari asked.

"That's exactly what I mean," said Christina. "Right, Dozer?" Her gelding tossed his head and his soft nicker sounded very much like laughter.

"Oh, thank the Great Earth Mother," Sora said. "Cross timbers—does that mean there is a chance that there will be at least a stream nearby so that I can actually wash?"

"Absolutely. The Pawhuska Cross Timbers has a sizable creek that flows through it. The water originates in the mountains, so it's always cold, but it will definitely be deep and clear and clean," said Christina.

"I know what I'm doing tonight." Sora lifted one of her long dark braids. "I will wash my hair and my body before we call down the moon."

"I will definitely join you," said Mari as she scratched her scalp. "I'm filthy."

"And I know what I'll be doing." Danita moved closer to Antreas and lifted his arm so that she could slide it around her shoulders. "I will find a certain Lynx and have an important discussion with her. *Then* I will bathe."

"Perhaps *then* I will join you," Antreas said softly.

"Will you help me wash my hair?" Danita asked.

"If you'd like," said Antreas.

"I'd like—very much." She smiled intimately up at him.

"They'll be fine," Sora said.

"I think so, too," Mari agreed with a grin.

"Oh, yes," said Danita. "We will definitely be fine." And then she kissed Antreas thoroughly to punctuate her point.

"I get the feeling that Bast is by the creek," Antreas told Danita after the caravan had stopped in an emerald valley that was framed on one side by Pawhuska Creek.

"Can you be a little more specific?" Danita asked. "It's a pretty big creek and I'd like to find her before it's dark. I need to get ready for Third Night."

Antreas closed his eyes. His brow furrowed as he concentrated. Then he opened his eyes and grinned. "She said she's exploring some caves that are on the steep western bank of the creek among the oaks. I asked if she was returning to camp soon, and she said *maybe*." He sighed. "I hope it's better after you talk to her. I'm having a hard time dealing with her lack of communication."

Danita hooked her arm through his. "It's a little like losing your best friend?"

He nodded sadly. "If that best friend was also your sister and your mother. That is one problem with Lynx pairs being so isolated. Since Bast Chose me, she has been my whole world—except recently when I met you and joined the Pack."

"That doesn't erase the years it was just the two of you. I understand. Try not to worry. I honestly believe that once I explain things to Bast you two will go back to how you used to be."

"Danita, I do not know what I'll do if we don't. I love you. I love our Pack, but I'm lost without my connection to Bast. It's more than mental— it's a physical link and it actually causes me pain to be isolated from her." Antreas spoke miserably, his eyes filling with tears.

Danita cupped his cheek in her hand. "Oh, love. I'll be back soon with your girl. All will be well."

"*Both* of my girls must come back to me," said Antreas.

She smiled and then tiptoed to kiss him softly. "I think you'll understand very soon that neither of your girls have ever really left you."

Danita knew she should hurry, but as she walked along the sandy bank of Pawhuska Creek she found it difficult to rush. After six days of hard travel where there was little rest and even less privacy, she enjoyed the sense of freedom being by herself granted her. Of course she had a slingshot and a bag of smooth, perfectly sized stones in the pack slung across her shoulder. She'd practiced consistently on the journey to the Wind Rider Plains, and Danita had been happy to discover she had a talent for hitting what she aimed at. Even Mari, who was an expert with the weapon, had said she was impressed by Danita's ability. But at that moment she didn't want to dwell on danger or the fact that sunset wasn't far away—or even that they still had at least nine days of hard travel before they reached the

Valley of Vapors. At that moment Danita just wanted to let her bare toes sink in the sandy creek as she walked slowly along it.

Danita was so distracted by the delicious privacy that she hadn't yet called for Bast—not even when the bank to her left lifted to form a rocky ridge that was dotted with what looked like several caves. *This would be an excellent place to create Earth Walker burrows*, she thought. Then she felt a thrill of another discovery. All along the ridge surrounding the caves were large old oaks. *And those would be perfect for the tree houses Nik and his people prefer. I wonder how far this place is from one of the Herd's settlements?* Danita was making a mental note to ask Mari about the possibility of settling the Pack here when she heard a bizarre sound. It was a call that at first made Danita think it was a child in distress, but as she listened she realized it was an animal—and it didn't seem to be in distress, just calling.

And then the answering call lifted the hairs on Danita's forearms as she recognized it as Bast's distinctive, chattering cough. The sounds were coming from up on the ridge and Danita held her hand over her eyes as she squinted against the setting sun. There she was. Bast was padding around the rocks above Danita to greet—Danita gasped in shock—*another big feline! Mihos? How could he get out here? His paws are still too raw to walk on very for long, and he definitely shouldn't be climbing rocks.*

Danita watched as Bast and the feline touched noses and then rubbed affectionately against each other. Quietly, Danita stepped out of the creek and put her shoes on, and then she started moving up the ridge. Within just a few feet she realized that the other feline definitely was not Mihos. It didn't even look like it was the same kind of Lynx as Bast. *Are there more kinds of Lynxes than just one?* Danita had no idea. It was then that she stepped on a dry branch. The sound of it breaking seemed deafening in the silence of the shady cross timbers. Both felines turned to face Danita. The mystery Lynx hissed and disappeared over the ridge. Bast watched it go and then she turned her attention to Danita and coughed her normal greeting as she picked her way down to her.

"Hey there, beautiful." Danita crouched beside Bast and petted her friend as she circled Danita, purring and rubbing against her. "You and I need to talk. It's really important."

Bast sat beside Danita and cocked her head, as if waiting for the important talk to commence.

"So, you're in estrus, which means you're ready to mate, and we need to talk about that, but I really wish you could tell me about that other Lynx. If that's what he or she is." Danita sat and leaned against a moss-covered rock as she studied Bast. "I know you understand everything I'm saying to you. This would be a lot easier if I could hear your response in my head like Antreas can."

Bast's purr got louder.

"Yeah, I love him, too. He's miserable, though. He misses you terribly. Have you really looked at him lately? He's not sleeping or eating much. Bast, you can't shut him out. It's like losing you, and you know Antreas couldn't survive your loss, right?"

Bast meowed pitifully.

"I'm going to take that as you agreeing with me. Okay, so, Antreas needs you and misses you. Everyone—well, by that I mean Antreas, Mari, Sora, and me—believes that you're avoiding Antreas because you need to mate and you're worried if you're as closely connected to him as you usually are you'll share your desire or lust, or however you want to put it, with him and then he'll be all filled with an intense passion, which will frighten me. Is that right?"

Bast's rolling purr stopped. She stared into Danita's eyes as if willing her to understand. Then she chirruped and meowed—as she typically did when she "talked" to Danita—before the big feline opened wide her mouth and made a sound that was a lot like a screaming child.

"Oh, Great Goddess! I'm sorry. Did I say something wrong?"

Bast chirruped softly and rubbed against Danita as if to comfort her before she made the scream call again.

"Okay, okay. You're not upset. I get that. I just don't understand what you're—" Then Danita went completely silent as the other feline, the one she'd watched Bast greet, reappeared on the ridge above them.

Bast purred and rubbed against Danita again before calling to the feline, only this time the sound was less scream-like and more coaxing. The feline didn't move for several long breaths, and then the beast began to pick its way slowly down the ridge. Bast's purrs got louder, and as the feline came closer she began chirruping and coughing, which she interspersed with sweet little meows.

When the feline stopped several yards from them, Bast padded over to him. Danita could see that he was a male who was not quite as big as Bast. She nuzzled him in greeting, and then trotted back to Danita, whom she nuzzled as well, and then purposefully leaned against her.

Danita barely breathed as the male inched forward toward them. When he was only a few feet away, Bast moved so that she could lie between Danita and him. Bast faced the male and continued purring and chirruping encouragement until finally the feline was within touching distance of the Lynx. He sat then, though Danita thought he looked like he might bolt at any moment as his golden eyes darted between Bast and her.

Bast looked over her shoulder at Danita and meowed, then turned back to the male. They nuzzled each other, which seemed to help him relax. Silently, Danita studied the new feline. She didn't think he was a Lynx—or at least not the same kind of Lynx as Bast. He was smaller and his paws weren't enormous, furry snowshoes like Bast's. He didn't have the prominent black ear tufts she did—and the color of his lush fur was different, browner, with dark spots. His face wasn't framed as thickly by fur as Bast's, though the general appearance of their heads was similar. As she continued to study him, Danita could see that they were actually more similar than different—and then she thought she might understand what had been going on with Bast.

"You've been hiding him from Antreas, haven't you?"

At the sound of Danita's voice the male skittered back several feet and hissed, but Bast didn't move and continued to purr and chirrup softly to him. Soon he returned to her, as if he couldn't stand to be parted from Bast.

"I don't understand why you've been hiding this from Antreas, but you have to tell him. And you need to listen carefully to what else I'm going to say."

At that, Bast shifted her position so she could meet Danita's gaze. The male did the same, staring at Danita as she continued.

"Bast, my precious one, I want you to mate—often and joyously. I want you to share that experience with Antreas as you were meant to do." Bast began to meow at her, but Danita stopped her. "No, you have to listen. When we met, I was broken and afraid, and you were and still are a big part of my healing. Your love and protection made me feel safe before I ever even considered loving Antreas.

"But I do love him—and you. Antreas and I have had sex. You know that." Danita grinned wryly and added, "You've witnessed it."

Bast coughed delicately. Danita laughed—a sound that seemed to intrigue the male as his head tilted from side to side as he watched her, which made her laugh even more. When Danita continued, her voice was still filled with good humor. "So you know that I absolutely am not afraid of Antreas's desire; I share it. And even if he is filled with your passion, I trust that he will still let me be in control because he knows that being in control of our physical love allows me to feel safe.

"Bast, you must mate, and you must let Antreas be close to you again. Please believe me when I say that I cannot think of anything I would love more than for you to bring a litter of beautiful kittens into our world. Please share that with Antreas and me. Please."

Bast held her gaze and then slowly dipped her head, as if she nodded in agreement.

"That's a yes, right?"

Bast's purr was deafening.

"Oh, good!" Danita looked from Bast to the male. "I'd like to sit here and get to know him, but it's a Third Night and I have to return to camp to join Mari and Sora—and I promise you Antreas is pacing back and forth somewhere worrying about both of us." Danita petted Bast's thick, soft coat while the male watched. "So, I'm going to go back. Please come soon."

Bast chirruped agreement.

"Thank you. Could you tell Antreas I'm on my way back and that there's nothing for him to worry about?"

Bast chirruped again and then her gaze became unfocused as she stared into the distance—a look Danita recognized as how the big Lynx looked when she communicated with her Companion—and Danita felt a wave of relief.

"Okay, I'm going to stand now and walk back to camp. Be sure he knows I'm going to move so I don't startle him."

Bast meowed at the male, who muttered a few strange feline sounds back to her before he stared at Danita again.

She stood, though slowly. The male leaned away but didn't actually move back. Danita waited, giving him time to get accustomed to her height.

Then she spoke to him. "I don't know what name to call you. Maybe you could tell Bast, so she can tell her Antreas—and then he'll tell me. For now I'll just call you Spot. I want you to know that I welcome you, and that I'm glad Bast found you. Bast needs to tell Antreas about you, but after she does we'll make sure the Pack and the Herd know—and then it'll be safe if you would like to travel with us." Danita reached down and petted Bast again. She would've loved to touch Spot, but she didn't want to push him. "Spot, it was wonderful to meet you. I hope I see you again soon, and I hope there are kittens to celebrate soon, too." Then Danita headed down to the creek and was surprised but pleased when Bast padded after her just a few minutes later. Danita glanced up to the rocky ridge to see Spot shadowing them. She looked down at the Lynx. "Now I understand why you want nothing to do with Mihos."

Bast grumbled and hissed softly, which made Danita laugh. She was still smiling as the two of them rejoined the busy camp and Antreas went to his knees and took both of them in his arms. He was hugging them when Danita felt his body go rigid just before he pulled back and stared at Bast.

"You've found a what?" The question seemed to burst from Antreas.

Bast chirruped.

"Wait. There are no Lynxes living on the Wind Rider Plains." Baffled, Antreas looked up at Danita. "Do you know about this?"

Danita grinned. "I just met Spot."

"Spot?"

"The male feline. He does look a lot like a Lynx, but not totally. It's like they could be cousins."

Antreas shook his head. "I do not understand this at all. No Lynx has ever mated with a feline who wasn't also another Lynx."

Bast made a pitiful little mewing sound, which had Antreas instantly cupping her face in his hands. "Oh, my precious girl! I am not upset with you and of course I will accept him. How could you believe you had to keep him from me? My sweet, beautiful girl—if Spot is your choice, then he is also my choice."

Bast chirruped.

Antreas chuckled. "Yes, I'll tell her."

"What?" Danita asked.

"Bast says his name isn't Spot, though he thinks it's funny that you called him that. His name is Rufus," said Antreas.

"Oh. Well." Danita scratched Bast's ears. "Rufus is an excellent name. Antreas, I think we need to tell River about Rufus so that she can spread the word to the Herd about him. I have a feeling we'll be seeing a lot more of him."

Antreas kissed his Lynx on her nose, which made her sneeze, before he stood and put his arm around Danita. "Oh, I promise you we'll see a lot more of Rufus. I'm pretty sure he and Bast will mate tonight."

"Tonight?" Danita felt her cheeks warm as Antreas's gaze became intimate.

"Bast says yes, if you are ready, it will be tonight." Antreas held her gaze.

"Oh, my love, I am definitely ready." And she sealed her words with a long, slow kiss that had Bast purring happily.

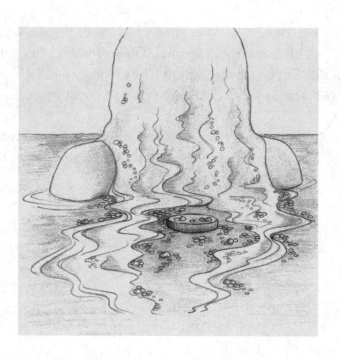

CHAPTER 17

River didn't think she'd ever get used to the Third Night drawing down of the power of the moon, or how it changed the Pack's Moon Women from mortals into beings who more closely resembled goddesses. "I love it when they start to glow with moonlight."

It is quite powerful. Anjo's voice drifted through her mind.

"I agree. And I'm finding that I truly like the Pack, especially Mari and Sora. They're easy to talk to."

The three of you are wise leaders and have much in common. I am surprised by how much I enjoy the canines—especially our canine. From her perch on Anjo's back Kit yipped sleepily before curling up in her riding basket and falling asleep almost instantly.

River, who was walking slowly beside Anjo as they followed the sandy bank of Pawhuska Creek, laughed and Anjo snorted with her. "I'd heard stories of canines. They're much different in person, though. The stories didn't talk about how precocious and affectionate they are—especially the puppies."

The Shepherds are wise and strong. The Terriers are loyal and funny.

"Not wise?" River whispered, and cut her eyes to where Kit was snoring on Anjo's back.

Anjo snorted again. *The older Terriers are wise—like Kit's mother, Fala, and the little blond Terrier with the bobbed tail. He sired the litter on that lovely Shepherd female.*

"Cammy is his name," said River as she bent to pick up a stone and toss it into the creek. "His mate's name is Mariah. I spend time with the litter while you're grazing. I like the adult canines, but I especially like the pups, and our Kit enjoys playing with them." River reached down and took off her shoes, slipping them carefully into Kit's basket. Then she blew out a long breath as she let her feet find the edge of the sandy creek and the cool, crystal water began working its magic. "I'm so tired."

Shall we head back to camp?

"No, let's stay out here a little longer. This evening has been a gift. It's probably the last time we'll get to break early for the night." River kicked at the water, sending droplets to catch the brilliant light of the moon and the stars that shined above the grassy prairie like awakened crystals.

I thought you were going to bathe.

"I am, but I'm procrastinating. The water is so cold!"

Anjo made a show of sniffing in River's direction before she replied, *You need to bathe. I can smell you. And the creek is not that cold.*

As if echoing her thought a shriek sounded downstream, followed by splashing.

"See, it *is* that cold," River said.

Let us join the bather. Perhaps you will find warmth together.

"Well, that's a strange thing for you to say. It isn't like two bodies can change the temperature of the creek." River found she was suddenly talking to Anjo's rear end as the mare trotted downstream toward the splashing noises. River sighed and followed more slowly. She'd been enjoying the solitude. When they were alone was the only time River could truly put aside the mantle of Lead Mare Rider and relax. But she fixed the annoyed expression on her face and jogged after Anjo, splashing in the sandy shallows. She was glad she'd already taken off her leather riding pants or they would've been soaked.

Anjo's rear end disappeared around a curve in the creek, and River forced herself not to grumble at the mare as her jog shifted into a sprint. She rounded the curve and almost ran into Anjo. "Hey, why are you rushing, then stopping in the middle of—" Her words broke off as River recognized the musical laughter that rippled over the water to her. She walked around

Anjo to see Tulpar standing knee deep in the creek and in front of him, sitting in the cold water so that it reached her shoulders, was Dove, who was laughing as the stallion dipped his muzzle in the creek and then flung water at her.

"Hey, I can hear you, which means I can splash you right back." Dove laughed and sent several handfuls of water in the direction of the golden stallion, who squealed playfully and jumped to the side.

"More to your left!" River called.

Dove startled and her head snapped in River's direction. "Who's there?"

"Oh, sorry. It's River. I didn't mean to frighten you. I'm with Anjo and Kit, but she's sound asleep on Anjo's back."

Dove's face lit with a beautiful smile. "River! You didn't frighten me. I was just startled because it is usually difficult to sneak up on me, but this giant horse was making too much noise." She laughed and splashed more water on Tulpar, this time aiming to her left and drenching his golden coat.

Tulpar snorted, backed quickly from the creek, and shook, sending droplets of cold water everywhere, which had Anjo moving away from him while River ducked behind her mare and was saved from being sprayed with the cold, horsy water.

"What's wrong?" River chided Anjo. "You were just telling me that the creek isn't *that* cold and I need to bathe."

The mare snorted and took several more steps away from the water. Tulpar did the same, then came to Anjo, and the two of them touched muzzles in greeting.

"Join me!" Dove called. "I even have this lovely soap that April gave me. She said it is made from the oil of lavender plants." She lifted the bar from the water and breathed in deeply. "It smells like a dream."

Join Dove. Tulpar and I will roll in the sand and then graze a little way up the bank. He says he found clover there.

"Okay. Go roll and graze. If I freeze, you'll have to come pull me out of the water like a block of ice, though." River took Kit's basket from Anjo's back and set it beside an old, water-whitened tree trunk that had partially fallen into the creek. The puppy yawned and went back to sleep. Then River slipped off her tunic and draped it over the trunk. The Herd was comfortable with nudity, and River was rarely self-conscious, so without hesitation she walked into the water but stopped when it reached her knees. "*Brr.* How can you sit in it?"

Dove smiled and turned her face toward River. "It isn't bad once you submerge yourself. Come on out here and sit with me. The water feels wonderful. It is the first time in days my body hasn't ached."

River felt foolish then, complaining about a little cold water when Dove, who had never ridden a horse until a little over a week before, had been suffering with the pace they'd been forced to set—and she had not once complained. River gritted her teeth and closed the rest of the distance between them. With a gasp River sat so that she, too, was covered to her shoulders with icy cold water.

"Oh, mare's tits! That is cold!" River sputtered.

Dove giggled. "Mare's tits. You sound like Sora. Her favorite thing to say when she is vexed is 'by the smooth thighs of the Goddess.' Would you like some soap, or did you bring your own?"

"I forgot and was just going to scrub myself with sand. Thank you. The Herd's lavender soap is much better."

Dove lifted the bar from the water and held it out in River's direction. River slid closer to her, took the slippery bar carefully, and immediately began to lather up. She was glad she'd thought to unbraid her hair and sighed happily as she rubbed the fragrant soap vigorously into her scalp.

"You're right. I don't know whether it's because I'm covered by the water, or whether it's because I'm grateful for the chance to wash my hair—but it's definitely not as awful as I thought it would be," said River.

"To be fair, I got used to bathing in cold water during our trip to your plains," Dove said. "I was surprised by how much I enjoy swimming. I had never learned how before I joined the Pack, but they taught me. I swam a lot during the months it took to cross Lost Lake."

"It didn't frighten you? Not being able to see and knowing you were in the middle of a huge lake that had drowned cities?"

"I think it was less frightening because I couldn't see," Dove said. "Everyone else talked about how there were places where they could glimpse the ruins below us. And the Pack was very uncomfortable when they couldn't see any shoreline, which was the case for much of our journey over the lake. Neither of those things bothered me. Instead, I concentrated on the water and teaching my body how to move through it." She shrugged. "It is difficult to be haunted by ghosts you can't see."

"When you put it that way it does make sense, though the trip here must have been grueling."

"I suppose, but I was just so grateful to be free of *Him* and accepted by Mari and Sora and the Pack that the only part I think of as really horrible was when the Saleesh people refused to listen to the words the Great Goddess gave me to tell them." She shook her head sadly. "And now they are no more."

"It is difficult to believe anyone would be so cruel as to slaughter an entire people," said River.

"Believe it. The God of Death is cruel. We must never forget that. I know. I experienced His cruelty. He cares for nothing except possessing that which He desires, and what He desires most is to rule the world."

River studied Dove. Her face appeared to glow as moonlight reflected off the water and onto her skin, which was slick and wet. Her long hair spread around her on the water, catching the light like a silver veil. Her shoulders were smooth and well-toned. River's gaze lowered to Dove's small, perfectly formed breasts—blush-colored nipples puckered from the cold. River felt her own nipples, hard from the frigid water, but she also felt more, lower, deeper in her body and despite the chill she was suddenly flushed with heat that was entirely new to her.

"River? You are probably exhausted from worrying about Death and His army and you simply wanted to come out here with Anjo and bathe in peace. Forgive me."

"No! I—I am glad for your company, and I assure you I will never underestimate the Death God. I was just considering what you said, about the fact that you have personally experienced His cruelty. Did He hurt you badly?" Just the thought of someone being cruel to Dove, who was nothing but kind and sweet and so empathetic . . . It made River want to gut the God herself.

"He could have hurt me much worse, and He would have had Lily not helped me escape, though I will be eternally sorry that His obsession with me has led Him to your world." Dove lowered her head.

"No." River touched Dove's cheek and then lifted her chin gently. "We already heard from Dax that the true reason Death left the Tribe of the Trees was because He poisoned the forest. You are not responsible for that."

"But the reason He chose to travel here, instead of north to the Whale Singers, or south to the Sky Talkers, is because of me."

Reluctantly, River forced her hand to fall from Dove's warm, smooth skin. "We don't know that for sure. Our plains are fertile and vast—our Herds are prosperous and powerful. Those things are well known. You said Death desires to rule the world. The Plains of the Wind Riders is an excellent world to rule."

"He destroys everything He touches," Dove said.

"Then He will not touch us," said River.

Dove's bow-shaped lips tilted up. "You say that with such conviction."

"No one can defeat the Wind Riders," River said firmly. "Now, here is your soap returned. If you aren't careful, I will use the whole bar. I usually enjoy our migration to the Valley of Vapors, but this rush to get there has made me long for the lazy winter days we spend in the valley, relaxing in the hot springs, washing our hair, soaking our bodies—especially after we slather thick mud all over ourselves, let it dry, and then wash it off."

"Why would you put mud on yourselves?"

"It is special mud, filled with the healing properties of the springs. It draws out pain and toxins and leaves skin glowing. I will show you when we get there." Just thinking of the Herd's sanctuary in the Valley of Vapors filled River's voice with contentment.

"That sounds magickal. Lily used to wash my hair often. It was one of my greatest pleasures." Dove sighed.

River spoke before she could stop herself. "I will wash your hair if you'd like."

"Would you? That would be so wonderful." Dove sent the water swirling as she turned so that her back was to River. "Oh, you will need this." She smiled over her shoulder as she offered the bar of soap to River.

River took it and began gently rubbing it through Dove's long blond hair—starting with her scalp and working down the soft, fine length of the mass. Then River let the bar float beside them as she used both hands to massage the creamy lather into Dove's scalp.

Dove moaned softly and leaned back, allowing River better access. "That feels wonderful."

"Your hair is so soft and beautiful," River said.

Dove laughed. "I do not know how you can tell under all of that filth."

"I can tell because it is no longer filthy. Here, lean back more and float. I'll rinse the lather from it."

Dove sighed happily and did as River asked. The moonlight glistened off Dove's naked body, illuminating her breasts and thighs. As River guided her floating body out to deeper water, she couldn't stop herself from staring at Dove. She was heartbreakingly lovely, and her beauty filled River with the need to touch her, caress her—to show her just how beautiful she was.

"There. It's clean and rinsed now." River's voice was barely a whisper.

Dove stopped floating and faced River. She held out her hand. "You will have to guide me back. I am afraid I'm turned around and do not know which way it is to shore."

A low nicker came from behind River as she took her hand, which made Dove's smile widen. "Yes, I hear you and now I do know which way it is to shore. Do not be distressed—River will guide me." She called to her stallion. Then she lowered her voice and said, "Tulpar is such a worrier."

Slowly, River led Dove back to the shallow water near the bank. "He's right to worry about you. It would be easy to drown out here."

Dove's laughter was musical. "Not at all. Were I alone, I would simply float and be still. The current would move me and then I would know to swim to my left or right to find the shore. I might find the wrong shore, but I certainly would not drown."

"I forget that, until Tulpar, you have spent your lifetime without sight," said River.

"I have and it is wonderful to be able to see through his eyes, though I can tell you that when I am not touching him, not seeing through his eyes, the darkness is comforting. There are things that are more special in darkness." Dove was turned so that she faced River. They were so close River could feel her heat through the water.

"Like what?" River asked breathlessly.

"Like how I used to see people."

"How did you see people?"

"By touch. I map faces and hold them in my memory," Dove said. "May I—" Dove pressed her lips together and shook her head quickly, sending little droplets of lavender-scented water in a spray around them. "Forgive me. I do not know the Herd's customs well enough yet to ask that question."

"I am not the Herd. I am just River right now and you are just Dove. What is it you would ask?" *Please ask to touch me—please.*

"I would like to see you as I did before I had the use of my Tulpar's eyes." Dove hurried on before River could reply. "I know I have seen you already, thanks to my golden stallion, but it is different when I look with my fingers." Her voice lowered to a whisper. "More intimate. More permanent."

"I would like you to see me through your touch. Very much."

"Thank you." Slowly, Dove reached for River. Her fingers found River's shoulder first. She followed the curve of her shoulder up to her neck. Then both of Dove's hands were touching River's face—gently, caressingly, she used her fingertips to trace her forehead, nose, cheeks, jawline, back down to her shoulders. "You are strong and beautiful, and now I have mapped your face and can memorize it."

River didn't know what to say. Her skin tingled wherever Dove touched, and even though the water they sat in was frigid, she was filled with heat that bloomed deep within her.

Dove's hands were still resting on River's shoulders. "Have I made you uncomfortable?"

"No," River said quickly. "Not at all. It's just strange."

Dove's lips tilted up. "Strange to see through my fingers?"

"No, that actually makes sense," River said.

When she didn't continue, Dove prodded. "Then what is strange?"

"That your touch makes me feel so many things." River spoke softly, afraid she would offend—or worse disgust—Dove. She already knew that the Pack had no archaic rules against same-sex love, but River had no idea whether love between women was accepted by the people who had raised Dove. And then she realized Dove's hands had not left her shoulders and instead she was caressing River's skin, tracing slow circles with her dexterous fingers.

"What things?" Dove murmured.

"Heat when I should only feel cold. Desire when I have only focused on duty to my Anjo and my Herd—until now." As River spoke, she couldn't take her gaze from Dove's lips.

"I have only loved one man, and he is dead," Dove said. "I did not think I would ever feel desire for anyone again, but I cannot deny that I am drawn to you." Her smile grew. "Though I suppose discovering new love in wartime is probably not wise."

Dove's words sent ripples of delight through River's body. "I think discovering love during wartime proves that life goes on—that we will all go on."

"I like that," Dove said softly. "It proves that we will all go on. River, would you please kiss me?"

River's answer was to put her arms around Dove. Their bodies slid together as their lips met. Dove's warmth filled River as that first, sweet kiss deepened and their embrace tightened. Their tongues met. River thought Dove tasted of lavender and spring rain—and felt slick and hot, soft and welcoming—and her body answered in kind. Need cascaded through River. Her hands began to move down Dove's supple back, and Dove shivered. River reluctantly pulled away, though she found and held Dove's hand. "You're shivering. You must be freezing."

"I am cold, but I do not think that is why I shiver," Dove said.

River leaned into her and kissed her again before saying, "Let's get you dry and warm."

Dove nodded. "That sounds wonderful."

Together they stood. River held Dove's hand and carefully guided her to shore. As they climbed out on the sandy bank, Anjo and Tulpar began meandering their way back to them, pausing to bite off and chew hunks of grass.

"I brought a blanket to dry with. It should be beside my clothes on a large rock somewhere close by," Dove said.

"I see it." River hurried to the blanket, shook it out, and returned to Dove.

Laughing through chattering teeth, they each used an end of the blanket to dry, though as River turned away to retrieve her clothes Dove's hand on her arm stopped her.

"River, may we kiss again? Soon?" Dove asked hesitantly.

River took Dove into her arms, and right then kissed her thoroughly. Against her lips River whispered, "Dove, I don't think I will ever want to stop kissing you."

CHAPTER 18

"W hy is this line not moving?" Death strode up to Thaddeus and shouted into the icy morning at the column of men who appeared to be frozen hulks dotting the snow-packed trail. The day had dawned clear—the first time in more than a week that they had awakened to no snow—but the clear sky did not last. By midmorning sharp flakes of ice mixed with snow began falling so that the army was barely able to shuffle forward as the wind and snow battered against them and blocked their path.

Thaddeus straightened himself. As more time had passed since he'd melded his flesh with his beloved Odysseus he'd found that walking hunched over and even sometimes letting his hands touch the ground—especially if he wanted to move quickly—was more comfortable than walking upright. He didn't mind the change. He welcomed it. It just made him closer to his Terrier, but it seemed to irritate Death, so whenever the God was close he made an effort to stand upright. At that moment he wanted nothing more than to drop to his hands and knees, snarl at and bite the God, and then tell Him what a complete idiot He was, though the rational part of his mind kept him from doing so. Instead, Thaddeus straightened his curved spine, rubbed his arms to attempt to warm them, and shifted from numb foot to numb foot before he responded to the God in a much more sedate manner. "My Lord, they cannot move quickly because the snow has packed the pass." *And it has packed the pass because You are an utterly incompetent leader and did not require the army to move quickly when You should have.*

"But the Milks are not bothered by the cold. They are of the dead, and the dead understand and accept the cold," said Death.

"Yes, but their bodies are still human and in order for them to move they need the pass to be cleared," said Thaddeus, though he chafed at explaining something that should be obvious to a creature Who called Himself God.

"Where are your men, Thaddeus?" Death asked sharply.

"They forage ahead, breaking through the snow as they try to hunt for something, anything, that will help sustain us." Then Thaddeus added more of the truth in a voice he kept carefully neutral. "We have eaten through the stores we confiscated from the Saleesh. I do not know if the Milks can starve, but I assure you my men and I can. We need food, and this snow prevents the Hunters from foraging very far from the pass and into the mountains after game." *And it was YOU who ate through the stores from the Saleesh. YOU with your God-sized appetite for everything. Though the last of Your little half-rabbit, half-human women froze and died three days ago, which is obviously part of why You seem so frustrated.* Thaddeus couldn't stop a growl that rumbled deep in his chest as he shouted the words in his mind, wishing he could scream them at Death and then push the God off the side of the mountain, call his Hunters and Warriors to him, and return to the Tribe of the Trees. *Odysseus, surely by now the poison has died out. Surely by now our forest is safe again. By all the gods I wish I had never begun this fool's trek with Death. We need to return to our home, my Odysseus. The home we should have never abandoned.*

"Thaddeus, you seem discontented."

Thaddeus's attention snapped back to the God, Who was observing him with a knowing expression.

"You growl at Me? *Me.*"

Thaddeus rubbed his arms more vigorously. "No, no, no—of course not, my Lord. I am only concerned. I am worried for our army. If we keep losing men, how will we defeat the Wind Riders?"

"I have already told you. I will seed them with poison and then the cure shall make them Mine. But I do acknowledge your worry, though your growl is inappropriate. Defeating the Wind Riders will be much easier and quicker if I do so with an army of My own." Death scratched His dark beard of thick, wiry hair that looked like bison scruff as He stared off into the distance.

Down the path not far from them the glowing form of their bison spirit guide turned to look back at the god to whom he was shackled. The beast shook his great head impatiently and pawed the earth.

Death chuckled. "This bull pleases me. He and I share the same impatience to reach the plains."

Thaddeus looked from the bull bison to the God of Death, Who was becoming more monstrous every day. *Odysseus, this fool thinks the bison spirit is eager to reach the plains when it is easy to see that the creature loathes Death and is only eager to rid himself of the God.* But Thaddeus nodded and made the sounds of agreement as the God expected. "It is a mighty beast. It is a shame that the bull isn't still living. He is so huge that by himself he could almost plow a path for your army to follow."

Death's head jerked around to face Thaddeus. "That is it. You have given Me an excellent idea, and a way to feed our army. Follow Me. I would have you serve witness so that when My Storyteller is returned to Me you will provide details to her so that she may complete My ballad accurately. Come." Death stomped away, pushing unfortunate Milks out of the way as Thaddeus struggled to remain upright and keep up with Him.

Do you hear Him, Odysseus? Thaddeus maintained a mental commentary to his long-buried Terrier. *He still believes Ralina is lost and will be miraculously returned to Him.* Thaddeus had to stifle a bark of sarcastic laughter. *She escaped, and if I ever find her I will slit her throat. That bitch will never lord anything over me again.*

"Thaddeus, come!" Death shouted.

Thaddeus hurried to the God, Who had reached the front of the army. It hadn't been difficult to do. The army was barely able to shuffle forward. The only way Thaddeus could overtake them, though, was because he literally walked in the God's hoofprints, and even then he still had to slough through knee-deep snow.

"I am here, my Lord," Thaddeus said between panting breaths.

"Ah, excellent. Now, observe and remember—and try not to speak. Your voice annoys Me."

Everything about You annoys me, Thaddeus shot back, but only silently, within his mind.

The God cupped His hands around His mouth and bellowed a cry that shook the snow-blanketed pines that clung to the mountainsides that surrounded the pass. Again and again the God called until Thaddeus began to consider how he was going to tell Death to shut up before His bellowing caused an avalanche that would sweep them all away.

Death stopped His calls abruptly and pointed to the spirit of the bison, who had been watching Him closely but was now turned away from Death, staring up the path as if in anticipation.

"Ah, he knows they come," Death said.

"They?"

"Of course. Those whom I called." Death frowned down at Thaddeus. "Did I not command you to be silent?"

Thaddeus bit the side of his cheek to stop himself from telling the God that he cared little for what Death commanded. Instead, he nodded quickly, bowed, and shuffled a few feet back from the God. *If I am out of sight, perhaps I will also be out of His mind—at least for a little while.* Thaddeus didn't wish for Ralina to return, but he did wish Death's attention wasn't so focused on him. *Odysseus, I need to distract Death. It is annoying that all His women froze. More of Death's foolishness. He preferred them unclothed, even in a blizzard. I cannot abide His shortsighted stupidity that—*

Thaddeus was pulled from his imaginary monologue with his dead Companion when the earth beneath his feet began to tremble.

"My Lord!" Thaddeus rushed forward to the God. "The earth shakes. We must get to higher ground before we are thrown from the pass."

Death glanced down at him with utter disdain. "Be still. I already said they come."

Thaddeus wanted to ask again who *they* were, but his eyes were drawn to the snow-filled pass that snaked through the mountains before them. The earth shook and a sound echoed through the pass. It was as if another army approached from ahead—and that army had hooves instead of booted feet. Finally, the smell hit Thaddeus—musty and thick like stags in rut as they sprayed their urine to mark themselves and get ready for battle.

Then through the icy snow and the low-hanging clouds that had shrouded the pass for days, the first of the creatures became visible. The lead bison bull was immense, almost as big as the glowing spirit of Death's guide. The bull plowed through the snow with surprising speed for something so large, and was followed by a long line of more bulls. Thaddeus quickly counted a dozen of them and then he was too busy backing away to do anything but stare as the huge male lumbered directly to Death.

Thaddeus thought that would be it. The enormous bull would gore the God, knock Him from the pass so that He would be lost somewhere below them in a world of white and gray and ice. But the creature stopped a few yards in front of Death. His breath was visible as he panted.

Death threw off the bison pelt cloak He wore wrapped around His massive shoulders, so that His naked chest was exposed. Thaddeus couldn't stop staring at the God. His torso was completely covered in thick fur the color of a fertile field. It hung in hunks from His shoulders and back, though it did little to cover the massive cords of muscles that had misshaped His chest and arms to something that was too hulking to be human. Death threw back His head and bellowed a war cry.

The bison bull answered. His roar reverberated around them as the creature tore the snowy pass with his hooves before he lowered his head and charged.

It happened so fast that Thaddeus didn't have time to run, though in retrospect he realized that had Death not defeated the bison there would've been no escape for him, or those behind him. But Death thundered another challenge and then He rushed forward to meet the bull's charge. The God caught the bison by his horns, turned to the side, and wrenched the mighty beast's head around so that the creature could choose to succumb and fall to his side or continue to struggle and have his neck broken.

The creature succumbed. He fell heavily to the ground and Death straddled him as He stared into the bull's eyes.

"*Surrender to Me!*" Death's preternaturally deep voice boomed around them.

The bison struggled for a moment more before he went limp. His only movement was the rise and fall of his mighty chest as he took in gulps of air.

"You will do My bidding, Prince of Bison." Death stared into the creature's eyes as He spoke. "Lead us from this place and into the plains where there is lush summer grass and bison cows to service aplenty. Once we are through the mountains I will reward and release you. Or choose to leave this world today, now, and still I will shackle you to Me. And know this—should you choose poorly I will not release you, ever."

The bull blew out a long breath and then he seemed to collapse in upon himself and his muzzle dropped to touch the God of Death's hoof in submission.

Death waited for several heartbeats and then He released the bull's horns and got off the creature. Slowly, the bull stood and shook himself, never taking his eyes from the God.

"Now go! Lead the lesser bulls!" Death commanded.

The bison turned to retrace his path past the line of bison who stood silently watching. As he reached each bull, the creatures turned and the line of enormous males began to follow him. As they did, they plowed a thick furrow through the snow that blocked the pass, clearing it enough that humans could navigate it.

Then Death glanced at the glowing spirit of the bull who had led them thus far. "You are no longer needed as my guide, but I do not release you, Bison King. I find that I enjoy your company. You shall continue to lead us truly!"

Death turned His back to the spirit and began shouting at the army to move forward and follow the line of bulls, but Thaddeus continued to watch the spirit. His glowing red eyes were filled with loathing as he stared at the oblivious God.

Death has no idea how much hate He inspires, Odysseus, and I believe it will lead to His undoing. Thaddeus imagined Odysseus looking up at him with his canine smile as he wagged his tail and yipped. *Yes, I agree. It is a good thing we are not hated as much as Death.*

"Thaddeus, move up the line and call your Hunters. They need not search for a few pathetic rabbits. We shall slaughter the smallest of the bison and feast at dusk," Death said.

"Yes, my Lord, right away." Thaddeus gritted his teeth against the loathing he felt for the God, Whose back was now turned to him so that he could drop to all fours, which made it much easier for him to maneuver quickly around and among the line of snow-plowing bulls. *Yes, I do believe hatred will lead to His undoing, and Odysseus, you and I shall be there to witness it and to celebrate. Until then, at least we will feast.*

Ralina had begun to be able to tell what time of day it was through study-ing the slate-colored sky, as well as observing the doe. For the first half of the day the doe pushed them hard, but as afternoon slid into evening she slowed, understanding that their strength was waning. So, Ralina had just checked the sky, wiped sweat from her forehead with the back of her sleeve, and thought, *It is about midmorning*, when the bellowing cry lifted from below and behind them. The sound was so shocking after the silence of the snow-shrouded mountains that even the doe stopped to listen.

The cry came again several times and Ralina shivered—from disgust, not the cold.

"It's how Death sounded when He called the bison bull He killed and then bound to Him as His new spirit guide," Ralina said.

"I wish we could tell how far away He is," said Daniel.

"He isn't close." Renard put his arm around Ralina's shoulder. "Do not let the strength of His voice fool you."

"That we can hear Him at all means He is too close," said Ralina.

The doe met her gaze, and Ralina saw concern as well as intelligence within those brown depths. Then she turned her beautiful, delicate head and began moving forward again—this time the doe picked up the pace and didn't relent until the slate sky shifted to coal. She led them off the path a short way to a rocky outcropping that offered almost as much shelter as a cave—and was surprisingly warm and dry after they built a fire. As had become their norm, the humans cooked whatever game had magickally crossed their path that day while the doe contentedly chewed whatever foliage was found in their nightly shelters—and there was al-ways something, whether it was a pile of long grass, strips of bark, or a mound of acorns and persimmons. Then she would curl her legs under her and sleep by the entrance of the shelter, and because of the Goddess-touched doe's presence snow did not blanket them at night, so that the humans and their two canines slept undisturbed and were ready to begin their trek anew with the rising of the snow-veiled sun.

Ralina and Renard leaned against each other, with Bear and Kong flank-ing them and Daniel—as both Shepherds adored the older man.

"Expect that the doe will keep up the hard pace she set today every day in the future." Ralina spoke softly so as not to wake Daniel or their Companions.

Renard nodded. "That is just what I was thinking. She didn't slow this afternoon at all."

"Death's voice was too close."

"I believe the doe has a timetable only the Goddess of Life understands, but the main part of it is for us not to be captured by Death," said Renard.

Ralina rested her head on his shoulder. She was exhausted, but the freedom escaping Death had granted them was such a relief that she did not mind the aching muscles and the unending trudging through snow. "I have a strong feeling that we must get to the plains far enough ahead of Death and His army that we are able to find a Herd and warn them of what's to come."

"We will. You will. The Goddess of Life is our ally."

Ralina sighed. "But the Sun God was the ally of the Tribe of the Trees—and our people are no more."

"Perhaps the Sun God isn't strong enough to defeat Death. Perhaps the only thing strong enough to defeat Death is Life," said Renard.

"I'm going to believe that," Ralina said. "If I didn't, I couldn't keep going." She felt that she was being watched and Ralina looked from the fire to the doe, who was staring at her. She met the doe's gaze and was filled with warmth and comfort. "Thank you," Ralina told her softly.

Renard held her close. "The doe is connected to you. She is a gift sent by the Goddess of Life, and I think she was sent for another reason than just to lead you from Death and into the Wind Rider Plains."

"What other reason?"

Renard smiled. "To give you—and Father—and me hope. I believe the Goddess knows that we have been too long without it."

"You sound like you wish to worship the Goddess of Life." Ralina studied his face carefully. The Tribe of the Trees had always worshiped the Sun God. Their skin absorbed their god's blessing every morning. Their canines were attached to them because the God of the Sun supported their ancestors when they refused to give up their pet dogs and guided them to the trees, gifting the nascent Tribe with the life-saving Mother Plant. It was unthinkable for a Tribesman to worship another deity.

Renard had been silent as Ralina's mind whirred, but when he finally spoke his voice was filled with quiet joy. "I will. I choose the Goddess of Life from here on until the day I die."

Their gazes met. "As do I," Ralina said.

Together they looked at the doe, who was watching them with gentle, knowing eyes that seemed to hold their future in their depths.

CHAPTER 19

Tulpar's greeting whinny trumpeted throughout the Herd causing all of the Riders and their Companions to turn and look to the west. Hearing it, River was filled with joy.

"Anjo, is it them?" River asked her mare breathlessly.

There was a listening pause and then Anjo's voice, likewise filled with joy, was a shout in River's mind. *Yes! It is our Dawn and our Echo! They have caught up with us. Tulpar says they are well.*

River felt dizzy with relief. She'd begun to worry. Without carts and supplies and people on foot, her mother traveled much faster than even the grueling pace River had set for the Herd. By her calculations, Echo should have caught up with them the day before, but she hadn't really worried until the sun began to fall into the western horizon that day. Too many things could have gone wrong. Clayton could have held Dawn hostage. Skye could have betrayed them. Skye . . .

"Anjo, are Skye and Scout with Mother?"

Indeed. They are well, too. There is no one else with them.

River wasn't sure whether she should feel relieved or angry that Clayton and his traitorous followers hadn't accompanied her mother, but whether she should be or not, the truth was she was relieved. Traveling at the pace they had to set to arrive at the Valley of Vapors within their two-week deadline was stressful enough. River hadn't been looking forward to the added problems Clayton's presence would cause, although she was highly interested in what the betrayer had to say for himself—that is, *if* Dawn had been able to find him.

"Let's go greet Mother and find out how it went with Clayton." Anjo turned neatly and kicked into her rolling gallop.

"River! It is so good to be with our Herd again." Dawn's smile was as beautiful as it was familiar. She was relaxed on Echo and had obviously been chatting with Dove, who sat confidently astride Tulpar.

"River, isn't it wonderful that Dawn has returned?" Dove's beautiful face glowed with joy.

"It is." River tried not to stare at Dove, which was difficult because she looked so spectacularly happy astride Tulpar. Anjo nickered to Echo, and the two mares affectionately touched muzzles; then Anjo surprised River by warmly greeting Scout as well, which pulled River's attention from Dove.

"I didn't know you like Scout," River whispered to her mare.

Scout does her best to help her Rider mature. I support her in that, said Anjo in River's mind.

And then River had no more time for silent discussions as Anjo brought her close enough beside Echo that she could lean over and embrace her mother. "I was beginning to worry. I expected you to catch up with us yesterday."

Dawn kissed her daughter's forehead. "You did not need to worry. Echo and Scout took excellent care of us. Tulpar and Dove have greeted us gloriously." Dawn turned her beatific smile on the Stallion-Rider pair before she continued. "You have traveled well. The Herd will definitely arrive at the Valley of Vapors within the two-week time frame."

"River, you look well," Skye said.

River wanted to snap at Skye and tell her had she shown better judgment and come to her about Clayton's treachery sooner there would have been no need for them to ever leave the Herd, but she felt her mother's sharp gaze resting on her—and beyond that River understood her responsibility to Skye. The girl was a member of Herd Magenti, and because of that and that alone, River either treated her with care or failed to be a fair and just Lead Mare Rider.

"Thank you, Skye. You look—" River broke off her platitude and really studied Skye. The girl looked terrible. Dark circles bruised her puffy eyes and she was pale and looked as if she hadn't slept in days. "You look exhausted," River finished.

"It has been a difficult journey," Dawn said, catching her daughter's eye. "Perhaps Skye can ride ahead and get some help with wiping down Scout while she rests?"

River nodded slightly to her mother before she turned to Skye. "Yes, of course. April is near one of the lead carts with Deinos. Skye, let her know that I've called a short break so that Scout and Echo can be cared for, but then we must ride hard to make it to our campsite."

"Scout and I will be ready to ride as soon as she's been wiped down and fed." Then Skye clucked at Scout so that the mare trotted to the waiting Herd.

River watched them go. "Scout doesn't look nearly as exhausted as Skye. Is she well?"

"She is with child," said Dawn.

River felt a jolt of shock. "Clayton's child?"

Dawn nodded. "Yes, but she asked us to keep the news private. At this time she wants no one to know she carries Clayton's child."

"That sounds like you come bearing bad news," said Dove from Tulpar's back. The stallion turned his head so that his Rider could look from Dawn to River.

"Not bad or good. Would you have me tell you here, or shall I wait to speak before Morgana?" Dawn asked.

"You shouldn't have to repeat yourself," River said. "But let us find Morgana now while the Herd rests. We have been eager of news . . ." She paused and asked, "You did find Clayton?"

"Oh, yes, and his Herd, Ebony," Dawn said.

"Tulpar says Clayton has no right to begin a new Herd. Criminals do not have that right," Dove said, and Tulpar snorted to punctuate her words.

"Tulpar is correct," said Dawn. "But as Clayton claims Herd Ebony as his own we must deal with his claim."

"We must refute his claim," River said grimly.

"Yes, but we have more serious issues than Clayton's minuscule Herd," said Dawn.

River nodded in agreement. "Come, Mother. Let us find Morgana and you can tell us your news. Dove, you and Tulpar should join us. This deals with the security of our Herd."

"Of course, River." Dove's smile was soft and intimate.

River felt her cheeks warm, especially as her mother was studying her. River cleared her throat and continued. "I would also like Mari and Sora to join our discussion. They have knowledge of those allied with the Death God from their Pack members who used to belong to the Tribe of the Trees." River cued Anjo to turn and head back to the Herd, and like they had been a mated pair for years, Tulpar turned with her so that the golden stallion and the silver mare returned to the Herd side by side. The sight of them together with Dawn and Echo close behind was met with a happy cheer from Herd Magenti.

Morgana, Mari, and Sora joined River, Dawn, April, Dove, and their Companions in a little grove of post oaks just a few hundred yards off the road where the Herd waited. They stood in a tight circle as they listened to Dawn recap what had happened since Clayton revealed himself to her and led them to his camp. When she was finished, Morgana shook her head sadly. "So, is your belief that Clayton will not join us to fight Death?"

Dawn lifted her hands and then let them fall at her sides. "Truthfully, I cannot say for sure whether he will or won't."

River met her mother's troubled gaze. "But what does your wisdom and experience tell you?"

Dawn shared a long look with her mare before she answered her daughter. "Echo is in agreement with me. We are sad to say that we do not think Clayton will join us. His arrogance has only increased since he named his Herd and created their camp in the ruins, and that arrogance will make him believe he and his Herd can take on Death so that he can be the hero of this story."

"That is a fool's belief," said Dove.

Sora scoffed. "As if he and two dozen Riders could defeat a god and His army when the entire Tribe of the Trees failed to do so."

Mari cleared her throat and then said, "What about the influence of the one Rider who did show you respect and stayed with Clayton to try to reason with him? I think you said Rand is his name. Is it possible Clayton—or maybe some of his people—will listen?"

Before Dawn could answer, River spoke. "I know Clayton. Well. He will not join us, and the reason has nothing to do with whether Rand can make him listen or not. He will not choose to regain his honor and fight Death with us because he does not believe he has lost his honor."

Dawn nodded slowly. "Sadly, after speaking with Clayton I agree with my daughter's reasoning."

Morgana's lined brow furrowed with disgust and her voice was grim. "Clayton is the most dangerous type of person—one who has no desire for self-reflection. His unwavering belief in himself overshadows everything—logic, common decency, and even the care he should take with his followers. Leaders like Clayton prey on the needy, and it matters not to him if he leads his people over a cliff so long as they chant his name as they plummet to their deaths." She looked at River. "What is your decision, Mare Rider?"

River didn't hesitate. She'd already gone over several scenarios in her mind—discussed them with Anjo and April—and she knew what she must do, though it brought her no joy. "When my mother went to Clayton to show him mercy and compassion, at first I disagreed with her, though ultimately I understood that she was showing the wisdom my anger kept me from seeing. So I have decided to also be compassionate—to a point." She turned to her mother. "You gave him three days after we arrive for him to join us in the Valley of Vapors, correct?"

"That is correct."

"I will honor that. Three days have already passed since you left Clayton. If he intends to join us, he and his Herd must leave their campsite no later than today, or it will be impossible for them to reach the valley in time, correct?" She looked to the Mare Council elder for the answer.

"Indeed," Morgana said. "Even Herd Magenti's golden Tulpar could not cover that much ground unless he began the journey from the ruins today."

Tulpar tossed his head and snorted, and Dove smiled lovingly and stroked his neck.

"Then I will ask our Herd Stallion to choose three pairs of Riders who are most accurate with their bows, and their Companions. They will leave in the morning and retrace the path Dawn and Skye just traveled. They should meet Clayton very soon—or see sign of him. If they do meet him then they will escort him swiftly to our valley," said River.

"And if they do not meet him or his herd?" Morgana asked.

River turned to stare into Tulpar's intelligent eyes. "Then our Riders will go stealthily to the camp of the traitor and carry out the death sentence my mother already appraised them of. Do you understand me, Herd Stallion?"

Tulpar tossed his head and then Dove said, "He does. He must choose Rider/Companion pairs who will carry out the death sentence with mercy—quickly and thoroughly."

"Exactly," said River grimly.

Dawn saluted her daughter by fisting her hand over her heart. "Lead Mare Rider, I ask that Echo and I be allowed to lead those Riders."

River's stomach felt hollow. "Mother, are you sure? It is most likely that Clayton and his Herd will have to be put down. Even done stealthily with merciful quickness it will be a horrendous thing to witness."

"I know that, but I would ask to be there. I will pray to the Great Mother Mare for their souls and, should any linger, I will be there to provide comfort as they transition from this world to the next."

River blew out a long breath. She wanted to save her mother from something so heartbreaking and horrible, but River could easily see the logic—and the compassion—in allowing this spectacular Rider and her mare to oversee the gruesome death sentence. *I cannot treat my mother with bias.* "You have my permission to lead the team to Clayton."

"Thank you." Dawn bowed respectfully to her. "I have one more favor to ask."

"If I can grant it, I will," said River.

"Rand showed Skye and Scout, Anjo and me, the respect we deserved. He treated us with kindness and care. He admitted he made a terrible mistake in following Clayton, and the only reason he remained behind is because he desperately wants to change Clayton's mind. I ask that you allow me to show him mercy."

"Granted. The death sentence is lifted from Rand and his Merlin. I do not know if Herd Cinnabar will accept him back, so I can only speak for

Magenti, but if he returns with you and fights honorably against Death then I will allow him to wear the purple," said River.

"And what of the others?" Dove asked. "What if they ask for mercy?"

River turned to Dawn. "Mother? What are your thoughts on that?"

"My thoughts are sad, but resigned, my daughter. I spoke to the entire Herd. The others had the opportunity to come to me—or to simply show me the respect I am due as a Lead Mare Rider. None did. Not even when Clayton and those closest to him slipped away before sunrise on the morning we left. Rand was the only Rider to show remorse."

Mari spoke softly. "Clayton has poisoned them as surely as Death poisoned so many members of the Tribe of the Trees. I saw what that kind of hatred and arrogance can do. It destroys."

Dove nodded. "And it is contagious."

"We cannot fight ourselves *and* Death's army," said River. "Rand and Merlin may be granted mercy. The others need to be put down swiftly and as painlessly as possible. Use arrows tipped in Flyer poison. That is the only mercy they deserve. It is agreed?"

"It is agreed," said Morgana.

"Then it has been said," River finished. She looked from Mari to Sora. "I want you to know how rare it is that a Lead Mare Rider passes a sentence of death on Herdmembers. We are peaceful people. We honor life. It sickens me that Clayton has forced us into this position."

"We understand," said Mari. "Nik has told me that even his father, who was Sun Priest of the Tribe of the Trees, looked away and allowed anger and entitlement to flourish and spread—which, ultimately, brought about their destruction."

"What you are doing is going to make sure that doesn't happen to the Wind Riders," said Sora.

Morgana's aged voice was filled with sadness. "I have lived longer than any other Council Member, and during my life there has never been a death sentence like this passed. River is correct to be sickened. It should sicken us all. Our Herds are led by wisdom and compassion and tradition that have allowed us to prosper for more than five centuries. Let us all work to be sure Clayton's sedition never happens again."

"From your lips to the ears of the Great Mother Mare," said April.

"For my part I will work to be sure no Stallion Rider ever feels unheard again," said River. "That is my pledge. Now, we must get the Herd moving. April, would you see to that?"

"Of course." April's Deinos took a knee so her Rider could mount, and then she galloped back to where the Herd waited.

"I will rejoin the Herd as well," said Morgana. "My soul feels heavy, and I need to be surrounded by Magenti."

"We will return with you, Morgana," said Dawn.

Morgana nodded and then stiffly Ramoth knelt, and River moved quickly to aid the old woman astride. River patted the mare's soft side before Ramoth turned and, much more slowly, with Dawn and Echo beside them, they followed April and Deinos.

"River, is there anything Sora and I can do to help you?" Mari asked.

River brushed a braided strand of long dark hair from her face. "There is. I know yesterday was a Third Night, but I would ask that tonight you draw down the moon and Wash my mother. I know she does not look it, but what she has done—and most likely will do—causes her terrible grief. Can your moon magick help ease that?"

"It cannot ease grief, but it can fill her with strength," said Mari.

"And we can also Wash Echo. It will help her be strong for her Rider," Sora added.

"Thank you, my new friends." River's smile did not reach her sad, dark eyes.

Quietly, Mari and Sora—with Rigel and little Chloe by their sides—headed back to the Herd. Which left River and Anjo alone with Dove and Tulpar. Without speaking, Dove slid from her stallion's golden back and closed the few steps that separated her from River.

"I know I had to do it—to agree to carry out the death sentence on Clayton and his followers—but I hate it. If there was a way I could change it without putting the rest of us in danger, I would gladly rescind the order and—and just let whatever is going to happen to Clayton happen to him." River's shoulders bowed and she stared woodenly at the distant line of horses and people who waited for her return to continue their journey.

Dove reached out and found River's shoulder. She slid her hand down her arm until she could press her palm to River's and weave their fingers together. "One mean, selfish man enabled Death to swallow the Tribe of the Trees. You gave Clayton a choice. It is not your fault that he is too blinded by his own desires to choose wisely. What you are doing is ensuring what happened to the Tribe does not happen to our Herd."

"Do you think I will be damned for this?" River whispered. "Will the Great Mother Mare reject me?"

Before Dove could answer, Anjo was there, pressing her muzzle to her Rider's face and sending waves of love to her. Then Tulpar was there on the other side of River. He stood close to her and nuzzled her gently, nickering soft reassurance.

"I cannot speak for the Great Mother Mare, but I believe She could very well be the same deity as the Goddess of Life, Who does speak through me. And I can say that I feel strongly that the Goddess loves you and absolutely will not damn you for doing everything you can to save the Wind Riders from Death," said Dove.

"Do you promise?" River's voice trembled.

"I will never lie to you, my River." And then gently she pulled River into her arms so that the Lead Mare Rider could sob her grief into Dove's shoulder while their Companions supported and loved them both.

CHAPTER 20

That night Mari and Sora held an intimate Washing ceremony, calling down the moon to empower Dawn and Echo. They decided to include Skye and Scout as well because Mari had noticed that Skye appeared so frail it seemed she might have been on the verge of tumbling from Scout before River called a halt for the night.

Mari had just settled down beside Nik, Sora, and O'Bryan with a haunch of rabbit and a steaming bowl of something delicious April had told her was baked prairie turnips when River and Dove suddenly appeared. Dove's hand was wrapped intimately through River's arm. Sora's foot quickly tapped Mari's. Their eyes met, and Sora waggled her brows knowingly, which had Mari looking with new eyes at the pair. *Huh, there's definitely something going on between River and Dove.*

"I hope I'm not interrupting your dinner," River said.

"Of course not," Mari said. "Join us. There's plenty."

"We ate while you were Washing Dawn and Echo, Skye and Scout," said Dove. Then she smiled. "But I will be glad when we have reached the Valley of Vapors so that Sora is able to bake her cloud-like bread again."

"We will all be happy about that," said Nik as he grinned at Sora.

Mari noticed Dove seemed much more at ease than River—who looked thin and tired. "River, be sure you present yourself for Washing tomorrow. I have not led this many people, but even our small Pack can be exhausting, and that's during the best of times."

"Hey, we try not to be too awful," O'Bryan said playfully.

"I think 'try' is the key word there, Cuz," Nik joked back.

River nodded. "Third Night is tomorrow, is that correct?"

"It is," Sora said.

"I will remember to present myself and Anjo. Thank you." Then River cleared her throat before continuing. "Mari, Sora, Dove tells me that your people are exceptional shots with the crossbow, and that some of you—like Nik—are even expert archers."

"Dove is correct, right, Nik?" Mari said.

"The Tribe of the Trees long prided themselves on accuracy with crossbows," said Nik.

"And my cousin here is the best of the best," added O'Bryan.

"Then I have a difficult request. It is something I wish I did not have to ask of you, and please know I would not ask it if I did not believe it was completely necessary," said River. "You all know that the Rider, Clayton, who attempted to kill Tulpar and me during the Stallion Run has been sentenced to death, along with his followers, if they do not join us to fight Death and His army."

Somberly, Sora nodded. "Yes, we all know."

"It seems most likely that Clayton will not choose to join us," said River.

Dove spoke grimly. "Which means Clayton and his followers must be put to death, or we risk a repeat of what happened with Thaddeus and the Tribe of the Trees."

Nik nodded somberly. "You cannot allow Death to use Clayton or his people to spread disease and hatred as Death did with Thaddeus and my old tribe. Your sentence is wise and just."

Mari realized then why River had come to them. "You want Nik to go with the Riders to carry out the death sentence. You're worried what will happen to your people if they kill fellow Riders."

"Yes, Mari. I am afraid the Herdmembers will not recover from such a thing. I am sorry to ask it of you, but none of your people know these Riders. It is my hope that it will not devastate them the way it would those who grew up with Clayton and his followers. So I came to you to humbly ask that the best archer you have join my Riders. The sentence will be carried out quickly and as mercifully as possible. My plan is to dip arrows in Flyer poison; it works swiftly. Flyer poison first paralyzes and then stops the heart, so that an expert archer could be effective without having to get close. So, yes, if Nik is the best I would ask that he join the Riders and put down Clayton before the God of Death takes control of him and his Herd," said River. "With Mari's permission, of course."

"You have my permission, but whether Nik goes or not is solely his decision," said Mari.

"River, I believe you are being wise," said Nik. "When he was a young man, my father was tasked to carry out a death sentence on a Tribesman and his Companion. It haunted him for his entire life." Mari reached over and covered Nik's hand with her own, lending him the support of her touch, her understanding, her forgiveness. Nik held her hand tightly as he continued. "I will gladly help you, but will I not slow your Riders down? I know from what I have learned from your Herd already that a horse being ridden double is much slower than those with one Rider." At his side, Laru whined pitifully. Nik automatically reached out and stroked the big Shepherd. "And as fast and strong as Laru is, he is no match for your horses. He could not keep up."

River frowned and pushed her hair back from her face. "You have seen the small, light carts that can be easily pulled by one horse?"

"Yes, but there isn't room in one of those for a driver, me, and my Laru," said Nik.

"That is true. There is no room for your big, beautiful Laru, and I must be honest with you. It is very likely that you would be parted from him for a week or more," said River.

Mari could feel the waves of anxiety radiating from Laru. He'd stopped whining, but he was staring up at Nik as if he was drowning and his Companion held his only lifeline. She spoke quickly. "River, normally it would only be uncomfortable for one of us to be separated from our Companion for that amount of time, but Nik and Laru are different. You already know that Laru was Nik's father's Companion and that he Chose Nik at Sol's death. They have been parted only once since Laru's Choosing, and during that time Nik came very close to dying." Mari's gaze went to Laru, who met her eyes and flooded her with fear and dread. "Yes, sweet boy, I know. I'm telling River now." She turned her gaze from Laru to River. "I do not believe Laru can bear to be parted from Nik again."

"River, I want to help you, but I'm afraid even if Laru could bear it I cannot guarantee that my worry for him wouldn't affect my aim," said Nik as he continued to stroke Laru. Then Nik sat up straighter and smiled. "But I do have a solution for you." He reached across Laru and slapped his cousin's shoulder. "My cousin has no Companion—yet—and his aim is second only to mine."

"Cuz!" O'Bryan blinked in surprise. "My aim isn't as good as yours."

"I said *second* only to me."

"But what of Wilkes? Or Sheena? They're actual Warriors," O'Bryan said.

"*You're* an actual Warrior," Sora said.

O'Bryan shook his head. "No, to be a Warrior I have to be Chosen by a Shepherd."

"*No*," Mari said emphatically. "Those were the rules of the Tribe of the Trees—not our Pack. You have proven yourself to be as much a Warrior as Wilkes or Sheena or Nik."

"And I've been watching you," said Nik. "You rarely miss."

"You bring me more game than Davis or Rose, and their Companions are Hunters," said Sora.

"Well. Huh." O'Bryan looked up at River. "I will join you and carry out your death sentence, but someone must spend extra time with Cubby while I'm gone."

"Chloe and I will take care of your Cubby," Sora said, and Chloe yipped in sleepy agreement from where she was curled up on Sora's feet.

"It is a gruesome thing I ask of you," said River. "But I do thank you."

O'Bryan nodded. "I hate even the thought of killing Riders and their incredible Companions, but what would be more tragic is to allow Clayton and his people to be used by Death. I lost an entire Tribe because Thaddeus wasn't stopped before Death could manipulate him. I cannot imagine the Wind Rider Plains poisoned by His sickness and destroyed as He did the Tribe of the Trees. I will go with your Riders and do what must be done." He turned to Mari. "I only ask that when I'm back you and Sora Wash me, whether it's a Third Night or not. I hope that will help to take some of the sadness from my spirit."

"Of course," said Mari.

"We will willingly Wash you every night until your spirit recovers," added Sora.

"Then I will be ready to leave when your Riders are," O'Bryan told River.

"Thank you. As soon as you break your fast after first light, Tulpar will come for you," said River.

"He's going to draw the cart?" O'Bryan looked from River to Dove.

"Oh, no," said Dove. "Tulpar must remain with Herd Magenti. He is in charge of getting us safely to the Valley of Vapors, but he has carefully chosen the Riders who will go with you on your journey."

"I will be ready in the morning." O'Bryan wiped his hands on his pants and stood. "But now I need to be with my Cubby."

"I'll go with you." Sora picked up sleepy Chloe and kissed her nose. "If Chloe and I are going to take care of Cubby while you're gone, I'd like to see her now and get to know her a little better while you're still here."

"I would appreciate that," said O'Bryan.

Formally, with great respect, River fisted her hand over her heart and bowed to O'Bryan. "I will not forget this great and terrible deed you do for us. Our Herd will never forget."

O'Bryan turned to Mari. "Would you come with Sora and me to see my Cubby? I know you can hear Companions who are not yours, and I would like you to try to speak with Cub and tell her why I will be gone."

"Of course." Mari patted Rigel on his head. *Stay here with Laru. He still feels worried.*

Rigel flooded her with warmth. Tail wagging with energetic enthusiasm, Rigel trotted to his sire and licked his face before he lay close beside him. Mari smiled at her young Companion and blew him a grateful kiss before she followed O'Bryan from their little group.

🐎🐎🐎

A ball of furry blond enthusiasm trotted out from the snug travel tent that held Davis, Claudia, their Companions, and the litter of pups—plus one very young wolverine baby.

"Cammyman! It's good to see you." Mari knelt and petted the sweet Terrier as he huffed and jumped up to greet her with very wet kisses.

"Oh, Cammy, I forget how happy you make everyone around you." Sora bent and kissed the little Terrier's blond head. Chloe yipped insistently and Sora put her down so that she, too, could greet Cammy. "I should come see you more often."

"Cammy, are you bothering—" Davis began as he ducked out of the tent; then he grinned at his visitors. "Never mind! Looks like you're greeting guests instead of bothering Riders."

"Cammy bothers Riders?" Mari shook her head as she petted the happy Terrier. "I can't imagine that."

"Well, he is a little obsessed with horses." Davis smiled warmly at his Terrier. "He's decided the way to get close to them is to make every Rider in Herd Magenti fall in love with him. I assumed he was out here loudly wooing a Rider who got too close to our tent."

"Sounds like Cammy has a plan," said O'Bryan. "A wise plan."

"An annoying plan." Davis smiled at his Companion, taking the sting from his words. "But you didn't come here to talk about Cammy—or did you?" Davis gave his Companion a stern look. "Cameron, have you done something I don't know about?"

Cammy planted his butt on the ground and yipped at his Companion.

"He says he hasn't done anything. Or at least he doesn't *think* he's done anything." Davis lifted his brow and turned to Mari. "But, really, what did he do?"

Mari grinned and ruffled Cammy's ears. "Nothing. Cammy is absolutely perfect." The Terrier jumped around Mari huffing happily. "Sora and I were just escorting O'Bryan to see Cub—and let you know that he's going on a mission for River and will be gone for several days, perhaps for as long as it takes us to reach the Valley of Vapors."

"Oh, well, that's fine. Mariah and Claudia and the pups are asleep, but you can be sure we'll take good care of Cubby while you're gone," he told O'Bryan. "Would you like me to go in and get him for you?"

"Yeah, Sora and Chloe are going to help with him as well, so they wanted to see him, and Mari is going to try to let Cubby know that I have to be gone but will definitely be coming back," explained O'Bryan.

"That's a good idea," said Davis. "And I'm curious to see if Mari can communicate with Cubby. He's definitely an interesting little creature."

"He hasn't been causing problems, has he?" O'Bryan was instantly concerned.

"No, not at all. He's well behaved and smart. The pups like him a lot,"

Davis said, and Cammy yipped in agreement. Davis patted Cammy's head. "That's right, little father." He looked up, smiling, at his visitor and whispered, "Cammy is very protective of his litter—and he's included Cubby in that."

Because Cubby is part of our family!

Mari grinned as Cammy's emphatic response resonated through her mind as well as his Companion's. She laughed and crouched beside the sweet Terrier. "That's right, Cammyman. Cubby is definitely part of our Pack family."

"You want to go get him, Cammy?" Davis asked.

Cammy huffed several times before he trotted into the tent.

"He can go get him?" Sora asked.

"Cammy has gotten excellent at corralling puppies," Davis said. "He knows exactly how to carry them so that he doesn't hurt them. Watch. He'll be back in just a moment, and I'd wager that he returns without waking Mariah or Claudia."

Davis was right. It wasn't long before Cammy returned, ducking under the tent flap to trot back to them with O'Bryan's Cubby held gently in his mouth. The Terrier went directly to O'Bryan, who bent and took the sleepy baby from Cammy. "Thank you, little man." O'Bryan scratched Cammy under his chin after taking Cubby and cradling him carefully against his chest.

"He's really grown since last time I saw him." Mari stroked the small creature with one of her fingers.

"He's handsome, isn't he?" O'Bryan tickled Cubby under his chin, which caused the little animal to make happy grunting noises.

"He really is cute," said Sora. She lifted Chloe so that the two young ones were nose to nose. Chloe yipped playfully and wagged her tail, and Cubby sniffed her and made more happy grunting sounds.

"O'Bryan, let's sit," Mari said. "Hold Cubby so that I can look into his eyes and let me see if I can reach him."

"This is really going to be interesting," said Davis, sitting quickly with Sora, Mari, and O'Bryan. Cammy barked in agreement. "Hey, you should probably be quiet. Mari is going to try to talk to Cubby."

Cammy went to Mari and looked into her eyes. *Sorry, Mari.*

"Oh, sweetie, you didn't do anything wrong." Mari hugged the Terrier. "You can sit here beside me while I try to talk with Cubby."

Where is Rigel? Cammy asked as he sat beside Mari.

"He just finished eating. He stayed with Laru and Nik," she told Cammy. Then Mari turned to look at the little wolverine. "Hey there, Cubby." She leaned over to scratch the young one under his chin as she'd seen O'Bryan doing earlier to Cammy. The baby looked up at her with dark, curious eyes and held Mari's gaze. "Do you think we could talk? O'Bryan—" Mari pointed to him. "He asked me to speak to you for him. Is that okay with you?"

Mari concentrated on the little wolverine. In her mind she sketched an image of herself talking with Cubby, just like she talked with Rigel, and Cubby responding.

The baby wolverine went very still.

"Yes, like that," said Mari softly. She glanced up at O'Bryan, who seemed to be holding his breath, and then met Cubby's gaze again. "Do you understand me?"

For a few moments Mari felt nothing, and then she was filled with a wash of warmth and in her mind she heard one word very distinctly.

O'Bryan!

Mari smiled. "Yes! O'Bryan is your Companion."

"Did he do it? Did he talk to you?" O'Bryan spoke softly, but his voice was filled with controlled excitement.

"So far he's said your name, which is an excellent start."

"Can you tell him how much I love him and how glad I am that he's here with me?" O'Bryan said quickly.

"I'll try." Mari returned her attention to the baby wolverine. In her mind she sketched another picture—one where O'Bryan was holding Cubby up and smiling at him. She filled the sketch with warmth and light, and sent it to the wolverine.

This time there was no waiting. Mari was instantly filled with happiness.

My O'Bryan!

"He is definitely your O'Bryan," Mari said, and the baby grunted happily and snuggled against O'Bryan's hand. She looked up at Nik's cousin. "He adores you."

He grinned. "The feeling is mutual."

"I'm going to try to make him understand you're leaving." Mari concentrated again, and Cubby turned his attention back to her, staring up at her with bright eyes. Mari drew a picture in her mind of O'Bryan waving goodbye to Cubby and leaving with a small group of Riders. Immediately Cubby started to whine and move restlessly as he burrowed into O'Bryan, though he kept his intelligent gaze on Mari. Quickly, Mari drew another imaginary sketch, where O'Bryan returned and Cubby rushed happily to meet him.

Cubby's frantic sounds and movements stopped. She stared at Mari. *My O'Bryan no go.*

"He has to go." Mari punctuated her words with a repeat of the first sketch, which showed him leaving camp with the Riders, and then she hurriedly changed the scene to his joyous return where Cubby greeted him. "But he will come back to you."

Must come back!

The words blasted Mari's mind with such power that she had to blink several times and rub her temple before she sent Cubby another scene where O'Bryan ran into camp to lift the baby into his arms and hold him close.

"Yes, O'Bryan will be back," Mari said.

My O'Bryan be back.

The words were strong, but this time they weren't a mind-numbing onslaught. Mari nodded. "O'Bryan will always come back for you. And while he's gone Sora and Chloe will visit and play with you." Mari added a quick sketch of her friend and Chloe frolicking with Cubby.

Cubby turned her head to look at Sora, who sat beside O'Bryan with sleepy Chloe curled on her lap.

Sora?

"Yes, that's Sora." Mari reiterated by sending him a smiling sketch of her co–Moon Woman.

"Should I . . . um . . . ," Sora began.

"You should definitely pet him," Mari said.

Sora reached over and stroked the little wolverine. "Please tell him I think he is very handsome."

Handsome!

Mari laughed. "He can understand you, and he likes that you call him handsome."

"He can really understand what we say?" O'Bryan's voice was hushed, as if he spoke a prayer.

"He absolutely does," said Mari. "He's not very articulate, which isn't unusual. Not all of Rose's pups were easy to understand when they were babies."

Sora snorted. "Chloe has always been easy to understand, but of course she is advanced."

Mari stifled a grin. "Of course Chloe is, but even though Cubby isn't completely articulate yet, he can definitely understand us."

O'Bryan grinned. "Well then, Cubby, can you tell Mari if you like your name, or if you would rather I call you something else?"

The wolverine looked up at him and grunted.

I Cubby.

"He likes to be called Cubby," said Mari.

"Then Cubby it is," said O'Bryan.

Then Cubby met Mari's gaze again. *Love O'Bryan. Love Cammy. Tell Cammy love Mariah and sisters and brothers. Love them and Davis and Claudia—but O'Bryan first!*

"Thank you for sharing that with me, Cubby." Then Mari turned to Cammy. "Cubby wants you and Mariah and Davis and the puppies to know that he loves all of you."

"Ah! Ah! Ah!" Cammy huffed happily and wagged the stump of his tail that was left after the attack of the Mouth on Lost Lake.

"He loves all of you, but O'Bryan first," added Mari.

"As it should be. The love of your Companion comes first," said Davis. He leaned over and stroked the wolverine. "You're a good boy. I'm glad you're part of our family."

Family!

"He likes that," said Mari.

Sleep with O'Bryan and Sora now. Cubby jumped from O'Bryan's lap, made three circles, and fell instantly asleep between O'Bryan and Sora.

Mari laughed softly. "He says he's going to go to sleep now—with you and Sora."

"Oh, well, I—uh—think he misunderstands," said O'Bryan as his cheeks heated bright pink. "Sora and Chloe are going to spend time with him *after* I'm gone."

Mari shrugged and winked at Sora. "Too late to correct that now. He's asleep."

"Well, you do take him to your bed every night," said Davis.

"Excuse me? O'Bryan has *never* taken me to his bed," said Sora.

Mari giggled. "I think he was talking about O'Bryan taking Cubby to his bed, not you."

"Oh. Well. That does make more sense." Sora stood, cradling a complaining Chloe. "So, you sleep with him every night?" she asked O'Bryan.

"Yes, but you don't have to. Just show him some extra attention and I'm sure that will be fine, especially now that we know he can understand us," O'Bryan said quickly, his cheeks still on fire. "And remind him I'm coming back."

"I can do that," said Sora. "And don't worry about him. If he seems lonely, Chloe and I will take him to our tent. It's really not that big of a deal. Be well, O'Bryan. We will see you when you return. Good night, everyone." Sora nodded to Davis and Cammy and Mari before she and Chloe disappeared into the night.

"Is she mad?" O'Bryan asked.

"No, I don't think so," said Mari. "She's just Sora, that's all." Mari had more to say as she watched her friend fade into the shadows, but if what she suspected was true Sora would have to come to terms with it, and it wasn't her place to say anything to O'Bryan until then.

The next morning, not long after dawn pinkened the eastern sky, Tulpar and Dove came to O'Bryan's campsite. He'd already taken down his tent, which Nik would pack for him. All he was carrying with him was a small bedroll and waterskin, his crossbow, and a large cache of arrows. His stomach felt tight and strange, so he'd broken his fast with dry bread and some bison jerky. He sat on a stump, murmuring soft reassurances to Cubby, who curled sleepily against his chest.

"Good morning, O'Bryan." Dove's voice was as soft as the blushing sky.

He stood and lifted the bedroll, hooking the arrow quiver over his shoulder and securing his crossbow's leather strap across his back. "Good morning, Dove and Tulpar." The horses intrigued him, and O'Bryan couldn't help but stroke Tulpar's golden neck.

"The Riders are ready to depart. Through Tulpar's eyes I see that you are, too. Shall we go?" Dove asked.

"Yes, but I'll need to return Cubby to Mariah first."

Dove smiled at the little wolverine. "If you allow it, Tulpar and I will return your boy to his family. That way he can be with you for a little longer."

O'Bryan lifted the sleepy baby and looked into his eyes. "Dove is going to take you back to Mariah and the pups. Okay?"

Cubby grunted and wriggled his little body enthusiastically.

O'Bryan looked up at Dove to see that she and Tulpar were studying him with open curiosity. "Oh, Mari found out last night that Cubby can understand us. He spoke to Mari." Even with the seriousness of his forthcoming mission, O'Bryan grinned.

"That is wonderful, though I am not surprised. It is obvious that Cubby adores you, and he seems quite intelligent," said Dove. Tulpar snorted and Dove smiled. "He says that he likes Cubby's color."

O'Bryan tucked Cubby inside his shirt so that just his little head peeked out as he walked beside Tulpar and Dove. "Well, Tulpar, he won't stay this color for long. He'll turn dark like a wolverine."

Tulpar snorted again and Dove laughed.

"What did he say?"

"Only that he hopes he will always smell like a canine. He says wolverines usually stink terribly," Dove said.

"Well, I've been bathing him whenever we stop near a creek or stream," said O'Bryan. "I've been aware that his scent might get off-putting, but so far he just smells like a puppy to me."

"That's what he smells like to Tulpar as well, so whatever you're doing is working," said Dove.

"That's good . . . that's good." O'Bryan thought that he should probably keep up a conversation with Dove. He liked her, thought Tulpar was magnificent, and usually would have enjoyed the opportunity to speak with both of them, but O'Bryan's mind kept circling around and around replaying River's words. He was going to have to kill Riders and their Companions—and that thought blotted out small talk as surely as snow clouds blotted out the sun.

It didn't take long to reach the group that had gathered near the rear of the Herd's temporary camp. River and Anjo, of course, were there—as were four Rider/Companion teams—one of which was hitched to a strange-looking small cart. Then O'Bryan blinked in surprise as he saw that Sora and Chloe were there as well.

"Good morning to you, O'Bryan," said River.

"Good morning, River and Anjo." O'Bryan bowed respectfully to the Lead Mare Rider team before greeting her mother. "And good morning to you, Dawn and lovely Echo." He bowed again.

Dawn saluted him. "What you do for us shall not be forgotten," she said somberly.

"Never," said River firmly. "We will never forget. Now, let me introduce you to the team Tulpar chose for this grim mission. You, of course, already know my mother and her mare, Echo."

"Of course." O'Bryan smiled at Echo, who stretched out her muzzle to greet him. He stroked her gently, marveling in the softness of her coat.

"And this is Stanton and his Dodger." River gestured at a tall, dark-skinned man who stood beside a muscular sorrel stallion.

"Good to meet you," said O'Bryan.

"Thank you for what you have agreed to do," Stanton said.

"This pair is Lace and her mare, Lovie," River introduced.

"Hello," said O'Bryan to the tiny woman who leaned against an athletic-looking brown and white paint mare.

"Please know that we are grateful for you," said Lace.

"And Ian will be your cart driver. His Dozer is an expert with the light cart. They will take good care of you," River said.

"I am glad you are with us," said Ian as he patted Dozer, a big dapple-gray gelding, on his shoulder. He met O'Bryan's eyes and spoke frankly. "You save us from having to kill a fellow Herdsman."

O'Bryan breathed a sigh of relief. He was glad the Riders were going to speak openly about what he must do. "Thank you. I will not say I am happy to join you on this mission, but I can say that I understand. I can imagine how horrible it would be if we had to pass this sentence on any of our Pack. I give you my word I will be swift and aim true."

"That is all we can ask of you," said River. "Dawn will, of course, lead the team. Stanton is our expert on Flyer poison and its uses. He will guide you on how to dress your arrows. Lace is our best tracker. Should Clayton and his people not be at their camp she will track them." River went to O'Bryan and saluted him formally. "My wish is that you return to us soon, O'Bryan, and may a mare's luck be with you."

Then Sora was there, standing in front of him. Her full lips tilted up as she scratched Cubby under his chin. "I thought you would probably bring him with you. I can return him to Mariah for you."

"Th—" O'Bryan began, but found that he had to clear the emotion from his throat and begin again. "Thank you. Cubby and I appreciate that."

Sora looked from the little wolverine up into O'Bryan's eyes. Something flashed across her face, and then she took his hand. "I have to speak to O'Bryan alone for a moment. We will be right back." And without saying anything else, she led him away from the group to a small stand of pecan trees.

"What is it?" O'Bryan felt a tremor of worry. *I hope she hasn't changed her mind about taking care of Cubby.* Hastily he said, "I really don't think Cubby is going to be a problem, but I'm pretty sure Mari and Dove will help you if she gets too much."

Sora made a shooing gesture. "Cubby won't be a problem. Chloe and I are looking forward to spending time with him." At her feet, the black Terrier pup yipped agreement. "It's you I'm worried about."

"Me?"

"Well, yes, of course. You're going to have to shoot and kill Riders and their horses. It's going to be horrible."

O'Bryan looked down at his feet while his hand caressed Cubby and held his warm little body close to his chest. "I didn't sleep much last night."

"That's normal. O'Bryan, look at me."

He lifted his head and met her eyes.

"What you are doing for the Herd—for all of us—is important. It's terrible, but from what I've learned from Dove and Nik, Wilkes and Sheena, and the others had Thaddeus been put down Sol would be alive today. The forest fire would never have happened, and Death would not have been able to defeat the Tribe of the Trees . . ." She paused and snorted. "Not that I have any fondness for your old Tribe, but putting down one evil person would've saved so, so many lives." She moved closer to him. "That is what you are doing—saving many lives by taking a few. Do not forget that.

And do not forget that your family is waiting for your return. Now, bend down," Sora commanded.

Confused, O'Bryan bent, and then Sora utterly shocked him by putting her arms around his neck and kissing him. It wasn't a long kiss. It wasn't a deep kiss. Their tongues did not meet, nor did their bodies come together, but it was warm and sweet and full of promise—and when they parted Sora smiled up at him.

"There. Think of that when the horror of your mission begins to overwhelm you, and remember that there are those who care for you—who know how kind and gentle you are—and we wait for you. Come back to us. We will heal your spirit of the horrors you survive." Then she reached out and pulled Cubby from his shirt. "Now, kiss your little boy goodbye."

"Goodbye, sweet Cubby." Still stunned by Sora, O'Bryan scratched Cubby under the chin and then kissed his little black nose. "Be good while I'm gone. I will come back to you." His gaze went from the wolverine to Sora as he finished, "Both of you. I promise."

"Good." Sora cradled Cubby close to her. "Cubby and I will hold you to that promise." At her feet Chloe yipped. Sora grinned. "Chloe will hold you to it, too. Safe travels, O'Bryan. May the Great Earth Mother be with you."

Then Sora turned and, with hips swinging, she headed back to the heart of the busy camp. As O'Bryan watched her, his fingers lightly touched his lips.

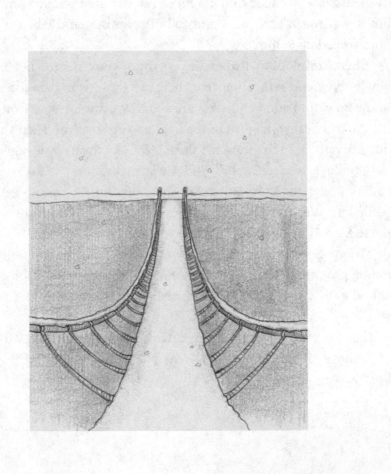

CHAPTER 21

Had O'Bryan's mission not been so horrible he would have loved every moment of traveling with the small group of Wind Riders. Their horses were magnificent and kind and strong. He was enthralled by the beauty of Dawn's Echo, but his favorite was Dozer, the big, friendly gelding who effortlessly pulled the light cart in which he and Dozer's Companion rode. Not that the light cart was comfortable; it decidedly was not. O'Bryan had never been so bruised or battered, but he adored the big gelding. He adored everything about the horses.

The pace they set was faster than even the Herd had been traveling. With such a small group they didn't have any elderly or very young with them and they could push the incredibly athletic horses to the limit of their endurance. They made camp only after all light had fled from the sky and began traveling again every morning as the sun lightened the darkness just enough for the horses to move safely.

It took three days to reach Clayton's camp. Dawn alerted them when they were within half a day's ride of the rogue Herd. They chose a site in the heart of a thickly wooded grove far enough away from Herd Ebony that even one of Clayton's Hunters would have difficultly discovering them. There they waited, silent and somber, while Lace stealthily made her way to the place Dawn had described as being Clayton's campsite.

They didn't have to wait long. Lace returned before dusk on the third day. Her paint mare was soaked with sweat, and Lace's expression was grim. As she dried off Lovie and tended to her, Lace filled in her team.

"Clayton and his people are long gone," said Lace. "Their campfires have been cold for days—at least six. They left their tents up, though—like fools."

Dawn shook her head sadly. "I explained to Clayton and all of his people that there is an army descending upon our plains. Logic says they will most likely emerge from the Rock Mountains on or near the same path Mari and the Pack took, and that path is only just a couple days' hard ride from Clayton's camp."

"Yet he made no attempt to cover their tracks into camp or camouflage their tents. His arrogance has become willful ignorance," said Lace as she vigorously toweled sweat from Lovie's coat.

"Could you tell in what direction Clayton headed?" asked O'Bryan.

Lace snorted. "Easily. He also made no attempt to cover their departure. He's heading to the Rock Mountain pass."

"And into the arms of Death," said Dawn.

"And poison and more horrors than he is capable of comprehending," added O'Bryan. He met Dawn's gaze. "What now?"

Her answer came without hesitation. "We track them and hope we catch them before they find Death."

"We cannot go any farther today," said Lace as she mixed water Stanton had already warmed with the sweet mash the mare would need to restore her strength. "But by first light Lovie will be fully recovered." She shook her head and frowned as she gave the tired mare the sweet mash mixture. "Clayton is utterly unfit to be Herd Stallion Rider. He might as well have sent up a signal fire to blaze the location of his Herd. You don't need me to find them. You don't need anything but eyes and a little sense. It's like he's taking his Herd on an outing with no care in the world."

"Clayton knew we would come after him. In his arrogance he thinks only of taunting us—of showing us how superior he believes he is." Dawn's voice broke and she had to pause to collect herself before continuing. "He does not think of his Herd. He does not think of any of the Great Herds or of what destruction his unearned confidence will cause."

Dodger, Stanton's big sorrel stallion, squealed and tossed his head. His Rider went to his side and stroked his neck soothingly. "Yes, my boy,

I agree. We all agree." He glanced up, met O'Bryan's curious gaze, and added, "Dodger says Clayton is not fit to be a Stallion Rider—that it is an abomination to put his own needs over the safety of his Herd."

"Do all Stallion Riders feel like that?" O'Bryan asked.

"Yes," said Stanton. "Except for the fools who followed Clayton."

Dawn spoke up quickly. "Not all of them are fools. Rand and his Merlin showed me proper respect. He acknowledged his mistake in joining Herd Ebony and, though he clearly did not have the ability to sway his course, only remained with Herd Ebony to try to reason with Clayton."

"I hope Rand can be saved," said Lace. "I got to know him when I tracked with Cinnabar's Riders a couple summers ago. He was kind and had a good sense of humor."

"I hope he can be saved, too," Dawn murmured as she began to mix Echo's sweet mash.

O'Bryan said nothing. He busied himself with spitting the pheasants they'd shot earlier and placing them over the fire to grill as he thought, *I hope someone describes Rand and his stallion to me. How will I be sure I do not shoot them?* He drew a deep, steadying breath when his hands shook. *How will I ever shoot a horse?*

The snow had finally sputtered and stopped, though Ralina kept eyeing the low-hanging, slate-colored clouds that were so close she could reach out and run her fingers through their damp coldness.

They had been climbing straight up for days. Ralina's legs felt as if they'd turned to iron—if iron could be sore and exhausted. Finally, the doe stopped their uphill climb and turned directly into the shrouded rising sun to follow a steady eastward path. Then, unexpectedly, just after they'd paused for their brief midday meal the doe chose a thread of a path that was really more like a rutted water runoff than trail. It took a downward turn that was so abrupt it seemed to Ralina that they were scaling the side of a gorge, and she was glad of the cloudy mist that concealed much of their surroundings. And then they climbed below the clouds and the world dropped off to nothingness beside them.

"Bloody beetle balls! I could've gone the rest of the day not knowing that was there." Renard jutted his chin at the slash in the mountain that fell away into fog and emptiness just off to their left.

"I'd rather know." His father's voice was muffled through the wrap that covered all but his eyes. "Looks too easy to fall from here if we didn't know."

As Daniel spoke the doe turned to look at them and tossed her delicate head, walking carefully as far from the edge of the ravine as possible.

"She agrees with you," said Ralina as they continued trudging after the Goddess-touched deer. "I just hope she's not leading us all the way to the bottom. I can't imagine climbing back up on the other side—if that's where we're headed."

"Wherever she's leading us we know it's the will of the Goddess of Life, and life will always find a way, no matter how difficult," said Renard.

From his position on the sliver of a trail just ahead of Ralina, Bear barked in agreement. The doe whirled around. She charged back at them, covering the few feet quickly and stomping her dainty hooves at Bear.

Ralina grabbed her Companion and pulled him back away from the suddenly angry doe. "Stop." She called to the doe, "Don't hurt him!"

The doe froze and met Ralina's gaze. Her large brown eyes showed not anger, only concern—even fear—and Ralina loosed her hold on Bear. "What is it?" she asked the doe. "Why did you—"

SILENCE!

The word blasted through Ralina's mind as the doe's gaze went from Ralina to Bear, and then back to Ralina again.

And Ralina understood.

"Bear and Kong have to be quiet," Ralina said quickly. "They can't bark."

The doe tossed her head again—her compassionate gaze going from Bear to Kong.

"That's it." She crouched before Bear. "Sweet boy, you have to be very quiet. No barking, okay?"

Through their Companion connection, Bear flooded Ralina with the warmth that was his way of telling her he understood.

"Renard, be sure Kong knows he must not bark, too," said Ralina.

Instantly, Renard turned to crouch before his big Shepherd, who walked between him and his father. "Hey, buddy, like Ralina said to Bear, you have to be very quiet until the doe lets us know it's safe."

Kong's tail wagged and he huffed soft agreement. Renard stood and turned to face the doe, who had been watching them closely. "Thank you for warning us. They'll be quiet now." He bowed respectfully to her.

The doe dipped her head in acknowledgment before she turned and continued their downward trek.

Slowly, the three humans and two canines followed.

"That means Death's army must be close." Renard spoke softly.

A shiver of terrible foreboding skittered down Ralina's spine as she nodded in agreement with her lover.

It seemed they had only continued walking for just a few minutes when their path bottomed out and fed into another, much wider trail that wrapped around the side of the mountain. Though it was more like a proper road, it was so snow packed that had the doe not displaced the drifts ahead of them, they could have only inched their way forward.

Ralina turned her head to look behind them, half expecting to see Death lurking in the misty shadows that hugged the side of the mountain, but all she saw was the trail being swallowed by snow. She was just beginning to wonder how the doe would find shelter that night when she heard it—a strange bellow. It wasn't a roar or a growl, but it was male and powerful, and definitely animalistic.

The doe's head snapped around to glance behind them, and then she increased her pace so the humans and their Companions had to jog to keep up with her.

It's Him. It's Death.

Ralina didn't speak the words aloud. She couldn't. If she spoke them, she was afraid she would conjure the God. Just the thought had her gazing to her right at the abrupt drop-off that was only a few yards away.

He won't take me. He won't take Bear. If He catches us, I will jump. Bear will follow, and I know Renard, Kong, and Daniel will also follow.

And then the winding path straightened, revealing a snow-covered suspension bridge that stretched over the open maw of the seemingly bottomless ravine. The doe led them to it and then paused as she waited for them to join her. As they did, Renard clapped his mittened hands and smiled fiercely.

"This is perfect. Ralina, your doe is brilliant!" He hugged Ralina exuberantly.

"Well, at least we don't have to climb up from down there." Ralina eyed the gorge nervously. "Not that we can even see what is down there."

Daniel's hand rested briefly on her shoulder. "Do not fret. It is only a gorge, and this is only a bridge. Were it not safe, your doe wouldn't have led us to it. We shall cross it and continue on our journey—ahead of Death."

"Exactly." Renard's smile got broader. "And after crossing it we can be sure that we'll remain ahead of Death."

And then Ralina understood why Renard was so joyous. "Oh, Goddess! We'll cut the bridge after we cross."

"Indeed we will." Renard gestured to his father. "We'll need the best knife in your backpack."

As Renard dug through his father's backpack, snow began to fall again—hard, icy pellets that stung so that it seemed the clouds had dropped down to them and then crystalized. From her position at the mouth of the suspension bridge, the doe stomped her hooves and tossed her head restlessly.

"We need to hurry," said Ralina. Her words were punctuated by another bestial roar that drifted eerily up the trail from behind them, this time closer and louder than the one before.

The doe snorted and moved onto the bridge, which swayed under her weight. She didn't pause to look behind her to be sure they followed. She trotted quickly, her hooves displacing the snow so that they clattered against the wooden slats and echoed around them.

Bear whined and looked up at Ralina, who bent to stroke his wide head. "It's okay. We'll be okay. Like Daniel said, the doe wouldn't lead us into danger. She's leading us *away* from it. Come on, Bear. We can do this." Purposefully, the Storyteller kept her gaze focused on the doe. She did not look for the opposite side of the gorge as it had already been obscured by the snow. She did not look down—for that way lay fear. She strode with confidence out onto the swaying bridge, holding tightly to the rope railing, and followed her Goddess-given guide, only glancing once behind her to be sure Renard, Kong, and Daniel followed.

Though the bridge swayed with their weight and the wind that whirled up from the gorge below them, it was surprisingly easy to cross to the other side. Of course, that was mostly because the doe displaced the snow and ice that coated the wooden slats, but it seemed little time had passed when Ralina's feet were once again on solid, but snowy, ground. As the others spilled from the bridge, they took off their backpacks and each of them grabbed a knife, though only the blade Renard used was sharp enough to saw completely through the thick ropes that held the suspension bridge above the seemingly bottomless gorge.

The doe stood close to them, ears pricked as her gaze was focused on the opposite side of the bridge. Every few moments she would stomp her hooves and toss her head restlessly.

Ralina felt her impatience like a hot poker fresh from the fire. "We need to hurry," she murmured to Renard and Daniel as the three of them sawed at the ropes, fat as tree boughs.

"Got it!" Renard said victoriously as he severed the last rope that held one side of the bridge. Then he quickly moved to continue the work Ralina and Daniel had been doing on the other arm of the bridge.

Ralina stepped back, acknowledging that the men were stronger and able to saw through the thick rope faster by giving them room to work. She wiped her sweaty forehead, glad at least to feel warm from the effort of trying to hack through the almost impossible thick— and frozen—braided rope. For a moment the icy wind that swirled up from the gorge felt good against the heated skin of her flushed face, but then she realized that the wind, eddying up and around them from the slash between mountains was intermittently blowing the falling snow away so that she could, occasionally, glimpse the opposite side of the bridge.

What she saw chilled her blood and had fear spiking through her body.

A dark line of huge, shaggy beasts had plowed through the snow and stood, paused, staring across the length of the bridge at her. Leading the line of beasts was an enormous creature shaped like the others, but this one glowed, much like the beautiful spirit of the doe Death had entrapped to guide them through the pass. Ralina blinked, thinking all those days of trudging after the doe had caused her to hallucinate. But then she realized that she stared at the glowing spirit of the bison bull Death had battled and killed and whose living heart He had gorged on right before the snowstorm began—right before she escaped. *The bison is bound to Death. He must be close!*

Suddenly, Ralina was filled with an overwhelming urge to run—to bolt away in panic—to put as much distance between her and the glowing spirit as possible.

The doe snorted and butted Ralina gently with her muzzle before she whirled around and trotted a few feet away. She paused there and stared back at Ralina as the Storyteller was flooded with an undeniable urgency to *run*. She stared at the doe, meeting her expressive brown eyes that seemed to beseech her to understand.

Ralina nodded. *Yes. Yes, we need to get out of here.*

The doe tossed her head again, snorted, and trotted backwards several paces, compelling Ralina to follow.

"Renard, we have to go. *Now.*" When he glanced up at her, she pointed across the gorge and his eyes widened as he stared at the glowing beast and the stationary line of creatures behind him.

"Bloody beetle balls, it's Death's spirit guide. Father! Hurry. The army. It can't be far behind the bison spirit," Renard said.

His father followed his gaze and then nodded as he bent over his rope, sawing with renewed vigor

"Why have you stopped?"

The bellow drifted across the bridge with the wind. Ralina's body went numb with fear. She would know His voice anywhere.

As she stared in horror, He strode into view, shoving aside the enormous beasts with such disregard that several of them tumbled soundlessly over the edge to be swallowed by the eddying snow and mist.

"Ah, I see. You pause before a bridge." Death spoke to the spirit of the bison who stood closest to the bridge. The God threw back His head and roared a parody of laughter. "Ignorant beast. It will not harm you. Cross. It is not that far to the other side."

And then, as Ralina's soul was filled with dread, Death turned His dark gaze from the spirit of the bison to the far end of the bridge. Even through the drifting snow, she saw Him startled in surprise.

The God of Death's first response to seeing her shocked Ralina. His face, changed to something more bestial, more bull-like than the stag He had been becoming, radiated joy as He smiled beatifically at her.

"My Storyteller!"

His shout was joyous, too—though His happiness was short-lived.

The smile slid from His face as rage furrowed His thick brow. His smile turned feral as He bared his teeth at her.

"My treacherous Storyteller!" This time His voice was filled with rage.

The need to flee blasted through Ralina's body as the doe squealed and stomped her delicate hooves, thawing Ralina's fear.

"Leave that side. The weight of the army will probably snap the rope anyway." Ralina grabbed Renard's shoulder, pulling him up and away from the last rope he and his father were still attempting to saw through.

"STORYTELLER!" Death bellowed, adding, *"THADDEUS, WARRIORS, TO ME."*

Ralina's frantic gaze went to Death as Thaddeus rushed up to the God *on all fours*. The disgusting little man crouched beside Death, staring across the gorge at her as his malicious laugh echoed around them.

"Renard, now! Kong, Bear, let's go!" Whining pitifully, the canines trotted toward the doe, who was impatiently prancing in place just a few yards down the trail from them.

Daniel stood and turned to his son and Ralina. "Give me the good knife. Go. I'll cut through the rest of the bridge and then join you."

"No!" Ralina cried.

"We aren't leaving you!" Renard said.

"Like Ralina said, the weight of the army will snap through the rest of the rope anyway," said Daniel. "I'll be fine, but you need to get out of here. Now."

As he spoke the final word, "now," Daniel staggered forward as a spear blossomed from the middle of his back.

"You got 'em!" Thaddeus shouted. Hunched, he danced around Death, more doglike than human.

Then from behind Death, Warriors Ralina barely recognized rushed to join the God, pulling their crossbows from slings across their backs.

Daniel dropped to his knees beside the bridge, a wicked-looking spear lodged in the middle of his back. His son knelt beside him.

"Go." Daniel's voice was weak, but edged with steel. "I stay willingly. I die willingly. The Goddess of Life will welcome me. I know it." The older man's gaze found the doe, who solemnly bowed her head to him.

Ralina didn't know what to say, so she crouched beside Daniel and put her arms around him. "I will be sure stories of your bravery will be told for generations."

There was the twanging sound of crossbows being fired, and all around them arrows began to clatter against the side of the gorge, the mountain beside them, and the snowy ground around them.

"Survive. Destroy Death. Love my son. That is all I ask," Daniel whispered to her before he took her arms from around him and turned to his son. "I love you. I will always love you. Now—*go!*" With his waning strength Daniel took the knife from Renard and pushed him toward the doe. Then the older man returned to sawing through the last rope that held the bridge.

"No, Father! I cannot leave you!"

An arrow whizzed past Renard, missing him only by inches.

"*STORYTELLER!*" Death bellowed.

The bridge began to shake and Ralina tore her gaze from Daniel to see that a line of Milks had begun to trudge through the snow that blanketed the suspension bridge.

Daniel did not pause. He did not even look at his son. He simply said, "Go! This spear will kill me. If you do not leave now, my death will mean nothing. Let my last act as a father to be to save you. Go. Now. With my love."

As arrows rained around them Ralina grabbed Daniel's arm again. This time he came as she pulled him, though he was sobbing brokenly.

"I love you, Father!" he called as he allowed Ralina to pull him with her while the doe sprinted down the path with their canine Companions padding after her.

"Hurry, we have to hurry!" Ralina panted as she continued to half drag, half lead her lover after the doe.

Renard came, but as he staggered with Ralina he kept craning his neck around, attempting to keep his father in view as long as the snow and mist would allow. He saw two arrows embed themselves into his father's arm and thigh, but he didn't appear to notice them. He kept sawing at the rope. And then the icy droplets swallowed Daniel and Renard could see him no more. Still sobbing, Renard turned his attention forward and ran with Ralina, their Companions, and the doe.

They had only run for just a few more minutes when they heard a sharp crack, like a tree snapping in a windstorm.

"He did it," Ralina said as she wiped at the tears washing down her cheeks. "That's the bridge breaking. Daniel did it."

At that moment both canines paused, raised their muzzles to the gray sky, and howled with grief.

"He's dead. My father. He's dead," said Renard.

Ralina threaded her arm through his and kept propelling him forward. She had no words to help his grief. All she could do was keep him moving and support him with her touch, her love, and her understanding.

Thank you, Daniel. I will never forget, and may the Goddess of Life welcome you into Her arms.

The doe's head turned once to look back at them and Ralina saw that tears made icy tracks down her face.

CHAPTER 22

Well, at least we only lost a few of the Milks." Beside Death, Thaddeus stared down at the bottomless gorge where just moments before a dozen or so Milks had fallen silently to their true deaths when that idiot old man had finally sawed through the rope holding up the bridge. That the old fool had lurched forward and tumbled into the gorge after the Milks was little consolation. Thaddeus had been looking forward to what Death would do to Daniel.

And then pain spiked through Thaddeus as Death backhanded him—though not hard enough to knock Thaddeus from the trail to join the doomed Milks and the stupid old man.

"*Do not make light of losing soldiers!*" He roared at Thaddeus, raining rancid spittle on his cringing face.

"Forgive me, my Lord. I simply was relieved that You did not fall, too." Thaddeus wiped his face with the back of his sleeve and lied to the God.

Death scoffed, "I was never in danger. *I am a God.*"

Thaddeus badly wanted to roll his eyes and tell the god that with the stupid decisions He'd been making during the trip it wouldn't have been surprising that Death had too little sense to keep from falling from the side of the mountain. But Thaddeus was a survivor, so he kept his true thoughts to himself, only sharing them with his beloved Odysseus. Instead, he spoke in a servile voice that nauseated him but kept him alive another day.

"My Lord, what now?"

Instead of answering, the God paced to where the spirit of their bison guide stood motionless by the entrance to the now-useless suspension bridge that flapped in the wind, beating against the side of the gorge like a dying bird.

Curious, Thaddeus moved close enough so that he could eavesdrop.

"Find another path," Death commanded the bison spirit. "Now. I must reclaim My Storyteller."

The glowing, transparent bison bull tossed his head and snorted soundlessly.

"Go. Now. Return when you have found another way across the gorge. And do not forget that you are bound to Me. You *must* return if you ever want to be granted peace."

The bison bowed his huge head slightly, though his eyes glowed red with malice, and then he lumbered back along the winding trail that hugged the snowy mountainside. Thaddeus shivered as the bison brushed past him. It was perpetually cold on the damnable mountain, but the bison spirit caused the air around him to be preternaturally frigid. Even Death didn't stride too close to the wraith, for when He did His thick black beard and the bison-like mane that had begun to frame His face, shoulders, and neck became matted with icicles.

Death's shadow fell over Thaddeus, causing him to startle and hastily bow low.

"You asked what now, Hunter? You see My answer. My bison shall lead us. Meanwhile, slaughter the smallest of these bulls. Build a magnificent fire. We feast while we wait." Death strode away, causing the army to press carefully against the side of the mountain to keep from being accidentally being thrown over the edge by their mercurial god.

"I hate Him, Odysseus." Thaddeus punctuated the sentence with a very Terrier-like growl. Then, on all fours, he scrambled back along the line of bison, mutating soldiers, and empty-eyed Milks until he rejoined the small group of Hunters who were his favorites. They turned to him eagerly, though their Terriers remained curled together—their dark eyes that followed Thaddeus's movements were the only evidence that they were awake and aware. *I need to talk to the Hunters about their Terriers, Odysseus*, Thaddeus thought as he glared at the pile of canines. *They have not been showing their Companions or me proper respect.* But his Hunters showed him respect and loyalty. They practically wriggled like puppies as he approached.

"What is it, Thaddeus?" said Wilson, the Hunter Thaddeus considered his right-hand man. "Why have we stopped?"

Before he responded Thaddeus peered down the trail to be sure Death wasn't within hearing range. When he didn't see the hulking form of the God, he allowed his voice to reflect the disdain he felt. "Seems that bitch of a Storyteller didn't freeze. She and Daniel and Renard beat us to the bridge that crosses over the gorge—something we would have come to days ago had that damned god not been so lazy."

The Hunters growled and nodded their shaggy heads, though they, too, kept nervously glancing around in case Death came within hearing.

"But if they beat us to the bridge, why have we not rushed across it to capture them?" asked Wilson.

"Because when Daniel was half-dead he somehow managed to cut the ropes that held the bridge over the gorge. He and the bridge fell—along with a bunch of Milks!" snarled Thaddeus.

"Milks . . . No loss there." Wilson shuddered, and the other Hunters growled agreement. "Now what?"

"Exactly what I asked Him." Thaddeus shrugged. "He sent the dead bison to scout another way across. Meanwhile, we're to slaughter the smallest of the bulls and feast. Probably before we all freeze to death stuck up here on this mountain."

"I will not freeze here," Wilson grumbled as he squinted his small eyes against the pelting snow and searched back down the trail for the God. "We should leave. We should return to the Tribe of the Trees. The poison could be gone by now."

"No!" Thaddeus snarled, and snapped his teeth at Wilson, who cringed and whined. "We will not quit so close to getting everything we deserve. We will get off this mountain and claim the rich land beyond. We will start our own Tribe far away from this blustering god and His army of dead things."

The Hunters huffed and nodded and wriggled, which made Thaddeus bare his teeth in the only version of a smile his face was still capable of making. "Now, get your knives ready. Let us prepare to feast."

The doe did not halt as dusk stained the sky dark. Instead, she shifted from the steady trot she'd been maintaining since the bridge to a brisk walk. She continued to hug the side of the mountain as the wide trail curved around it. The doe did glance back at Ralina and Renard frequently, as if to be sure they were still there—still following.

Ralina wished they could stop, but she didn't think she could have rested anyway. Not after she'd seen Him. Not after she knew how close He was to them. She was grateful that the trail was wide and curved instead of going straight up or down. She was also grateful that it allowed her to walk beside Renard. She remained close to him, as did Kong and Bear. All they could do was lend Renard their love and strength through touch.

They trudged after the doe until the snow was so stinging and the night so black that even the magickal creature had trouble making their trail passable. Finally, she paused and then began to climb up the side of the mountain. She continued for so long Ralina had begun to stumble, and wondered if this would be it—their end—frozen here. *At least Death didn't capture us. At least we're still free.*

Then the doe stopped before a clump of prickly junipers stubbornly clinging to the mountainside. As she had all those many nights since their escape, the doe entered the little grove, her presence sweeping away snow to expose shoots of tender foliage on which she began grazing while Renard and Ralina used sticky juniper boughs to feed their precious fire, over which they roasted the two hares that had crossed their path earlier that day.

Dinner was mostly silent. Renard's face was pale and tearstained. Both Shepherds remained close to him, using touch to comfort him. When he spoke, his voice was weary, but firm.

"Did you look at Him? Death? Did you see how He'd changed?" Renard said.

"Yeah, I saw Him and—" Ralina's words broke off as she thought back. Until then she had tried not to think about how He looked. She'd only thought about keeping moving—staying ahead of Death and His army— and of Daniel's courageous sacrifice. Now she replayed the scene where the God had bellowed her title across the gorge, studying the remembered image in her imaginative mind. Ralina sat up straighter and met Renard's sad gaze. "He's becoming more and more like the bison he killed."

Renard nodded grimly. "His form is turning as monstrous as His rotted heart."

Ralina shivered and nodded. "I'm going to make sure we beat Him. I'm going to make sure Daniel's death—*all* the deaths that led us here—are avenged."

"I know you will, and I will be right beside you to watch it happen. Father would want me to be there."

Ralina curled up beneath Renard's arm and snuggled against him. "He'll know. I believe Daniel will know when Death is defeated." Her gaze drifted to where the doe rested across the fire from them. Her compassionate brown eye met Ralina's. Very slowly and distinctly, the doe nodded her head before closing her eyes to sleep.

Death feasted on the slaughtered bison, and then He paced. All night He paced back and forth, making a rut in the snow that blew and drifted around them and covered the wide path that ended at the broken bridge.

Thaddeus wouldn't have cared what the God did, but in the absence of His other distractions—the Storyteller and the rabbit women who used to cater to His every whim—Death had taken to forcing Thaddeus to remain close to His side. This meant Thaddeus had to constantly be on alert, for the God's moods were ever changing, and there was no easy way to predict when or why He would lose His temper.

"Odysseus," Thaddeus whispered to the memory of his faithful Companion, "I hate to say it, but the Storyteller handled Him better than I do. She was good at keeping him calm." The Hunter snorted. "Of course she was. Women can be good at calming men. It's a shame He let those rabbit women freeze."

Thaddeus had commandeered a pelt from one of the Milks. He'd taken it from the dead-eyed thing and then silently pushed it off the mountain path while Death's back was turned. He placed the pelt on the snowy ground, sat on it, and then wrapped it, cloak-like, around himself as he pressed against the side of the mountain and watched Death pace.

"Did you say something, Thaddeus?" On all fours, Wilson scrambled up to him, pleasantly obsequious as always.

Thaddeus glanced behind Wilson where the rest of his Hunters clustered together between the huge, sleeping bison. A little way apart from the men their Terriers were curled around one another like puppies. "Why do your Terriers not sleep with you anymore?" Thaddeus surprised himself by asking Wilson.

Wilson shrugged his hunched shoulders and glanced behind where his blond Terrier, Spud, slept in the center of the canine pile. "Haven't given it much thought. Didn't really even notice it until you mentioned it." He shrugged awkwardly again and jutted his chin back down the path. "Same with the Warriors and their Shepherds."

"Do your Terriers still show you proper respect?" Thaddeus narrowed his small, dark eyes as he stared at the pile of sleeping Terriers.

"They hunt well. They come when called. What more is there?" Wilson said.

Thaddeus's gaze went from the canines to Wilson. "Your connection. Do you still speak with Spud through your connection?"

Wilson paused and then barked what sounded like a canine laugh. "Spud has never been one for saying much, though I haven't asked him much lately, either."

"Interesting . . . ," Thaddeus said. *Odysseus, something is happening between Companions and their canines. See how wise we were to change our relationship? You and I will never grow apart.*

"*Thaddeus, to Me!*" Death bellowed. At the sound of the God's voice Wilson flinched and scrambled back to join the other Hunters.

Thaddeus sighed and hurried to the God. "Yes, my Lord?"

"Build a fire. A roaring one. Here, near the entrance to the bridge. It will help Me think."

"Yes, my Lord." Thaddeus pulled out the tinderbox he had kept carefully packed with his things since the early days of their hellish journey. He brought it out and shouted at his group of Hunters, "Collect boughs! Our god wants a fire near the bridge!" Wearily, but without complaint, the Hunters scattered to find places down the trail where they could climb up the mountainside and strip any pines they found of their boughs. Early on the mountain they'd discovered that even green pine boughs would burn if they had enough sap. Soon Thaddeus had a fire burning high and bright. Flames licked the side of the cliff, creating bizarre shadows.

"Do not let the fire go out!" Death shouted at Thaddeus when his head had begun to nod sleepily in the warmth.

"Yes, my Lord," Thaddeus said quickly, throwing off the pelt cloak so that the frigid night wind kept him awake.

Death paced all night, and Thaddeus struggled to stay awake and aware enough to feed the fire. Just after dawn, the Hunter almost shouted with relief as the spirit of the dead bison finally trotted up along the path and directly to Death.

The creature stopped before the God and bowed his massive head.

"Well? Lead Me. How do we cross this chasm?" Death asked.

Slowly and carefully, the spirit of the bison bull went to the edge of the path to the place where the useless bridge hung loosely from its anchor and still flapped against the frozen side of the gorge. The beast tossed his head and pawed at the ground. He moved forward as far as he could and still be on solid ground, stopped, pawed at the snowy path again, and then craned his neck to look at Death.

"Ah. I thought as much. It is why I did not rest all night. No matter. I have, of course, thought of an alternative plan. Wait near. I shall require your services again soon . . ." The God paused, then bellowed, "*Thaddeus!*"

Thaddeus swallowed the response he wished he could give the God: *I am only feet away from You, You great blustering fool. You need not yell.* Instead, he hurried to Death's side and bowed. "I am here, my Lord."

"Excellent. I need rope—as long as we have. Get it. Now."

Thaddeus bowed again and scrambled back to his Hunters. "The God needs rope. Immediately."

Wilson nodded and bared his teeth in a Terrier-like smile. "We have rope. We use it to make snares."

"Get it. Tie it together so that it is as long as possible. Hurry," said Thaddeus. "Then bring it to me. I will be with the God."

Thaddeus scrambled back to Death, Who had stopped pacing and was squinting through the swirling snow and the grayness of morning at the opposite side of the gorge.

"My Hunters will bring You the rope, my Lord," said Thaddeus.

"*My* Hunters," Death corrected him, but without His usual malice.

"Yes, of course, my Lord," Thaddeus agreed quickly. Then, because the God seemed distracted enough that He might actually answer a question, he asked, "I know You must have a plan, my Lord. Will You share it with me?"

Death glanced down at Thaddeus and smiled. "I believe I shall surprise you."

That worried Thaddeus as much as it intrigued him, but all he could do was nod and bow—and wait for *his* Hunters to bring rope, which they did quickly.

"Ah, excellent," Death said as He tested the knots in the long length of braided hemp Wilson delivered to Him. "Now, which of the people who used to belong to the Tribe of the Trees is the best climber?"

"The best climber?" Thaddeus repeated.

"That is what I said. Is your hearing failing?" Death stared down at Thaddeus.

"Not at all, my Lord . . ." Thaddeus paused as he considered. Then he answered the God honestly, "Jason is the slightest of the Hunters. He easily scales trees. I say he is the best climber of the Tribe of the Trees." *Or at least of those who are left alive and with me*, he added silently.

"Hunter Jason, to Me," Death commanded.

On all fours, Jason scrambled up to Death. He cringed and bowed low before the God, his forehead pressed into the snow. "Yes, my Lord?"

"I need you to climb."

Jason looked up at the God. "Climb? There is an absence of trees here, my Lord."

"Then it is good that I do not need you to climb a tree," said Death.

"What shall I climb, my Lord?" Jason asked.

Death's smile was fierce. He pointed at the dangling bridge. "That. You shall scale the broken bridge." The God lifted the end of the rope. "You need not go far. Just a third of the way down it will be enough. Then I shall feed this rope to you. You will tie it securely around the bridge and simply climb back up."

"I do not understand, my Lord," said Jason.

Death's look darkened. "Do you understand that you must scale the broken bridge, tie the rope to it, and then return?"

"Y-yes, my Lord."

"Then that is all you must understand."

Jason looked over the edge of the gorge and shuddered. "But I might fall."

"I command that you do not unless you have already tied to the rope to the bridge. I will be quite annoyed should you fail me in this, Hunter," said Death.

Thaddeus could not stop himself from speaking up. *Was this fool really going to send one of my Hunters to a meaningless death?* "My Lord, I think—"

Death spun around and backhanded Thaddeus, knocking him into the rocky side of the mountain. "You do not think. I do." Then Death turned to the Hunter who trembled before His cloven hooves. "Climb!"

Jason nodded and drew a deep, shaky breath, and then on all fours he crawled to the edge of the gorge. He turned and his gaze lifted to beseech the God silently.

"Do it. Now," Death commanded.

Slowly, Jason descended over the sharp edge. Thaddeus crawled back to Death's side so that he could watch his Hunter as he disappeared.

"That is excellent," said Death as He peered down at Jason. "Keep climbing. I will tell you when to halt."

Time seemed to pass slowly as Jason carefully climbed down the ladder-like bridge. Thaddeus was amazed that he was able to find toeholds in the slats. Twice, the Hunter slipped so that he dangled, clutching the frozen bridge with hands white with cold and fear.

Silently, Jason's Companion, Midnight, a solid black Terrier, joined Thaddeus. The little canine stared over the edge with no expression, making no sound, as Jason continued to climb.

"There, that is far enough!" Death shouted against the wind. He wrapped one end of the rope around His thick waist. The other end He fed down to Jason. "Take the rope. Tie it securely to the bridge."

Jason looked up and nodded jerkily as Death let the rope down to him. The small Hunter wrapped his legs through the thick suspension ropes that served as rail and support for the bridge. Thaddeus thought Jason looked almost like the monkeys that lived on the ruins that jutted from the surface of Lost Lake as he clung to the bridge. He was actually able to free his hands enough so that when the rope reached him Jason quickly and efficiently tied it to the thick, braided cable.

Then he looked up at the God, baring his teeth in a wide smile. "It is done!"

"Well done. You may climb up now," said the God.

Jason began scrambling up, but after climbing just a few feet his toe slipped from the ice on a wooden slat. He hung by his hands for a moment. Even through the snow and morning gloom, Thaddeus could see that Jason's arms trembled with exhaustion. One hand let loose. Jason stared up. He met Thaddeus's gaze.

"Help me!" Jason cried just before the grip of his second hand failed, and with an agonized shout he fell.

Beside Thaddeus, Midnight stood very still—like a carving of a Terrier—for several long moments, and then the little canine's body jerked as if someone had hit him. He whined pitifully, drew in a ragged breath, and stepped silently over the edge of the gorge to follow his Companion.

Behind them, the Terriers raised their muzzles to the whitewashed sky and howled miserably.

"Shut them up, Hunter, or I will toss each of them over the edge," said Death.

Thaddeus raced back to his group of Hunters. Their canines were still huddled together, several feet from their Companions, howling.

"If they do not shut up, Death will be sure they follow Midnight," Thaddeus told his men, who immediately went to their Terriers, cuffed them on the side of their heads, and demanded, "*Enough!*"

The little canines went silent, but their gazes, filled with sadness and condemnation, never left their Companions.

I do not like it, Odysseus. I do not like what is happening to the Terriers.

But Thaddeus had no more time to consider the changes in the canines. Death was suddenly there on the path. The thick rope was wrapped around His waist. His cloven hooves bit the hard-packed snow as He moved away from the edge of the gorge, step by step, drawing the massive suspension bridge up with Him. Death kept trudging until the top third of the bridge rested up on the trail.

Then the God returned to the edge of the ravine. He bent, took the broken bridge in His massive fists, and hand over hand the God of Death pulled the entire rest of it up onto the trail until it was piled atop itself—an enormous mound of frozen wood and rope.

"*Thaddeus, to Me!*" Death roared.

Fighting a terrible feeling of foreboding, Thaddeus joined the God.

"Do you understand yet?" Death asked him.

"No, my Lord. Your wits are beyond mine. All I see is a pile of useless wood and rope."

"Watch and learn. Watch and learn." The God untied the knot Jason had made. With the rope in hand, He went to Thaddeus. "Stand like a man—unless you've forgotten how."

Painfully, Thaddeus forced his bowed spine to straighten as he faced the God, Who had made a noose-like loop in one end of the rope. He slipped it over Thaddeus's head and tightened it around his waist.

Thaddeus staggered back a step. "My Lord?"

"Oh, do not fear, Thaddeus. You are not as expendable as the other Hunters. I shall take care you do not follow Jason. Your death is not required—not yet." Death quickly and efficiently tied the other end of the rope tightly to the end of the bridge close to the frayed cable Daniel had so recently sawed through, so that Thaddeus could not move without the huge suspension bridge moving with him. "There. I have secured you to the bridge. The bridge is secured to this side of the gorge." Death pointed to the anchors. "All you need do is not slip backwards once you are on the other side, but if you do you shall not die. I will simply pull you up and we will begin again and again until we get it right, and when you do get it right anchor the bridge well enough that I can cross safely. I shall then join you and secure it so that the rest of the army may cross after us."

There was a strange humming in Thaddeus's head. Sweat had broken on his face and ran like melted ice down his neck and chest. "I—I still do not understand, my Lord."

"You shall. You shall. Now, as I said, do not slip backwards." Death grabbed Thaddeus by the fur that sprouted thick and Terrier-like at the scruff of the back of his neck, and lifted him so that He could also grab Thaddeus's leg. Then, as the Hunter whined in terror, with preternatural strength Death swung him once, twice, thrice—and released him so that he soared across the gorge, the broken end of the bridge strapped to and following him.

Thaddeus had no time to think. He could only act on instinct. He hit the far side of the trail so hard that the air was knocked from him. He expected to be pulled back and down with the broken bridge, but the God's aim was as true as His incredible strength. Enough of the bridge fell beside him that it piled on the wide landing and didn't automatically fall back.

"*Anchor it, Hunter. Now!*" the God roared.

Gasping for air and holding one arm tightly against what he was pretty sure were several broken ribs, Thaddeus crawled to the boulders that had been placed as anchors for the original bridge supports. Forcing himself to continue to move, Thaddeus painfully slipped the rope from around his waist. He flicked the rope out, so that the noose was wide enough to fit over the top of the boulder. It settled around the frozen rock and snapped taut as the bridge began to slide back down into the abyss.

"*Well done, Hunter.*" The God grasped the rope rail and started across, hand over hand, the rest of His massive body swaying in the snowy wind as He crossed the gorge.

Thaddeus watched the God dangling from the bridge, and hoped beyond all hope that His grip would tire and He would join Jason and Midnight at the bottom of the gorge. He even briefly considered pulling the noose from around the boulder so that He would fall.

But Thaddeus did nothing. It was not possible to kill the God of Death. Trying would only enrage Him and make Thaddeus the target of that rage.

No, Thaddeus would wait. He would survive. And someday he would take his Hunters and make a new Tribe as far from Death as the Wind Rider Plains allowed—and Thaddeus already knew those plains stretched on so wide and so vast that he could easily settle well away from Death and the rest of His horrible army.

We will survive, my Odysseus. We will survive Death.

The doe roused them the next morning before sunrise. They quickly heated the watery soup made from rabbit bones and handfuls of juniper berries and broke their fast, and then they trudged after the doe, who did not return to the wide main trail. Instead, she headed up the side of the mountain, sloughing through the snow, displacing it just long enough for the two humans and their Companions to follow before white covered everything again.

This time she led them in a serpentine pattern in a northeasterly direction, and she pushed them harder than before. Time lost meaning. Ralina could not keep track of what day it was. All she or Renard had energy to do was follow the doe, gut and skin or pluck whatever game miraculously ran across their path, and keep moving, always moving, past sunset to begin again before sunrise.

Ralina couldn't tell if it was still snowing, or if the unending white that swirled around them came from the massive drifts the doe displaced. It really didn't matter. What mattered was that they put one foot before another and did not give up.

Though Ralina listened closely, and even asked Bear, with his superior canine senses of hearing and smell, to alert her the moment he caught sound or scent of Death and His army, Bear did not alert her—nor did Kong. And Ralina heard no more unnatural bellows drifting with the snow behind them.

"We haven't heard any sign of Death for days. Bear and Kong haven't scented or heard Him, either. Maybe your father cutting the bridge stopped the army completely," Ralina said one night to Renard before they gave way to exhaustion and slept.

"With all of my heart I hope so, but I think were that true the doe would not be pushing us so hard to get through the last of these mountains." Renard held her close as they talked softly, not wanting to wake either of their sleeping Companions.

Ralina sighed. "You're right. I just want it to be over. I want to be free of Him."

Renard kissed the top of her head. "We are free of Him. We have been from the moment we followed the doe away from His army."

"But to be truly free of Him we must reach the Wind Riders before His army does," said Ralina as she snuggled wearily against Renard.

"We will. I believe it with every fiber of my being. Sleep now. The doe will wake soon."

The next morning felt different from the very beginning. As had become their norm, the doe woke them before sunrise. They ate whatever was left from their evening meal and then followed the doe from their impromptu shelter. The first difference came when the doe led them down instead of up. They were still headed into the east, but now their serpentine path wound in a descending pattern along the side of the white-faced mountain.

The second difference was that around midday the fitful snow was replaced by rain—steady, soggy, cold rain.

This descent felt quicker, easier than the one that had led them to the gorge bridge, but it was still exhausting to slide and stumble, trudge and slip behind the doe, especially in the constant rain. While it was nice to be out of the snow, the rain turned the ground to mud and muck, soaked them, and made travel as miserable as it was treacherous.

Shortly after midday Ralina was so focused on staying on her feet and keeping them moving, one step and then another, that at first she didn't realize when their descent was over. She had no idea how long they'd been walking on level ground, surrounded by tall pines and winter-naked aspens, when Renard touched her arm to pull her to a halt.

Ralina wiped rain from her face. "What?" She squinted ahead, looking for their faithful doe, but though the muddy path they'd been following was clear, she didn't see the doe. "Where is she?" Ralina's eyes scanned the forest. "Did we lose her?"

"I don't believe we could lose her—not unless she wanted to be lost. She's probably just ahead past those trees, but look at Bear and Kong," Renard said.

Ralina's weary gaze easily found their Companions, who were not far ahead of them on the path. Both Shepherds had stopped. Their ears were pricked and their tails were lifted as they stood silent and tense, staring ahead.

"Bear? What is it?" Ralina reached out through the bond they shared. Bear had never been very articulate, but he was excellent at understanding her and sending her feelings that allowed her to understand him. As she relaxed and found their bond, Bear flooded her with excitement and anticipation—and some nervousness, too. She glanced up at Renard. "He's excited, but I can't tell about what. What's Kong say?"

Renard shrugged one shoulder. "Like Bear, Kong doesn't actually say much, but I'm getting the same excitement from him. Maybe you and Bear should stay here, on this side of the aspen grove. Kong and I will scout ahead. I'll see where the doe has gotten off to. You know she usually isn't far."

"No, Renard. I don't think we should separate. We need to stay together. I can't lose—"

Her words broke off as the two canines backed to their Companions. Bear whined and Kong barked twice—and then the outlines of huge beasts materialized in the gloom, creatures who moved quickly toward them, plowing through the mud and rain as if it was nothing.

Ralina stumbled back several steps with Renard. "Bear, Kong, stay close!"

The Shepherds pressed against their Companions' sides but showed little aggression, though they thrummed with excitement.

Ralina shielded her eyes with her hand and blinked against the rain—and the group of creatures got close enough to be identifiable.

"Oh, Great Goddess of Life," she murmured as her legs went numb with relief and she staggered to her knees. "Wind Riders! We did it! We found them!"

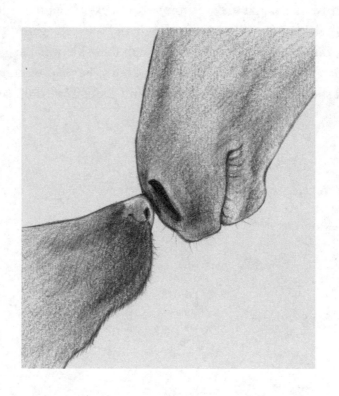

CHAPTER 23

The Wind Riders weren't as friendly as Ralina had hoped they would be, but at least they hadn't tied them up and were willing to listen to her. They were already aware that an army was on its way to their lands. Ralina knew that meant at least some of Nik and Mari's group had made it through the mountains, though Clayton ignored her questions about them.

Ralina understood that their sudden appearance ahead of Death's army must seem suspicious. She and Renard could be scouts or spies—that would be a rational assumption, especially as these Riders did not seem to comprehend that the army was filled with mutants and the dead.

"Please listen to me. Renard and I escaped Death's army to warn you," Ralina repeated.

"Oh, I hear you," said Clayton as the rest of his Herd listened silently. "But hearing and believing are different things. Believing comes with trust—or proof."

"We understand that perfectly," Renard said. "We watched as our Tribe, mighty and prosperous, was decimated and then utterly destroyed by the arrogance and selfishness of one man. It seemed impossible to us, too."

Clayton lifted his chin. His face lost all expression. "Are you calling me arrogant and selfish?"

Renard shook his head. "Absolutely not. What we're trying to get you to see is how easy it was for Death to infiltrate our Tribe and destroy us from within *because we refused to heed the warnings we had.*"

"We don't want the same thing to happen to your plains and your people," said Ralina.

"And you're telling me that the only reason the God didn't infect you and somehow cause you to mutate is because you're a Storyteller?" Clayton scoffed. "It doesn't seem probable."

"Death didn't infect me because of His enormous ego. It is important to Him that tales are told of His magnificence and songs are sung about His glory. I convinced Him to allow me to remain as I am, because otherwise I would not be able to properly tell His story or create ballads of His victories." Ralina kept a tight hold on the irritation that threatened to creep into her voice, though she was growing more and more frustrated by this Wind Rider's disbelieving attitude.

"And what of Renard? Is he, too, a Storyteller?" Clayton asked.

"No," Renard responded. "Ralina saved my father and me from infection by beseeching the God to allow us to remain as we are so we could serve her—and in so doing that Ralina could better serve Death."

"And, Clayton, let me be very clear—it isn't just disease that Death brought to the Hunters and Warriors of our Tribe," Ralina explained carefully. "It begins as a disease—a sickness that at first seems like a nasty cold. Then boils form on the skin. Eventually the skin sloughs off, leaving gaping wounds until it eventually kills.

"Then Death brought what He called a cure to our people, beginning with Thaddeus, the selfish, arrogant man of whom Renard spoke earlier," said Ralina.

"And this cure actually causes a mutation?" Another Stallion Rider who had been introduced to them as Rand spoke up. He'd been the one to suggest to Clayton that they pitch a shelter and build a fire so that they could interrogate Ralina and Renard out of the pelting rain.

Ralina nodded, eager to speak with someone who seemed more willing to listen. "Yes. To cure the sickness Death filleted sections of skin from the Tribesmen's living Companions—Shepherds like Bear and Kong . . ." She paused to nod at the Shepherds, who lay still and watching by their sides. "And smaller Companions, canines called Terriers."

Rand shuddered. "And they allowed their Companions to be abused like that?"

"That's where Thaddeus came in." Ralina continued to explain. "He had been sick, and then he seemed cured. When others fell ill it was easy for him to convince many of them to take the same cure—convince them it's what their Companions would want because without the cure they would die.

"But it isn't really a cure," said Ralina. "It begins a change that is horrible. Thaddeus and his men are becoming more and more canine-like, though without the grace and compassion, beauty and kindness, of canines."

Renard took up the telling then. "What they are becoming is bestial— not human and not animal, but something horribly *other.*"

"And what of their Companions?" asked a young woman who stood beside a female horse the brownish red of fall leaves. "Did they die?"

"No, but they, too, seem to be changing," said Ralina. "Not in appearance. They did not get ill and they are not mutating, but their attitude toward their Companions has very obviously changed."

Renard nodded. "Yes, it was more and more apparent just before we escaped. Their canines preferred to remain in packs—sleeping, eating, and hunting with other canines instead of their Companions."

"And that is unusual behavior in a canine Companion?" asked Rand.

"Absolutely," said Ralina. She reached down to stroke Bear's wide, intelligent head. He pressed against her leg and his tail thumped the damp ground. "After they Choose us, our Companions rarely leave our side."

Rand nodded and petted the neck of the big stallion who stood close to him. "That is how it is for our Companions as well."

"Your Companions are magnificent," said Ralina.

"Truly," added Renard. "We have heard tales of Wind Riders and seen depictions of them in the work of our artists who have journeyed to your plains, but nothing compares to seeing them in person."

"They are magnificent, indeed." Clayton stroked the flank of his big black stallion.

"Too magnificent to fall prey to what Death has planned for you Wind Riders," said Ralina. "He spoke of it frequently. He said He learned from poisoning our forest. He will not make the same mistake here, as He intends to rule your plains." Clayton snorted a sarcastic laugh, but she kept speaking. "Instead, He will capture a few of you, infect you with the skin-sloughing disease, and then force you to take the cure. Death is intrigued by what it would do to a human to be merged with a horse. Actually, I expect that He plans on absorbing a horse within Himself. I watched Him become stag-like, and then the stag was not powerful enough for Him, so He killed a bison bull, ate his still-beating heart, and absorbed his essence. Then I watched Him become bull-like." She met Clayton's dubious gaze. "I do not want to watch Him become stallion-like."

"What you are describing is difficult to believe," said Clayton.

"Indeed," agreed Ralina. "Had I not seen it for myself I, too, would be uncertain of the veracity of what we've told you. But I *have* seen it for myself. I lived through the nightmare of it so that I could bear witness to it."

"As have I," said Renard. "This journey has cost me almost everything I have ever loved." He had to clear his throat before he continued. "My father was with us. He even escaped the army with us. Several days ago we came to a suspension bridge that spanned a huge gorge. After we crossed it Death's army approached. My father gave his life to destroy the bridge and buy us enough time to flee so that we could warn you—so that you would not suffer the same fate as the Tribe of the Trees."

"I know that bridge," said Rand. "Two years ago I became friendly with a Lynx Guide, and I traveled with him from our plains to that suspension bridge. It is truly no more?"

"My father cut through the last of the ropes anchoring it as Death rained spears and arrows into him—and killed him," said Renard.

"How did you get away from Death and His army?" Clayton asked.

"The Goddess of Life sent me a dream. In the dream She showed me a white doe appearing in the middle of a snowstorm and told me to follow the doe—that it was time I left Death." Ralina wiped wearily at the rain that dripped from her hair down her face. "The next day it began to snow and the doe appeared. We followed her, and she led us up into the mountains and away from Death."

"And where is that white doe now?" Clayton said.

"She disappeared just before you found us," said Ralina. "Please believe us. Death destroyed our Tribe and our homelands, and He means to destroy your people, too. He says He will not poison the plains, but how will He control the spread of the skin-sloughing disease once it is loosed?"

She shook her head. "I do not believe He can or will. The disease does not hurt Him. He eats tainted meat and it does nothing to Him. And He is amused by the mutations happening to the Tribesmen. I can only imagine how much it would amuse Him to watch Wind Riders mutate." Ralina shuddered.

"This is all difficult to believe," said Clayton.

"But it wouldn't be should we see this army ourselves," said Rand. "The suspension bridge is just a few days' travel into the main Rock Mountain pass, and you say the bridge has been severed. Perhaps we should travel there and behold this army for ourselves."

"Death won't remain trapped on the other side of that gorge." Ralina's voice had taken on a hard edge. She was exhausted. She'd risked everything to get to these people and warn them, and they didn't believe her. "He will find some way to either repair the bridge or He will discover a different crossing place. He always finds a way. If you travel on the main trail, it is very likely you will see His army—as they capture you, infect you, and flay the flesh from your Companions to pack into your wounds."

"Did you not follow the main path through the mountains?" Clayton said.

"When we were with the army we did," said Ralina. "But to escape them the doe led us to paths that were so narrow and treacherous the army could not possibly have followed. It kept us ahead of them so that we arrived here first."

"Then call your goddess's doe." Clayton's voice was tinged with sarcasm. "Surely she can lead us into the mountains to a place we can safely glimpse this mutant army."

"I did not call her to begin with!" Ralina shouted in frustration. "The Goddess sent her to me. And the army isn't just made of mutants. It's also made of the reanimated dead bodies of the people they killed as they traveled to the mountains—more than a thousand of them! It is worse than you can comprehend. That is why we had to warn you. Why would we lie? Why would we make up a story like this?"

Clayton shrugged. "You are a Storyteller, are you not?"

Ralina stared at him, and within his eyes she saw an all too familiar arrogance. "I would like to speak with your ruling Council," she said. "Please."

Clayton laughed. "Oh, you won't find any of those old women near here. Herd Ebony does things differently. We don't follow the rules of crones and mares. We are ruled by the strength of stallions instead."

Renard touched Ralina's shoulder gently. "They are going to have to see to believe."

Ralina drew in a deep breath and exhaled it slowly. Then she met Clayton's gaze. "Then follow the main trail back into the mountains, but take only a couple men with you and leave your Companions here. While you do that Renard and I ask to be given directions to the ruling Council for the rest of the Wind Riders so that we may warn them."

Clayton scratched his chin. "We will enter the mountains, but we will not be separated from our Companions and Herd Ebony stays together. You will join us. If the army is as you say it is, we will happily give you directions to the archaic Mare Council. And while you flee to them Herd Ebony will skillfully attack Death's army, which should slow their progress out of the mountains."

Ralina shook her head incredulously as her gaze touched on the Wind Riders surrounding her. She counted a couple dozen people and horses. "You cannot fight an army with so few."

Clayton waved his hand dismissively. "Not face-to-face, but we know stealth. And we are experts with the bow. We can pick them off one at a time from a distance."

"Do you know the different roles of our canine Companions?" asked Renard.

"I know your big Shepherd Companions are Warriors," said Rand. "We have had them visit Herd Cinnabar with their Companions to train with our Warriors."

"Yes, Shepherds are Warriors," explained Renard. "Terriers are our other Companion canines. They are smaller than the Shepherds, and their greatest skill is in hunting and tracking. Many of the Tribe of the Trees members who followed Thaddeus and took the cure are Companions of Terriers—Hunters—who now are developing the ability to scent and track as well as their canines."

"He tells you this because they will come after you," said Ralina. "Thaddeus and his Hunters will track you, capture you, and infect you."

"You do not know us," said Clayton. "You do not know our skills. You do not know of the swiftness of our horses. You do not understand how well we know our land. You do not know any of these things, yet you sound completely convinced these mutants can overwhelm us."

"That is correct. I do not have to know any of those things about you," said Ralina—her voice like iron. "Yet I am completely convinced Death's army will overwhelm you if you go into the mountains and attack Him because I know the God of Death."

"Well, then, we shall have to see who is right and who is wrong, won't we?" Clayton made it clear his question was rhetorical by standing and clapping his hands together as if they had just had a lovely conversation about whether the rain would end soon or not. "It is too late to begin a mountain trek today, so let us camp here for the night. We have venison steaks to grill and ale to drink."

Ralina stared at Clayton. His demeanor had completely changed. Gone was the sarcasm and disbelief, and in its place was a lightheartedness that utterly baffled her.

"Oh," Clayton continued. "Many of us have never seen a canine until now, and my Bard tells me that several of the horses are very curious about them. Would they mind meeting our Companions?"

Ralina mentally shook herself. This man could not be reasoned with, but it would be unwise to make an outright enemy of him, especially as she and Renard, Bear and Kong, were their captives.

"Bear and Kong, would you like to greet the horses and their Riders?" asked Ralina.

Bear barked happily, and Kong wagged his tail and whined with excitement.

"That is a yes from both," said Ralina. "And I would love to be introduced to your horses." Her smile was authentic as her gaze went from Clayton's stallion to Rand's gray Merlin. Both horses had pricked their ears and were studying the two Shepherds.

"I have to say that I am intrigued by your horses, too," said Renard. "I would like to touch one, if that is allowed."

"It is definitely allowed." Clayton laughed magnanimously. "Herd Ebony, let us make camp and properly welcome our guests to the Plains of the Wind Riders."

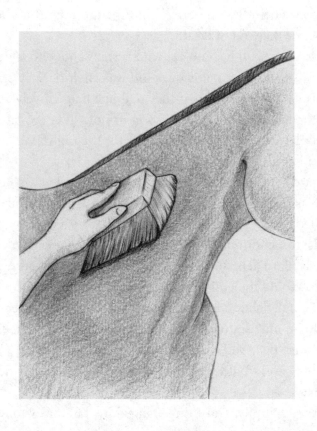

CHAPTER 24

U sed to rising early with the magickal white doe, Ralina woke before
dawn. She expected the camp to be stirring, but only a single Rider
tended the large central fire. Everyone else, even the horses, slept under
the interesting rain shelters the Riders had draped between trees. It was
still raining, so Ralina lifted her hood against the wet, motioned for Bear
to remain curled beside Kong and Renard, and joined the Rider at the fire.

Rand looked up and smiled a welcome. "Good morning, Storyteller."

"Good morning, Rand." Ralina looked around the silent camp. "When
will they wake? The earlier we begin the better. There is no way for us to
know how long it took Death to figure out how to cross that gorge. He
could still be there—or He could only be a day behind us."

Rand's sigh was weary. "Yes, I am aware of that and I agree with you
that we should be on our way soon, but I am not the leader of this Herd.
Clayton tends to sleep in." He stood and took a wooden mug from a bowl
of them near the fire. He dumped out the rainwater, poured steaming tea
into it from a pot that rested in the embers of the campfire, and offered it
to Ralina. "There will be soup to break your fast as well. It is almost warm
enough." He pointed at one of the two cauldrons suspended over the fire.

Ralina took the mug and sipped the strong tea slowly as Rand scooted
over and made room on his log for her to sit. Hanging above him was a
tarp that caught most of the unending drizzle.

"Rand, I need to speak with you about something. Perhaps you can advise me on how best to talk with Clayton about it," said Ralina.

"If it is about the army, I can tell you that Clayton has decided to enter the pass and nothing will dissuade him."

"Yes, he made that clear last night." Ralina sighed. "Sadly, I have already come to understand that I cannot convince him otherwise. But here's the thing—I cannot get near Death and His army ever again. Neither can Renard, Bear, or Kong. We will enter the pass with your people, but at the first sight or sign of the army we will stop."

Rand nodded. "That is understandable. Death will surely kill you should He capture you."

"Death will not kill me. He will do worse. He will kill Renard and Kong. He will torture my Bear." Ralina met Rand's gaze and read compassion and sadness there. "If it means Clayton kills us when we refuse to go farther into the mountains, then so be it. That fate is kinder than the one Death holds for us."

Rand nodded. "I understand. Let me handle Clayton."

There was a rustling in the soggy ferns and grasses that dotted the forest floor, and two large dark shapes ambled to the fire. Rand smiled warmly at his stallion. "Yes, my Merlin, I know you want your warm mash—and Bard as well."

"Can you talk to Merlin *and* Bard?" Ralina asked as Clayton's big black stallion, who was decidedly friendlier than his Rider, touched his velvet muzzle to her shoulder in greeting and allowed her to gently stroke him.

"Anyone can talk to a horse," said Rand as he stood and began mixing grains from two bags kept dry under the shelter into two large wooden bowls. "But only the horse's Companion can hear his or her response. Merlin told me that Bard is hungry, too."

"It's the same with canines," said Ralina. "Though they vary vastly in how articulate they are. My Bear understands everything I say, but he rarely speaks to me in words. Most often he sends me feelings and sometimes images. It is the same with Kong and Renard, though some of our Tribe's Companions are, or were, much more talkative."

"That's how it is with our horses. Merlin speaks to me in words—a lot of words actually." Rand grinned and patted his stallion's flank before he took a second pot that steamed over the fire and added the hot water to the two grain bowls, and continued to stir them with a long wooden spoon. He glanced up at Bard, who had remained by Ralina's side so she could caress his sleek neck. "He likes you."

Ralina felt a rush of happy surprise. "Really? Did he tell Merlin that?"

Rand chuckled. "No. I don't need Merlin to tell me that." Merlin butted Rand, making his Rider laugh outright. "But I do need him to tell me lots of things."

Ralina stood slowly and Bard lipped her hair gently. Her laughter joined Rand's. "Does he eat hair?"

"No, he's just playing with you." Rand put down the bowl he'd been mixing and reached into a travel pack that rested behind the log. He pulled out a wide, soft brush and tossed it to Ralina. "Bard would like it if you'd groom him. Horses like to be brushed."

Ralina touched the bristles woven into the wooden brush. "What is this?"

Rand's grin widened. "Horsehair. From their manes and tails. What better for brushing horses?"

"Huh. That makes sense. Um, how do I brush him?"

"Just go with his coat, not against it. Be firm but not rough. Bard will show you. If you're doing it right, his body will relax. He may smack his lips, though probably not, as he'll be eating his mash once it cools enough." Rand began stirring the two mixtures again. "You'll see. It's really not difficult."

Ralina decided that grooming Bard was the most enjoyable, relaxing thing she'd done in months. She worked her way along the big stallion's body, running her hand along his sleek ebony coat after the brush. She didn't speak, and neither did Rand, who, after he gave both horses their mash, began grooming Merlin. Ralina thought she could stay like that forever—under the rain shelter—near a campfire with her loved ones safely sleeping close by while this incredible horse allowed her to brush her stress away.

"Oh, sure. I'm up and *now* you're quiet?" At the sound of Clayton's voice Bard's head jerked up and his ears pricked. He nickered a sweet greeting to his Rider, but Clayton ignored him and frowned at Ralina. "We allow our guests to sleep in the morning." Though he clearly meant that his guests were expected to be quiet and allow *him* to sleep.

Ralina's hand still rested on Bard's flank, so she felt the stallion's body tense at his Rider's admonishment. She patted Bard gently once more and whispered, "Thank you for letting me groom you. You are magnificent." Before she strode to Rand's pack and dropped the brush back inside it. Then she turned to Clayton. "Good morning. Forgive me if I woke you. I have not had reason to laugh for quite some time. Your beautiful stallion lightened my mood, though I would have stifled my laughter had I not thought your camp was already waking. It is dawn and by your own decision we will travel today."

Clayton barely glanced at her as he picked up a bowl and began ladling soup into it. Then he cleared his throat and shouted, "Herd Ebony, let's go! We move out as soon as we break our fast."

As the camp began to awaken and Rand ladled soup for her, Ralina ate and thought how very much she hoped Clayton was not the norm for Wind Rider leaders.

The rain remained a constant companion as the group of Wind Riders and deposed Tribe of the Trees members made their way through a lush green valley into which a wide trail from the heart of the Rock Mountains emptied. To make better time, Ralina rode double behind Clayton and Renard rode behind Rand.

Ralina had been shocked when Clayton offered to allow her to ride with him, but Rand quietly told her that Bard had volunteered to carry her—just as Merlin had said he would be happy to carry Renard. Some of the stress of returning to the mountains was easier to bear for Ralina because of Bard. She sat carefully behind Clayton—not wanting to touch him and also not wanting to do anything that would bother the beautiful and kind stallion—but she often stroked his smooth coat and marveled at his strength. Bear trotted easily beside Bard, and Kong kept pace with Merlin. Ralina didn't even mind the constant cold rain. The warmth from Bard buoyed her spirits, and the few times the horses broke from their ground-eating trot to a canter—and once even a gallop—Ralina wanted to laugh aloud with joy at the speed, though she didn't. Clayton would not have been amused. She didn't think Clayton would be amused by anything.

The path that they followed into the Rock Mountains was wide and muddy, and Ralina was grateful she and Renard weren't sloughing through it on foot—though it was far easier to traverse than the threads of deer paths the doe had led them on.

Travel was so much faster on horseback! Far faster than the army had ever moved, and Ralina felt a little better about their chances of fleeing Death should they view Him from a distance.

At midday when they halted briefly to eat and feed and rest the horses, Ralina remained near the stallion, frequently stroking his coat as he ate while she stretched muscles already sore from the half-day ride. Bear rested close by, under the thick boughs of an evergreen, with Kong beside him. Renard decided his sore muscles required more than a stretch, so he walked briskly a little way up and down the wide path, though when he spoke about Merlin he had only praise for the stallion's power and speed—and good humor about his aching muscles.

Rand came to Clayton, who had allowed Ralina to mix Bard's sweet mash and feed it to him. His eyes were bright as he spoke, and he grinned at Ralina often.

"As we move more into the mountains I'm remembering more and more of the trip I took with the Lynx Guide, and I have an idea that I think will be helpful," said Rand to Clayton.

"What is it?" asked Clayton as he chewed on smoked venison strips.

"When we get a little higher into the mountains, the pass will change from this wide trail to a path that hugs the side of the mountains. I re-member because the Guide told me that there are deer paths that lead through the heart of the mountains; though the going is steep, it is actu-ally a faster way to cross than the main pass."

Clayton shrugged. "How does that help us?"

"We don't want to come face-to-face with Death's army. We just want to see where it is and *what* it is. We can do that safely from a distance if we are above the pass. So, when the trail changes, instead of continu-ing to follow it we should climb up. From high up within the mountains we'll have a good view of the main pass, which we can follow from above. When the army comes into sight, we will be able to watch and evaluate them, but from a distance," Rand concluded.

Clayton shrugged again. "That makes sense, though if the going is too rough we'll have to return to the main trail."

"Or we wait above. Death will come to you, versus you endangering yourself and your Herd by going to Him," said Ralina.

Clayton's voice hardened. "Like I said, it makes sense as long as the going isn't too rough for the horses. And let's move. All this talking isn't getting us anywhere."

As Rand passed by her, Ralina smiled and nodded her thanks to him before Clayton remounted Bard and Renard boosted her up behind him.

It didn't take long for them to come to the part of the pass Rand had described—where it changed from a wide, ascending road to a narrower trail that curved, hugging the mountain on one side with a sheer drop-off on the other. Ralina's stomach tightened. It was much like the part of the pass the army had plodded through, following a god who cared more about His own desires than those under His care.

"There!" Rand shouted as he pointed at a narrow, muddy path that was more a water runoff than actual trail. "I recognize this as where the Guide said he could break off and head up to a faster, though more treacherous, pass through the mountains."

"We'll try it, but like I said, if it gets too rough, we return to the main trail," said Clayton. Over his shoulder he told Ralina, "You'll need to hold on. This is going to be steep. Try not to slide off. It'll upset Bard if you do."

Ralina glanced at Renard, who was chuckling as he wrapped his arms around Rand's waist. For a moment she was envious that her lover got to ride with someone so much more pleasant than Clayton, but then she stroked Bard's sleek coat, and the big stallion turned his head so that he could meet her gaze. She saw such warmth and kindness and understanding there that she patted him again and then, without complaint, held tightly on to Clayton's waist.

It was a lot more difficult to stay astride Bard as he climbed the steep, narrow trail than it had been when they were on the wider, main part of the pass. The horses had to go single file, with Bard leading. As Ralina became more confident in her seat, she was able to loosen her hold on Clayton and look around. This part of the mountains hadn't been blanketed by snow—or at least not yet it hadn't been—but it was soggy from days of rain. Mud splashed under Bard's hooves. Ralina wanted to ask Clayton questions about Bard and the other horses, as well as the other Wind Rider Herds, but the one time she attempted to draw him into conversation his responses were so gruff and monosyllabic that she gave up and instead focused on the mountain and the amazing creature she rode.

It was midafternoon when everything changed forever.

Bard had just climbed a particularly steep area of the slender path and come to a spot that was surprisingly level. Ralina was just going to ask Clayton if they could stop for a moment so she could relieve herself and walk around to restore feeling in her numb legs and feet when Clayton pulled Bard up sharply.

"Is that the army?" He leaned to the side so she could see around him.

Ralina peered through the drizzle to see that the pass stretched below them. It clung to the side of the huge range of mountains in tiers, winding around, going up and up. In the distance she could see that it changed from mud to a blanket of thick white. She could even see that it was still snowing in the higher altitudes.

And there, like a stain on the pass, was Death's army—led by the glowing spirit of the bison bull. Behind the bull's spirit was a line of living bison who were plowing their way through the snow—and still farther back was Death, leading the mutants and His Milks. Even from this distance Ralina could see His horns and the immense size of Him. The God made everyone around Him, even the mighty bison, look like children. If she squinted hard enough, she could even see someone she thought was probably Thaddeus. The evil little man was close behind Death, walking so stooped that every so often he dropped to all fours so that, canine-like, he padded after his master. After him came a group of similarly hunched men and then their canines, who followed grouped together, not by their Companions' sides. Lastly the Milks paced, their ranks stretching out of view along the winding pass.

Ralina had to swallow the bile that suddenly filled her mouth before she could speak. "Yes. That is Death. That is His army, and we need to get the horses behind that clump of trees and stay low. If He sees us, you are worse than dead."

Clayton grunted a response and kneed Bard over to a group of tall pines that grew straight and proud on the flattened part of the mountainside. They dismounted and Clayton hurried to meet the rest of the Herd as they climbed up the trail, motioning for them to take the horses to the trees. When they were out of sight, Ralina and Renard joined Clayton and

Rand as they crouched behind a group of boulders to stare down at the distant army.

"What is that leading them?" Clayton asked.

"It's the spirit of a bison bull Death killed and then bound to Him to be the army's guide through the pass," said Ralina.

"But those are living bison behind it," said Rand.

Renard stared at the line of bulls. "They were not with the army when we escaped it."

"Death called them." Ralina's voice was strained. She felt as if her throat was closing. "If He has a link to them, He can command animals to Him. He called the bison bull to Him, and then killed him and ate his heart. Even from here you can see that He isn't human. Look at His horns—at His size. He's grown larger even than He was when last we saw Him. The bull He killed was enormous—like a king bison—so now Death must have command over the other bulls."

"They are plowing a way through the snow. It's how He's getting the army through the pass, even during such a storm." Rand shook his head. "I can see it with my own eyes, yet it is difficult to believe."

"Look behind the God." Ralina pointed. "See those men hunched over, who sometimes are walking completely on their hands and knees—like canines. Those are what the Hunters and Warriors of the Tribe of the Trees have become after taking Death's cure."

Renard continued. "And behind them you can see that long, long line of men. Watch them closely. You will not see them look around. You will not see them do anything except march after Death. Those are the Milks—the reanimated dead."

Unable to look any longer, Ralina turned and rested her back against the boulder. Her gaze found Clayton's as he glanced at her. At first she couldn't read his expression, though the sarcastic sneer had slipped from his face. Then she realized what it was she saw in his eyes—not fear or horror, but fascination.

"Is this enough?" she blurted. "Do you see now that Renard and I have been telling you nothing but truth?"

"It seems to be as you said, but as I have said since we first learned of this army, it should be easy to hide in the mountains and pick them off, one man or mutant or Milk at a time," said Clayton.

"There are more than a thousand men down there." Ralina wanted to shout at the ignorant young man. "You have what, two dozen or so members of Herd Ebony? You cannot pick off an entire army with so few Riders."

Clayton shrugged. "We can do some damage, though, and I would like to get closer and see exactly what these hunched creatures and their god look like."

"No." Ralina spoke quietly but firmly. "If you get closer, He will sense you. He is a god—not a man. He will capture you, infect you, and flay the flesh from Bard to pack into your wounds, and you will become a twisted version of yourself, which will also change your Companion forever, just as it did the Hunters and Warriors of my Tribe."

"I can see that you are afraid, but I am not. Bard is swifter than the army—swifter even than Death. Herd Ebony is small, but stealthy. If He discovers we are there, we simply flee. You will see."

"No," Ralina repeated. "I will go no farther into these mountains. My veracity has been proven. Unless you choose to make Renard and me your prisoners we insist that we leave this mountain and continue our journey. Just give us directions to the Mare Council. They deserve to know what is descending upon them."

"If I say you come with me, then you will come with me." Clayton's voice was as hard as his calculating gaze.

"Clayton, I think we can all understand Ralina and Renard's hesitation to get closer to that army, and what she has told you has been proven true." Rand's voice was reasonable. He smiled at Clayton. "Herd Ebony treats people fairly. Isn't that why you established it? To treat everyone more fairly?"

Clayton's eyes narrowed, but he nodded.

"Good, then it should be no problem to release them and their canines. We can even give them extra supplies to take on their journey to the Valley of Vapors—and then send them on their way. It is the fair thing to do," Rand concluded.

Clayton blew out a long breath, then said, "You have a point, Rand. I am fair. So, here is what we will do. I will take Herd Ebony with me to get a closer look at this mutant army, and you will remain here with Ralina and Renard and await my return. *Then* we will send them on their way to the old women."

CHAPTER 25

Ralina hated every moment of the wait. At first she paced back and forth behind the grove of pines where she knew Death would not glimpse her silhouetted against the gray sky should He happen to look up at the ridge. In the grove, Rand and Renard hung a tarp to keep the constant drizzle from them and their Companions. Then Rand helped to occupy her mind by asking her if she would like to groom his Merlin, which of course she readily did.

"It's calming, isn't it?" Rand said after she'd worked her way partially around the big gray stallion's body.

Ralina sighed. "It is, but it also makes me worry for Bard. He should be here on the ridge with us and not heading into horrors his Companion clearly does not understand." She turned to face Rand and asked the question that had been haunting her since she'd met Clayton. "Are the leaders of the other Herds like Clayton?"

The Stallion Rider ran a hand through his dark hair. "No. You might as well know the truth. You will learn it anyway when you meet more Wind Riders. There are five Great Herds."

"That's what I thought," said Renard as he joined them under the shelter. "Let's see—I used to have them memorized. They are Magenti, Virides, Cinnabar, Indigo, and Jonquil, correct?"

Rand grinned. "Absolutely correct."

291

"My mother was intrigued by horses. She was an artist who used to draw them for me when I was a child," he explained.

"What of Herd Ebony?" Ralina asked.

"Herd Ebony is new," Rand said, speaking slowly as he carefully chose his words. "The five Great Herds are all led by women. Wind Riders are matriarchal, as are horses. We are ruled by a Mare Council made up of retired Lead Mare Riders from each of the Great Herds. Clayton decided it was time to change that." He shook his head and sighed. "I was foolish enough to be swayed by the excitement of change and the possibility of power. I joined Clayton when he began this new Herd, though I did not realize that he would first break the greatest rule of our people—not to harm any Rider or Companion."

"Clayton hurt someone?" Ralina asked.

"Recently he attempted to. He wanted to win Herd Magenti's Stallion Run, which is how a Herd chooses who will be their Herd Stallion and Rider—the team that oversees the security of Magenti." Rand's shoulders slumped. "I did not know about what he attempted until it was too late. I'd already followed him, and then when I realized what he had done and discovered there was an encroaching army I chose to remain with Herd Ebony to try to temper Clayton's rashness."

"How did Herd Ebony learn about Death's army?" said Ralina.

"The retired Lead Mare Rider of Herd Magenti came to us with Clayton's sentence for what he attempted, and to inform us of Death's army."

"How did she know about Death?" asked Renard.

"People made it through the pass ahead of you," explained Rand. "Dawn, the Lead Mare Rider, said the people have joined Herd Magenti. They call themselves a Pack and are made up of Earth Walkers and members of your old Tribe."

Ralina felt a wave of relief. "Mari and Nik—their group made it!"

"It has to be them," said Renard.

Ralina thought about what Rand had and had not revealed and asked, "What was the sentence passed on Clayton and his Herd?"

"Banishment from the Wind Rider Plains," said Rand. "Dawn came to give us that sentence and a way we might regain our honor. She offered us the opportunity to join Herd Magenti at the Valley of Vapors, which is their winter stronghold where the Herd has retreated to prepare for

Death's invasion. If we had chosen to fight with them, we would still have been banished, though our honor would have been restored."

"That sounds reasonable," said Ralina. "And you seem like a reasonable man. Why didn't you choose to join Herd Magenti?"

"I wanted to. I still want to. As I told Dawn, I chose to stay with Clayton to try and convince him to join Magenti, but Clayton will not listen to any counsel but his own. He won't even listen to Bard." Rand reached out and stroked Merlin's neck. "None of Herd Ebony's Riders are listening to their Companions. I was arrogant enough to ignore my Merlin's advice to *not* follow Clayton. I will never make that mistake again."

"We should leave," said Ralina. "Now. You, Renard, and our Companions. We should retrace our way out of these horrible mountains and go to the Valley of Vapors, where you will regain your honor and we will warn the Herds."

"The Herds have been warned," said Rand.

"The Herds do not know Death's true agenda," said Renard as he rested his hand on Kong's wide head.

Rand's brows lifted. "Which is?"

"To awaken the Goddess of Life and rule the world with Her," said Ralina. "The Goddess knows that would be disastrous for our world, which is why She helped us escape."

"You," Renard corrected. "The Goddess helped Ralina escape because she knows how to stop Death."

Rand stared at Ralina. "How do you stop Death?"

"I don't. You don't. No human does. He can only be stopped by the Goddess of Life, and I know how to awaken Her," said Ralina.

Merlin turned his head and butted his Rider. "Yes, yes, I know." Rand squared his shoulders. "Merlin and I pledge our word that we will aid you in getting to Herd Magenti."

Ralina's legs felt weak with relief. "Can we go now? This moment?"

"Let us check on Clayton's progress," said Rand. "Perhaps he will just get a closer look at the army and then return. In that case I will petition him to allow one other Rider team to go with us so that we can travel on horseback and make much better time. It would take months for you to cross the plains to the Valley of Vapors on foot."

As they made their way to the group of boulders, careful to stay out of view of anyone looking from below, Ralina said, "I understand the logic of what you say. Your horses are much swifter than we are on foot, though perhaps Renard and I should leave now. You could join us with another Rider when Clayton returns."

"If you leave before he returns, there is no way he will allow me or any Rider to leave," said Rand.

"Even if you explain to him why?" Renard asked.

"Yes."

Ralina shook her head. "Clayton isn't fit to lead."

"No," Rand said somberly. "I finally understand that he is not."

They crouched behind the boulders and looked over them at the main pass through the Rock Mountains. The army was there, a distant dark blot on the pass, but closer than Ralina thought they would be. For such big beasts, the bison moved quickly, and the army followed behind in an inky line. Ralina's gaze went from them to search the upper parts of the mountain. Clayton and the Herd were not within sight.

"Do either of you see any sign of Clayton?" Ralina asked.

"No," said Renard grimly.

"No, but there are many dips and rises in the mountains, and of course plenty of tree cover. They'll be stealthy. They do not mean to be discovered," said Rand.

Ralina's gaze went back to the army. They trudged ever forward. A terrible premonition shivered its way down her spine to lodge in her belly. Ralina squinted and studied the line of men. *What is it? What is bothering me?*

She continued to study the pass. There didn't seem anything too remarkable about it—actually, like the part of the pass she'd traveled with Death and His army, it was rather monotonous in its never-ending winding road. Farther ahead of the army there was an area of the pass that widened considerably, though only for a brief area. *That's probably where they'll make camp tonight*, she thought. Frowning, she looked at the line of men and beasts again—and she saw it.

"Renard, where are the Tribesmen? *Any* of the Tribesmen? Or Death? Where is He?" Frantically, Ralina's gaze scanned the line of men.

"I do not see them. Not one of them. But there are the canines—the Shepherds and Terriers. See, they're together near the front of the line, just behind the last bison." Renard's voice shook. "But there are no War-riors or Hunters with them."

"The army is much nearer than I expected them to be." Rand's voice sounded strained and then he gasped and pointed. "Oh, Great Mother Mare, no! There they are!"

Pouring from the side of the mountain, being herded by the missing Warriors and Hunters, came Herd Ebony. They were all on foot, followed by their Companions—and bringing up the rear, forcing the horses to keep moving, was the God of Death. The Warriors and Hunters had cross-bows trained on the Herd as they circled around them on the unusually wide section of the main trail Ralina had noticed. Death made His way to stand before the Herd. They were much too far away to hear what the God was saying, but even from that distance He appeared highly animated. His massive arms were raised above His head as He gestured and paced.

Ralina felt as if her blood had frozen in her veins. She couldn't move. She couldn't speak. All she could do was stare down at the distant scene in horror.

"This can't be real. This can't be happening." Rand wiped a shaky hand across his forehead.

"I told you all. *I told you.*" Ralina was barely keeping control of herself. She wanted to scream and cry—and more than anything she wanted to run away, fast and far, and never return. "Herd Ebony is no more." Her words hitched as she remembered Bard's kind eyes and his sleek coat.

"What can we do?" Rand asked frantically.

"Nothing. Not one thing except get out of here and pray to the Goddess of Life that we reach one of the Great Herds before Death and the Riders He will mutate do," said Renard.

"But I—I have to do *something*," said Rand as his voice broke.

"You can witness the end of the Herd and then help us get out of here." Ralina held Rand's tortured gaze. "Clayton is enough like Thaddeus, the traitor who betrayed our Tribe for power, that I can predict what will hap-pen. He will tell Death Renard and I are here. I promise you the God will come after us, so we cannot remain here much longer or we will join your Herd and they will infect you and flay Merlin's flesh into yours."

"I will ready Merlin. We leave immediately." Rand hurried to the stand of trees and Renard went to help him take down the temporary shelter and repack their bags as Rand tacked up Merlin while Bear and Kong paced and growled.

Ralina didn't allow herself to look away. She stared at the group of captured Wind Riders and their beautiful horses. She tried to find Bard, but the horses were grouped too closely together and they were too far away to distinguish individuals. She did recognize Clayton, though. He had stepped away from the rest of the Herd and stood facing Death, Who continued to speak animatedly to the much smaller man.

"You are a fool, Clayton. What happens next is your fault and yours alone," murmured Ralina. Then she breathed a whisper of a prayer. "Great Goddess of Life, please don't allow Bard to suffer. Please, oh, please, if there is any way let that magnificent horse's end come swiftly without pain." Ralina wanted to look away, but as she had done since they paddled away from her beloved Tribe, she forced herself to watch so that she could accurately tell their story.

"Ralina, we're almost ready!" called Renard.

Ralina still didn't move from her place behind the boulders. She kept watching and memorizing every detail—every moment—as her thoughts raced. *Clayton will betray us. Death will mutate him and the rest of Herd Ebony. How will Rand and Renard and I get away from them if they have horses to ride? And we only have one horse for three of us, and two canines.* Feeling more defeated than she had since she'd left the army, Ralina swallowed bile and continued to record in her memory the last moments of Herd Ebony.

"Ralina." Crouching, Renard joined her at the boulder. "Rand has a plan. You are to ride Merlin. The stallion knows how to reach the Valley of Vapors, which is the closest of the five Herd strongholds. We will follow you."

Ralina shook her head back and forth, back and forth. "No. I will not leave you. I will not leave Bear."

Renard took her hand. "You must. Death will have mutant Wind Riders now. The Herds have to be warned."

"It's too much. I simply cannot, Renard. I will not—"

On the other side of the stand of trees where Rand had just finished readying Merlin there came a terrible thrashing and breaking, as if one of the bison bulls had smashed through the pines and scrub that dotted the mountainside.

"Kong! Bear! To us!" Renard shouted, and the Shepherds rushed to their Companions.

Rand grabbed his bow, notched an arrow, and turned toward the sound as Bard crashed through the mud and pine trees to them. He slid to a halt. His sides were lathered white and his eyes were wild as he stood, trembling and snorting.

"Bard!" Ralina rushed to him.

"Careful. He may not be in control of himself." Rand moved to stop Ralina, but she was too fast.

She reached Bard. His head shot up and he snorted and stumbled back. "Sssh. It's okay. You made it here, brave boy. You did it. Let me help you." Slowly, she held her hand out. Bard stared at her, and then he dropped his muzzle to her shoulder. She stroked his steaming neck and continued to murmur softly to him.

"Oh, Great Mother Mare," Rand said. "Merlin says Clayton sent Bard away—sent him here to carry you out of here, to get you to the Valley of Vapors. Ralina, Clayton did it to save us."

Ralina breathed in a shaky breath as she stroked the stallion's steaming coat. "He'll let me ride him by myself?"

"Yes, Merlin says. Definitely. First let me wipe him down. He has to rest for as long as we can allow it, and then we must get out of here." Rand grabbed a grooming cloth from his bag, hurried to the exhausted stallion, and started wiping him down.

"What can I do?" Ralina asked.

Bard was still fully tacked up, and Rand pointed at the waterskin that was tied on to Clayton's pack behind his saddle. "He needs water. Inside the pack the skin's tied to you'll find one of the hide feed bags. You know, like the ones you mixed mash in earlier. Get it and pour water into it, but don't let him drink all of it at once."

"Anything I can do?" asked Renard.

Rand nodded as he continued to wipe down Bard. "Search on the other side of the trees. See if you can find another trail. One that leads back the way we came but doesn't descend to the main trail like the one we took up here. We need to stay ahead of the army."

"Got it." Renard, with Kong shadowing him, hurried past the trees.

Ralina was surprised at how steady her hands were as she poured water for Bard and let him drink. She stroked his sweaty forehead and kept talking softly to him. Tears dripped from the stallion's eyes and ran down his face. He held his muzzle low, though he'd stopped trembling.

"Ralina, look!"

At the sound of Renard's excitement Ralina stepped around Bard to see her lover standing at the edge of the clump of pines. Not far from him was the white doe, gleaming like moonlight through the gray day.

CHAPTER 26

Before the doe led them into the heart of the mountains, Ralina returned to the boulder for one last look. The bulk of the army had still not reached Death and His captives. Clayton was separated from his Herd. He stood before Death, Who had taken a seat on a fallen log. Gathered against the side of the mountain was Herd Ebony, Riders and Companions, in a tight circle. The mutated Warriors and Hunters stood guard around them, crossbows at the ready.

It made Ralina sick.

She turned her back to the avoidable tragedy playing out in the distance below them and went to Bard. She stroked his side and looked into his eye. "Thank you. I know this is horrible for you. I know how much you love Clayton, no matter his mistakes. I know because Bear has always and will always love me no matter what. What you're doing is brave and good and wise. You're saving the Wind Riders. They will never forget. I will be sure no one ever forgets."

Bard pressed his muzzle to her cheek and blew softly. He'd cooled, eaten handfuls of grain, and drunk a skin of water—and through it all, even now, tears never stopped washing down his face.

Rand boosted her up on Bard's back before he mounted Merlin and helped Renard to sit behind him. Bear and Kong padded with them as they followed the white doe along the mountainside and then they turned abruptly to the east, away from Death and the horrors happening on the main trail, to find a slim, muddy path that wound around trees and boulders.

At first it seemed they were going to continue to climb and climb, but soon the doe took a fork in the path that opened up to a wider trail that headed almost straight down the side of the mountain.

"Lean back as we descend," Rand told them. "Try not to move around a lot. You'll throw their balance off. Merlin and Bard already know how to pick their way down a steep path. All you need do is hang on and don't hinder them—and don't fall off."

Ralina concentrated, leaning back to help Bard balance. Beside the horses, the Shepherds slithered down the muddy trail, careful to stay out of the way of hooves. This descent seemed unending, almost worse than the first time the doe led them out of the mountains, even though they were much swifter mounted on the horses. The drizzle had returned to a more steady rain, and they were losing daylight rapidly. Silently, Ralina cursed Clayton for delaying their start that morning. She didn't know how they'd make camp on this sheer side of the mountain, but even with her limited knowledge of horses Ralina reasoned that they couldn't keep sliding down the path after dark. The horses would misstep, and if they began to fall that would be the end of them—and their Riders.

We have to live. We have to warn the Herds.

And then so abruptly that it jarred Ralina's teeth together, the descent was finished and they surged out onto the grassy valley that flanked the mountain range. Merlin had been leading, following just behind the doe, with Bard and Ralina and Bear bringing up the rear. As they entered level ground, Bard drew up beside Merlin.

"She's gone," said Rand.

Ralina peered around, looking for the shining white doe, but she saw nothing.

"She does that," said Renard from behind Rand. "That's what happened right before you found us."

"What do we do now?" asked Ralina as she wiped rain from her face. "How long can we keep going?"

"We let Merlin and Bard decide that. They know how urgent this is and will not stop until it is too dangerous for them to continue," said Rand.

"First let's give them some water and let me check their saddles." Renard slid down from Merlin's rear and went to Ralina to help her dismount as Rand dropped to the ground with a lot more grace and began unpacking the waterskins.

Ralina was stroking Bard's neck when she felt the tremor that cascaded through the horse. It was as if he had been shaken from the inside out. The big stallion stumbled and dropped to his knees.

"Rand, something is wrong with—"

Bard lifted his head and screamed. It was like nothing Ralina had ever heard. There was such agony in that sound that she cringed and tears pooled in her eyes.

Then Merlin echoed the sound, screaming into the slate dusk.

"Rand!" Ralina rushed around Bard to see that Rand had collapsed against his stallion. The only reason he was standing was because he had wrapped his arms around Merlin's neck and was holding tightly to his stallion as he sobbed brokenly.

"Oh, Goddess! What is it?" Renard cried from beside Ralina.

Rand turned his devastated face to them. His dusky skin had gone so pale that he looked gray. "They're dead."

"Who?" Ralina asked as she frantically looked from Rand and Merlin to Bard, who was still on the ground, keening.

"All of them. Every horse. Every Rider. Herd Ebony is no more." Rand pressed his face into Merlin's mane and sobbed.

Bear and Kong lifted their muzzles to the darkening sky and howled in anguish at the loss of so many Companions.

Ralina rushed back to Bard. She dropped to her knees beside him. His head was still raised as he screamed over and over.

"Oh, sweet boy. Let me help you. Show me how to help you." Tentatively, she reached out to touch his neck and then his face. "Please, please let me help you."

The stallion's head drooped. He turned to meet her gaze. His intelligent brown eye was awash in tears. He looked broken, utterly defeated.

Ralina didn't know what else to do. Still on her knees she moved forward through the mud and rain and opened her arms. "Please let me comfort you. Please."

With a mighty sigh, Bard placed his head in her arms, and as she held him close to her and kissed his forehead she was flooded with emotions: desperate sadness and also need and warmth and love—so, so much love.

I am Bard. Will you be my Rider?

The words in her mind were spoken with such sweetness, such hesitancy, that Ralina's breath caught in her throat and then released with a shocked sob. "Yes! Yes I will! I will be your Rider!"

Bear instantly stopped howling and rushed to her side. He pressed against Bard, licking tears from the stallion's face and whining softly as his tail wagged so hard his whole body wriggled.

"Ralina?" Renard approached them.

Ralina looked up at him, smiling through her tears. "He Chose me. Bard is mine and I am his."

Then Rand and Merlin were there and Bard got unsteadily to his feet, careful to keep physical contact with Ralina and Bear. "It's true. Bard has Chosen you." Color rushed back to Rand's face as he bowed with the traditional Wind Rider greeting to Ralina. "May a mare's luck be with you and your stallion all the days of your lives."

Mari thought the Valley of Vapors was a marvel. The Herd had trudged up into the Quachita Mountains, which were rocky and inhospitable, but in the heart of the rugged mountains was a jewel. Even through her exhaustion Mari felt a thrill as the winter sanctuary for Herd Magenti came into view. The Herd had to enter the valley single file, as the only entrance was a narrow passage through the mountains, which ringed the Valley of Vapors like a crown of spikes. Instead of sitting on the head of a giant, it protected a lush raised plateau. There was a mineral scent that permeated everything, but it wasn't unpleasant—actually, Mari rather liked it. It reminded her of fertilized earth and green growing things. And all around them were crystals—clumps of them that winked magickally in the sunlight.

"This is incredible." Sora walked beside Mari, as everyone who had been riding in the horse-drawn carts had to make their way on foot at the end of their journey due to the treacherous pass. "But I think it's misnamed. This isn't a valley. It's more like a verdant mountaintop."

"I was just thinking the same thing," said Mari as she stared ahead of them. It was late afternoon and the waning fall sunlight caressed the sanctuary so that it blazed with color and crystals.

"River and I have been saying that for years. It really isn't a valley, but the name has stuck for generations, so the Valley of Vapors it is," April said from behind them. She walked next to her mare, Deinos. Little Cleo trotted past April to yap at Chloe, whom Sora carried in a sling close to her heart.

Sora laughed, kissed her pup on the top of her little black head, and put her down to play with her sister. "Yes, you may play, but stay close and watch the horses' hooves. The members of the Herd who are already here and are not accustomed to puppies yet."

"Rigel, keep an eye on the pups, please. Be sure they don't get into any mischief you can't get them out of," said Mari as she ruffled her big Shepherd's ears. He barked happily as the two Terrier puppies began chasing him around Deinos. Then Mari turned to April. "No matter what it's called, this camp really does look like a sanctuary. Is there any other way into it than the narrow pass?"

April smiled and shook her head. "Absolutely not. It's like the Great Mother Mare scooped out an area here atop the mountains, creating a safe place for Herd Magenti." April pointed to the sheer walls of rock encircling the valley. "The sharpness of the mountains protects the valley from intruders, as well as from the worst of the winter weather. Hot springs bubble throughout the valley, which doesn't just keep us warm but also allows us to grow crops, even when everything outside the barrier is frozen. Wait until you see our grow rooms. Your people will love them. The Mother Plants, along with all the crops you brought with you, will thrive here."

As they continued into the heart of the campsite, Mari gaped at the tall buildings that lined the main road. They were white and glinted in the afternoon sun like milky jewels. "Are those truly buildings of the ancients? And they're habitable?"

"Absolutely." April's voice was filled with pride. "They are maintained year round by Herdmembers who choose not to live a nomadic life. There aren't enough buildings to house all of Herd Magenti, but the Mare Council inhabits one building. Five others are where the Lead Mare Riders of the branches of Herd Magenti and their families winter." April's grin widened. "As Lead Mare Rider of the main Magenti Herd, it is River's right to claim the largest, most spectacular of the buildings. You'll see. And there's plenty of room. You and Nik and Sora—well, and also Davis, Claudia, and their family of puppies—should join us." Then her smile faded. "It is usually so joyful to retreat here for the winter. We feast and rest and soak in the mineral springs. It's something we look forward to all year. I wish you could be experiencing that for your first time in the valley, and not preparing for a siege and war."

After they poured through the pass, the road opened wide—so wide that half a dozen horses could easily walk side by side along it—and it was incredible. Made of flat stone, it stretched through the center of the valley with glistening buildings and colorful purple tents framing it. More of Mari's Pack hurried into the valley to join her. Nik rushed up with Laru and took her hand.

"This place is amazing. And River said those buildings are actually inhabited," Nik gushed. "I wonder if it'll be like living in a burrow."

Before Mari could answer, River trotted up to them on Anjo, with Dove and Tulpar following closely. River dismounted and turned to the Moon Women. "Mari, Sora, I'd like you to join Dove and me to meet the Lead Mare Riders of the other branches of Herd Magenti. We are the last to arrive as we were unusually far away because of the Stallion Run, and we have much to discuss as we get ready for Death's army."

"I would be happy to," said Mari.

"As would I," echoed Sora.

River nodded her appreciation. Then they all turned their attention to the four magnificent mares and their Riders who trotted together down the wide, well-maintained road toward their newly arrived group. Each woman's hair was dressed with striking purple ribbons and crystals. As with River's Herd, they looked healthy and strong—and were smiling in welcome.

"So, our Herd is called Magenti Central, correct?" Nik asked.

"Yes," River explained. "The other Herds are named for directions— Magenti North, South, East, and West."

"But Magenti Central is the largest of the five Magenti Herds," added April. "And Magenti is the only one of the Great Herds with multiple branches. We are quite powerful and—"

April's words broke off like someone had clamped a hand over her mouth. Mari had turned to see what was wrong when every horse and Rider in the valley gasped. Some cried out as if they were in pain. At the same moment each horse raised his or her muzzle to the sky and began keening the most horrible, heart-wrenching sound that Mari had ever heard. Beside them River and April staggered to their mares, stroking their necks and making inarticulate sounds of distress.

"By the smooth thighs of the Goddess! What is happening?" Sora shouted as she and Mari and Nik stared around them helplessly as their friends and Herdmembers sobbed while they attempted to comfort their horses.

"Oh, Goddess. It is finished." Dove spoke from Tulpar's back. The big golden stallion bowed his head as tears dripped down his face. "They have been successful."

"Dove," Mari said. "What is it?"

Dove slipped from Tulpar's back and wrapped her arms around her stallion as he keened with the rest of Magenti. Her words were heavy with sadness. "They mourn the death of Herd Ebony. The horses felt it—felt them die. It is quite horrible."

Ralina could hardly believe what had just happened, but it was true—so very true. Bard, *her* stallion, was exhausted, but after they took a short break he told her—*he told her*—that he was willing to continue until darkness stopped them.

Ralina encouraged Bard, stroking his neck and murmuring her love and support as they began again, heading eastward across the blessedly flat land through rain that had decreased from a steady downpour to a drizzle. Though Bard and Merlin were still moving, their pace was slower. The light was waning and, as Bard explained to Ralina, they must take their time when it was difficult to see so that they did not step into a gopher hole.

"Renard, Bard just told me that if a horse breaks a leg it is pretty much a death sentence. Is that true?" Ralina had been firing questions at the experienced Stallion Rider since Bard Chose her.

Rand nodded. "It is true. You will learn to help protect your stallion's legs against injury—that and hoof care are very important, but do not be overwhelmed. Herd Magenti will help you, and Bard will also guide you." His gaze went to the big black stallion. "It is a marvel that he Chose you."

Ralina reached down to stroke Bard's warm, wet neck again. "I think so, too . . ." Then she paused and added, "Does it not happen often that a horse Chooses more than one Rider in his lifetime?"

"No, almost never." Rand spoke quietly, his voice filled with great sadness. "Most horses suicide when their Riders die, and most Riders choose not to outlive their Companions."

"How long do horses usually live?" asked Renard from his seat behind Rand.

"Their life span is as long as their Riders," said Rand. "Legend says in ancient times horses only lived about thirty years. Thank the Great Mother Mare that changed when horses and humans became Chosen Companions. When you meet Morgana, the Leader of the Mare Council and Rider of the mare Ramoth, you will meet the oldest living horse and Rider team. No one knows for sure exactly how old they are, but I've heard rumors that they have been bonded for eight decades."

"That's incredible," said Ralina.

"It is very similar with our canines," said Renard. "Though their life spans aren't as long as your horses', they do often live thirty, forty, and even fifty years. They rarely outlive their Companions, but if they do our canines almost always choose to follow them into death. It is not often that a human is Chosen by another canine during his or her lifetime." Renard's gaze went to Kong, who padded through the muddy grass beside Merlin. "They are our biggest joy and thus our most desperate sadness when we lose them."

They rode on in silence for a while, and then—very softly—Ralina said, "I do not understand why Death killed them. Why did He not mutate them? That was His plan. He told me over and over what He intended. Why would He change His mind?"

Into her mind, Bard's sweet voice said, *My Clayton and Herd Ebony were not killed. They chose to die.*

"Oh, Bard, my precious boy. That is so horrible." She stroked his neck. Beneath her touch she felt his body trembling again.

"What is it?" Renard asked.

"Bard just told me that Death did not kill Herd Ebony, but that they chose to die."

Rand's shoulders slumped. "Will Bard tell you anything else about what happened?"

Bard, precious one, will you tell me what happened to your Clayton and Herd Ebony?

Bard shivered violently and his neck turned so that she could look into his expressive brown eye. Tears still leaked down his face. *I cannot. I must bear that alone.*

"You're such a brave, wonderful boy. Know that I am here for you—always—and that when you are ready you can tell me anything." Beside them Bear barked to punctuate her words. She glanced at Rand. "He knows what happened, but he won't talk about it."

Rand nodded sadly. "He won't show Merlin what happened, either. Perhaps someday he will."

They traveled on past sunset, until the sky went from ash to the black of a starless, cloud-covered night.

My Ralina, we cannot go farther safely.

Ralina wondered if she would ever get used to the miracle of Bard's sweet, soft voice in her mind. He was articulate and compassionate and amazingly gentle. She was already so connected to him that she could feel the terrible grief that he carried, as well as his guilt at surviving and Choosing another Rider.

"We must stop and make camp." Rand's voice came out of the darkness in front of them.

"That's what Bard just told me," said Ralina.

"Merlin says there is a grove of apple trees just ahead," said Rand. "We can pitch our tarps there and make a fire. It will be good for all of us to get dry and warm and eat something."

As the stallion's keen senses had noticed, just ahead of them was a grove of gnarled old apple trees. As they hung tarps, they discovered that the boughs still held plenty of ripe apples. The horses munched eagerly on them while their Companions built a blazing campfire over which they boiled water for sweet mash. In Clayton's packs Ralina discovered two pheasants, plucked, quartered, and wrapped tightly in a skin—ready to roast. Renard spitted them while she buried apples in the coals to cook.

Bard and Merlin ate and then stood resting by the fire. Merlin remained close to Bard, as did Bear, and Bard was always within touching distance of Ralina. She often stroked his smooth coat and sent him waves of love. She spoke regularly to him. Sometimes just calling him her precious boy. Sometimes she reminded him she was there, beside him, and told him over and over that she would never leave him. Bard returned her affection, but she could feel the weight of grief he carried and she desperately wished she could do something—anything—to lessen that burden for him.

As they were unrolling their sleeping gear, first Merlin's and then Bard's head went up, immediately followed by Bear and Kong, who had been dozing by the fire, coming wide awake. The Shepherds stood and growled and stared into the night.

Rand rushed to ready his bow. Bear and Kong went to their Companions' sides. The fur down their backs lifted as they continued to growl and peer into the night.

And then Merlin neighed a joyous greeting, and Bard echoed him, though with less enthusiasm as the sounds of large creatures moving through the grasses surrounding the apple grove came to them over the rain.

"Who is it?" Ralina's heart felt as if it would beat out of her chest. *It can't be Death! He must be a day behind us!*

Bard's voice, thick with relief, sounded in her mind. *Wind Riders. Not enemies.*

Into the dancing firelight came several horse and Rider teams, as well as a horse pulling a small, light cart.

"Dawn! Echo!" Renard dropped his bow and hurried to the Riders. "Thank the Mother Mare."

A beautiful woman with skin the color of fertile earth slid from the back of a horse so white she seemed silver. Renard halted before her and bowed low, crossing his wrists over his heart. "Greetings, Dawn, Mare Rider of Echo."

"Rand, you live!" Dawn embraced him. "We felt the death of Herd Ebony and were just turning to head back to the Valley of Vapors when a white doe appeared to us. She behaved so oddly that it was clear she wanted us to follow her, which we did until we saw your fire. The doe disappeared and we understood she'd been leading us here." The woman's gaze went from Rand to find Ralina and Renard—and their Companions. "Bard? He lives, too? Where is Clayton?"

Rand opened his mouth to respond but was interrupted when a man leaped from the light cart to rush past them.

"Ralina! Renard! Is it really you?"

Ralina felt a jolt of shock. "O'Bryan?"

And then her friend and Tribesman pulled her into an embrace, which Renard joined. O'Bryan thumped their backs before he let them loose to greet their Shepherds. "Bear, Kong! Come here, boys." The Shepherds eagerly went to O'Bryan as he dropped to his knees to hug and pet them while they covered his face with wet kisses. His smile beamed at the Wind Riders accompanying him as he announced, "This is Ralina, Storyteller to the Tribe of the Trees. It is she who Dax spoke of—she helped him escape Death so that he could warn the rest of us." He turned back to Ralina. "I can't believe you're here. How did it happen and where did this stallion come from?" O'Bryan gestured at Bard, who stood so close behind Ralina that his muzzle rested on her shoulder.

"They are a bonded pair," said the woman Rand called Dawn. She met Ralina's gaze. "Which means Clayton is no more."

CHAPTER 27

Around the campfire Ralina told her story to the Lead Mare Rider, O'Bryan, and the three Wind Riders in their group. She did not rush. Ralina spoke slowly, carefully, and with accuracy. She told of the death of their beloved Tribe of the Trees as O'Bryan wept openly and the Shepherds comforted him. She recounted to the small group the atrocities Death had committed, wiping out the Saleesh people and reanimating their dead with spirits of the ancients. She explained Death's goal— subjugating the Wind Riders and awakening the Goddess of Life to rule over their plains. Finally, she replayed for them the events of the day— how they'd found Death's army and how Clayton and his Herd had been captured—and all had died except for Rand and Merlin, who had remained with them, and Bard, whom Clayton had somehow sent to them and who had Chosen Ralina as his Rider after Clayton's death. As she finished, Dawn came to her and touched her cheek gently.

"You have been given a great gift," said the Lead Mare Rider. "Bard's choice to live and to accept you as his Rider is extremely rare and speaks to the integrity and compassion in your heart. Welcome, Stallion Rider, to Herd Magenti."

Then Dawn went to Bard, who stood beside his Rider, always within touching distance. The other horses had gravitated to Bard as soon as they had been cooled down and fed. They surrounded the stallion, remaining close, as if to lend him strength.

Dawn touched Bard's forehead and asked Ralina, "Has Bard told you how Clayton and the rest of the Herd were killed?"

Ralina had to swallow several times before she could answer the Mare Rider. She placed her hand on Bard's neck. "All he would tell me is that they weren't killed. They chose to die. When I asked more, he said it is something he must bear alone."

Dawn's breath hitched as tears tracked down her smooth brown cheeks. The striking white mare moved up so that she stood beside Bard, so close that their shoulders touched. She nuzzled him with her muzzle and nickered softly as Dawn took Bard's head in her hands and pressed her forehead against his. "Brave Bard, do you trust me?"

Bard's response resonated in Ralina's mind. *I do, Rider of Echo.*

"Bard says he trusts you," repeated Ralina through her own tears.

"Then listen to me, Stallion of Herd Magenti. This is not your burden to bear alone. The weight of it is too great. You must share it with your Rider and your Herd so that you may begin to heal. I beseech you, show Ralina and our Companions what happened."

Bard went very still. He breathed in a long breath—as if readying himself to plunge underwater—and then Ralina's mind was filled with images.

First she saw Herd Ebony in the mountains, surrounded by Thaddeus and the mutated, twisted Warriors and Hunters. They sprang on the Herd when they were in a low part of the path that flanked the main trail, raining arrows on them—wounding several of the horses and Riders, though not fatally. Then Death revealed Himself to them and Bard showed Ralina that was the moment Clayton finally realized the gravity of his mistake. It was in the chaos of Herd Ebony being captured that Clayton sent Bard away, begging him to return to Rand—to carry Ralina to the Valley of Vapors—and to forgive him.

Then there was nothing except visions from Bard's escape as he raced to do his Rider's bidding. Bard's body began to tremble again as Ralina's point of view went from seeing through Bard's eyes to a far different view from Clayton.

Ralina gasped and began to tremble with her stallion.

Dawn's voice was a lifeline of calm authority. "Bard was not physically present when Herd Ebony died. He will only be able to show you what happened through the memory of what Clayton witnessed."

"T-that's where we are. With Death and H-his army." Ralina's teeth chattered and her voice broke.

"Yes, I know. Our Companions watch with you and send the images to us. You can do this. You must witness this. We all must witness this—for Bard. He must share this great sadness with his Herd so that we might bear it with him," said Dawn, who was still holding the stallion's head between her hands. Though the Lead Mare Rider's voice remained steady, her tears fell from her cheeks onto the stallion's face to mix with his tears.

Ralina nodded and closed her eyes. She leaned against Bard and opened herself fully to the visions he sent her.

She watched Death rail at Clayton. First He told the Rider that the arrows that had wounded so many of Herd Ebony had been tipped in blood from those infected with the skin-sloughing sickness. Death spewed lies about how wonderful the cure was—how magnificent it would be for the Riders to be joined with their Companions on an even deeper level. She saw through Clayton's gaze as he looked from Death to the twisted beings who used to be tall, proud members of the Tribe of the Trees, but who were now hunched, malignant versions of themselves. Not human and not canine, but something less than either. She watched Clayton rejoin his Herd. She heard him whisper to them to forgive him, but that they must not allow Death to use them and their Companions to destroy their world.

Tears washed Ralina's face as she felt, with Bard, Clayton make his decision. As Death paced and spoke untrue platitudes about His magnificence and how Herd Ebony would be *more than* any of the other Riders on their plains—how they would be by Death's side as He subjugated the Wind Riders—Clayton, followed by his Herd, rushed forward to hurl themselves from the side of the mountain. The Warriors and Hunters tried to stop them. Death tried to stop them, but the Riders had chosen, and the rain of arrows did nothing but propel them from the trail. Through Clayton's eyes Ralina watched the Wind Riders fall to their deaths. Some wrapped their arms around their beloved Companions' necks so that they fell together. Some held the hand of the Rider falling beside them. Clayton was the last to go. He stood on the lip of the pass, witnessing the death of his Herd, until Death took a spear and drove it into his back, sending him over the edge to fall with Herd Ebony.

Ralina sobbed into Bard's neck. Around her she heard the sounds of the other Riders, crying brokenly, and of their Companions, who moaned and made desperate, whining noises as they pressed even closer to Bard as if trying to physically take his pain from him.

"Great Mother Mare, hear our plea." Dawn straightened, though she kept one hand pressed against Bard's forehead. "Though Clayton made many errors, he freely gave his life, and that of his Herd, to protect us. We shall not forget. Please take the burden of this awful grief from Herd Magenti's brave stallion, Bard, and his new Rider, Ralina. Allow Herd Magenti to share their grief so that it is bearable for all of us. It has been said."

"It has been said," spoke every Wind Rider together.

Then, miraculously, Ralina felt a lessening of the suffocating grief in which she and Bard had been wrapped. Her stallion lifted his head, turned, and pressed his forehead against her. She held him and sent waves of love to him while the Wind Riders and their Companions remained close, sharing their burden—and together, Rider and stallion, began to heal.

Thaddeus watched three more Milks misstep in the darkness and silently fall from the pass down the side of the mountain. He sighed and dropped to all fours so that he could move more quickly, though when he caught up with Death he stood, not wanting to provoke the God, Who always sneered at him when he walked on all fours.

"My Lord."

Death stopped and turned to face Thaddeus. The glowing spirit of the bison bull who stood in front of the God illuminated His body, which had grown to massive proportions and was covered with hunks of wooly dark fur. The black horns had completely replaced the rack of antlers that had grown from Death's head. They were hooked—their tips glistened malevolently—sharp as a blade.

"What, Thaddeus? I have no time to discuss banal things with you. We must rid ourselves of these mountains. There will be more members of Herd Ebony waiting for their brethren to join them, and this time we shall shackle them so that they cannot escape us." The God's voice blasted Thaddeus.

Thaddeus bowed and nodded. "I understand and, of course, agree with You, my Lord, but I know how much You do not like to lose Your Milks and in this darkness they have begun to stumble from the pass and fall. I am afraid if we do not halt for the rest of the night that You will lose several scores of them."

Death sighed heavily. "Torches. We should have torches. First we shall slaughter several more bison. We will not need them much longer as the pass at this altitude is not so snowbound."

"Yet," Thaddeus muttered.

Death turned on him. "What did you say?"

"I said yes. I agreed with You, my Lord," Thaddeus lied. "And we can, indeed, make torches so that we may continue to march into the night tomorrow. But this night You will lose many more Milks should we continue."

"Yes, yes, I hear you. At least the Goddess-be-damned snow has stopped. We shall halt, too. Tell your Hunters to slaughter several bulls—fat ones. Have the Warriors climb up into the mountains for firewood, mindful to chop long, straight branches from the trees. We shall use them as torches tomorrow, and in doing so I am confident that with one more day of travel we will be free of these mountains," commanded the God.

It is always us, Odysseus. Always my Warriors and Hunters who do His bidding while He blusters and boasts. That will change after we defeat the Wind Riders.

"My Lord, in this darkness it is too dangerous for the Warriors to climb into the mountains for fuel, which is why we loaded firewood on the backs of the Milks. Perhaps there will be some torch-worthy boughs with them. If not, at dawn the Warriors will be able to see well enough to climb from the pass," said Thaddeus as he squinted up at the mountains that hulked above them.

His cheek stung when Death backhanded him, throwing him against the rocky mountainside.

"*Do not tell Me no!*" the God roared.

Carefully, Thaddeus picked himself up and wiped blood from his mouth as he sucked in the air that had been knocked from his body.

And the Hunter froze.

He sniffed again, lifting his face like a true Terrier to taste the scents on the cold night wind. Thaddeus's sense of smell had intensified during their journey as the change that was happening in his body made him ever more like his beloved Odysseus than human.

Thaddeus knew what he had scented. He was sure of it. He had spent the past many months smelling her stench.

"Do you think I jest, little man-dog?" Death loomed over him.

Thaddeus shrank back and he spoke quickly to the mercurial god. "My Lord! I smell her! Your Storyteller!"

Death's demeanor changed immediately. "My Storyteller? Where? Where is she, Thaddeus?"

Thaddeus raised his face to the mountain again and huffed in the air. He caught the scent again. It was faint, but definitely there. Thaddeus walked along the side of the pass, moving forward past the bison spirit. The line of living bulls had pulled ahead of them as they trudged down the pass with mindless loyalty to the god who had enslaved them. Thaddeus reached a spot in the pass where there was a slender, muddy path between two huge boulders that led up into the mountains. Had her scent not been there, he would have walked past it with the rest of the army, thinking it was no more than a water runoff.

"Here. Her scent is here." Thaddeus pointed at the path. Then he caught another trace of the Storyteller—mixed with bison shit and musk. "And here, my Lord."

"Tell Me more," Death said excitedly from behind him.

Thaddeus breathed in, tasting the different threads of scent that wove through the air, lifting from all around them on the pass. "She was here. With horses and . . ." He paused, sniffing again before he grimaced. "And the stench of Renard, Bear, and Kong. They followed this pass before going up into the mountains."

Death scratched His thick, tenebrous beard. "They thought they would surprise us. They must have watched us from afar."

"Before Clayton made the mistake of believing he could sneak up on us," said Thaddeus.

Death nodded. "They underestimated the ability of My Hunters to scent them. And scent them still we shall. You can track her, can you not?"

Thaddeus had to suppress a sudden desire to wriggle with excitement. "Indeed I can, my Lord."

Death paced back and forth while the spirit of the bison stood, watching, his illuminated form throwing horrendous shadows against the rocky wall of the pass. "And you will still be able to track her tomorrow?"

"Of course, my Lord." Thaddeus's response was automatic, though truthfully, if the rain returned and they did not move fast enough the Storyteller's scent would dissipate. *I shall not tell Him that, Odysseus.*

"Then slaughter the bulls. Tomorrow we track My Storyteller."

CHAPTER 28

The next day Thaddeus had to suppress his Terrier-like desire to run around in circles and yip with glee when, just before dusk, the army finally left the Rock Mountain pass and entered the valley that opened to the Plains of the Wind Riders. His exuberance was short-lived, though, when Death bellowed for him.

"*Thaddeus!*"

Thaddeus hurried to the God's side. "Yes, my Lord?"

Death frowned down at him. "Why must I repeat Myself? You know I would find My Storyteller. You said you could track her. I can lose my bison guide now, but first I would know that you have her scent."

Thaddeus looked around them. There were a couple dozen living bison bulls standing around grazing hungrily on the winter grass. *Huh. Odysseus, I hadn't even thought about the fact that since Death called the bulls to Him they haven't eaten.* The glowing spirit of the bison bull didn't eat; the dead need no nourishment. He stood several yards from Death, staring at the God with such hatred that Thaddeus turned away from him.

"Yes, of course, my Lord. I can find her scent." Thaddeus wasn't actually sure he could track the Storyteller. A day had passed and it had rained since she'd passed this way, and the bison, his Warriors and Hunters, as well as the stupid Milks, were milling about, muddying scents. Thaddeus sighed and added, "But it would help me if the army would remain here and I searched ahead. They are interfering with her scent."

"You should have let Me know that earlier!" Death blasted the admonishment at Thaddeus. "I would have forced them to remain within the pass. Go on, dog-man. We shall await you." Death strode to the front of the army. "Remain here. Remain still. Do not wander. Thaddeus is on a mission for Me, and he does not need your interference."

The army instantly quieted. The Milks slumped to the damp ground in their groups, murmuring strange words to one another. Thaddeus's Warriors and Hunters sent him curious glances. Their Companions, Shepherds and Terriers alike, curled up together separate from the rest of the army, as had become their norm. He ignored them. They were not Odysseus, so their disloyalty was only an occasionally mild irritant—the Hunters and Warriors didn't seem to mind that their Terriers and Shepherds avoided their company, so why should he? For a moment Thaddeus considered asking for the help of his Hunters. Their senses had heightened as well as his, but Thaddeus decided he would rather not share the glory of tracking and capturing Death's favorite.

I will use this as a way to bargain with Death. I return His Storyteller to Him, and He will gift me with my own lands.

With the army contained Thaddeus moved out in front of them. When Death didn't follow him, he gratefully dropped to all fours as soon as he was out of sight of the God. Thaddeus moved in a serpentine path, tasting the air, testing the ground, sifting through the myriad of scents as he searched for that one particular odor that said *Storyteller*.

He'd almost given up and was trying to decide whether he would lie and just begin leading Death randomly to the east when he finally stumbled upon a small slash in the side of the mountain, well south of where the main pass ended. Like previously, it was not much more than a water runoff—at most a deer path. But he definitely caught the scent of Ralina, Renard, two canines, two horses, and one other Rider. Thaddeus raced back to Death.

"My Lord, I have found the Storyteller's scent trail!" Thaddeus remembered at the last moment to stand erect as he came within sight of the God of Death.

"Excellent. Lead, Hunter. We shall follow," said Death.

Thaddeus noted that Death didn't release the spirit of the bison, so the creature, still staring at Him with eyes filled with hatred, followed the God.

They had marched on for quite some time when the Storyteller's scent brought them to a cold campsite. There she and her small group had joined several other Wind Riders. They'd stopped for the night, and then their path led to the southeast.

"My Lord." Thaddeus hurried to the God. "Your Storyteller was here. I can scent that she has joined with more Wind Riders, though I believe only a group of three or four, and another man's scent I recognize."

Death gave him a dismissive look. "Of course. Renard is with her."

"No, not just Renard, my Lord. I recognize the scent of a member of the Tribe of the Trees—a young man named O'Bryan, who is cousin to the family that used to rule the Tribe." *Until I put an end to that, right, Odysseus?* He added the smug thought.

Death's heavy, bestial brow lifted. "Ah, that means the Tribe is ahead of us, with Dove and that magnificent woman I glimpsed so long ago as she brought down sunfire from the heavens and rained it on your extinct Tribe."

"Mari." Thaddeus said the name with disgust. "She's an abomination— part scratcher, part Tribe of the Trees."

"You say 'abomination.'" Death shrugged His huge shoulders. "I say 'interesting.' Can you track them?"

"Easily. They head out across the plains together."

"Excellent, Thaddeus. You have done well." Death clapped him on the back, almost knocking him to the ground. "Wherever they lead is where we shall go. No matter that it is a rather small group. This time we will be quite sure they cannot escape us by ending their lives before we can infect and cure them. *Then* they will provide us the information we need about where the main Herds are camped. Cured and changed, they will join our army and help Me bring about the destruction of those arrogant Wind Riders."

Thaddeus wanted to shout, *No one is as arrogant as You!* Instead, he nodded enthusiastically. "Exactly, my Lord. Excellent plan."

"How far ahead of us would you say they are?" Death asked as he scratched his shaggy black beard.

Thaddeus decided quickly to reply truthfully. "Easily one day, if not more, and they will keep pulling ahead of us. They have horses. We cannot possibly keep up with them on foot."

"Will you chance losing her scent should they pull too far ahead of us?" Death asked.

Thaddeus again decided he must be honest with the mercurial god. "There is always that possibility. It is weather dependent. Should it rain again I will most likely lose her scent, especially if they are more than a day ahead of us."

"But if we were able to move more swiftly?" Death said.

"Well, the fresher the scent the easier is it for me to track, even in the rain," said Thaddeus. "But You saw those horses. They can move unbelievably fast, even faster than our canines. That horse that escaped capture only did so because he was so swift he moved out of bowshot range before the Warriors could bring him down." He added as almost an afterthought, "Unless You can discover a way to move this army more quickly Your Storyteller might very well escape."

Death glowered at Thaddeus. "She will *not* escape Me."

Thaddeus would have liked to laugh in the God's face. Thaddeus didn't know a lot about Wind Riders, but even he was aware of how fast they were—faster than even the swiftest human or canine.

Then Thaddeus realized that Death had moved away from him. The God strode to the head of the army with the reluctant bison ghost at His side. He turned to face the large group. The bison bulls grazed around Him. Behind them the Warriors and Hunters had spread out on logs and rocks, resting. Their Shepherds and Terriers grouped together, as usual, well away from their Companions. The Milks, which made up the bulk of Death's army, stood or sat in silent groupings staring at nothing, speaking infrequently and only to one another.

Death cupped His huge hands around His mouth, tilted His head, and roared a clarion call that shook the pine boughs that flanked the verdant valley.

Every bison lifted his head at Death's bellow and stared at the God. Beside Death, the spirit of the king of bison echoed Death's call—eerily the cry lifted around them.

Again and again Death bellowed until Thaddeus wanted to scream at Him to *shut up shut up shut up!*

And then the earth began to shake.

Thaddeus moved away from the tall pines behind him. He'd experienced earthquakes before, though not often, but he remembered that it was safest to be free of trees and boulders and out in the open when the earth shook. Death was continuing to bellow, so he motioned for his Warriors and Hunters to join him—well away from any trees.

"What is it, Thaddeus? Why is Death causing the earth to shake?" asked Wilson, who rushed to Thaddeus on all fours.

"I don't know, but we should remain out in the open. It is safest here." Thaddeus threw a look at Death. The God was standing near several tall, shivering pines. "He's immortal. We aren't."

Thaddeus smelled them first—musk, shit, piss—familiar scents that had been polluting his nose since the bulls had plowed their way through the pass.

"Look!" Wilson pointed to a distant area of the valley where a dark line thickened as the shaking of the land reverberated through Thaddeus's body.

Thaddeus stared. As the line got closer, he realized what they were—bison. A herd of them raced toward Death.

"The earth doesn't quake," Thaddeus told his men. "It is a herd of bison. Get behind the trees!"

As they scrambled for cover, the dark herd stampeded to Death. For a moment Thaddeus thought that they would trample the God, and he wondered what Death would do. Get up and brush Himself off? Clap His huge hands together and cause the deaths of the herd?

None of those things happened. Instead, the herd of bison slid to a halt before the God of Death. Their muzzles dropped to the ground in submission to Him. Then they stood, silent except for their labored breathing, focused on nothing but the God.

Death's massive head swiveled around until His gaze found Thaddeus. The God's smile was feral. "What do you think, dog-man? Will you be able to scent My Storyteller now?"

Thaddeus moved from the cover of the pines to approach Death. "I do not understand, my Lord."

"Of course you do not," Death scoffed. "Were you as wise as a god I would not have to explain, but you are not—so I shall share my brilliant plan with you and My army. We ride the bison. They will carry us across the plains so that we do not lose My Storyteller, and I have a feeling she will lead us into the heart of the Wind Riders and the very Herd that I must overthrow to gain possession of this fertile land."

Thaddeus felt a jolt of shock. "We *ride* the bison?"

"That is what I said, dog-man. Tell the Warriors and Hunters to mount up." He turned away from Thaddeus to bellow at the Milks, commanding them to mount the bison. Like the mindless beings they were, the Milks ambled to the herd. Expressionless and mute, they mounted the giant beasts and waited for Death's next command.

Hesitantly, Thaddeus, followed by his men, approached the mass of huge creatures. They snorted and pawed the ground but remained still as each Warrior and Hunter climbed onto their backs. Then Death picked out the largest of the bulls and leaped astride him.

As an afterthought, the God of Death turned his gaze to the glowing spirit of the bull who had led them through the pass. "You shall not be free quite yet, King of the Bison. Remain with Me yet a little while. I may have need of you."

The bison spirit lifted his head. His red eyes glared at Death. He snorted and then roared his loathing at the God before he took position at His side.

Death threw back His head and laughed. "Ah, kings can be so temperamental. Now, dog-man, lead us. We shall follow."

Thaddeus owed the Storyteller bitch his thanks, and he enjoyed the irony of it. Had it not been for her, he would be stuck somewhere back with the rancid herd of bison, eating the dust of those in the lead, but because Death needed him to track Ralina by scent Thaddeus was allowed to go before the herd. He was decidedly uncomfortable astride the big, somber bison bull, but the army was traveling much swifter riding than on foot.

"*Dog-man!*" Death bellowed from behind Thaddeus.

Thaddeus had to grit his teeth to keep from shouting at the God to shut up and stop calling him dog-man. Of course he could never say such a thing and expect to live—and Thaddeus would always survive. So, he fixed his face into an amiable expression and turned to face the God, Who galloped up on the largest bull in the huge herd.

"So you still have her scent?" The God had posed this question to Thaddeus over and over as the days passed and they continued to cross the deserted plains chasing the group Ralina was with.

"Yes, my Lord. I have her scent," said Thaddeus truthfully.

"How far ahead are they?" Death asked.

"They continue to pull ahead," said Thaddeus. "My best guess is that we are almost three days behind them."

"All the more reason I will defeat these Wind Riders. Only a god should control beasts as swift as horses," said Death. "Though I am beginning to believe I shall not get the chance to experiment with merging horse with man before we attack their main encampment."

"You think that's where they are going?" Thaddeus asked the question only to keep the God engaged. It had been obvious to him since he scented O'Bryan that the Wind Riders had been joined by the group Nik and Mari led, which meant they had arrived weeks before, with plenty of time to warn the horse people so they could retreat to their stronghold.

"I am certain of it, which actually saves Me time," said Death, scratching His thick, wooly beard. "My plans have changed. I will not infect and cure a small group of Wind Riders. I shall infect and cure *all of them*." The God threw back His massive head and made a sound that was meant to be laughter but was more like the roar of a beast. "I am especially pleased that it seems likely we are being led to a stronghold wherein we will find the group that escaped ahead of us."

Thaddeus nodded. "That means Dove, the vessel You chose for your goddess, should be with them."

Death scoffed. "Yes, but upon more thought I have decided that she is too flawed for My beloved to indwell. I rather like the idea of a Sun Warrior being the vessel for the Goddess of Life."

"Sun Warrior?" For a moment Thaddeus wasn't sure of whom the God spoke—and then he realized who it was, and couldn't stop his sneer. "You mean the hybrid scratcher bitch Mari?"

With blinding speed, Death struck Thaddeus so hard that he was thrown from the bison and landed in the grass, struggling to find his breath.

"Do not *ever* disparage My beloved's vessel!"

Thaddeus cringed against the ground. "I am sorry, my Lord. It is just that I know the scratcher. She is unpleasant."

Death snorted. "It matters not what she is or is not. She will be no more when My love awakens, though like with this body, her talents will remain. The Goddess of Life may find it interesting to have the ability to call sunfire from the skies."

Thaddeus could only imagine how horrible that would be—especially if Death's *beloved* was even a fraction as volatile as Him. *Odysseus, this is just one more reason for me to settle my Tribe well away from them.* "You are right, my Lord. Forgive me. I hadn't thought of that."

Death bared his teeth in a feral smile. "Of course I am right. Now, re-mount and lead on, Thaddeus. Our future awaits."

🐎🐎🐎

Ralina was amazed at the speed with which the horses traveled across the plain. She kept glancing at the little light cart that held Bear and Kong, scrunched in beside Ian, the Companion to Bonnie, the gelding who pulled it. When they'd begun their sprint across the plains at sunrise, Dawn had decided it would be best if the canines rode in the cart and O'Bryan rode tandem on a horse, as it was impossible for Bear and Kong to maintain pace with galloping horses.

O'Bryan joined Rand on Merlin. Bard had told Ralina that he could easily carry Renard behind her, so her lover joined her.

Then they ran.

Ralina had never known such speed and strength. Bard was a marvel to her—as were the other Wind Riders. Dawn's Echo was especially magnificent. She led them, the swiftest of the horses by far.

They raced across the plain in a never-ending cycle of galloping for as long as the horses could manage to keep up such a fast pace. Then Echo would drop to a ground-eating trot. The other horses slowed and followed her at a trot, which they seemed to be able to maintain endlessly.

Periodically, Dawn would call a halt so that they could stop, water and feed the horses, and walk beside them as they cooled. Then Echo would toss her head and whinny impatiently, and Dawn would set out at a gallop again as the rest of their group scrambled to keep up with her.

Ralina thought her buttocks would never regain feeling. Her thighs

328

were on fire, and her feet were completely numb. But she did not complain. She could almost feel Death's hot, rancid breath on her neck; the faster they traveled the better.

They rode until the sky was black and Echo decided it was unsafe to continue, and then the group stopped and quickly made camp. The first night they settled by a lazy river. Without any discussion, the Wind Riders from Herd Magenti unpacked nets from their travel bags. Ralina watched with interest as she wiped down Bard while they cast the nets out into the river, pulling in clumps of fat, wriggling fish, which they quickly gutted and cooked, but their focus wasn't on filling the bellies of the humans.

"On a race across the plains we must always care for our Companions first," explained Dawn. "We can ride ill or exhausted or starving, but if our Companions are any of those things they cannot carry us."

"And if they cannot carry us, Death's army will catch us." Ralina completed the thought for her.

"Exactly," said Dawn. "Though an army on foot is no match for our swiftness. We will make it to the Valley of Vapors in less than six more days of travel. It will take at least three times that long for people on foot—and probably longer for a group the size of the army you describe."

Ralina groomed Bard and then carefully mixed his sweet mash. She knew what Dawn said was truth, but her intuition told her they were being pursued—and much faster than the Wind Riders believed.

The second day of travel started as the day before—when the predawn sky had barely begun to blush. They woke in darkness, ate hastily as they tended to the horses and broke camp, and began the race across the plains as soon as Echo decided the weak light illuminated the land just enough so that they could gallop safely.

Ralina ignored the pain in her body. Muscles she had never before used screamed. When they paused at midday, she had to bite her lip to keep from crying out as she slid from Bard's back and hobbled around her stallion to loosen his waterskin and mix his midday meal, but Bard made it all better. He knew she suffered, and he nickered soft encouragement to her. Dawn showed Renard and Ralina great kindness by offering them a healing salve that smelled astringent but when rubbed on their bodies helped the agony in their muscles.

They covered an unbelievable amount of ground in three days, though

Ralina could not shake the feeling that Death was closer than any of them realized. As the sun sank behind them on the third day, they came to a rise in the land. On it was a grove of oaks that stretched their gnarled branches, thick and mighty, to the sky. Running through the grove was a crystal stream, which the horses waded into eagerly. Echo chose then to allow them their last break before their final gallop when darkness would force them to halt and make camp.

"Let our Companions drink; then we will walk beside them until Echo says they are ready to run again. We will not break again until dusk," said Dawn.

Ralina slid gratefully to the ground after Renard. Bear and Kong came to them, huffing and pressing against them.

"You're doing so well," said Renard. "Ralina and I are so proud of you."

Ian smiled. "They've really acclimated to the cart. Their balance is excellent. Much better even than O'Bryan's."

"Hey, I tried!" called O'Bryan from where he was stretching beside Merlin.

Ian laughed. "You did a good job, but Dozer says you're heavier than the canines."

Ralina wanted to join their easy banter, but she couldn't relax. She kept looking over her shoulder.

"They cannot possibly catch us," said Dawn.

Ralina met the Lead Mare Rider's gaze. "My mind knows that, but my heart is still worried."

"I wish we had our Tribe's lookout towers here," said Renard. "From our tall pines we could see all around our forest."

"That's it!" Ralina said. "Dawn, if you allow, I can climb the tallest of those oaks." She pointed at the grove of giants. "From there I can see across the plains—particularly behind us."

"You believe the army is closer than we think."

Dawn didn't phrase it as a question, but Ralina answered, "Yes. I cannot stop thinking that He is just there—" She jerked her chin at the direction from which they'd come. "Right behind us."

"It seems impossible, but it also seems impossible that humans would mutate into beasts," said Dawn. "Yes. Climb and look. We will wait."

Renard, Bear, and Kong went with Ralina to the tallest of the oaks.

"I can climb," said Renard. "I know how sore you are."

Ralina snorted. "No sorer than you. And I'm lighter, which means I can safely climb to the higher boughs that would break under your weight." She shrugged. "It'll be good for me to use my old skills. There is one thing every member of the Tribe of the Trees does well, and that is . . ."

"*Climb*," she and Renard said together as Bear and Kong barked in agreement.

Renard boosted her up to a low bough and Ralina began to climb. It felt odd at first. There were no intricately carved bridges connecting this tree to its neighbor. There were no homes, dangling like ornate nests of giant birds from the upper branches. There was no scent of pine and cooking—no sounds of a happy, prosperous Tribe. Though even without those famil-iarities Ralina quickly relaxed, happy to be far above ground again, where she felt safe and at home—so very much at home.

Ralina hadn't realized she was weeping until she had to brush tears from her face, which she did quickly. *I don't have time for loss or longing. Later. Not now. Later.*

Ralina climbed.

She came to the crown of the oak sooner than she expected—too soon. Ralina could have remained in the embrace of the ancient tree forever, especially had Bear and Renard and Kong been up there with her. She longed for a family nest and the comforts and safety of the past, but as she steadied herself, holding tightly to the uppermost branches of the oak, Ralina felt the touch of Bard's mind.

You will have a new home with me, my Ralina.

Yes, precious one, I know. Ralina sent warmth and love back to Bard through their connection. *I do not mean to upset you by my remembrance.*

You do not. I will always remember my Clayton, but if we choose life we must move on.

Indeed, agreed Ralina.

She pulled herself up, hooked her feet in a fork in the topmost branches, and peered around her.

It seemed she could see forever. It helped that the plains were mostly flat. From her tall vantage point she could see distant clusters of ruins, which they had avoided in their race across the land. Ralina's gaze didn't pause on the ruins. Death wouldn't stop at a ruin. He was single-minded in His need to conquer the Wind Riders, and they would not be found in crumbled remains of the ancients.

Ralina lifted her hand to tent over her eyes as she gazed into the west, squinting against the glare of the setting sun. At first she didn't understand what her eyes saw. In the far distance, against the horizon, it seemed clumps of black, like huge mounds of earth, were moving forward—toward them—leaving a dust cloud in their wake. Ralina stared and finally understood. There, only perhaps a day behind, was a herd of bison, but the bison were misshapen. Ralina squinted harder and continued studying them. Then her stomach roiled. They appeared misshapen because they were being ridden! At the front of the herd was the glowing shape of a bison spirit, dead and shackled to a malevolent god. She had been right. Death was closer than any of them—except her—had believed.

Resolutely, Ralina descended.

"Your face tells me that your news is not good, Storyteller," said Dawn as Ralina and Renard hurried back to their little group with Bear and Kong on their heels.

"Death is only a day behind us, and He is mounted—as is His army," said Ralina slowly as she stroked Bard's neck.

"Mounted?" Rand blurted. "How could that be possible? Except for Merlin and Bard, all of Herd Ebony's horses are no more."

"Remember the bison He was using to clear the snow from the pass for His army?" Ralina said.

Rand nodded. "I will never forget that sight."

Ralina swallowed the bile that had risen in her throat. "Death and His army are riding bison, and from what I can see He called more of the beasts so that His entire army is mounted."

"Oh, Mother Mare!" Dawn said. She reached out for Echo as if to steady herself, but quickly the Lead Mare Rider recovered. Her voice was steel. "Then we ride even faster and rest even less. Bison can sprint at speeds that rival horses, but they are not used to running for long periods of time, and never burdened by riders. We are swifter. We will make it to the Valley of Vapors before them." Echo snorted and tossed her head as the other horses whinnied their agreement.

"Yes we will, Lead Mare Rider," said Rand. "You ride. We follow."

"For Herd Magenti!" shouted Dawn.

"For Herd Magenti!" the group responded.

Then they rode with renewed speed and determination, and Ralina understood intimately exactly how the Wind Riders had earned their name.

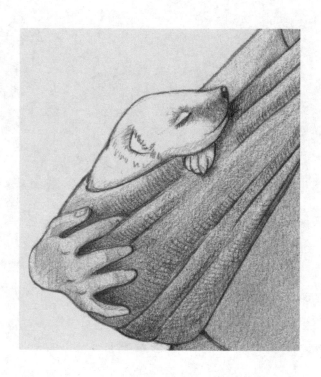

CHAPTER 29

Herd Magenti and the Valley of Vapors had been in constant motion since Mari, the Pack, and River's Magenti Central had arrived a week before, but there was no hysteria—and no whining or complaints. The Magenti Herds worked together with consideration and mutual respect. They listened to each of the five Lead Mare Riders, as well as the Mare Council, who had chosen to join Magenti at this, the largest and most well-appointed sanctuary of the five Great Herds.

One of the first tasks River set the Herd to accomplishing was to clear all trees from the area just outside the huge, rocky wall that ringed the valley. The trees were felled and chopped up, and then horses dragged the wood on litters into the campsite to be stacked for cook and hearth fires.

Mari was still amazed by the beauty of the valley, as well as astounded by what incredibly snug shelters the buildings of the ancients provided. For her entire life Mari had been warned against going anywhere near the ruins of the ancients. *Of cities beware—Skin Stealers are there!* Her mother had drilled into her that the cities of the ancients were dangerous and ruins were places only to be carefully pillaged, but never inhabited.

It was so, so different in the Valley of Vapors. The ruins of the city of the ancients had been meticulously restored. Any building not habitable had been torn down and salvaged to maintain sturdier buildings with structural integrity. And those buildings gleamed—they were pearl-like white stone from which ivy and flowers draped and perfumed the mineral-scented air.

In the areas where buildings had been torn down, purple Magenti tents were erected, boasting banners and streamers, feathers and glass and beads. Beautiful, spacious tents spread throughout the valley, especially in the areas surrounding the places where hot mineral waters bubbled up from beneath the valley, warming everything.

The main road leading through the heart of the valley was miraculous. Flat stones carefully fitted and mortared together served as a wide walkway for Companions and their Riders. Mari thought it was a marvel that even when it rained they were able to traverse the length of the settlement without sloughing through mud.

Everyone was busy; everyone had a task, and even amidst their preparation for war, the Herd was filled with beauty and serenity—and a sense of community that permeated everything.

But by far Mari's favorite area of the valley was the largest of the restored buildings. The Herd called it the plant nursery. Though not a burrow, it gave Mari the same feeling she'd had tending the Clan's many gardens with her mother. It was solace and a connection to the earth's green growing things that all Earth Walkers craved, and Mari often visited the nursery just to ground herself, which was where she was when Rigel rushed up to her, barking and wagging and leaning against her in a joyous doggy greeting. Not far behind was Laru, who greeted her with greater maturity but no less exuberance. And behind Laru came Nik—her mate and lover.

"There you are." Nik grinned and bent to kiss her. "I had to ask Laru to track you. It's easy to lose you in this place."

"Well, if you ever can't find me, just come here. You can pretty much count on the fact that I'll make my way to this building eventually," said Mari as she sighed happily and gazed around the huge white marble building.

"Me as well!" called Sora from where she was weeding a bed of winter spinach.

"And the rest of us!" From even deeper in the nursery came the voices of other Earth Walkers as they busied themselves tending the riot of plants that filled the place.

Nik gazed up at the elaborate system of mirrors that were mounted along the top of the tall marble walls. They were positioned to catch sunlight and direct it down inside the building at the beds of herbs and vegetables that thrived within. Like in all of the buildings of the ancients, hot water from the mineral springs on which the valley had been built ran beneath the floor, heating the plants that thrived there year round.

"And how are the Mother Plants doing?" asked Nik.

"Spectacularly." Davis grinned as he and Sora, with Cammy and little Chloe padding beside them, made their way from the center of the nursery. "Mari, what do you think of the image of the Great Mother Goddess?"

Their small group turned their focus to the center of the main floor of the nursery where Davis and the Earth Walker women had been lovingly re-creating the Earth Goddess idol Whose carved face Davis had brought from Mari's burrow. The Goddess image was new, so Her body—made of fertile earth covered by velvet moss—was still taking root, as were the ferns that cascaded down Her shoulders. She appeared to be rising from Her resting place on the earth, as if awakening from the winter, and the beautiful carved obsidian oval that was Her face was radiant, especially when a beam of sunlight refracted from the mirror system to illuminate Her.

Mari's smile was bittersweet. "Davis, I think my mother would approve. This image is verdant and lovely. It's like She's always been here."

"All of the plants we brought with us are thriving," said Sora as she wiped sweat from her face. "They love this heat and humidity, and the Herd's watering system is incredible.

"River was explaining to me about the pipes, wheels, and windmills that keep water, both mineral and lake water, pumping throughout these buildings." Nik's voice was filled with excitement. "It is amazing that even though the lake is outside the walls, all we need do is lift a lever and water spills from it."

"It is delightful," said Sora. "I know we're preparing for a terrible war, but I have never been surrounded by such luxuries." She patted her thick, curly hair. "And my hair is spectacular. It loves the mineral water—as does my skin."

Mari nodded. "I have never soaked so long in a bath in my life. When the water begins to cool, I just lift the lever and hot water pours in!"

"It is a special type of miracle," said Sora reverently before adding,

"Mari, have we no word of O'Bryan and the Wind Riders he left with? They have been gone for days and days—well over a week. Dove told me Herd Magenti has sentries placed in the mountains surrounding the valley—lookouts watch for our people as well as Death and His army. Why haven't they been spotted?"

Mari sighed. "I spoke with River this morning while Nik and I were breaking our fast, and there has been no sign of them."

"I wish O'Bryan would return," said Nik. "I worry for him."

"As do I." Sora's voice was heavy with concern. "He is so kind—so compassionate, especially toward animals. It could break him to kill the Wind Riders' Companions." She shuddered. "It almost breaks me just to think of it."

From behind them River's voice rang against the smooth marble wall. "It almost breaks many of us." She entered the building with Dove's arm hooked through hers.

"Our sentries have announced that Dawn and her group have been sighted," said Dove, whose eyeless face was somber.

"Is O'Bryan with them?" Sora asked quickly.

"I assume he is, though they were too far away yet to recognize individuals," said River. Then she added, "The sentry did count two additional horses, and Companions riding double."

"What does that mean?" asked Nik.

"It means that there are Wind Riders who are Companionless—or that my mother's group has picked up people who are not part of our community, but who are important enough that she believed they need to be brought to us quickly," said River.

"Is that good or bad?" Mari asked.

River shrugged. "We cannot know until they arrive, but I thought you would like to join us as we greet them."

"I would very much like to greet O'Bryan," said Sora as she patted at her wild mane of hair and wiped at her sweaty face.

A little mewing sound that also could have been a growl came from the pouch slung across Sora's chest. Mari frowned as she glanced down at Chloe, who was chasing ever-patient Cammy around tomato beds. *If Chloe is down there, then who is in Sora's pouch?*

"Oh." Sora smiled and rearranged the pouch so that her friends could see that it held a small white creature whose bright, intelligent eyes looked around at the humans surrounding him. "It's just Cubby. Claudia told me he misses O'Bryan and has been restless. Chloe is getting too big for this pouch anyway, so I've started carrying him around with me."

Mari raised one brow at her friend. "Really?"

"Really." Sora frowned. "Would *you* leave a baby to pine for his Companion?"

"Of course not." Nik spoke up right away, and his sentiments were echoed by River and Dove while Mari just watched Sora knowingly.

"How soon will your mother's group arrive?" Sora changed the subject neatly.

"Soon. They were spotted not far from here, and they're moving fast," said Dove.

"Which means you don't have time to bathe and primp," added Mari.

River coughed to hide her bark of laughter. "Well, um, we should make our way to the entrance. By the time we're there Mother and her group should be arriving."

"If you do not mind, Cammy and I will stay and continue to work on the Mother Goddess idol," said Davis as Cammy huffed beside him.

"I do not mind at all. My mother's welcome by the Herd will be crowded enough." River looked from Davis to the idol. "And what you're creating is lovely."

Davis smiled. "Thank Mari for that. The Goddess's face came from a burrow tended by Moon Women for generations."

"I didn't know that," said River. "That makes the statue even more precious."

"Yes," Mari said. "It does."

The nursery was in the middle of the row of buildings that lined the wide main walkway of the Valley of Vapors, and together Dove and River, Mari, Sora, and Nik walked toward the narrow entrance to the impressive site. Laru and Rigel padded beside them, ignoring little Chloe, who made a game of trying to jump up and bite their tails. Within just a few paces, Anjo trotted up to join River, with the Terrier pup Kit balancing carefully on her wide rump.

"It's amazing how quickly the pups have acclimated to horseback," said Nik as he reached up and scratched Kit under her chin.

"My Kit has an excellent seat," said River, grinning at her pup, who yipped happily.

The small group walked down the main walkway of the valley and Mari marveled at the busy Herd. Everyone worked together, and as it was past midday the enticing aroma of meals being prepared for dinner mingled with the ever-present earthy scent of minerals, making her mouth water.

A huge, sphere-shaped boulder marked the entrance of Herd Magenti's winter sanctuary. Shortly after they had arrived River had explained a lever and pulley system allowed it to be easily rolled to block the only entrance to the valley, though for as long as she had been alive she couldn't recall any time it had been moved from its resting place beside the entrance—until now. Now it had been cleaned, all plants and dirt from around it cleared, and new ropes and levers had been anchored to it, and the Herd daily practiced closing and opening it.

And each night the boulder was rolled to seal the entrance so that the Herd rested snugly, secure in the knowledge no one could enter their sanctuary uninvited.

As they waited for the group to arrive, Mari gazed around the walled city. The Herd had spent the preparation days wisely. The area outside the tall, spikey rock wall was completely clear. There were no trees, not even any scrub bushes, that an attacking army could use as cover. Atop the wall the Herd had set up bow stations where Riders could easily ascend rope ladders and find quivers full of arrows, slings and rocks, and even throwing spears—though they were much more effective when launched from horseback.

"It looks like we're ready for Death's army," said Mari to River.

River smoothed back her long braided hair and leaned against Anjo, still holding Dove's hand. "I hope we have another seven days or so until Death arrives. The valley is secure, but our Riders are still working at setting up traps outside the walls."

Nik nodded. "Wilkes, Davis, Sheena, and I have been helping with that and it's going well. We have several surprises for an invading army, though it would be nice to have more time to prepare."

"Tulpar says you and your group have been great help," said Dove as she smiled in the direction of Nik.

"Your stallion is magnificent," said Nik enthusiastically. "He doesn't ever seem to rest but is always overseeing our preparations."

Dove sighed. "Indeed he is. I have to remind him nightly that he cannot protect the Herd if he becomes ill from not taking care of himself."

River patted Dove's hand where it rested on the crook of her arm. "You should have told me that Tulpar was overextending himself. Anjo will speak with him. Our Herd Stallion must be in top shape for the coming battle." Anjo tossed her head and snorted in agreement.

Then, as if speaking of him invoked his presence, the beautiful golden stallion galloped through the entrance, his hooves clattering against the flat stone of the walkway. He slid to a halt before Dove and nuzzled her gently.

"Yes, sweet boy. I hear you, but I do not need to tell River as here they are."

Only paces behind Tulpar, Dawn and Echo galloped through the entrance, followed by the three Rider/Companion teams they'd left with— including Ian, driving the light cart his Dozer pulled. The horses were soaked with sweat and blowing hard, and their Riders looked disheveled and exhausted. The instant they entered the campsite two big Shepherds leaped from the cart. Rigel and Laru rushed to them, barking a riotous welcome.

"Bear! Kong!" Nik shouted as he raced to the Shepherds. "Is it really you two?" Then Nik laughed joyously while the big canines jumped around him, barking happily. "But where are—"

"Nik, thank the Sun!" cried a woman who slid quickly off a tall black stallion and staggered to Nik to be swallowed in a huge, welcoming hug.

"Ralina?" Mari said as she hurried to join them.

The Storyteller looked up and smiled wearily at her. "Mari, it is so good to see that you are safe."

"Nik!" A man followed close behind Ralina to greet Nik.

"Renard? You're here, too?" Nik pounded his back and then had to steady him as he almost fell to his knees. "Sorry, my friend. I didn't realize."

Renard was gaunt and pale, but his smile beamed as he gripped Nik's arm. "It has been a long journey."

Nik turned to face River and Dove, as well as the crowd that had begun to form around them. "This is Ralina, Companion to Bear, and Storyteller to Tribe of the Trees. And this is a talented young Warrior, Renard, Companion to Kong."

"Greetings." River crossed her fists over her heart. "Welcome to the Valley of Vapors."

In the middle of the greetings, the big black stallion pushed his way through the group until he was beside the Storyteller, who rested one hand on his sleek coat.

"Bard?" River moved to stand before the stallion. She looked from him to her mother, who was just dismounting from Echo.

Dawn embraced her daughter quickly and brushed her hair back from her dirty, sweaty face before she made the announcement that had the growing group of Riders surrounding them gasping in shock. "Clayton is no more, and Bard has Chosen Ralina as his Companion."

Then the last member of the small, weary group came through the narrow entrance. Rand led his gray stallion, Merlin, and went immediately to River. He bowed low to her. "Greetings, Lead Mare Rider of Herd Magenti. I would beg entrance to your sanctuary."

River looked from the Stallion Rider to her mother. "I do not understand. We all felt the death of Herd Ebony, yet here is Rand, his Merlin, and Clayton's stallion, Bard—alive and well. Mother, please explain."

Dawn spoke in a clear voice that carried throughout the group. "Clayton's Herd Ebony is no more, but not because we were able to fulfill their death sentence. Clayton and all of his Herd except Rand were captured by Death and His army."

"Oh, Great Goddess, no!" Dove said. She staggered and would have fallen had Tulpar and River not been there to steady her.

"Death did not kill Herd Ebony." Ralina's voice, seasoned by years of storytelling, commanded silence in all within listening distance. "Clayton and his Herd ended their own lives instead of allowing Death to use them. Bard is here with me because Clayton helped him escape as Death captured his Herd. He finally understood and believed the truth of what Dawn and I had warned, so he sent Bard to us so that we could travel quickly to your valley and warn you of what is to come."

Dawn nodded and into the silence added, "Clayton regained his honor at the end, though it cost him his life, and the lives of his Herd."

"Rand, how did you and your Merlin survive?" asked River.

"Clayton thought he could spy on Death and His army." Rand's voice was rough with emotion. "Ralina and Renard knew better. They refused to follow Clayton as he sought to get closer to Death, and I agreed with them. Merlin and I remained with the Storyteller and her mate while Clayton and the Herd stalked Death's army." He shook his head and his shoulders bowed. "We watched as they were captured. Bard rushed to us and we fled. That is why Merlin and I survived."

"Rand listened to and helped us," Ralina said. "He was the only member of Herd Ebony who did."

"Daughter, I ask you to pardon Rand and his Merlin. Though he chose to follow Clayton, he has more than atoned for that mistake," said Dawn.

River's gaze returned to Rand. The Stallion Rider bowed low to her.

"I acknowledge my mother's wisdom. Rand, Rider of Merlin, you are pardoned."

He straightened and wiped tears from his cheeks. "Thank you, Lead Mare Rider. I will spend the rest of my life atoning for my mistake."

"As you should," River said.

Sora approached O'Bryan. "You are whole and not broken by your journey?"

O'Bryan's open, kind face was pale, and he was thinner than when he'd left. Dark circles bruised his eyes. He nodded wearily. "I am whole and unbroken."

Sora reached up and tugged on his shirt so that he bent down. There, in front of everyone, she kissed him—passionately and completely. Then, while he stared at her with a dazed smile lifting the corners of his lips, she reached into the pouch slung across her chest and pulled out the squirming, grunting Cubby, who immediately began covering his dirty face with kisses.

"Good," Sora said. Then she turned and pushed her way through the crowd.

"Mother," River drew the group's attention back to her. "How many days behind you is Death's army?"

"One for sure, but we hope two or more," said Dawn grimly. "We have raced here, pushing our Companions to the edge of exhaustion to try to pull farther ahead of them."

"What? One? How could that be?" River shook her head. "An army on foot cannot possibly be as swift as our Companions—not even one led by the God of Death."

"They are not on foot," said Dawn. "Death enslaved a herd of bison. The mighty beasts carry Him and His horrible army across our plains. They will be here soon."

"Oh, Great Goddess!" Dove cried out, and pressed her face against Tulpar's golden neck.

"We will not panic." River's voice carried throughout the crowd. "We are safe within the walls of our sanctuary. We are prepared. Herd Magenti will not be ruled by Death."

Tulpar trumpeted his agreement. His voice was joined by each stallion in the Herd and echoed by Anjo.

"As my daughter said, we will *not* be ruled by Death, especially as we have with us one who knows how to defeat Him," said Dawn as she turned to Ralina. "Speak, Storyteller. Tell them how Death will be vanquished."

Ralina straightened her shoulders. Even exhausted, thin to the point of emaciation, and covered with travel dirt and sweat Mari thought she looked regal and confident—and when she spoke her voice was filled with a strength that belied the haggard look of her body. "Death will be vanquished by the Goddess of Life, and I know how to awaken Her."

The Lead Mare Riders and Herd Stallion Riders spread the word throughout the valley that Death's army approached. There was no panic—no weeping or hysteria. There was only action. Arrow stations along the valley wall were filled. Vats heavy with fat were added to the stations. They could be lit and poured down on soldiers foolish enough to attempt to breach the walls.

At dusk River called for Ralina, Mari, and Sora to join her, Dove, April, and Dawn with the Mare Council in the gleaming white building that housed the older women and their Companions. The building was large, though not as big as the nursery. In the main room was a fireplace so massive Mari thought she and Sora could have easily stood within it. It burned steadily—as did a myriad of candles placed all around the spacious room. The light from the flickering flames turned the white room golden and made shadows dance across the walls.

They met in a semicircle before the great hearth fire. The Mare Council, including Dawn, sat on carved wooden chairs facing out at the room where River and Dove, Mari, Sora, and Ralina stood. Behind them were their Companions, including canines, silent though observing everything carefully.

River opened the meeting by introducing Ralina and Bear to the Council. Ralina, who had bathed, changed out of her filthy travel clothes, and eaten a warm meal, looked substantially better, though still too thin and pale. She faced the Council with her back straight and her chin lifted. Bard was the only Companion present who refused to remain on the fringe of the group. Instead, the big black stallion was always within touching distance of his new Companion—something no Rider questioned.

"Ralina was Storyteller to the mighty Tribe of the Trees," said River in a clear, strong voice. "Her canine Companion is the Shepherd Bear." From where he lay beside Rigel, Bear barked at his introduction, which had the Mare Council smiling. River continued. "And you see her stallion, Bard, here beside her." Instantly, the Council sobered, bowing their heads in acknowledgment of the new Rider pair. "Ralina traveled as Death's captive, escaping only with the help of the Goddess. Her story impacts us all. Not only does she have intimate knowledge of Death and His army, but she also knows how to defeat Him." River motioned for Ralina to take her place before the Mare Council.

With Bard at her side, Ralina stood in front of the semicircle of wise women. Mari stood not far from the Storyteller, beside Sora and little Chloe, who was asleep in the pouch she was almost too big to fit in comfortably. Mari listened raptly as Ralina told her gruesome story.

The brave Storyteller began with the extinction of the Tribe of the Trees—recounting in detail how Death had lured what was left of the sick Tribe to see off Him and His army of mutating Hunters and Warriors as they launched their boats on the Umbria River, only to loose an arrow and set aflame the forest, murdering what was left of the once mighty Tribe.

Mari closed her eyes and wiped tears from her cheeks. She loved Nik and those members of his Tribe who had joined their Pack so very much. Even though the Tribesmen who followed Thaddeus in taking Death's cure were reprehensible and beyond salvation, she pitied the poor Tribe members who had been innocent of Thaddeus's betrayal and had been slaughtered by Death. *I'm so glad Nik isn't hearing this. He knew they were likely dead, but this fiery end would break his heart.*

Ralina's strong, clear voice continued, taking them with her on a horrendous journey. She recounted the end of the Saleesh people, and the reanimation of their corpses by spirits long dead.

"Storyteller." Morgana raised her hand to interrupt Ralina. "Do you know what spirits dwell in the reanimated bodies?"

Ralina sighed and brushed back her hair. "The Milks, which is what we named them for their dead, white eyes, are very difficult to communicate with, so this is only a guess, but I believe they are the spirits of the ancients that died in the gorge during the sunfire that ended their world."

"Do you know why they reanimated?" River asked Ralina.

"All I know is what Death told me—that they must atone, though for what and how not even the God knows," said Ralina.

"Can these Milks be killed?" Morgana asked.

Ralina nodded. "Oh, absolutely. They died in hordes during our journey. They drowned as we crossed Lost Lake. They fell from the side of the Rock Mountains pass. But they also show no fear at all for their lives, which makes them dangerous soldiers."

"Interesting . . . Go on, Storyteller," said Morgana.

Ralina continued, taking them into the Rock Mountain pass and recounting how Thaddeus and his Hunters and Warriors had continued to change physically and emotionally—until they were more beasts than men—and how their Shepherds and Terriers began to avoid them.

"Even at the very end, when Renard, Rand, and I watched Death approach and capture Clayton and his Herd, it was obvious. We could see that the behavior of the canines was unusual. They grouped together—well away from their Companions." She glanced back at Mari and Sora. "You know how strange that behavior is."

Mari gave Rigel, who was curled up only a few feet from her, a fond look as Sora caressed her sleeping pup's head and said, "We do."

"As do April and I," said River, who motioned to their pups, Kit and Cleo, who slept on the rumps of their horses.

"The cure changes humans—that much is obvious," said Ralina. "But what no one realized at first was that it also changes the humans' Companion animals. Though I can tell you it didn't seem as if Death, or Thaddeus, or any of the Hunters and Warriors noticed the difference in their Companions. My intuition says that is important information for us to know."

"The more we know about Death and His army of horrors the better prepared we are to defend ourselves and defeat Him," said Morgana. "Continue, Storyteller. You have our full attention, as well as our appreciation."

Ralina told of how Death called the doe and then murdered her and shackled her spirit to Him as His guide and when she disappeared how He drew to Him the king of bison—to murder and enslave. "But what is most interesting about Death's two guides is that the God told me the Goddess of Life was responsible for freeing the doe's spirit from serving Him. It was about then that the Goddess sent me a vision in a dream. She told me that my time with Death had ended and when it began to snow I should follow the white doe to freedom, which is what Renard, his father, Daniel, and I did . . ." She paused and added, "Daniel died cutting the suspension bridge from over the gorge. We tried to slow Death, though He managed to continue through the pass anyway."

"You did what you could," said River. "It was you against an army and a god."

"I wanted to leave. Every single day I wanted to leave, or I wanted to follow that poor young priest who was the only Saleesh Death allowed to survive. I watched him drown himself in Lost Lake." Ralina's gaze fell to the smooth marble floor. "I would have done the same had it not been for Bear and Renard, Kong and Daniel. Back then they were all that kept me alive, but as we got farther and farther into the mountains I began to believe that I was alive for another purpose. That I must gain all the information I could from Death Himself—and with that information I would discover a way to defeat Him. I believe I have that information."

Morgana leaned forward on her chair. "Tell us, Storyteller. How do we defeat Death?"

"We do not," Ralina said. "He cannot be killed. I am sure of that. He must return to sleep in the arms of the Goddess of Life. Only then will order be restored to our world, but the Goddess is on our side. As I traveled with Death I hoped She would be, and now I know She is. She sent the doe to save me—not once but twice."

Dawn spoke up. "I can attest to that. The doe led us to Ralina."

"What do we need to do to help the Goddess defeat Death?" River asked.

"We must awaken Her," said Ralina. "And hope that by our doing so, the Goddess of Life can take Death into Her arms and return to the bowels of the earth with Him again."

"And how do we do that?" Morgana said.

"Death told me how He planned on awakening Her," said Ralina, her voice bright with excitement. "He is going to infect a woman with the skin-sloughing sickness and then pack the living flesh of a doe into her wounds and bleed her until she is on the verge of dying. Then He will command the Goddess to awaken in the body of the vessel He chose, and She will be compelled to come."

"Did Death say which woman?" River asked.

"Early, He did not speak with me about a specific woman, though I overheard Him talking with Thaddeus about her." Ralina turned to Dove. "Death spoke of an eyeless girl named Dove."

"He will not have Dove." River's voice was filled with anger.

"It wasn't just Dove Death spoke of," said Ralina. Her gaze found Mari. "He calls you the Sun Warrior, Mari. Death watched you call down sunfire just before His people attacked the Tribe. He is obsessed with you."

A chill fingered its way down Mari's spine, but her voice was strong and sure. "Death will not have me, either."

"Death will not have either of us," said Dove from her place astride Tulpar. Her golden stallion turned his head so that his Companion could gaze through his eyes at the group. "Death's description of how He will call forth the Goddess is much like how He was awakened. My Dead Eye, the boy I loved, was infected with the sickness. One night he cut himself and almost bled to death at the base of the idol our people used to worship—though Dead Eye and I always railed against the belief that the idol was anything but an empty shell." She shook her head, suddenly looking much older than her tender years. "Dead Eye must have shouted at the God—commanded that He awaken—and then He did, though my Dead Eye was still there, still within his body, but only for a short time. Death packed the living flesh of a stag in Dead Eye's wounds, and my love was killed—forced from his body so that Death might live." She turned to

Ralina. "Any human who calls forth the Goddess will suffer the same fate. She will be no more."

Ralina nodded. "Yes, I believe that, too, which is why I think together we should call Her forth. The Goddess of Life made it clear that She does not wish to awaken—not permanently. She told Death as much, though He refused to listen."

"Then one of us will have to sacrifice our life to the Goddess," said Dove.

"Perhaps not," said Ralina. "Look at the strength of the matriarchy surrounding us."

Dove said, "Ralina, you said the Goddess spoke to you in a dream, correct?"

"Yes."

"She has also spoken to River and Mari and me," said Dove. "That seems to support your belief that matriarchs might awaken Her, but the truth remains—a human may not be able to survive the indwelling of an immortal."

"Yes, I agree, which is why I believe matriarchs should try to awaken the Goddess, but with a surrogate who can be a temporary vessel for Her," said Ralina.

"A temporary vessel? Explain," said Morgana.

Ralina lifted her hands and then let them fall by her sides. "I do not know. All I know is that the Goddess of Life led me to you and put the thought of a surrogate in my mind, so there must be an answer here."

"The idol!" Sora stepped forward to stand beside Ralina. "The Earth Mother idol we have fashioned in the nursery building!" She spoke quickly, her words filled with excitement. "What better vessel could there be for the Goddess of Life? We have created Her from fertile earth and clothed Her with verdant plants. The Goddess could inhabit the idol and then go to Death!"

Ralina turned to Dove. "Could it work?"

"I think it is worth trying," said Dove.

"Then after Death's army arrives we will attempt to call forth the Goddess and awaken Her within the idol," said River. "Dove, Ralina, do you know what we will need to do this?"

"Our matriarchs," said Dove. "Those the Great Goddess has already touched."

"Blood," said Ralina.

"The power of the moon," said Sora and Mari together.

"Then that is what we shall do," said River.

"It has been said!" Morgana shouted.

"It has been said!" Women's voices echoed eerily from the marble walls as firelight made their shadows dance.

CHAPTER 30

I t was a Third Night, so after the meeting with Ralina and the Mare Council Mari and Sora drew down the power of the Moon and Washed the Earth Walkers and any of the Herd who so desired free of Moon Fever and illnesses. Dawn insisted her whole group, including Ralina and Renard, be Washed. Then the Herd ate as they did every night—communally. The nights had turned cold and the trees within the valley were showing off with bright crimson, rust, and yellow displays of their changing leaves, but it was still warm enough for the Herd to gather outside around campfires as they ate. They were subdued. The Herd usually played music and even danced on the wide, flat main street of the valley by torch- and firelight. This night there was no music, no singing, no dancing.

Sora loved the Valley of Vapors. They had only been there a relatively short time, but the green growing things spoke to her. The scent of minerals that perfumed the air grounded her. The gorgeous crystals were amazingly beautiful, and the hot springs intrigued her almost as much as did the white marble buildings of the ancients that turned golden in firelight.

"When this battle with Death and His army is over, where do you see us living?" Sora asked Mari, who sat beside her picking meat from the last of her pheasant.

Mari's brows lifted. She kept her voice low as she answered, "On the Wind Rider Plains, of course."

"Well, I know that," said Sora. "But I mean *where* on the plains? Herd Magenti is nomadic. Is that what you'd want to be?"

Mari shrugged. "I haven't given it a lot of thought, though the cross-timbers area at the Pawhuska Creek by the Tribe's spring settlement did have lovely caves that could be converted to burrows, as well as strong oaks in which our Tribesmen and -women could build nests."

"So you're not thinking of being nomadic?" Sora pressed.

"I would be surprised if we decided to travel with the Herd," said Nik, who sat on the other side of Mari. He tossed bones to Laru and Rigel before he continued. "Of course Dove will travel with Magenti. She won't be separated from Tulpar. And I also wouldn't be surprised if Jaxom traveled with the Herd, but I think most of us want to put down roots."

Mari gave Nik a surprised look. "Jaxom? Really?"

Nik lifted a shoulder. "Why not? Any Earth Walker who has been Chosen by a canine is free of Moon Fever. Jaxom was Chosen by Fortina, so he can travel without worrying about returning to a Moon Woman every Third Night to be Washed." His gaze went to Sora. "He'll never forgive himself for what he did to you when he was infected with the skin-sloughing disease."

Sora said nothing. Though she'd come to be easier around Jaxom, she agreed with Nik. She would not deny that seeing Jaxom could jar her back to that terrible day when he and two other Earth Walkers, infected by the skin-sloughing sickness and out of their minds with Moon Fever, attempted to brutalize and rape her.

Mari nodded. "You're right, Nik. It would probably be the best thing for Jaxom to start anew traveling with the Herd."

"I do not disagree," said Sora slowly. "But you're thinking that you will make a permanent settlement for the Pack?"

"Yes, probably," said Mari. "But I won't try to stop any Pack member from traveling with the Herd. A few of the Pack are even young enough to be presented at the next Choosing to be a Wind Rider." She grinned at Nik. "Wouldn't that be something? If another one of our Pack was Chosen by a horse?"

Nik grinned. "I'll be envious, but it would definitely be something."

Mari's attention returned to Sora. "Why do you ask? Do you wish to travel with the Herd?"

"Oh, by the tits of the Goddess, no! I have had enough traveling for my entire life," Sora said. "I was just wondering what you were thinking."

Mari studied her. "You love it here."

"You mean here in the valley?"

Mari nodded. "Yes, that's what I mean."

Sora twirled a dark curl around her finger. "Yes, I do love it here. I love it so much that—"

"Excuse me. Could we have your attention, please?" Antreas's voice interrupted Sora as everyone within hearing distance looked up to see that the young Lynx Guide and his mate, Danita, stood before the largest of the campfires. Beside them was Bast.

"What's this about?" Nik asked Mari.

"I have a guess, but I don't want to ruin the surprise," said Mari as she slipped her hand within Nik's.

When the conversations around them died, Antreas cleared his throat and continued. "Danita and I aren't sure how these things are announced within the Herd, but we have good news we would like to share with everyone."

Grinning, Danita added, "Because we all need good news right now."

"Good news is always welcome in the Herd." River sat beside Dove, close to the main fire on a thick blanket. They held hands, with Dawn and April, as well as all of their Companions, close by.

Antreas nodded at Danita, whose grin widened as she announced, "Our Bast is pregnant!"

There were happy shouts of, "Congratulations!" and some spontaneous applause. When the Herd quieted again, Antreas said, "The Bobcat many of you have seen shyly lurking about is the father."

Danita bumped him with her shoulder. "Rufus does *not* lurk." Bast punctuated Danita's sentence with a low grumble.

"Well, he is definitely shy," said Antreas. "And we thank the Herd for being patient with him. From what some of you have told me, Rufus is a Bobcat, which is not a Lynx, so he has never Chosen a Companion and is still uncomfortable around humans."

"Though he's going to be around a lot more after the kittens are born," said Danita happily. "Or at least that's what Bast told Antreas." Bast chirruped her agreement. "So, please continue to be patient with him while he gets used to all of us."

Dax, along with his Lynx, Mihos, still recovering from their rush through the mountains to warn the Herd of Death's army, asked, "Do you think the kittens will Choose Companions?"

Sora watched the faces of the surrounding Herdmembers light up with interest.

"We hope so," said Antreas. "Though you and I have talked about the fact that we know of no other Lynx who has Chosen a Bobcat mate, so we cannot be sure until the kittens are weaned and ready to Choose."

"How many kittens does a Lynx usually give birth to?" Dawn asked.

"Lynxes usually give birth to two to three kittens," said Antreas. "But sometimes litters have been as small as one, or as large as eight."

"Well, I hope it's a big litter and each of them Chooses a Companion," said April from beside her mother. "Bast and Mihos are beautiful and smart and brave."

"I agree," said Dawn as she smiled at Bast, who purred loudly. "Adding kittens to the Herd would be delightful."

"How long before Bast gives birth?" asked Sora.

"Two to three full phases of the moon," said Antreas. "Which means Bast will probably give birth in the middle of a snowstorm."

"Then the valley is the perfect place for her," said River. "No matter the weather out there"—she jerked her chin at the land outside their valley—"we will be warm and protected in here. Thank you for sharing this happy news." River stood and raised the mug of winter beer she'd been sipping. "To Bast and Rufus and their kittens!"

"To Bast and Rufus and their kittens!" the Herd echoed before returning to their subdued conversations.

"I cannot wait to see what baby Basts look like," said Mari. She glanced at Nik. "Have you ever seen a Lynx kitten?"

"No. They're usually so solitary that their kittens are rarely seen," said Nik. "But I'm with you. I can't wait to see them."

"I hope they Choose Companions," said Sora. "That would mean that they'll stay close, even after they're adults, and I know that would make Antreas, Danita, and Bast happy."

"Sora? Is this a good time to speak with you?"

Sora looked up to see O'Bryan standing in front of her. She could tell by the bulge in his shirt that he had Cubby with him. "Yes, of course. Is

Cubby well?" Worried, Sora started to stand so she could check out the baby wolverine, but O'Bryan shook his head quickly.

"Oh, no. I mean, yes. Cubby is perfect. You took great care of him." Hearing his name repeated, Cubby stuck his little white head out of O'Bryan's shirt and made the strange little purring sound that said he was happy and well.

Sora smiled up at the baby. "Good. I liked getting to know him. He's really very smart, and was no trouble at all. I'm happy to watch him for you any-time. He and Chloe have become good friends." Sora stroked her fat, sleepy pup who had curled by her side. When O'Bryan said nothing else but con-tinued to stand before her, clenching and unclenching his fists nervously, she added, "Did you need to speak with me about something privately?"

O'Bryan blew out a long breath as his cheeks flushed pink. "Well, yes and no. I'd like to say this next part privately, but because you're a Moon Woman I'm not sure of the exact rules, so I want to do this publicly to show you the respect you deserve . . ." He paused and then added, "I am just now realizing that I should have spoken to Mari or Danita or one of the other Earth Walkers about this. But, well, too late now."

Sora exchanged glances with Mari, who shrugged her shoulders. She glanced at Nik, who also looked confused. Then she turned back to O'Bryan. "I'm intrigued. What is it you want to say to me?"

"Ask, really. Not say." O'Bryan cleared his throat. "I want to ask if you would allow me to officially court you. Please say yes and accept this gift." He reached into his shirt and felt around beside Cubby, and then pulled out a necklace made of delicately braided thread. Dangling from the cen-ter of the braid was a stone that glistened deep purple in the firelight.

Sora stared at the crystal. It was about the size of her thumb and ex-quisitely beautiful. Her stomach gave a little flutter of happy nerves as she realized that everyone within hearing distance of them had quieted and was watching her expectantly. She looked up from the crystal to O'Bryan. He was still offering the necklace to her—and his face still flamed scarlet.

Mari bumped her shoulder and whispered, "Answer him."

Sora finally found her words as she looked into O'Bryan's compassion-ate green eyes. "Yes. I will allow you to court me, and I will gladly accept your beautiful gift." Then she raised her brows and teased, "It took you long enough."

O'Bryan's smile blazed. "Well, I had to practice my braiding skills and then find the perfect crystal."

Dawn was suddenly there beside O'Bryan. "This is why you asked me to show you how to braid thread." Her gaze went to Sora. "Every night on our journey O'Bryan practiced, even when he was exhausted." She turned back to O'Bryan. "And you made an excellent choice in this amethyst. It is appropriately Herd Magenti colored, and amethyst is a highly protective crystal. Well done, O'Bryan." She smiled at Sora. "Congratulations, Sora. You have made an excellent choice."

"I agree," said Nik as he stood and clapped his cousin on the back.

Though O'Bryan grinned and thanked Dawn and Nik, his gaze never left Sora, who stood gracefully and turned her back to him. When he did nothing, she glanced over her shoulder at him. "You're not going to put my gift on me?"

"Yes!" O'Bryan placed the necklace over her head so that when Sora turned to face him the purple crystal sparkled between her breasts. "It looks even more beautiful on you."

This time Sora didn't have to tug on his shirt to get him to bend to her. Eagerly O'Bryan leaned down and cupped her face between his hands. With his lips almost touching hers he murmured, "Thank you for accepting me."

"Thank you for finally asking," Sora whispered back.

And then their lips met as the Herd cheered.

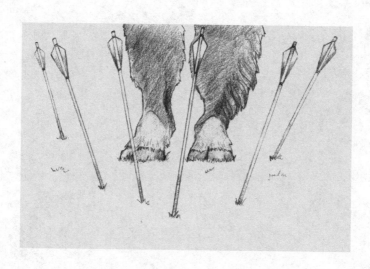

CHAPTER 31

Three days later, as midday was turning into afternoon, Mari had just finished lunch and was heading from the marble house she, Nik, and Sora shared with River to the nursery when a sentry thundered through the narrow entrance and into the Valley of Vapors as he shouted for River—who was quickly located and rushed to the sweaty stallion and his Rider.

"The army has been spotted," he reported to River. "They will be here by nightfall."

River nodded somberly. "You have done well. Care for your stallion and yourself." *Anjo, find Tulpar and Dove. Reach Morgana's Ramoth. Mari is already here with me. She will gather Sora and Ralina. Death arrives this night.*

I hear you, my River.

River turned to Mari. "We need Sora and Ralina."

"Of course." Mari nodded solemnly. "They were at the baths. I'll send Rigel for them." She ruffled the fur on her Companion's head. *Sweet boy, go to the baths. Find Chloe and Bear. Tell them Sora and Ralina must come. Death's army has been spotted.*

Rigel barked acknowledgment before he sprinted off toward the main bathhouse.

"Is the ramp finished?" River called to Riders who had been laboring on a horse-sized ramp that led up to the top of the wall that ringed the valley.

One of the men turned to nod. "It is almost complete."

"Death's army will be here by dusk. It must be ready by then," said River.

"It will be," the Rider assured her.

"Will we be ready?" Mari asked River much more quietly.

River blew out a long breath. "As prepared as we can be to battle a god, though I agree with Dove and Ralina. I believe the Goddess of Life is on our side, and She will guide us to victory."

"And now all we have to do is awaken Her," said Mari.

"Is Her idol ready?" asked River.

"I was just heading there, but Davis and the Earth Walkers had already created a lovely idol *before* we knew we would be attempting to awaken the Goddess within it. In the past days they have transformed lovely to exquisite. Were I a goddess, I would be pleased with what they've done."

"Let's hope She is," said River.

The valley buzzed with activity all afternoon. Last-minute preparations for a siege were completed. The final corn and wheat from outside the walls were harvested and brought within. The last trees were felled and the firewood dragged to fuel piles.

And then the Herd readied themselves for the arrival of the God of Death and His army.

River led them. Bonfires were lit all along the wide main road of the valley and the people and Companions gathered. They were dressed in their finest. They braided their hair and their horses' manes and tails with ribbons and feathers, beads and bits of glass and shells. They took thick, sticky dye paste made from cherry tree roots and painted themselves and their horses with it.

Mari and Sora moved among the people with River, helping them to dress their hair, paint their bodies, and just in general bolster their confidence. Mari was impressed by the positive attitudes of the Herd. Only Ralina and Dove were subdued, though they, too, painted their bodies and dressed their hair.

And then the Herd waited.

"My Lord, I scent many people, horses, and canines close ahead. I cannot tell for sure that Ralina is within, but her trail leads there." Thaddeus pointed ahead through yet another miserable mountain range as the God's bison trotted up to join him at his position well in front of the army. "I believe we have come to the stronghold of the Wind Riders."

"Yes, I can tell that we approach the summit of these mountains. We are at the end of our journey." Death bellowed back at his army, "Wait here!" Then He dismounted and gestured for Thaddeus to join Him.

Thaddeus was incredibly glad to dismount from the beast he'd been riding for what seemed like an eternity. If horses were anything like bison Thaddeus did not understand how Wind Riders could abide them. Bison stank. They were mean and rather stupid. And riding them was torture.

Not that Death cared. The God didn't seem to care about anything except reaching the Wind Rider encampment and infecting Riders with the skin-sloughing sickness so that He could cure them—mutate them—and rule them. It was almost as if the awakening of His Goddess had become an afterthought.

"Are you not excited that we have arrived?" Death asked Thaddeus as the Hunter scrambled to keep up with the God while He strode through the colorful forest, following the same wide path they had come to the day before.

"Yes, my Lord. I look forward to never having to travel again," Thaddeus said.

Death barked a laugh. "I cannot disagree with you. I look forward to ruling this new world."

Thaddeus spoke without thinking. "I thought you were most looking forward to awakening the Goddess of Life." The moment the words left his mouth, Thaddeus pressed his lips together, berating himself for being a fool, but the God was in one of His rare good moods and just laughed.

"Ah, My lover will come *after* I have defeated these annoying Wind Riders and readied the plains for Her magnificence," said Death. Then the God sighed. "Though I do wish Her by My side sooner. My bed has been quite cold without Her."

His bed has been cold since He let His stupid little rabbit women freeze to death in the middle of the Rock Mountains, right, Odysseus? Thaddeus amused himself with the thought.

They came to the edge of the forest, and though the road continued, the trees abruptly ended. Death halted inside the tree line and stared ahead of them at the end of their road, which disappeared within a wall of rock.

"What could that be?" Thaddeus spoke his thought aloud.

"It is their sanctuary," said Death. He nodded and seemed pleased. "They have chosen well, which means I will enjoy ruling from this place on high . . ." The God paused and added, "Get your Hunters and Warriors. I need them to circle the parameter of this walled place and report back on entrances and exits—and any weaknesses they discover. Do not allow the Wind Riders to see them." Death stared down at Thaddeus. "Now, dog-man."

"Yes, my Lord." Thaddeus didn't bother with remounting the bison he despised. As soon as he was out of sight of Death, he dropped to all fours and sprinted back to the army where he shouted for his men, who obediently ran to him. "There is a walled fortress in front of us. It is where our journey ends, and the god wants us to search the circumference. Look for entrances. Look for weakness. Do *not* let the Wind Riders see you. Go, now."

Like Thaddeus, his men had become more comfortable on all fours, and like man-sized canines they sprinted off through the woods. Thaddeus noticed none of their Companions followed them. He didn't even see any of the canines, though he was fairly certain they were still with the army—or at least they had been the night before. He'd watched them gnawing on discarded bison bones and entrails. *Their Companions no longer feed them, and why should they, Odysseus? They avoid their humans as if they are no longer attached to them,* Thaddeus scoffed. *All of them together are not as loyal or brave as you, my Odysseus.* Thaddeus put the cowardly canines from his mind as he hurried back to the God.

"The Hunters and Warriors have gone to scout out the wall as You commanded, my Lord." Thaddeus bowed low as he approached Death.

"Then why are you still here?" Death asked without taking His gaze from the walled city.

"I thought You meant for the men to—"

"Dog-man," Death's voice cut him off. "I do mean for *My* men to scout the walls. You are one of My men. Scout the walls. Now."

"Yes, my Lord." Thaddeus slunk back into the forest before he dropped to all fours and padded around the tree line. *His men? My men, Odysseus. They are my men, not His.* *His* men were well ahead of Thaddeus, so he did not move with haste. He decided he would not tax himself but would find one thing he could report to Death and then return to the God.

Thaddeus had to remain within the tree line as the area between it and the sheer, rocky wall was completely cleared of any vegetation that might hide him. He had to admit to himself that he was impressed by the immense size of the walled city, though he named it a city without actually seeing it. His nose told him inside those walls teemed with people and horses. As Thaddeus followed the wall around he also scented canines— familiar canines. He bared his teeth and growled softly as he identified the Shepherds Laru, Mariah, Bear, and Kong for sure and the traitorous Terriers Cameron and Fala. Odysseus's Fala! Thaddeus hadn't known Rose had escaped the fire. "You should have perished with the rest of the Tribe with your honor intact," he muttered. "No matter. Soon things will be very different for you, and you will beg me to save you." Thaddeus's laughter was cruel. "Perhaps I will. Perhaps I will not."

As Thaddeus considered how satisfying it would be to be Rose's savior—or not—he continued to slink around the walled city until he could go no farther because he came to a large lake that butted up against the far curve of the rocky wall. Not able to see to the other side of the lake, Thaddeus glanced up at the sky. The sun was quickly falling into the west. He would not have enough light left to travel around the lake to continue following the wall, so he turned back and was pleased to see that his men were also hurrying from the forest around them to report to the God.

"Well? What did you find?" Death asked impatiently.

Thaddeus spoke up quickly. "My Lord, I found a large lake that laps against the base of the wall more than halfway around the city. I could not see to the other side of it, and wanted to return to You before dusk."

"And the rest of you?"

"The wall is quite high," said Sean, one of the Hunters.

"Yes, I can see that from here." Death frowned. "Does anyone have any useful news?"

Wilson cleared his throat and spoke up. "My Lord, as far as I went around the wall I observed that it was well maintained and meticulously cleared of all trees and brush. There is no way to approach the wall without being seen."

Death nodded. "Yes, that does not surprise Me. Dove is weak but not stupid. She would have warned the Wind Riders to prepare for us. They have readied themselves for a siege." The God smiled viciously. "I do enjoy a good battle. So, I shall speak with our Wind Riders and give them the opportunity to surrender before they begin a fight they cannot possibly win."

"My Lord, how will You speak with them? They are behind those walls," said Thaddeus.

"Watch and learn, dog-man. Watch and learn."

"Someone approaches!" The shout came from one of the sentries stationed atop the front wall of the well-secured city. "He rides a bison and carries a flag of truce."

Astride her white mare, River faced her people and was filled with pride at the sight of them. They were strong and brave and proud. There was no panic—no tears—no complaints. They had come together as a Herd, and as a Herd she absolutely believed they could not be defeated.

We are ready, my River. Anjo's voice was filled with confidence. *Speak to the people. They will listen.*

I will, my beauty. I agree. The Herd is ready.

River lifted an amplifying crystal and addressed her people. "Stand straight. Stand tall. Death is outside our walls. *Remember that!* Death is *outside* our walls. He will not get within." She turned to Dove, astride Tulpar. Her long blond hair was dressed with purple ribbons to match those woven in her mighty stallion's mane. Lines of thick purple paint striped her face and her bare chest, as well as Tulpar's neck and flanks. She looked magnificent and River was filled with pride that this wise, strong, beautiful woman loved her. "Speak your truth to the Herd, Stallion Rider."

Tulpar faced the silent crowd. Dove's voice rang along the street. "Show Death no fear. Without being tempered by the Goddess of Life, He is a mean bully looking for a fight. Weakness excites Him. Strength angers Him. When He is angered, He makes foolish decisions. So, be strong, Herd Magenti. Be strong!"

The Herd shouted in response.

"Ralina, we save your reveal for last." River glanced at Nik and O'Bryan, who stood beside Mari and Sora. "Are you ready to do as we discussed?"

"Absolutely," said Nik as he patted the crossbow he held in the crook of one arm.

"Always," added O'Bryan.

River smiled. "Good. You will follow me to the wall. Spread out to my left and wait for my signal."

"We will be close beside you," said Mari.

River nodded her thanks and gazed around the crowd. The entire Pack was there. They, too, had dressed themselves in their finest. The Herd had gifted their newest members with purple ribbons that they'd braided into their hair. They'd also followed Herd tradition and painted their bodies. Around the necks of their canines, the two Lynxes, and even Rufus, the Bobcat, were braided strips of purple cloth with dyed feathers hanging from them. They looked fierce and proud and ready to take on anything—including Death.

"April, Mother, and the Mare Council, when I make this motion"—River made a small beckoning gesture with her hand—"follow Ralina. Spread out next to her along the wall. Lend her and Dove your strength," said River.

Morgana bowed her head slightly. "It has been said." Behind her the rest of the Mare Council, all dressed in regalia that reflected the colors of all the great Herds, echoed, "It has been said."

"*Wind Riders! I would parlay!*" Death's voice blasted over them.

River's smile was confident. "Let us show this bully what it is to trespass on our lands."

Anjo whirled around and sprinted up the wide ramp that had just that day been completed. It led to the only ledge along the wall that was big enough to accommodate horses, and only two fit comfortably, but two were all River required.

Mari, Nik, Sora, O'Bryan, their Companions, and the rest of the combined peoples of the Tribe of the Trees and the Earth Walkers who now called themselves a Pack followed closely behind her. They spread out along the top of the wall and stared stonily down at the lone god. The rest of the Riders—except for Dove, Tulpar, Ralina, and the Mare Council—scrambled up rope ladders so that in seconds the walled barrier was filled with her people who stood silently, holding weapons at the ready.

River looked down on the God. Alone, He carried a stained white piece of cloth on a long branch and rode a huge bison bull—though He dwarfed the bull. The God was enormous. If He straightened His legs, His cloven hooves would drag on the ground. His shoulders were impossibly wide. His chest was bare, so that the bison pelt that covered his torso was on full display—as were the black, razor-tipped horns that curled in deadly crescents from His head.

He was terrifying.

Remember, my River, our love is stronger than anything—even the God of Death. Hold your head high, Lead Mare Rider. Share my strength. We are together in this—as in all things.

River was filled with a rush of love and warmth that burned away her fear. She lifted her chin and spoke with the confidence of a true leader. "I am River, Rider of Anjo, Lead Mare of Herd Magenti. Why do You trespass upon Wind Rider land?" River held the amplifying crystal in one hand but kept that hand low and hidden.

Death smiled. "Ah, a woman leader with an unusually loud voice. How interesting. My beloved, the Goddess of Life, will enjoy ruling a people led by women." His smile faded. "But as She has not yet awakened I must tell you that I find females who lead much less amusing than those who warm My bed." He shrugged His wide shoulders. "But no matter. Lead Mare Rider River, you ask why I am here, and I shall tell you. I am here to usher a new era into the Wind Rider Plains—one where man and horse will be even closer than you are now."

River's laughter rang around her and was picked up by the others standing along the wall. "What do you know of the bond between Rider and horse? Our people have already shown that they would rather end their lives than be bound to you."

Death's look darkened. "That does not amuse me."

"Good," River said. "I do not intend to amuse you as my people are not interested in being ruled by Death."

"Young Rider, how do you know what it would be like to be ruled by a living God? Perhaps you should take the time to get to know me." He gestured with His meaty hands. "Come down from your wall. Let us speak together of the future in a civilized manner."

River ignored the God's invitation. "That is an interesting question, but

I have an equally interesting answer for You. I already know what kind of ruler You would be because among my people are those who have been ruled by You." She nodded, and from behind her Tulpar surged up onto the landing, followed by Mari and Nik, Sora and O'Bryan.

Death's gaze focused first on Mari. His dark eyes widened as if in sudden recognition. Then He tore His attention from her at the sight of Dove sitting bare breasted and proud astride her golden stallion. Death leaped from the back of the bison bull and strode several paces closer to the wall.

"Now, Nik," River said softly.

So fast that his hands blurred, Nik—the best bowman in all of the Tribe of the Trees—fired six arrows, one right after another, which landed in the grass in a perfect crescent barrier just inches in front of the god.

Death halted, looked up at the wall, and laughed—a cruel sound that grated on River's nerves. "Did these informants not mention to you that *you cannot kill the God of Death*?" He roared.

River shrugged nonchalantly. "I may not be able to kill You, but I imagine even a god finds being struck by dozens of arrows rather uncomfortable."

Death's dark gaze returned to Dove. He ignored River and spoke directly to her. "Ah, little bird, you tried to fly away from Me but landed in My path anyway. How fortuitous—for one of us."

Dove said nothing. She sat regally astride her golden stallion, whose eyes blazed hatred at Death.

"You refuse to speak to Me, little bird? But we are old friends," Death cajoled.

"You usurped my lover's body. You brutalized and raped me. We have *never* been friends. *I was willing to die to rid myself of You.* God of Death, You are nothing to me." Dove's sweet voice had taken on a hard edge and she spoke with no fear.

River watched the God grow more and more furious. It was clear that He was barely in control of Himself. It was also clear that He kept shifting His focus from Dove to Mari, and back to Dove again. For a moment she thought He would charge the wall, climb it, and hurl Himself at them. She felt an instant of panic. What would happen then? A god couldn't be killed—but could a god kill an entire Herd?

Death did not charge the wall. Instead, He bared His teeth in an attempt at a smile. "So, you have poisoned the Herds against Me, little bird. No matter. The truth will be revealed soon enough." He turned dismissively from Dove and refocused on River. "Do not swallow whole what this eyeless, broken child has fed you, Lead Mare Rider. I can offer you power you cannot imagine."

"And yet here I am, leading the strongest, most prosperous of our Herds. I stand looking down on You—a god. I do not want Your power. I do not need Your power. Keep traveling east. Cross the wide Miss River to the lands beyond. There You may settle and rule. Not here. Not among the Wind Riders," River said.

"You have misjudged Me and My people," said Death. "Perhaps 'power' was the wrong word. The correct word is 'intimacy.' I offer you an intimacy with your Companions that will forever change your lives."

River made a small, beckoning gesture with her hand and from the ramp Ralina and Bear emerged to stand to the right of Dove and Tulpar. The Mare Council followed, spreading out beside her. They looked wise and formidable with their masses of silver hair and their aged faces and bodies that bore the signs of decades of leadership and wisdom. They remained utterly silent as Ralina's voice rang like a clarion call, amplified by rage and righteous indignation.

"You lie!"

Death's body jerked as if He had been stuck. His eyes blazed with a yellow, animalistic sheen. *"Storyteller, you betray Me!"*

"Betray You?" Ralina's voice was rich with sarcasm. "I was never Your ally. I was Your prisoner."

"You were My Storyteller!" He bellowed.

"I have never been *Your* anything." Ralina turned away from Him and spoke to River, though she pitched her bardic voice to carry to the God. "Death does not offer intimacy with our Companions. He offers mutation, abomination, and estrangement." Then she looked back at the God. "*That* is the only story I or anyone else will ever tell about You— how You were a stain upon our world. How You brought poison and madness and destruction—*and nothing else.*"

Death opened His mouth to roar again, but River's calm voice interrupted. "And there You have it. We know the truth from the woman You brutalized, the Tribesmen whose lands You poisoned, and the Storyteller who survived to record in detail what she is calling *The Ballad of Doomed Death*, wherein your atrocities are documented. Leave our plains. Now."

"*You do not command a God!*" Death yelled as white foam spewed from His mouth and His cloven hooves tore the grass.

"Nik and O'Bryan, now." River spoke quietly.

The two men responded instantly. They lifted their crossbows and fired arrow after arrow after arrow into the God. He roared and swatted at the arrows, knocking some away while others embedded themselves to the fletching feathers in His massive body. Nik and O'Bryan continued to fire until it appeared as if the God had sprouted scarlet quills.

"That is all," River said to Nik and O'Bryan, who stood down. She spoke to the God. "No, we cannot kill You, but we will *never* succumb to You—and we will make Your life a misery until You leave our land. Begone, God of Death. This is not Your land. We are not Your people." Anjo whirled around and disappeared down the ramp, followed by Tulpar and Dove, then Ralina and Bear.

The other members of the Herd remained staring down at the God, their weapons at the ready, until He remounted the bison and thundered away.

CHAPTER 32

"My Lord!" Thaddeus rushed to Death as He slid from the bison, pulling arrows from His body as if He brushed away flies. Thaddeus had waited for the God just within the tree line with the Hunters and Warriors, and the glowing spirit of the gloomy bison bull. He had heard everything the leader of the Wind Riders had said to Death—as well as eyeless Dove's admonishments—but what Thaddeus would never forget were the insults the Storyteller had hurled at the God. Thaddeus almost liked her for them, but he kept his expression under control and appeared only concerned. "Have You been injured?"

Death backhanded Thaddeus, knocking him against the base of an ancient white oak several yards away. *"I am Death! I cannot be injured!"*

Thaddeus blinked rapidly as his vision fragmented into sparks and stars, and he struggled to remain conscious.

"Oh, get up, dog-man. We have much to do." Death pulled the rest of the arrows from His body as He strode past Thaddeus.

Thaddeus staggered after the God, Who strode to the bison spirit. Death stared at the beast, whose small red eyes looked steadily back at Him—filled with malevolence. "I want no more traitors around Me. I release you!" Death shouted.

The bison's head lifted suddenly, and, as his spirit faded, he opened his mouth and roared hatred at the God.

Death turned away from the disappearing spirit and faced the mutated men. "Do you hear Me? I will have no more traitors in My midst! If you are not for Me, leave now. Go!"

The men shuffled their feet nervously and bowed their heads as they cast surreptitious glances at Thaddeus, who had limped up to stand beside Death.

Thaddeus knew this was his chance. Not to escape Death. No matter what the God said, he knew Death would never allow any of them to leave His army—at least not while they were still living. Had there been any chance of that, Thaddeus would have fled even before the Storyteller did. But the God had just been served one blow after another to His ego by first the Wind Rider leader, then Dove, and finally Ralina—and Thaddeus would use that to his benefit.

"My Lord, the Hunters and Warriors are all loyal to You. We will be true to You. Always." Thaddeus caught the gaze of Wilson and gestured quickly for him to follow his lead, so when Thaddeus bowed low, first Wilson and then the entire group of ex-Tribesmen bowed as they murmured their agreement.

Death blew out a long breath. "That is the loyalty I expect."

"My Lord, it is the loyalty You deserve," Thaddeus lied.

"Indeed, indeed," Death said. "Half of you make camp here, within the tree line. The other half shall slaughter a fat bull. Attend Me, dog-man."

Death strode away, crashing through the forest underbrush and into the herd of bison, who were quietly grazing beside the army. Death continued to wade through the herd until they were well away from the watching army before He halted before a rather diminutive bull who snorted in alarm and took several steps away from the God.

"Hold," Death commanded, and the bison froze, though he stared at the God with eyes filled with fear and loathing.

"Dog-man, come here."

Thaddeus had no choice but to swallow his fear and approach the God. Then was shocked when the God said, "Give Me your hand."

"My Lord?" Thaddeus was sure he hadn't heard Death correctly.

"I thought your senses had been heightened. Have you lost your hearing?" Death asked with a deceptive smile.

"No, my Lord," Thaddeus answered quickly, offering his hand—which only trembled slightly—to the God.

Death grasped Thaddeus's arm and roughly pulled up his sleeve to expose his forearm. The God snorted. "You are covered with dog fur. It amuses Me."

Not knowing what to say, Thaddeus simply nodded and smiled.

With one swift motion, Death pressed His claw-like fingernail into the flesh of Thaddeus's forearm and slashed downward, leaving a long line that wept crimson.

Thaddeus grunted in pain and automatically pulled his arm away as he cringed back, waiting for Death to knock him senseless again.

But Death only chuckled—a low, cruel sound. Then He whirled around, grasping the bison bull by the horns. The God wrenched his head back until the creature was forced to fall to the ground.

Death sat on the bull's thick neck. He leaned forward. With one hand the God wrenched back the bull's neck even farther, and with the other He pried the creature's jaws open.

"Drip your blood into the bull's mouth. Now, dog-man," Death commanded.

Utterly baffled, Thaddeus did as he was commanded. He hurried to the bull's head and held his arm over the beast's open mouth. As the bull impotently bucked and bellowed, Thaddeus turned his arm so that the blood that flowed freely from the long laceration dripped into the beast's mouth.

After the bull swallowed several times, Death finally stepped off the bison and freed him. The bison stood, tossing his head and trembling as his red gaze speared the God.

"Dog-man, you will watch this bull. Come to Me the moment he sickens," Death commanded.

As Death strode back through the herd, retracing His path to the campsite the army was erecting, Thaddeus called to His broad back, "My Lord, I do not understand!"

"Of course you do not, dog-man. That is why I am the God and you are My servant. Again, just do as I say and watch and learn. Watch and learn . . ."

The matriarchs gathered in the nursery. Mari wished her mother had been there to see how strong and wise the women were—and how they worked together harmoniously. She, Sora, Dove, River, and Ralina stood on the fringes, watching as the finishing touches were added to the Goddess idol.

The big building felt deceptively small, filled as it was by women and their Companions. Rigel and Chloe and the other bonded Terriers were there, padding around the plants. Horses found places between the beds where they stood watching their women with open curiosity—though Dove sat astride Tulpar so that she could see through her stallion's eyes, and Bard always had to be within touching distance of Ralina.

Space had been made by moving beds of plants so that the idol, which reclined in the center of the large room, could be circled by women—and one man. Davis was there, with Cammyman huffing happily beside him, as he worked with the women to complete the exquisite idol they, and he, had created.

Mari felt a swell of pride and love as she studied the beautiful statue. Her skin was moss. Her hair was made of ferns and white, fragrant jasmine flowers. Vines cascaded around her body as if she wore a fringed gown, and her face was the perfect oval obsidian that had rested on the idol over Clan Weaver's Moon Woman burrow for generations. Davis, who had received the Goddess's blessing to remove the face stone and bring it with them to the Wind Rider Plains, approached Mari's group as he smiled and nodded respectfully to each of them before he spoke.

"If you believe the Goddess idol is ready, I will leave you now and wish you—as our new Herd family would say—a mare's luck tonight," said Davis.

Mari's intuition made her speak up immediately. "Stay. Please. You are the first Tribesman to hear the Great Earth Mother and choose to worship Her. Though She does not speak to me as She does to you, I believe She would want you here."

Davis's eyes filled with tears. "Truly? I may stay?"

Mari looked to River. "Davis has a special connection with the Goddess. I would very much like him to stay."

River nodded. "Then Davis stays."

Cammy huffed as he jumped around his Companion, wagging his stumpy tail so hard his rear end looked like it was going to wiggle off as

Davis, smile blazing, returned to the circle of women surrounding the Goddess.

"What else do we need?" River asked as she surveyed the room.

Ralina sighed and leaned against Bard. "Well, Death always talked about how blood was required to awaken the Goddess of Life—blood, illness, and the melding of animal flesh with human." She turned to Dove. "He spoke of you. How He had planned to use you as the vessel for the Goddess. You were there when Death awakened, were you not?"

Dove nodded. "I was there when He usurped my lover's body, but it is my hope that we do not have to behave as Death to awaken the Goddess."

"It would make sense that we do not," said Mari. "The Great Goddess has sent dreams and visions to us and made it clear that She is invoking our aid against Death awakening Her."

"She warned Death against it," said Ralina grimly. "He, of course, made light of Her warnings by laughing them off by saying the Goddess is a worrier."

River shook her head. "His arrogance will be His undoing."

"Like many men," Dawn added as she joined their little group. "The idol is ready. As are the Mare Council and Davis." She smiled at her daughter. "I am pleased you allowed him to stay. His connection with the Mother Mare, or Great Goddess as the Pack calls Her, is clear."

"Thank Mari. She thought to ask him to stay," said River. "But I agree with you, Mother. Davis has definitely been Goddess-touched."

"Well, I shall join the other Council Members. We await your pleasure. And may a mare's luck be with us all." Dawn returned to her place in the circle beside Morgana, whose ancient mare, Ramoth, stood next to Echo, watching everything with interest.

"So, how do we do this?" asked Sora.

"My gut says use that." Mari motioned up at the mirrors that captured silver light from the full moon. "Let's blow out the candles and torches and concentrate on the power of the moon."

"I agree," said Dove. "But I also believe we must call the Goddess with blood—and not because Death used it, but because blood is always present during birth, and the Goddess of Life will recognize that."

"That sounds reasonable," said River. "So, we have knowledge from our Tribe of the Trees matriarch." Her gaze went from Ralina to Dove and her expression softened. "Advice to use blood from one who used to be part of the People." She looked from Dove to Mari and Sora. "And moon magick from our Earth Walkers. I, too, would like to add something from Herd Magenti." She reached into a pocket pouch in her tunic and pulled out a glistening crystal. "Quartz, clear like this, amplifies communication with the spirit realm. Each Lead Mare Rider always carries one."

"That is an excellent idea," said Dove, smiling at River. "Each Mare Council Member should place her crystal before her in a circle around the idol."

"And what about the blood?" Sora asked.

"I think blood should be offered from a representative of each of our peoples," said Mari. "Unless one of you has a better idea."

"That makes sense to me," said River. "Anything else?" When none of the women had more to offer, she continued. "Then let us begin."

"I'll get a gardening knife to pass around," said Sora. "Who is going to bleed?"

"I will bleed for my people," said River.

"And I for mine," Dove said, adding with a smile, "As Lily is not yet a matriarch, I am the only one of my people here."

"I will bleed for the Tribe of the Trees," said Ralina.

"And I will bleed for Earth Walkers," said Sora. She glanced at Mari. "While I'm bleeding you draw down the power of the moon, and then I'll join you."

Mari nodded and repeated the traditional Wind Rider acknowledgment. "It has been said."

"It has been said," the women murmured together.

"I will tell the Mare Council to place their crystals around the Goddess," said River.

The women prepared quickly and efficiently. When all were ready, they extinguished the candles and torches so that the Goddess idol was bathed in the silver-white light of a full moon that ruled a clear night sky. With the idol encircled by women—and Davis—ringed with clear crystals that winked and twinkled like visiting stars, watched by loyal Companions, Mari thought she had never seen anything so beautiful or magickal. She went to stand before the head of the reclining statue, and it seemed that the smooth stone eyes gazed at her with expectation.

To Mari's right was Sora, who held a carefully cleaned pruning knife. Its sharp blade glittered in the silver light. To her left was River. Beside River, Dove was astride her golden stallion, who stood still and somber. On Sora's right was Ralina, who leaned against Bard. The women and stallions made a crescent shape in front of the idol.

"Whenever you are ready, Mari," said River.

Mari nodded. "Sora and I will need the help of you all—including our Companions. Intent is always important with moon magick, so set your intention, which is to awaken the Goddess of Life, known by Earth Walkers as the Great Goddess and Wind Riders as the Great Mother Mare. She is all those things and more."

Around her the women and Davis nodded. They focused on the idol as they set their intention.

"Sora, bleed first so that you can join me in the drawing down of the moon."

"I will," said Sora.

Mari closed her eyes and drew several deep breaths in and out. *Please, Great Goddess, You have never spoken to me, but I ask in honor of my mother, Leda, who You loved and spoke to often, that You hear me.*

Mari felt a familiar warmth fill her and she slitted her eyes to see Rigel, who sat with Bear and the Terrier pups just outside the circle, wagging his tail in encouragement. Then her mind was flooded with voices as her body brimmed with warmth.

You can do this, Moon Woman. Anjo's voice was the first Mari recognized.

Be strong, came Tulpar's encouragement.

We shall lend you strength. Mari's gaze found Echo, whose sweet voice drifted through her mind.

Yes, Mari.

We believe in your power.

Call the Goddess, Mari.

Mari had to smile as the voices washed through her mind, and the warmth of the Companions filled her. She shook back her hair and tilted her gaze upward to the full, fat moon. When she began speaking the ancient invocation she and Sora had altered earlier, Mari felt the hairs lift on her forearms. Sora strode confidently forward, cut her hand, and turned it so that her blood dripped into the moss packed around the base of the idol.

> *"Moon Women we declare ourselves to be*
> *greatly gifted through blood and ancestry.*
> *This night we gather for Thee*
> *in celebration of love and life and matriarchy."*

Sora gave the blade to River before she returned to her place at Mari's side to grip her hand tightly and lend her even more strength. River stepped forward, cut herself, and dripped blood into the moss.

> *"Your people ask a great boon tonight.*
> *We cannot stop Death without Life's light."*

River returned and raised her hand to give Dove the knife. Tulpar went forward, positioning himself perfectly so that his Rider could cut herself and add her blood to Earth Walker and Wind Rider scarlet.

> *"Your children we are, faithful, loving, and true.*
> *Find us here as we beseech You."*

Tulpar backed to once more stand beside River as Dove gave Ralina the knife. The Storyteller and her Companion walked forward; she cut herself quickly, and added the blood of the Tribe of the Trees to the offering before the Goddess. Ralina left the knife there, on the reddened moss, before she and Bard returned to their place beside Sora.

> *"Come, precious silver light—fill us to overflow.*
> *Lend us power so that the Goddess of Life shall know.*
> *By right of blood and love and birth, channel through Sora and me*
> *the Goddess gift that is our destiny.*
> *Wake, Great Earth Creatress, this very hour,*
> *for Death can only be halted by Life's divine power!"*

Mari and Sora held hands so tightly that their knuckles whitened, but neither woman cared. Both concentrated on calling down the silver-white power of the moon.

"Remember, channel it through you." Mari spoke softly to Sora. "Imagine it going into the crystals. Then think of that light reaching down, down, down into the earth to awaken Her."

Sora didn't speak, but she nodded tightly.

"Reach up for it, Sora! Reach with me!" Mari shouted as she lifted her hands, including the one grasped by Sora, who mimicked her so that the two women looked as if they would embrace the moon. Within her mind, Mari sketched a powerful picture of moonlight cascading down from above and into Sora and her.

And then the mirrors flashed with blinding white light as moon magick shot down so that it poured into the Moon Women, who in turn directed it to rain into the circle of clear crystals spaced before the Mare Council all around the idol. The crystals lit as if on fire.

"Now, channel it deep into the earth," Mari said.

Together, the Moon Women let loose each other's hand. With a motion much like throwing a stone, they channeled the power through the crystals and into the moss-covered earth at the base of the idol, which began to glisten like emeralds.

"Don't stop!" Mari ground between her clenched teeth as she tried not to be overwhelmed by the power cascading from the moon. "We don't keep it. We don't contain it. We only move the power. It is not ours, but our goddess's."

"It is not ours, but our goddess's," repeated Sora.

Then from his place in the circle, Davis picked up the cry. "The power is not ours, but our goddess's!"

River and Dove shouted together, "The power is not ours, but our goddess's!"

Ralina's voice added strength to the cry. "The power is not ours, but our goddess's!"

Then every person in the room—each elder, each leader, each follower of the Goddess—shouted together until their strong voices lifted in joy.

"The power is not ours, but our goddess's!"

A blinding flash of light exploded from the idol. Mari's concentration faltered as she blinked and tried to clear her vision. She lost her connection to the moon power, and wanted to cry out in despair, *What do we do now? How could we have been so wrong?*

Then Sora's hand grasped hers again, and in a voice filled with reverence she said, "Mari, look at Her face!"

Still blinking, Mari's gaze went to the smooth stone that was as familiar to her as her beloved mother's face had been.

The idol turned Her head and opened Her eyes to look directly into Mari's.

"Merry meet, Mari, daughter of Leda."

Mari gasped and dropped to her knees before the living idol. "Merry meet, Great Goddess." All around her everyone went to their knees as they stared at the animated statue.

The idol had been fashioned in a reclining position, and when She stretched and then sat, cross-legged, She moved with the fluid grace of grasses dancing with the breeze. Her face was lovely. Not lifeless obsidian anymore, but pliant and indescribably beautiful. Her dark eyes glistened with intelligence and compassion as She gazed around the room. Her voice sounded familiar—even though the Goddess had never before spoken to Mari.

"Merry meet, My children." Her gaze paused on Davis. *"I see you there, Davis. Where is your sweet Cammyman?"*

Huffing joyously, little Cammy padded from the group of canines to the Goddess. He bowed his blond head before Her and then danced around Her huffing and wagging.

"What a delight you are!" The Goddess looked from Cammy to Dove, who was still astride Tulpar. Both Rider and stallion had their heads bowed reverently. *"Dove, Merry meet. I have visited your dreams often, but it is good to be here with you."*

"Great Goddess of Life, I am honored to be Your Seer," said Dove breathlessly.

The Goddess's gaze went to Ralina, who was on her knees beside Bard, her head bowed.

"Brave Ralina. I have asked more of you than anyone in this world. You

have not disappointed Me. It is because of your courage that I have awakened even this much."

Ralina's head lifted. "But are You not truly awake, Great Goddess?"

The Goddess's laughter was rich, honeyed, and the moment Mari heard it she knew why Her voice was so familiar. *It's Mama! She sounds like Mama!*

"*Oh, child, no. This is only an exceptionally real dream to Me—as well as to you, all of you,*" said the Goddess.

"But we need You!" The words seemed to burst from Ralina. "Death is outside our walls. He plans on destroying our lives—poisoning us and twisting us like He did my Tribesmen before He awakens You completely."

The Goddess shook Her head, causing the scent of the jasmine flowers in Her hair to fill the room with perfume. "*That would destroy the world. Gods were not meant to walk with humans, but only to lend them magick and guide them to paths that lead them to become their best and brightest selves.*"

"We understand that, Great Goddess," Dove said. "But can You not awaken long enough to take Death into Your loving arms again and return to the womb of the world with Him?"

"*Yes, I could. But not in a form such as this.*" She glanced down at Herself. "*Though I do find your idols made from my fertile earth quite lovely. Were I to fully awaken, even for the short time it would take to embrace the God of Death, I would need a living vessel to incarnate.*"

River stood and took a step forward. "Then use me as Your vessel, Great Goddess! I am ready. I am willing."

The Goddess cocked Her head. "*You would make a lovely vessel, River, Mare Rider of Anjo, though should I do that—should I inhabit your body and go to Death—two things would happen. First, Death would know it a trap and not come into My embrace. Second, you would perish.*" The Goddess's gaze roamed the room again until it lit on Mari. As She continued to speak She stared into Mari's eyes. "*All present must understand that your soul cannot survive an immortal awakening within your body. The indwelling of an immortal severs the tether that holds the soul to its mortal shell. It will flee. It will always flee.*" She finally took her gaze from Mari and turned her focus to Dove. "*My brave Seer witnessed this when the soul of her beloved fled from the God of Death.*"

"I understand," said River in a clear, strong voice. "And still I willingly offer myself as Your vessel."

The Goddess gazed down on River. *"You do your people proud, Lead Mare Rider. But what would your Anjo do should your soul flee your body?"*

River's deep brown skin paled and she fisted her trembling hands at her sides. When she replied, her voice broke with emotion. "My Anjo would follow me. She would not survive."

Bard dropped his head and pressed against Ralina, who stroked him soothingly. The Goddess turned from studying River to the big black stallion.

"Faithful Bard, you remained with a corrupted Companion until your heart was broken. It pleases me that you opened yourself to Ralina. She is worthy of you, and you are worthy of loving her in return—without heartache or regret." The Goddess leaned forward, towering over the stallion, who stood motionless. Then She bent and kissed him softly on the middle of his forehead.

A shudder rippled through Bard and Ralina gasped. The Storyteller turned to her Companion and put her arms around his neck, sobbing tears of joy into his sleek coat.

"It's gone! His grief is gone!" Then Ralina turned back to the Goddess and dropped to her knees again. "Thank You! Oh, thank You so much."

Instead of speaking to Ralina, the Goddess turned to River. *"When Clayton died, Bard's grief almost killed him, even though he and his Companion were poorly matched. River, your Anjo and you are perfectly matched. Consider carefully the pain your loss will cause your Companion and your people."*

River's head bowed. Her shoulders shook with her silent sobs, but when she lifted her head to meet the Goddess's gaze she wiped away her tears and spoke firmly. "I have considered. Anjo and I are in agreement. I remain willing to be Your vessel. Great Goddess, if Death is not stopped our plains—our world—will be filled with far more grief than the loss of one mare and her Rider."

"You and Anjo are worthy to lead your people," said the Goddess. *"And I honor your willingness."*

River drew in a deep breath as Anjo trotted to her side. River lifted her hand and rested it on her mare's neck. "We are ready, Great Goddess."

"Oh, brave child, I know you are, but you are forgetting the first thing of

which I spoke. Death would know it is a trap. I can return Him to the womb of the world and bespell Him to sleep again, but for Me to do so He must willingly come into My embrace, and the only way He will do that is if He believes He awakened Me."

"How do we make Death believe He awakened You?" Mari's stomach roiled as she asked the question because she feared she already knew the answer.

"*I must be awakened by Him, as He planned.*" The Goddess yawned mightily. "*But now I leave you. I cannot fully awaken here—so I must return to My slumber. My Storyteller knows what needs be done.*" The Goddess moved back to Her original position of recline. Once more, Her gaze locked on Mari's. "*What needs be done . . . what needs be done . . . what needs be done . . . ,*" the Goddess's last words echoed around them as the light went out of Her eyes, Her head rested against the mounded bed of fertile earth on the marble floor, and She was again just dirt and moss, fern and flowers, and a lovingly carved obsidian image.

CHAPTER 33

The Herd was subdued that night. Word of the Goddess's short-lived awakening and the details She provided the matriarchs spread quickly through the valley. As River sat beside Dove at her usual evening place around the Herd's main campfire, Herdmembers approached. One at a time, they came. Without speaking, they saluted her and left gifts in a sacred circle around her. Some left beautiful feathers. Some left beads. Others placed crystal pendants, wrapped in wire or woven thread, around their Lead Mare Rider. They also honored Anjo, who stood near her Rider, solemn and attentive. River often raised her hand to stroke her mare.

Mari sat across the fire from River. Rigel lay beside her, watching everything. Every few minutes Mari put her hand on him—taking comfort in his warmth and nearness. Nik and O'Bryan were with the Stallion Riders as they made weapon checks, but Sora was there with Mari. She sat quietly near her, sipping a calming tea she'd brewed for their group after they left the nursery. With them were Ralina and her Bear, as well as April, who kept sending her sister worried glances.

"The Herd shows you great honor," said April. Her voice sounded uncharacteristically soft.

River nodded as she stroked Anjo. "Yes, they do."

Dove didn't speak. She just held River's hand and remained close to her.

"How should I do it?" River asked when the trickle of Herdmembers began to slow. She caught Ralina's gaze. "What steps do I take?"

"I should do it. You have an entire Herd to lead." Ralina shuddered. "But I cannot. Forgive me, all of you. I cannot go back to Death. I would rather end my life."

Bard nickered with low urgency and nuzzled his Rider as Bear whined pitiably and pressed against her.

"I know that's horrible for you and Bear to hear, my precious boys, but I would rather die than be captured by Death." She looked around their small campfire circle. "Forgive me for not being braver."

"It has nothing to do with bravery," said Dove. "I understand you. I, too, could present myself to Death. He quite possibly would use me as the vessel to call forth the Goddess, but it is more likely that He would not use either of us but simply brutalize us and then slit our throats—causing our Companions horrible grief and ending their lives as well."

"It cannot be either of you," said River. "But Dove, Ralina, I look to you for guidance. How do I make Death fall into the Goddess's trap?"

Mari sat up straighter, listening attentively.

"He must capture you," said Ralina.

Dove nodded slowly. "Yes, I agree, and He must not realize you mean for Him to capture you."

River chewed her lip as she considered, then said, "Do either of you believe Death will send His army against us immediately?"

"No," Ralina said quickly. "It is more like Him to bluster and lie, cajole and manipulate—like He attempted to do today."

Dove nodded. "Only after it is clear that you see Him for the monster He is and that you will not succumb to Him will He attack."

"So, perhaps after He attempts to parlay a few more times I agree to meet with Him in person. Would He try to capture me then?" River asked.

"Perhaps," said Dove.

"To be sure of it you should insult Him," said Ralina. "Misunderstand what He says to you on purpose and laugh at Him. When He is angry, He acts on instinct."

"But wouldn't He just kill her?" Mari asked.

They turned to her and Dove sighed. "Yes. That is a definite possibility."

"We could pretend to need something outside the walls," said April.

"Death has no way of knowing how well provisioned we are. Wait through a full turn of the moon phases, then be seen sneaking from the valley with a group of Hunters. When He captures you, struggle against Him, but do not overly provoke Him."

"He wouldn't just capture me," said River, shaking her head. "He would capture any Rider team with me. He would infect them. I cannot allow that."

"Going to parlay with Him in person seems your best option," said Sora. "But instead of angering Him, treat Death as you would any other leader." Sora's gaze found Ralina. "What do you think?"

"He is more likely to be amused by River if she is charming. He will be impressed by her intelligence and beauty—and He will be obsessed with Anjo." Ralina shuddered again. "But you cannot let Him flay the flesh from your mare. It changed the canines. It will change her as well."

River gazed up into her mare's eyes and spoke softly. "She will not survive when my soul flees my body. Death will not be able to change my beloved Anjo."

April sobbed and wiped at her face. "I-I'm sorry. I don't know how to bear this."

"There is still time," Mari said. "River cannot just walk outside the walls and offer herself to Death. The Goddess made it clear that He would know it's a trap. So, there is still time."

April nodded and wiped away more tears. "Yes, there is still time. Perhaps we will discover another way of awakening the Goddess or something—anything—else than sacrificing River."

Mari said nothing. She only rested her hand on Rigel, who leaned against her.

"What are you thinking?" Sora whispered.

Mari shook her head and answered her best friend quietly, "Nothing. I'm just sad that it has come to this." Then Mari cleared her throat. "I'm going to sleep. If Nik comes by, please let him know I'm in our chamber."

The group called good nights to her as Mari left. She could feel Sora's gaze on her back, and walked faster. She would have to avoid the other Moon Woman. Sora knew her too well. She would get suspicious and ruin everything.

Walking at her side, Rigel whined softly.

Mari let her fingers play through the soft fur on his head. "It's going to be okay. At first it will be awful, but then it will be okay. I promise. I'll make sure of it."

Rigel whined again and sent her a wave of sorrow.

She blinked quickly. There was no time for tears. Not yet. Maybe never.

River and Dove slowly made their way to the marble building and the lovely chamber the two of them had been sharing since the Herd arrived at the Valley of Vapors. It was late. They'd sat by the campfire long after Mari and the rest of their friends had gone to their own beds.

Even then the two women hadn't retired. Instead, with their Companions they'd climbed the ramp to the top of the wall and looked out at the forest where they caught glimpses of the yellow fires of Death's army, flickering through the trees like giant, swollen fireflies. River and Dove didn't speak. They only gazed out at the army's fires as they stood together, the four of them, warm and safe and loved.

When River and Dove finally retired to their chamber, their Companions lay down beside each other. Anjo and Tulpar, exhausted from the events of the evening, fell asleep immediately—though both stallion and mare slept restlessly, as if their dreams were filled with nightmares.

From the thick pallet they shared Dove opened her arms. "Come, beloved."

Gratefully, River went into Dove's embrace. They held each other without speaking. River could feel Dove's heart beating against her own chest. It seemed they shared a heartbeat, as well as breath.

When River finally spoke, she couldn't keep the fear and sorrow from her voice. "I do not want to die."

Dove's arms tightened around her. "I know."

"But I see no other way."

Dove's voice was barely audible. "I know."

"Please tell me you and Tulpar will survive. Promise me. I do not think I can go through with it if I know you will not live."

"Tulpar will survive, though Anjo is the mate of his heart. And because he would not survive my death, you have my promise that I will live," said Dove.

River kissed her gently. "I wish we'd found each other sooner. We haven't had enough time."

"I will always be yours," said Dove. "And I will find you again someday, should the Great Goddess allow."

"Do you think She will?" River whispered.

"Yes. I believe it with all my heart," said Dove.

River nodded. "Then I will believe it with all my heart, too. Now, let us use the days we have left to love each other as if we have loved already for a lifetime."

"Yes, beloved. Yes."

Their lips met and passion burned away sorrow as their bodies came together. When they finally slept, their dreams were filled with laughter and joy and love.

"Mari?"

Nik's whisper had Mari turning over and beckoning for him to join her under the thick fur she'd burrowed beneath. Rigel was pressed against her back, sleeping fitfully. Laru sighed as he jumped up on the pallet, circled, and lay down at her feet.

"I saw Sora," he said as he kicked out of his pants and pulled off his tunic before he slid into their pallet beside her. "She told me you went to bed early."

"I couldn't stay out there and watch River's people leave her offerings. They honor her, but it makes it seem as if she's already dead."

Nik pulled her into his arms so that she rested against his chest. "Is there no other way to awaken the Goddess?"

"River does not believe so," Mari said.

"What about you? What do you believe?"

"I believe it's going to be very difficult to trap Death into awakening the Goddess," Mari prevaricated.

"How soon is River going to give herself to Him?" Nik asked.

Mari chose her words carefully. "She started discussing it tonight. Ralina and Dove believe she needs to wait—have Death come to the wall a few more times, and then perhaps she agrees to meet with Him in person. But they can't decide whether angering Him would work for or against River."

She could feel Nik nod. "Ralina says His arrogance can be used against Him. River just needs to remember that and decide at the time whether it is best to flatter or threaten . . ." He paused before he added, "I saw Death watching you today. It made my skin crawl."

"Mine, too," Mari agreed. "I've felt His gaze on me before, when we paddled away from the Tribe of the Trees that awful day I called down sunfire. I thought He watched me then. Today I realized that I'd been right."

"Just remember that within these walls you are safe, and that we're going to defeat Him." Nik's voice was filled with confidence. "The Herd is strong and capable. The Goddess of Life is our ally. What does Death have? Mutants whose Companions cannot abide them and reanimated dead things. No, they will not win."

Instead of speaking, Mari pulled Nik to her and kissed him with a passion fueled by heartache and the knowledge of what must come next.

It was barely dawn when Thaddeus woke, uncomfortable and annoyed that he'd had to sleep outside the shelter the Hunters erected for him because Death had commanded he watch the bison who had swallowed his blood. Thaddeus stretched, grimacing at the sore spot sleeping on a root had caused in his back. *Tonight, Odysseus, if I still have to watch the damnable bison I will tie him to a tree outside my tent. Death did not say where I had to watch the beast.*

Thaddeus sniggered at his own cleverness and then a strange sound had him sitting up and staring around. He recognized the sound. He'd definitely heard it before. An animal was coughing and gasping for air.

"Odysseus?" Thaddeus lifted his face, tasting the air hungrily as he sought the scent of his dead Companion. "Odysseus?"

The wheezing cough came again, calling Thaddeus's attention to the far side of an enormous old oak. On all fours, the Hunter made his way to the tree to find the bull standing with his head down behind it, wheezing and coughing bloody phlegm into the grass. His eyes were glazed with fever. His nose was matted with green snot. He looked terrible—and smelled worse.

. . . watch this bull. Come to Me the moment he sickens.

Death's command lifted from his memory and Thaddeus huffed. *Well,*

Odysseus, let us tell Death the bison sickens. Tonight we will for sure sleep snug in our shelter once again.

The God was easy to find. All Thaddeus need do was follow the scent of roasting meat and campfire. Though they'd had to leave Death's ridiculous throne in the Rock Mountains pass, the army had fashioned Him a new one. It was not much more than a huge fallen tree they had rolled beside the camp's main fire and then hacked at until it was chair-like, but the God sat on it as if it had been fashioned of gold, as He chewed a hunk of bloody bison meat.

"My Lord." Thaddeus bowed low before the God. "The bison sickens."

"Ah, it happened as quickly as I intended." He stood and tossed the rest of the hunk of meat at several Warriors who sat across the campfire. On all fours, the men snarled and fought for the piece of bison meat, which made the God laugh before He turned to Thaddeus. "Dog-man, lead Me to him."

Thaddeus did so quickly, moving through the outskirts of the bison herd back to the lone bull, who still stood beside the tree, head down, struggling to breathe.

"Excellent, excellent! Now, dog-man, yesterday did you not say that you found a lake that adjoins the walled city?" Death asked.

Thaddeus nodded. "I did, my Lord."

"Good. Take Me to the lake, but we must remain inside the cover of trees and move quickly. There is no time to waste. I am eager to have the walls of the Herd's city fall to Me."

"My Lord?" Thaddeus wasn't sure he'd heard Death correctly. The walls of the Herd's city were high and wide and appeared unbreachable. How could a sick bison cause them to fall?

"Just take Me to the lake. As I must remind you often, *too often*, watch and learn." Death jerked His pelt-covered chin in the direction of the Herd's fortress. "Now, dog-man."

"Yes, my Lord." Thaddeus hurried off.

Behind him he heard Death order the sick bison to attend Him, and the beast obeyed, though he staggered and coughed and struggled to breathe.

Thaddeus tried not to speak, but he could not contain his curiosity. Finally, he decided to ask Death the question foremost on his mind as the

God probably would not hurt him too badly for questioning Him—or at least He wouldn't until they arrived at the lake.

"Um, my Lord. I shall watch and learn. On that you have my word. But might I ask one question?"

"Go on. All is going according to my plans and I am feeling magnanimous." Death gestured for Thaddeus to speak.

Thaddeus swallowed hard and then asked, "How did you know the bison would sicken?"

Death chuckled, a low, bestial sound more like the snorting of a bull than laughter. "Because I used you to sicken it, dog-man."

At Thaddeus's shocked look the God chuckled cruelly again. "You carry within you the sloughing sickness. All of the Warriors and Hunters do."

"But we were cured."

"Well, 'cured' is not an entirely accurate word. Perhaps 'changed' would be a better one." Death shrugged His wide shoulders. As had become His custom, the God wore only a short leather skin tied around his waist so that His massive body was on full display, including His inhumanly thick muscles and the dark fur that covered Him. "Yes, 'changed' is much more accurate. The sickness will always live within you. I would think that would be obvious to you, as you, and the other Tribesmen, keep evolving—keep *becoming*."

"Becoming what?" Thaddeus could not stop himself from asking.

Death simply shrugged again. "I am not entirely sure, but it is an interesting experiment, is it not?"

"Y-yes, my Lord," Thaddeus stuttered.

I am becoming more like you, my Odysseus. That is all. And that is good. It is good. There is nothing for me to fear if I am only becoming you.

"My Lord?"

"Ask one more question," said Death.

"How will the walls fall?"

"There are many ways that could happen, and they all begin this morning. Ah! Is that the lake I see through the trees?" Death asked.

Thaddeus sniffed the air. Scenting water, he nodded. "Yes, my Lord."

Death grunted and took the lead from Thaddeus. They moved through the forest with the sick bison stumbling behind them. Death kept glancing at the walls of the city and the Riders who were posted there, looking out upon the forest. Then they were at the edge of a large, clear lake flanked by willows whose long green branches swayed gently in the dawn breeze.

Death halted inside the tree line, hidden there from the sentries on the wall. He paused and glanced back at the bison, who had lagged several yards behind.

"Attend Me," Death growled at the poor, sick beast, and with a last spurt of energy he trotted to Him. The God pulled a knife from the waist of the leather wrap He wore. "Now, dog-man, watch and learn."

Quickly, brutally, Death stabbed the sick bison—in his shoulders and flanks. They were not mortal wounds, but they bled freely. The bison did not flee, though he grunted in pain and his ravaged body trembled.

"Now, noble beast, your suffering is almost at an end. I have one last command for you. Go into the lake. Swim to the city wall. There you may take your eternal rest and sink within the arms of the lake."

The bison blinked his glazed eyes, shook his huge head—spraying snot and saliva and blood around him—and then the poor beast seemed to have a spurt of strength. He trotted to the lake and entered it, swimming strongly toward the distant wall.

Death wiped the knife on his clothes, tucked it back into his waistband, and turned from the lake, retracing their steps.

Thaddeus was staring at the God when he finally understood. *He's poisoning their drinking water!* Thaddeus almost laughed at the simple brilliance of Death's plan.

"Come," Death said to Thaddeus from well within the tree line. "Let us return. Killing always makes Me hungry."

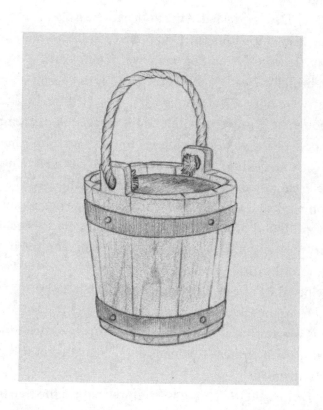

CHAPTER 34

The Goddess didn't ease Mari into the dream. Instead, it was an instant immersion, as if she'd been thrown into water. The Great Goddess was suddenly there, sitting beside Mari. She looked much as She had earlier that night—an idol fashioned lovingly from earth come alive—only She was human sized and perched on the edge of Mari's pallet beside Rigel. In the dream Rigel woke and Laru woke, though they remained still as they stared in awe at the Goddess while Nik slumbered peacefully beside them.

The Goddess smiled and spoke to Mari in her mother's voice. "For your entire life you thought that I refused to speak to you. It was never that, beloved child of Leda. It was only that I knew I must wait for this day for you to truly hear Me and to understand the importance of what I must say."

In the dream Mari brushed the hair back from her sleepy face and rubbed at her eyes. The Great Goddess was still there, smiling at her as the canines watched.

Mari blurted the first thing that came to her mind. "Your voice sounds like my mama's!"

The Goddess's smile was tender. "I thought that you would enjoy hearing Leda's voice again. Was I incorrect?"

"No! I've missed Mama so much. It is a gift to hear her."

"It makes me happy that My gift pleases you. Now, sweet daughter, are you ready to fulfill your destiny?" asked the Goddess.

Mari sat, glanced at Nik's sleeping form, and then nodded. "I am. But how? River talked about it most of the night. She and Ralina and Dove have not been able to decide on a plan that will work."

"And they will not. What happens next is not their destiny; it is yours."

Mari felt a shudder of fear.

The Goddess reached out and touched her cheek. "There is nothing for you to fear. Some of what comes next will be unpleasant, but know that your mother waits to embrace you."

Mari swallowed the fear and terrible sadness she felt whenever she thought about leaving Rigel and Nik, Laru and Sora—and her people, her beautiful, strong, amazing Pack. *But they won't be beautiful and strong and amazing if Death wins. They will be slaves to His desires and pawns as He mutates them all.*

"Tell me what I need do. I will not disappoint You," said Mari.

"Of course you will not disappoint Me. You never have, Mari, daughter of Leda, Moon Woman for Clan Weaver and the Pack." As the Goddess spoke, images began to form in the air between them, as if she sketched them for Mari. "Here is where you must go. Now. Before the others awaken. Death will already be there, but that is expected. You need only stop what He attempts *and* use it as well. This morning He unwittingly provides you the key to unlock My incarnation."

Mari gazed at the scene forming before her. She recognized the setting as the part of the wall where the lake fed the aqueduct that provided fresh water for the Valley of Vapors. Not long after they'd arrived April had given Mari and Sora a tour along the wall that ringed the city, and they had spent quite some time at the part of the wall that met the lake. April had explained how there was a system of sluiceways and canals that flowed from the lake throughout the valley where the fresh water could be mixed with the hot mineral water that bubbled from beneath the valley. Mari had been intrigued, so April had also shown how the sluiceway could be closed, which they often did in the spring when rain swelled the lake to flood levels.

"I know this place," Mari said as she studied the image that floated like a mirage in the air between them. "Why it is important?"

"You will understand all when you witness what Death does, but you must hurry, and take a bucket and a rope with you—one long enough to reach from the wall down to the lake," explained the Goddess. "You and Sora will reverse what Death attempts to do, but you must first allow Him to complete His vile act. As I said, it is key to My incarnation."

"Within me." Mari was embarrassed by how weak and afraid she sounded.

Once again, the Goddess touched her cheek gently. "As I said, after the unpleasantness all will be well. You need not fear. I am with you. I will be with you. I have always been with you."

Mari nodded. Rigel whined softly and pressed his face against her leg. She stroked his head gently and met her goddess's gaze. "May I ask one favor?"

"Yes, brave one."

"When I am gone, Wash Rigel's grief away, like You did for Bard, so that he may Choose another Companion and live a long, happy life."

The Goddess bowed Her head slightly. "I give you My oath that I will not leave gentle Rigel to suffer."

"Thank You, Great Goddess." Mari kept stroking Rigel's head as her Companion gazed up at her with tears dripping from his expressive eyes.

"You must go now, my brave Mari. I will not speak to you again until I incarnate. Do not fear, daughter," said the Goddess.

Mari felt a spike of panic as the Goddess began to dissolve from her dream. "But how do I make sure Death will find me and awaken You within my body?"

"I shall help you. That is why I cannot speak with you again. I will be communing with My beloved. He will be ready. He will believe that He finds you, when in truth *you* shall find *Him*." The Goddess's body had become transparent.

"I won't take Rigel with me. I cannot," said Mari.

"I shall help you with that, too. Gentle Rigel must wait within the walls, safe and far from Death's grasp. I will send a creature My beloved will not be able to resist. Please know that she will not truly experience pain. I am with her, too. And, Mari, a mare's luck shall be with you, on that you have my oath . . ." The Goddess faded away completely.

With a gasp Mari awakened. Nik slept at her side. Laru was still curled at their feet. Only Rigel was awake. Pressed against her he stared at her. Tears made dark paths down his face to drip to the pallet from either side of his muzzle. Mari opened her arms, and her Shepherd moved closer into her embrace as they wept silently together.

Mari reluctantly broke their embrace. She put her hands on either side of his face and whispered, "I will always love you. Always." Sending him images of the two of them—some from when he had been a puppy, newly arrived at her burrow, bloody and beaten from fighting his way through a swarm to get to her. She sent him pictures of the three of them—Rigel, Mari, and Leda—as Earth Walkers found a way to live with a Companion. Other images flowed from Mari to Rigel: of him growing and walking proudly beside her after she'd revealed herself to the Clan, of Rigel and Laru on either side of her, taking on the Tribe of the Trees to rescue Nik, of Rigel, Laru, Nik, and Mari all curled together on their pallet, snug and safe in their cocoon of love. "Always, Rigel. You will always be my favorite memory of this life. And my greatest wish is that after I am gone you will find joy and love again."

Rigel closed his eyes and pressed himself against her as tears dripped down his face.

When Mari could bear it no longer, she whispered, "I must go. And I cannot wake Nik or Laru."

Rigel sent her a picture of him padding by her side, and she nodded. "Yes," she said softly. "You may be with me for as long as you're able, but when I tell you to stay within the walls you must . . ." She paused and added, "You were part of the dream, too, weren't you?"

Rigel sent her an image of the Goddess sitting on the edge of their pallet, touching Mari's face gently.

Mari felt a wave of relief. "Good, then you do understand. Okay, sweet boy, let's go face my destiny."

Quietly, Mari and Rigel moved from the pallet. She dressed and looked back at Nik and Laru, who slept so soundly that they had to have been touched by the Great Goddess. Mari was glad. She couldn't have faced Nik or Laru just then. Later, yes. After it was too late, but not now. Mari bent and kissed Nik on his forehead, and then Laru before she and Rigel tiptoed from the chamber.

First Mari went to the nursery building and collected a long rope, which she coiled inside a wooden bucket. She was relieved that it was so early that no one was tending plants yet, which allowed her a moment to stand before the Goddess idol, bow her head, and whisper a prayer. Beside her Rigel whined softly and leaned against her leg.

The sun was just beginning to peek above the horizon as she and Rigel made their way to the wide ramp the horses used to climb to the top of the wall. There were, of course, sentries posted there, as well as all of the way around the city, but none of them questioned her as she and Rigel followed the narrow ledge that framed its circumference. Sentries did greet her, and Mari forced herself to smile and return their good mornings. Rigel remained by her side, subdued and silent.

By the time they'd made their way around the city to the rear area of the wall that met the lake the sun had cleared the horizon and the sky was blushing pink. Mari stopped there, above the lake, which lapped rhythmically against the rock wall. She had chosen a place between sentries that was still shadowy in the wan dawn light. She did not wait long. A slight sound from the forest drew her attention. Carefully, she peered out at the tree line. Within it she could barely make out a dark hulking form. Then a creature stumbled from the trees. It was a bison who rushed into the lake and began swimming.

Mari glanced at the guards. She saw that they noted the bison but were not concerned. And why should they be? Animals bathed in, drank from, and swam across the lake frequently. They were stationed there to guard the sluiceway from any who would breach the city's defenses via its system of canals and aqueducts.

But Mari's Goddess-given intuition told her the truth. The bison was the threat and the way the city walls would be breached. She shifted her gaze from the big creature who struggled through the lake toward the wall back to the tree. For an instant the rising sun illuminated the forest edge just enough for her to see that Death was there, turning to fade into the forest.

There was another person with him, and with a start of realization Mari recognized him as Thaddeus. Though Ralina had described the mutations that were happening to the men from the Tribe of the Trees, it was different actually seeing it. Thaddeus's body was furred and bent. His arms and legs looked odd, and Mari understood quickly that he would probably be much more comfortable on all fours. His face had changed, too; though he was still recognizable as Thaddeus, his mouth and nose had elongated, appearing more muzzle-like, and she could see pointed Terrier ears poking up through thick, matted hair.

Then he, too, faded into the forest and Mari's gaze returned to the bison, who was much closer to the wall—close enough that she could see the blood that spread from the injured beast to taint the clear water around him. She stared at the bison, and realized that his glazed eyes were matted and snot ran thickly from his nose. The creature's forward momentum faltered, and without a sound his body relaxed and he sank below the surface. The stain he left in the water around him began to spread, and with every ripple of the lake it got closer to the city wall and the sluiceway there.

The beast had been infected with the skin-sloughing sickness.

"Death means to poison our water supply so that we sicken and He can overrun us." Mari closed her eyes and prayed. "Thank You, Great Goddess, for this warning." She opened her eyes and stared down at the expanding scarlet stain in the clear lake. "And for this opportunity."

Mari turned and shouted at the guards to her left and right, "Close the sluiceway! Death has poisoned the lake!"

That set off an explosion of activity. Both sentries slid down the rope ladder, shouting for help as they raced to the huge wheel system situated inside the wall where lake met rock. Men and women joined them—half dressed they raced to the wheel.

Working quickly, Mari tied the long hemp rope to the handle of the wooden bucket, and threw it out into the lake and the poison spreading there. She dragged it back, hand over hand, and lifted it to her on the wall. While the Herd rushed to the wall, Mari lifted the bucket. The water was stained a rusty color. As it met her lips she grimaced. It reeked of decay and sickness and tasted rancid, but she drank swallow after swallow, until it was completely gone.

Mari and Rigel made their way back to the wide ramp. They descended, and as Mari passed the large, ever-burning campfire just outside River's building she tossed the wooden bucket directly into the flames.

Rigel whined and she stroked his head as she murmured, "I don't want to take a chance anyone else will get sick."

"Mari! What has happened?" River rushed from the building with Dove's arm through hers and Tulpar and Anjo trotting behind.

Mari was determined to tell as much of the truth as she could. "The Great Goddess came to me in my dream. She showed me a vision looking out from the section of the wall that meets the lake. I felt a great sense of danger, and then the Goddess compelled me awake. So that is where Rigel and I went this morning—to where the lake meets the wall—in time to see a sick bison bleeding out into the lake, and Death sneaking away in the forest."

"Oh, Great Goddess!" Dove gasped. "He means to poison us!"

Mari nodded. "Yes, but because of the Goddess's warning He did not. The sluiceway has been closed."

"Thank the Mother Mare," River said. "But the lake is still poisoned, and we cannot drink undiluted mineral water." She shoved her hair back from her face. "So, He has not poisoned us, but He has greatly impacted our ability to remain safely within these walls."

Ralina appeared, yawning as she joined their group. Then she registered their somber expressions. "Oh, no. How bad is it?"

"Bad," River said, and quickly explained what Mari had discovered.

When she was finished, Mari spoke up. "Well, yes. What Death did is horrible, but not as horrible as He intended."

"I don't understand why you don't seem more upset," said River. "Not only has Death poisoned our drinking water, but we can no longer fish from the lake, and any animal that drinks from it will sicken. That sickness will spread across the plains."

Dove blew out a long breath. "So He will poison these beautiful plains as He did the forest of the Tribe of the Trees and Clan Weaver. I agree with River. It is quite terrible."

Mari's smile was authentic. "Death does not understand what it means to have Moon Women as allies."

"Did you say 'Moon Women'?" Sora joined them, nuzzling little Chloe, who wriggled within the pouch she had mostly outgrown.

"I did," said Mari. "Death sent a diseased bison into the lake that feeds our water supply. The sluiceway has been closed."

"But the lake is still poisoned," repeated River.

Sora's smile mirrored Mari's. "Oh, only until moonrise, Lead Mare Rider. As Mari said, you have Moon Women as allies."

River blinked several times before she spoke. "Do you mean you can heal an entire lake?"

Sora and Mari shared a look. "Yes, we absolutely can," said Sora.

"Thank the Mother Mare!" said River. "What do you need from us? How may we help you?"

"We only need moonrise," said Mari. "But River was right. Anyone who drinks from the lake before then will carry the sickness. We will all have to be vigilant and not eat from any animal who acts oddly or smells rancid."

"More than that," added Ralina. "Death cannot know you have healed the lake. Let Him believe we're here, within these walls, succumbing to the skin-sloughing sickness. It will make Him overconfident and that will cause Him to make mistakes."

Dove nodded. "Ralina is correct. Death will be celebrating with His army, believing He simply has to wait a few days for us to become so ill we cannot protect ourselves." She reached out and grasped River's hand. "Perhaps during that time we will figure out an alternative to River sacrificing herself."

Mari nodded. "That is a really good point. We should all take a breath. Death believes He has the upper hand, so we know He won't attack."

"You must tell the sentries stationed at the lake to watch for large animals entering the lake, like bison or deer, who look ill or act strange," said Ralina. "Death probably will not add any more sickened animals to the lake, especially as He believes we are ignorant of the sick bison, but we need to be sure."

"If He does, Mari and I will just Wash the poison from it again," said Sora firmly.

"Yes, but let us hope Death believes one sick bison will suffice," said River. "It is wonderful that our Moon Women can heal the lake, but we still must think of the creatures that will be poisoned and the toll that will take on our lands."

"Even after the Great Goddess embraces Death and takes Him back to the womb of the earth with Her we will have to remain vigilant," said Dove.

Ralina nodded grimly. "I agree. We cannot allow Him to turn these fertile lands into the poisoned nightmare our forest became."

"We will be vigilant," said River. "And we will also be grateful for our Moon Women. Mari, Sora, do you need the Pack with you when you Wash the lake?"

"No," Mari said. "Sora and I need to Wash the lake quietly."

"We'll be careful and not draw any attention to us when we heal the lake," added Sora.

"We should call down the moon as the sun sets," said Mari to Sora. "The moon begins to rule the sky then, but it will still be light enough that a sudden flash of silver on the lake won't be visible to Death through the trees."

"If He has returned to His camp," said River.

"Oh, He has," Ralina assured them. "He'll be celebrating and blustering and completely unaware of what Mari and Sora do. That is one good thing about His ridiculously inflated ego—it often makes Him blind to the abilities of others."

"And in His blind arrogance He will not bother to watch and be sure the poisoned waters of the lake keep pouring into the valley," said Dove. "Yes, I agree with Ralina. What Death has actually done is give us several days' reprieve." She slid her arm around River's waist. "Now, beloved, let us break our fast with the Mare Council and update them. We have extra days to come up with a plan that does not involve sacrificing our Lead Mare Rider."

"Would you mind if I came with you?" Ralina asked. "Perhaps there is some piece of information that I learned from my time with Death that might help with an alternative plan. I don't know what it could be at the moment, but if I continue to talk about it and think on it maybe I will remember something I have forgotten—or not realized was important."

"Of course," said River. "That's an excellent idea." She turned to Mari. "When I thought of a lake attack, I only imagined Death's army attempting to get within our walls through the sluiceway, not through poison. Again, thank you. You have saved the Herd and Pack from terrible illness."

"Thank the Goddess," said Mari quickly. "She is the reason I was there."

"We shall," said Dove with a smile.

As Dove, River, and Ralina walked toward the building that housed the Mare Council, Mari stared into the campfire and slowly stroked Rigel's soft head.

"Is something wrong?" Sora asked quietly, for her ears alone.

Mari startled and then shook her head, forcing herself to smile at her best friend. "I am just sad for River and Dove."

"You do not think they'll find another way for the Goddess to incarnate?" Sora said.

"No. I do not think they will," said Mari.

"Mari, Rigel, there you two are." Nik stretched and scratched the stubble on his chin as he and Laru joined Sora and Mari. "Where did you get off to so early?"

"Mari caught Death trying to poison us," said Sora. "Pull up a log, Nik. O'Bryan should be joining us any moment. We'll fill you in when he does, but until then I have bread and cheese and robust morning tea with which to break our fast."

"That sounds delicious." Nik grinned and sat on a log near where Mari and Rigel stood looking into the fire. Laru went to Rigel, sniffed him, and whined softly. Nik tilted his head and studied his Companion's son. "Mari, is Rigel feeling okay?"

Mari forced herself to shrug and respond as she normally would. "What we witnessed upset him."

"Did Death do something to you? To Rigel?" Nik stood and hurried to Mari's side.

Mari stepped into his arms and rested her head against his chest. "Death did not even know we were there, but what He did reminded us of how He destroyed the Tribe of the Trees. It was a lot for Rigel and me."

"Of course it was!" Nik held her close and stroked her back. "Hey, Rigel, it's going to be okay. Promise."

Rigel looked up at Nik and whined before he sighed heavily and lay next to Mari, careful to remain in physical contact with her as if touching her could keep her there—alive—with him.

Mari closed her eyes and wished more than anything that she could freeze the four of them in that moment and keep them all safe, together, and alive.

Just before sunset Sora and Mari, Nik and O'Bryan walked along the ledge that framed the walled city. Rigel was the only Companion with them, as there was little room on the narrow ledge, but Mari refused to leave him beyond. As they reached the area where wall met lake, River greeted them. She was there with two odd-looking rope contraptions, which instantly intrigued the Tribesmen.

"I see what these are." Nik held up one of the two wide wooden planks onto which ropes were securely attached. "Look at this, O'Bryan."

O'Bryan studied the things and nodded. "This is good, but we can definitely help them create a cage system like the Tribe used, which would be better."

"Cage system?" River asked.

"That sounds ominous," said Sora.

"Oh, I know what Nik and O'Bryan mean and it's not ominous at all," said Mari. "I'm assuming Sora sits on one of these planks and I sit on the other and then you lower us to the bank of the lake, correct?"

River nodded. "Yes, exactly." She pointed to wooden wheels that had been built into their side of the wall. "We wrap the ropes around the wheels and this lever system allows one person to lower another easily to the ground. We created it to make quick repairs and checks of the sluice-way."

"Nik and O'Bryan and the Tribe of the Trees had a much more elaborate system," said Mari. "It allowed one person to lift or lower several people inside something that looked like a beautiful carved cage for giant birds."

"We can show you how to replicate it," said Nik.

"It would be our pleasure," added O'Bryan.

"That would be wonderful," said River. "Until then let us strap the two of you in and lower you to the bank."

"We won't fall?" Sora looked at the contraptions dubiously.

"No, you sit on the planks and wrap the shorter ropes around your waists to secure you. Then if you slip you will not fall to the ground," said River matter-of-factly.

"That does not actually make me feel better," said Sora.

O'Bryan put his arm around her shoulders. "I will not let you fall."

Sora gazed up at him and sighed. Her hands trembled as she sat on the planks and O'Bryan strapped her in, but she bravely only squeaked a tiny terrified sound as they lowered her and Mari side by side while Rigel whined softly from above them.

When they reached the ground, the women untied the security ropes, waved to River, Nik, and O'Bryan, and made their way quickly to the nearby bank.

"Ready?" asked Mari.

Sora nodded. "Ready. And we need to hurry because the sun has set." She jerked her chin toward the forest, where the sun had disappeared beneath the horizon—though the sky still held its dying light in watercolor swatches of coral and flaxen.

"Completely ready," said Mari. Then she had to clear her throat of phlegm before she began, though when she began speaking the magickal invocation her voice was firm and clear.

> "Moon Women we declare ourselves to be.
> Greatly gifted we bare ourselves to Thee.
> Earth Mother, aid us with Your magick sight.
> Lend us strength this moon-touched night."

Sora took up the invocation from there.

> "Come, silver light—fill us to overflow
> so that which has been poisoned your healing touch shall know."

The two Moon Women lifted their hands to the gloaming sky and finished the invocation together.

> "Through right of blood and birth channel through me
> that which the Earth Mother proclaims my destiny!"

Cold, silver power flowed down into Mari. She gritted her teeth and fought against her natural instinct to keep some of it—to allow herself to be healed of the sickness that had already taken hold within her body—but Mari did not keep the power. Within her mind she painted an elaborate picture of silver power flowing down and through her and into the lake.

"Now!" Mari told Sora.

The Moon Women flung the silver magick out into the lake, which blazed like a shooting star for a moment, and then that light, and the light in the sky, faded to darkness.

"Wow, that was a lot easier than I thought it would be," said Sora as she looked up at their eagerly watching group and gave then a victorious wave.

Mari coughed, cleared her throat, and nodded. She forced herself to smile and lightened her voice. "I wouldn't have imagined a lake would be easier to heal than a Clan, but it seems it is."

Sora watched her as they returned to the chair lifts and began strapping themselves in. "Would you like to do this again inside the walls? I could draw down a little more power and channel it through you. You seem off."

Mari waved her hand dismissively. "It's nothing. Rigel's having a tough time. Seeing Death poison the lake brought back all sorts of feelings about the Tribe of the Trees and their forest being poisoned."

Sora seemed satisfied by Mari's explanation but continued to watch her.

I need to avoid Sora between now and when I leave the city, Mari told herself as Nik and O'Bryan worked the wheels and they lifted to the wall. Sadness filled Mari at the thought of not being able to say a proper good-bye to her best friend. *She'll understand when it's over. Nik will understand when it's over. They'll be alive. They'll thrive. It will all be worth it.* In the darkness Mari wiped away a tear as Rigel whined softly.

CHAPTER 35

The Great Goddess of Life followed Her innate connection to Death and slipped into His dream. She took Death into Her soft arms and pulled Him close to Her naked body. The God moaned with desire.

Ah, My love, You have returned to Me, Death spoke against her lips.

I have never left You, beloved. It is You Who left Me.

But only temporarily. It is You Who has been reluctant to be awakened so that We can be together again. He stroked Her hair and let His fingers trail down Her throat and over Her full breasts, where He lingered on Her dark, firm nipples.

The Goddess gasped with pleasure and when She spoke Her voice had become husky with desire. *That is why I come to You this night, beloved. I understand now that You will not return to sleep within My arms, and I cannot bear to be without You any longer.*

In the dream Death raised Himself from Her lush body and met Her eyes. *My love! Is it true? Are You ready to awaken?*

I will not lie to You, My own. You know that.

Then I shall awaken You as soon as I defeat the Wind Riders. I have found the perfect vessel for You within their city. She is moon and sun touched—and a beauty as well as a Warrior.

She sounds perfect. But, beloved, I miss You so terribly that I would choose not to wait. Can none other be My vessel? None of the women with You on Your journey?

Death scowled. *Those foolish women allowed themselves to die. They were unworthy of You, My love.*

So, there are no other women with You?

No. But there are women aplenty within the walls of the Wind Rider city.

The Goddess paused. Her full lips formed a pout. *But I have waited long enough.* Then she smiled and said in a happy rush, *I know, beloved! Tell Me the name of the vessel You have found for Me. I shall attempt to enter her dreams and compel her to leave the walls of her city so that You may capture her and awaken Me sooner.*

Death scratched the thick pelt that was His beard. *She is Mari—a leader and magick worker. She may, indeed, listen to You, especially after she is infected.*

Infected?

Nothing to concern You, My love. Just the first step to awakening You.

The Goddess nodded with enthusiasm. *Beloved, if she is a magick worker she will be familiar with healing plants. I could compel her to search for an obscure healing plant outside the walls of the city. If she is ill, that could be enough to get her to leave her fortress.*

Indeed, agreed Death, *especially as she will not be the only person to have been infected with the sickness.*

Beloved, could she be ill already?

She could be. It happens quickly.

The Goddess threw Her arms around Her lover and pressed Herself against His mutated body. *Then I shall go to her dreams this very night. Watch for her, beloved. Watch for her . . .*

As Her body began to fade away from Him, Death still attempted to hold His goddess tightly. *I shall, My love, and then I shall awaken You.*

Yes, beloved, yes . . .

Mari felt horrible, and what was even worse than feeling horrible was having to hide how she felt *and* avoid the people with whom she most wanted to spend her final hours.

Thankfully, Nik and O'Bryan had already begun instructing the Herd carpenters on how to build a Tribe of the Trees lift, which was keeping both men busy as well as absent.

She coughed wetly and wiped her nose on the back of her sleeve—and then scratched the inside of her elbow. Rigel looked up at her and whined, and Mari stroked his head.

"Sssh, it's going to be okay, remember? The Great Earth Goddess will make it all okay, sweet boy." She coughed again and then realized what the itchy pain in her arm—in both of her arms—meant. Mari had been heading to see Jenna, Danita, and Davis one last time, but she froze, looked around her, and stepped into the shadows behind a large tree. Quickly, she pulled up her sleeves.

They were there. Pustules that would soon turn into open, weeping sores she would not be able to hide. Her stomach twisted, and she bent at the waist and vomited the tea she'd recently drunk to try to keep her cough under control.

Rigel whined again, and Mari went to him and dropped to her knees. She put her arms around his neck and breathed in his warm, familiar scent. "I love you so much," she whispered into his thick fur. Then she stood and brushed her hair back from her sweaty face. "I can't see them like this. Danita and Jenna know me too well. They'll realize I'm sick. And Davis is Goddess-touched, which means he is more observant than most men. I must leave without seeing them." Mari glanced up at the sky and breathed a sigh of relief. Dusk wasn't far away. "It's tonight," she said softly. "Ralina said after the sores appear is when the cure is administered." Mari attempted to smile at Rigel. "I know how to go without worrying anyone—or at least not worrying anyone at first. But I *must* say goodbye to Nik, even if he won't understand that it is goodbye. He will later, though." She coughed and had to take several long breaths to stop from vomiting again. Then Mari straightened her sleeves, wiped the sweat from her fever-heated face, and she and Rigel began to make their way slowly to the area where Nik and his cousin were working with the Herd carpenters.

Strangely, it seemed to take forever and no time at all to reach the big, open-sided tent that smelled of freshly cut wood and the sweat of the men fashioning it into what would eventually be a lift that was beautiful as well as functional.

"Mari! I was just going to send Laru to find you and Rigel." Nik grinned and walked toward them with Laru padding at his side. He was carrying a thick hunk of bread that had meat and cheese stuffed within it. "Sora brought us all dinner so that we could keep working." He gestured at the rest of the carpenters, who were talking as they ate. O'Bryan caught her eye and waved, which Mari returned. "Sorry that we won't be eating with you."

Just the thought of food had Mari's stomach churning. She swallowed quickly and forced a smile. "Well, that's actually good. Rigel and I are going to go soak in one of the mineral pools." She lowered her voice and Nik leaned down to her. "Rigel has been really upset since Death poisoned the lake. He needs to spend some alone time with me."

Nik nodded and kissed her cheek. "Laru agrees. He says Rigel is extremely upset but won't share with him exactly why."

Mari hated lying to Nik, so she tried to tell as much of the truth as she could. "He probably doesn't want to share with him because he knows how troubling it would be for any of the Tribe to have to relive what Death did."

Nik rubbed Rigel's head. "He's underestimating us." Then he squatted down in front of the Shepherd. "Hey, boy, you don't have to carry this alone. Laru and I can share it with you."

Rigel whined and licked Nik's face. Nik laughed and stood, putting an arm around Mari. "Well, I tried. You should definitely Wash him next Third Night."

"That's a good idea," said Mari. Unable to stop herself, she turned away from Nik and coughed.

"Hey, are you feeling okay?" Nik touched her face and frowned. "Your skin is hot."

Mari forced a bright smile. "I'll be fine, but you might want to stay away from me. I may have caught a cold from one of the Herd children who like to hang around the nursery building."

Nik hugged her close. "I am not afraid of a little cold. My Moon Woman can Wash that away, but only after she Washes herself first."

"I will definitely remember that next Third Night," Mari said. "But take your time tonight. I'll soak in a mineral bath and sleep early."

"There is a lot of work to do here, not that I'm complaining. I thought it might be upsetting to teach the Herd how to build our lifts, but instead I find that it's soothing and nicely nostalgic. I know Father would approve."

"I know he would, too." Mari looked up into his kind green eyes and searched his face, wanting to memorize every detail of it. "Nikolas, Companion of Laru, Sun Priest of our Herd, son of Sol, I love you completely."

Nik blinked in surprise and then he grinned happily. "And I love you, Moon Woman Mari, Companion of Rigel, daughter of Leda."

He bent to kiss her, and Mari wanted so, so badly to let him—to lose herself in his taste and touch—but she would not dare take that chance that she might infect him. She would not leave him sickening, even though Sora could Wash him of this disgusting disease.

Mari turned her head and coughed into his shoulder. She made herself laugh and then kissed him quickly on the cheek and stepped out of his embrace.

"Just because I can Wash you free of illness does *not* mean you'd enjoy catching this." She turned away and coughed again as Nik grimaced. "And now I'm going to soak." She met his gaze. "I love you."

"You already said that."

"Can I say it too much?" she asked.

He grinned. "Never. I love you, too. Have a good soak."

Mari watched him join O'Bryan, who waved at her again. She returned the wave and felt Laru's gaze on her. The big Shepherd hadn't left Rigel's side, though he stared at her, not his son.

Mari touched his mind and painted a picture of the four of them together, curled up in her Moon Woman burrow, cozy and safe.

In return Laru filled her with warmth and love. Before he turned to go to Nik she saw that tears leaked from his eyes.

Mari and Rigel took the long way to the front of the walled valley. They did not walk down the wide main street where the Herd and Pack gathered to share dinner. She could smell roasting meat, which made her so nauseous she struggled not to throw up again. She could hear the indecipherable sounds of conversations drifting on the cool night wind. Mari wanted so badly to join them—to ask Sora to draw down the moon and Wash her free of this terrible disease. Mari wanted so badly to live.

But as she moved silently through the shadows, first to the nursery where she grabbed a long, triple-braided rope, and then to the wide ramp that led to the top of the wall, she concentrated on the good that she was doing. Her life as an exchange for the lives and futures of all those she loved was a small price to pay. She was keeping the beautiful, lush plains of the Wind Riders from becoming a place of disease and death—of slavery and darkness. She was keeping her people safe, which was the ultimate destiny of every Moon Woman.

Mari and Rigel paused in the shadows by the ramp. She waited a few minutes until she was sure people would be distracted with filling their plates, and then she made her sore, feverish body hurry up the ramp. She nodded at each sentry they passed but spoke to no one. Mari knew where she was heading. River had made sure there were sentries posted to look out over the lake, but she remembered an area of the wall, just before it curved to meet the sluiceway, where the rock formation created a natural alcove. It would not be easy, but Mari had no choice. Hidden within the alcove, she would tie one end of her rope around one of the jutting rocks that created the wall and the other around her waist, and then she would climb down the side of the wall, much like she had rappelled with Nik from his city in the trees to the forest floor.

They arrived at the alcove much faster than Mari had anticipated. It seemed to her that time had begun to behave strangely. It had taken so long to move through the shadows to the ramp that Mari had been worried she wouldn't have the strength needed to do what must be done. And then it was like she'd blinked and suddenly she and Rigel were there. Stiffly, Mari tied the end loop of the rope securely around a nearby rock, wiped the sweat from her face, coughed, and crouched before Rigel.

It was time to say goodbye to him, and she wasn't entirely sure she could do it. How could she leave him? How could she break his heart and hers? He was part of her, and she him. She sobbed silently as she pressed her face into his thick fur and tried to find her lost courage.

"You infected yourself, didn't you?"

Sora's voice came from behind her. Mari stood and whirled around as she wiped tears from her face. "What are you talking about?" She lifted her chin and tried to sound indignant, but her outrage disintegrated in a bout of coughing that had her leaning against the wall for support. When she could speak again, she met Sora's gaze and nodded. "I did."

"And now you're going to go to Death." Sora didn't phrase it as a question, but Mari answered.

"I am."

Sora looked down for a moment before she met her gaze again and asked, "The Great Goddess spoke to you?"

Mari nodded. "Twice. That night in the nursery when She manifested I thought the Goddess meant for me to be Her vessel, but I did not know how—or even if it was just my imagination. Then She came to me in my dream the night Death poisoned the lake."

"She did more than just warn you about the lake?"

Mari nodded again, coughed, cleared her throat, and continued. "Yes, She told me how to defeat Death. I drank from the poisoned lake. The Goddess said She would prepare Death—that She would make Him believe She wants to awaken, and set Him up to use me as the vessel. Now all I need do is get beyond the wall so He can believe He's captured me . . ." Mari had to pause as she coughed up blood and bile again. "Sora, please don't try to stop me. It has to be this way. It is the will of our Great Earth Mother. You know River should not make this sacrifice. She leads this valley. They need her."

"We need you!" Sora brushed angrily at the tears that had begun to leak from her eyes.

"No, my beautiful, capable best friend. You will be their Moon Woman." As Mari spoke, she felt the truth of what she said and knew the knowledge was another gift from her goddess. "You will train Danita and Isabel to be Moon Women, as well as the daughter I know you will bear O'Bryan. You will lead our Pack to establish a home on these amazing plains where they will prosper for generations."

Tears flowed down Sora's cheeks, but her voice was steady. "We were supposed to watch our children play together. We were supposed to grow old together. I do not want this. I do not want it to be this way."

"Neither do I, but it is the Goddess's decision and I have made the choice to accept my destiny."

Sora's gaze went to Rigel, who sat silently pressed against Mari's leg. "Will Rigel go with you?"

"No! He must stay here. I—I can't do this if Death can harm him. The

Great Goddess promised me She would not allow him to be in pain. Remember what She did for Bard?"

Sora nodded.

"The Goddess will touch Rigel, too, so he will be free of the pain of losing me." Mari's hand went to her Companion's head. "I want him to Choose again. I want him to be happy and have a long life. Please tell his new Companion that."

"I will." Sora drew in a deep breath, wiped her face, lifted her chin, and said, "Come with me. I will help you."

Mari's brow furrowed. "How?"

"Just come on. Try not to cough, which means don't talk, because I had that terrible sickness and talking only makes the coughing worse." Sora turned and headed along the narrow ledge toward the lake.

Mari was too sick and weak and sad to argue with her, so she followed silently with Rigel beside her. When they came to the familiar part of the wall above the sluiceway, Sora greeted the sentry stationed there.

"Hey there, we're your dinner relief." Sora spoke in a soft, conversational tone. "And no need to hurry back. We'll keep watch over the lake tonight."

The young Rider who had been standing guard smiled in surprise. "Truly? I expected to be here until the moon was well over the trees."

Sora shrugged. "We're early. We like looking out on the forest. It reminds us of home."

"Well, then, thank you." The Rider nodded to Sora and Mari, and then moved past them with a light step.

After he was out of sight Sora went to the wooden box that held the ropes and planks they'd used the day before to descend to the ground. While Mari coughed and petted Rigel, Sora readied one of the lifts, wrapping the ropes around the lever and wheel system.

"It's ready," Sora said.

Mari nodded and crouched before Rigel again. She took his face between her hands. "I'm sorry this causes you pain. If I could change that, I would. If I could make any other decision than this one, I would. Please know that you have been my greatest surprise in this life, as well as my greatest joy. Stay close to Sora. Help Nik and Laru. And always, *always* remember that I love you with every part of my being." She kissed Rigel on his muzzle and pressed her face into his fur one last time. She breathed in his scent, trying to embed it into her memory. Rigel pushed his head against her as he whined softly. Then she kissed him again and stood. "Be brave, my sweet boy." She turned to Sora and wiped her face with her soggy sleeve. "I'm ready."

As Sora helped her onto the plank and secured the ropes around her waist, she asked, "What is your plan to find Death?"

"It has to appear as if He finds me. I will go directly into the forest from here so that no sentries see me. Then I'll simply wander toward where I know His army is camped." Mari jerked her chin in the direction of the many campfires that glowed through the forest. "I'm close to delirium already, so when I'm found I've decided to say the most logical thing—that I was searching for an herb to relieve my fever and got lost. I have to trust that the Goddess has taken care of the rest of it." Mari cleared her throat again and added, "Keep Rigel with you tonight and for as long as you can. Nik thinks I have a cold and Rigel is upset because of what Death attempted to do to us. I told him we're going to soak at one of the mineral pools."

Sora stroked Rigel's head. "I will take care of him."

"Thank you."

Sora tied the last knot. "It's ready for me to lower." She put her arms around Mari and hugged her tightly. "You became my sister. Thank you for saving all of us."

Mari couldn't speak. She only nodded and clung to Sora. Finally, Sora stepped back, wiped the tears from her face, and smiled. "Tell Leda I said hi."

Through her own tears Mari nodded and managed two words. "I shall." Then she cleared her throat and added, "I love you."

"I love you, too, my sister."

Sora lowered Mari slowly to the ground and then Mari walked as quickly as she was able to the distant tree line. She glanced over her shoulder constantly, memorizing the two faces that stared from the top of the wall down at her. Sora stood beside Rigel, who had lifted his front paws to the top of the wall so he could stare after her. Mari saw Sora put her arm around Rigel. She felt her Companion; she would until the moment she died. Even through his grief he sent her warmth and strength and love, always love.

CHAPTER 36

Thaddeus woke shortly after dawn. He stretched and scratched and then on all fours crawled from his tent—the biggest and most well-appointed tent in the army except for Death's ridiculously huge shelter. The morning was so cold the browning grass was covered with frost, but the cold didn't bother Thaddeus. He barely felt it, which made him smile. *It is our thick fur that keeps me warm, Odysseus!*

The dog-man made his way to a tree far enough away from the sleeping area that he was free to relieve himself. Instead of standing, Thaddeus lifted his leg and, huffing with humor exactly as his Terrier would have, urinated a dark, steady stream onto the trunk.

He did stand then, but only so he could stretch again. Then he scratched himself behind his ears, which had become pointed and considerably larger than they were before he'd merged with his Companion. It felt so good to scratch that Thaddeus lost himself in the sensation as he wandered in the forest—going in no particular direction except purposefully not toward the heart of the army where Death would surely be.

There would be time enough for the God to order him around as the day progressed, but Thaddeus had discovered that, unlike the Storyteller, Death did not call for him immediately upon rising, which mean Thaddeus sometimes had most of the morning to himself. *I need the quiet time, Odysseus. We must plan where we will go after the walled city falls.* Thaddeus remembered the lush valley at the base of the Rock Mountains. *Perhaps there, Odysseus. It is weeks away from here, which means Death cannot easily meddle in my business. Yes, I think that would be perfect, my—*

His thoughts broke off as a tantalizing scent lifted with the cold morning breeze to his enhanced nostrils. Thaddeus froze. He raised his head and sniffed, tasting the scent in the wind.

Disease was unmistakable. Thaddeus would never forget that particular scent. But it was paired with something much more delectable—a female. A human female. Panting, Thaddeus kept scenting the breeze. He dropped to all fours and stealthily followed the delicious smell. Soon his Terrier-sharp hearing caught another all too familiar sound—that of someone coughing.

Thaddeus was pleased by the coughing. It helped to spew her scent into the forest, leading him to—

Once more, Thaddeus froze as he finally recognized the female's scent.

It was that bitch of a scratcher, Mari! The whore who had caused the death of his beloved Odysseus—the one Death had called Sun Warrior and stared at greedily when she appeared on the city wall just days before.

For a moment Thaddeus considered not taking her to Death. He could track her and capture her and do whatever he wanted to her out here in the thickness of the woods, away from Death's censuring gaze.

Thaddeus's body stirred with lust. He hadn't been with a woman since they'd left the Tribe of the Trees. During the journey Death had made it clear His little bunny women were off-limits to all but His touch, and Thaddeus suddenly realized that he craved the release the scratcher mutant would provide him, especially when that release came after he had made her pay for all that she'd done to him.

But Thaddeus was no fool. After they defeated the Wind Riders and he had his own Tribe, he could take any female desired, whenever and however he desired. But first Death must allow him to leave—to establish his own Tribe—and Death would be most likely to do that if Thaddeus kept Him happy.

Bringing the scratcher bitch to Death would definitely keep Him happy.

The night had passed like a waking nightmare. The one good thing about the fever that burned through Mari's body was that it kept her warm. There was nothing else good about the skin-sloughing disease. Her cough was terrible, and the green phlegm she kept spitting up had turned pink with blood. She thought she might be done vomiting, which was a nice reprieve, but her skin felt on fire. Mari had checked on the pustules once. They'd gotten substantially bigger and were weeping rancid liquid.

Had she not still been able to feel Rigel and his love and strength and belief in her Mari might have just sat down, closed her burning eyes, and slept forever.

Mari realized she'd stopped walking and shook herself, grimacing at the pain in her swollen neck. "I cannot stop. I must keep going."

"Must you, scratcher bitch? Why? Where exactly are you going?"

Mari blinked her blurry vision clear and looked around the lush forest for the source of the voice. What she saw had her questioning reality. Surely this was just a fever dream.

"W-who are you?" she asked, and then coughed and spit blood onto the forest floor.

"I am offended you do not recognize me," he said.

Mari stared at him. Then her mind cleared enough that she recognized him. From the wall he'd appeared changed, but seeing the *thing* he'd become up close was almost incomprehensible.

"Thaddeus?"

On all fours, the mutated man circled Mari. "So you do remember me. How touching. Now, answer my question. Where exactly are you going?"

"Into the forest. I—I need herbs to ease my fever," said Mari as she turned to stare at him. Except for his mean little eyes, he was utterly changed. Thaddeus was covered with black fur. His spine was curved. The shape of his legs and arms had changed. His face was horrible—not man and not dog but something in between that lacked the beauty and grace of either. "I got lost. I don't want any trouble. I'm sick and need to gather willow bark and medicinal herbs I cannot find within the walled city. That's all."

"You made a fatal mistake today, scratcher." Thaddeus's voice was different, deeper, and even crueler than before. "Now you will come with me."

Mari coughed violently and wiped her mouth before she could speak again. "Please, Thaddeus. Just let me go. I'm really sick and just want to collect some herbs and bark."

"Oh, but you will do so, so much more than that. That way, scratcher. Move!" On all fours, Thaddeus began nipping at Mari's calves and heels, herding her back the way he'd come.

Mari let him. She knew Thaddeus was taking her to Death, which had been her plan all along, but she was too ill to feel victorious and too filled with grief to do much more than stumble along, only once in a while complaining as the creature that used to be a man bit her legs and drove her forward.

When they reached the edge of the army's encampment, Thaddeus stood upright and kept shoving her in front of him. Mari observed everything through a fever haze, which intensified the strange, nightmare intensity of the day. There were bison everywhere. Most were grazing quietly. Several were being roasted over open fires. There were more Terrier-mutated men like Thaddeus. They joined him, occasionally pushing her and laughing when she tripped and fell or had to stop to cough and gasp for breath.

Then more mutating dog-men joined them, only these men were clearly becoming Shepherds. They were even more horrible than Thaddeus and the Terrier men. The most disturbing thing about Shepherd men was what was happening to their faces. Fangs had grown in mouths meant for human teeth, pushing their jaw structure to elongate with their noses. Mari thought they were the most horrible living things she'd ever seen.

She stumbled past men that stared at nothing with white eyes and skin the color of old bones. They were silent and unnaturally still.

These are the Milks. The reanimated corpses Ralina told us about.

Mari would have liked to study them, perhaps even speak with them, but the dog-men would not allow her to pause. They kept driving her forward until they came to an area that had been cleared. She noted that at the edge of the clearing canines, Terriers and Shepherds, huddled together in a circle, which reminded Mari of how Cammy and Mariah's puppies had clustered when they were very young and had not yet opened their eyes. But these were adult canines. They turned their heads to look in her direction but made no other movement or sound.

Not far from them scores of other men huddled around small campfires. They, too, were grotesquely changed. Some appeared to be boar-like. Some reminded Mari of deer, a few horrifically looked like they had been merged with rats, and some appeared reptilian. They stared at her with hungry eyes and she turned away from them.

In the center of the clearing was a huge tree trunk that had been cut and hollowed into a crude replica of a throne and placed near a large, brightly burning campfire. On the throne sat Death, and Mari quickly decided that *He* was truly the most horrible living thing she'd ever seen.

He was more bison bull than man. Naked from the waist up He sat on the throne and took bites from a huge hunk of meat. Fat and blood dripped down the dark pelt that formed His beard. His body was massive. His torso was so muscular it looked misshapen. Like Thaddeus and the dog-men, He was covered with fur, but His was clearly bison and not canine. His legs were like tree trunks and ended in cloven hooves that gleamed the same black as the razor-tipped horns that curled up from His head.

When Mari first entered the clearing, He glanced her way, frowning at the Hunters and Warriors who circled around her.

"Thaddeus! What is the meaning of this? You interrupt My breakfast!" Death bellowed.

Thaddeus grabbed her arm cruelly, pulling her with him to approach the God. When she stumbled and fell, he dragged her.

"I bring You a gift, my Lord." Thaddeus pushed her so that she fell at the God's feet, coughing wretchedly on her hands and knees as she stared at His cloven hooves.

Death said nothing for several heartbeats as Mari regained her breath and then struggled to her feet. She stood, swaying and feverish, and looked into Death's dark eyes.

He smiled, threw back His enormous head, and laughed. "My Goddess acts quickly when She makes up Her mind!" His gaze went from Mari to Thaddeus. "You have done well to bring her to Me. Now, get My guest water and something to sit on, dog-man."

"Yes, my Lord." Thaddeus scurried away to return quickly rolling a stump with another dog-man following with one of the beautiful blue mugs stolen from the extinct Saleesh.

"Sit—sit." Death gestured magnanimously at the stump. "And drink. You are clearly not well."

"Th-thank You. My Lord," Mari added as she sat and gulped the water thirstily.

"I believe I remember my Storyteller saying your name is Mari, and explaining that you are a hybrid born of a Tribe of the Trees member and an Earth Walker. Is that true?"

"She is a scratcher." Thaddeus spit on the ground beside her. "Her father was killed for creating her. According to Tribal law she should have been killed then, too."

With a speed that was incredible for a being so big, Death moved from the throne to Thaddeus. He backhanded the twisted little man so hard that he was knocked almost into the fire.

"She is My guest! You will not disrespect her!" Death roared before He returned to His crude throne. Then, as Thaddeus crawled from the edge of the fire and bowed low to Him, the God smiled warmly at Mari. "Where were we? Ah, I know. I'd asked about your name and your lineage. Are you the Mari the Storyteller spoke of?"

Mari coughed and wiped her mouth. "I am Mari, daughter of Leda of Clan Weaver and Galen of the Tribe of the Trees."

"Is it true that you can call down the power of the moon and the sun?" the God asked.

Mari had no reason to lie to Him and every reason that He should believe her to be so powerful and special that He would be sure to choose her as a vessel for His goddess. She nodded wearily. "It is." Mari coughed again. "Though I can do neither at the moment. As you can see, I have contracted an illness."

Death scratched the pelt that formed His beard. "Indeed. I can see that. I wonder, Mari, if the rest of the people within the wall also have contracted your illness."

"I do not know," said Mari quickly—purposefully not meeting the God's dark gaze. "I left the city to hunt for remedies in case others did become ill."

"Of course you do not wish to tell Me the truth. I understand that. It would be betraying your people, and there is no need for that. I am a God. I know what will happen next." He leaned forward and steepled His thick fingers. "The people within the walled city will sicken. Then they will die."

Mari began to speak, but the God's raised hand silenced her.

"But as I am a god, I have the ability to save your city and cure the people within," He said.

She did meet His gaze then, and spoke with complete honesty. "Ralina told us of Your cure."

Thaddeus spoke up from where he knelt beside the God's throne. "Do not let her fool You, my Lord. This scratcher can cure the skin-sloughing sickness. I have witnessed it."

Death looked from Thaddeus to Mari. He cocked His head and studied her before asking, "Is that true?"

Mari coughed and then nodded. She would speak the truth as much as possible. "I am a Moon Woman—a healer among my people. I have cured this sickness before. In the Tribe. Before You defeated them. But I was not infected with the sickness then . . ." Mari had to pause to cough and catch her breath. "I give You my word that I am too ill to call down the power of the moon right now, whether to cure my people or myself. That is why I snuck from the walled city to forage for healing herbs in the forest. If I could get better, I could help myself and my people."

Death nodded. "That is just as My Goddess foretold. But you may rest easy, Moon Woman Mari. As I said, and as My absent Storyteller corroborated, I can cure this sickness."

Mari looked around the clearing, her eyes lingering on the mutated dog-men and the other men who were changing even more strangely before she returned her gaze to the God and continued. "The Wind Riders will never take Your cure."

Mari thought the God might explode in anger. Instead, He simply leaned back in His throne and contemplated her. Soon He nodded, and spoke more to Himself than to her. "The Wind Riders are problematic. I am loath to wipe them from the earth, as I am intrigued by their equines, but they do seem very stubborn." Then Death's expression shifted and He smiled wryly as He focused His attention once more on Mari. "Perhaps they simply need a very public demonstration of My power, Mari." When He spoke her name, the God's voice softened. "Are you a follower of the Goddess of Life?"

Mari did not have to feign surprise at the question. "Yes, but my people have always called Her the Great Earth Mother."

"And what of the Wind Riders? Do they worship the Goddess of Life as well?" Death asked.

"Yes, but as with my people they call Her by a different name—the Great Mother Mare," said Mari.

427

Death nodded His massive head and the firelight glistened against His onyx horns. "Indeed . . . indeed . . . this is quite interesting. Perhaps I do know how to move the stubborn Wind Riders to accept their fate. My love, the Goddess of Life, has shown Me the way by sending you to Me."

Mari's stomach twisted and she almost vomited again but swallowed bile and sickness. *This is exactly what I want. And it also means I will soon be with Mama. Just a little while longer. I only have to be brave a little while longer.*

Mari cleared her throat. "My Lord, I do not understand. The Great Earth Mother did not send me to You. I only wished to find plants to cure this illness."

Death ignored her words. His eyes glinted slyly and His next question had Mari's heart fluttering around in her chest as if it searched for a way to escape her body.

"Where is your Companion? I was quite certain the Storyteller said you were bonded to a large Shepherd."

Mari lowered her gaze. Her thoughts went to Rigel. Their bond was there and would be until she was no more. He felt her and sent warmth and love to her. When she lifted her gaze to Death again, tears streamed down her face. "Ralina told You the truth. I did have a Shepherd Companion named Rigel. He died on the journey here."

From where he crouched Thaddeus snorted.

The God's head snapped up and He narrowed His eyes at the dog-man. "You disbelieve her?"

"Yes, my Lord. The Storyteller would have told her of Your . . ."—Thaddeus paused and enunciated the word carefully—"*interest* in our Companions, especially the Shepherds. When the scratcher left the walled city, she probably told her Shepherd to stay behind in case she was caught—and I can prove it."

Mari felt a stab of panic. *Prove it? If Thaddeus can prove I lied will that change Death's decision about using me as His vessel?*

Death's gaze went from Thaddeus back to Mari as He commanded, "Then prove it, dog-man."

Thaddeus turned and spoke to another mutant who looked to also be morphing into a mixture of Terrier and human. "Wilson, get Spud over here!"

The man whistled and called, "Spud, come here!"

The pack of canines remained still and curled together.

Wilson stood, though he was almost as stooped and twisted as Thaddeus. His voice blasted across the clearing with anger Mari had never heard any member of the Tribe use when speaking to their Companion. "Spud! Come here or I will go get you and drag you here!"

A small blond Terrier emerged from the group of canines. His ears and tail were down as he padded reluctantly to Wilson.

Death snorted and spoke softly, for Mari's ears alone. "The canines have become more and more disobedient. Soon it will be time to rid ourselves of them."

Wilson glared down at his Companion. "When I call you, come. Now, run to the walled city. Get close. They won't shoot a canine, so you have nothing to worry about. Reach out to any Terrier or Shepherd within. You know them. At the very least Laru is there with the traitor, Nik. Ask if—" Wilson looked from his Companion to Mari. "What did you say his name was?"

Mari had to answer. She had no choice. "Rigel."

Wilson continued speaking to Spud. "Ask if Rigel is dead or alive and then return with the answer." When the little Terrier didn't move, Wilson shouted, "Now!" And kicked at Spud, who darted off toward the walled city.

Mari noted how odd it was that Wilson had to order Spud to return to share information with him. At that moment, as far outside the city walls as they were, she could reach Rigel and he would relay to her any information she requested. *They are losing the ability to communicate with their canines.*

Death's deep voice broke into her inner musings. "While we wait would you like something to eat? Perhaps some bison broth?"

Mari shook her head. "No, my Lord. I cannot eat. But I would drink more water."

"Get her water, Thaddeus," Death commanded.

Thaddeus did as he was ordered, returning quickly with another mug full of water, which Mari drank thirstily. She tried not to think about what would happen when Spud returned. *Will this all be in vain?* Mari was desperately trying to reason through the fog in her mind when Spud raced back to the clearing to his Companion.

"Well?" Death asked.

Wilson stared at Spud and then his gaze went to the God. "Spud says he spoke with Laru, and Rigel is truly dead."

Mari almost fainted with relief. *How? He couldn't have spoken with Laru; Laru wouldn't lie.* As the Terrier padded back to join the other canines, his gaze found hers and in Mari's mind came his compassionate voice. *I will keep your secret, Mari, loyal Companion to Rigel. We will all keep your secret.*

"Thaddeus, do you hear that? Do not question Mari's veracity again. She has spoken provable truth," said Death.

Mari thought she heard Thaddeus growl, and wished fervently that she would be alive to witness the hateful little dog-man's downfall.

"So, I do have a plan that will sway the stubbornness of the Wind Riders," Death was saying. "But I need the perfect joining for you, sweet Mari. You did say you are a healer, correct?"

"Yes, I am, but I cannot channel the power of the moon when I am ill," Mari said truthfully.

He waved away her words. "Oh, that is not why I mention it. I only wonder how much longer until your body succumbs to the illness. Do you happen to know?"

A fit of coughing allowed Mari to consider and discard several answers, but when she had finally recovered enough breath to speak, Death abruptly stood. A feral smile lifted his meaty lips and his voice roared across the clearing, "Ah, My Goddess, My love! You fulfill My needs before I even ask." Death strode to Mari and gently turned her.

Just within the opposite side of the clearing stood an exquisite white doe.

"To Me," Death ordered the doe, and she trotted gracefully to Him. When she reached the God, she dipped her head, bowing to Death. His laughter made Mari cringe and want to cover her ears. Death's huge hand rested on her shoulder. "Do not fear, Mari. Your cure is here and your suffering shall soon be over. You do a great thing this day. You forge the way that will allow the Wind Riders to live—to accept my cure—though they will be changed." He laughed again, more cruelly. "Ah, yes, they will be changed."

Mari knew exactly what Death planned, but she continued to play her part, glad her waking nightmare was nearing its conclusion. "I do not understand, my Lord."

"Of course you do not, child. Watch and learn. Watch and learn." Death shouted across the clearing, "Iron Fist, to Me!"

One of the non-canine mutants hurried from the group of men who had been silently watching and rushed to bow low before the God. He seemed boar-like, with a thick body and several rows of curled tusks that muffled his deep voice. "My Lord, what is Your command?"

"Gather what I need for a public Harvest as we once did in the city."

Iron Fist's strange face became animated as he almost danced around the God with excitement. "Yes, my Lord! Here? Do we Harvest here in the clearing?"

"No, Iron Fist. Set up what I need within easy sight of the walls of the city. The Wind Riders shall witness the awakening of their goddess. It will be magnificent, and herald the end of life as they have known it."

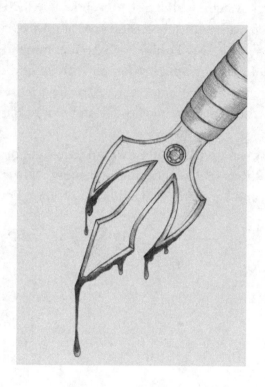

CHAPTER 37

Mari hadn't expected this. She'd understood she would sicken. She knew if Death accepted her as the vessel for the Goddess He would flay the flesh of an animal into her wounds and then probably bleed her until she was almost dead—then the Great Goddess would awaken within her and Mari's spirit would be untethered and she would go to join her mother.

What she hadn't expected was that Death was going to do all of that while everyone she loved and everyone who loved her watched.

Helplessly, Mari sat on the log as the mutated men, canine and otherwise, exploded into action around her. They chopped logs and then bound them together in the shape of a cross. One man, who looked as if he was more opossum than human, sharpened a long dagger with a trident blade.

All the while the white doe stood near Mari. Her presence was soothing. Though the doe rarely looked at her, she radiated peace and calm—and often Mari reached out and stroked her smooth, snow-colored coat.

Death sat on His throne. He commanded and observed and spoke to Mari about what He incorrectly believed the Wind Riders would do after His *little demonstration*. She only listened long enough to realize that the God was incapable of understanding that some people would never surrender to Him.

Mari's fever had increased, and had Death not kept ordering her mug refilled with fresh water, she realized she probably would have passed out.

Part of her wished fervently that she would lose consciousness, but that was the cowardly part of her. Mari knew she wasn't quite done with this life yet. She must finish what she had begun.

So Mari drank the water and waited.

The sun was at midpoint in the clear fall sky when the creature named Iron Fist bowed low before Death's throne.

"My Lord, all is ready."

Death stood and stretched. "Doe, with me." Then He smiled down at Mari. "Little Moon Woman Mari, it is time to end your suffering. Are you ready?"

Mari had to clear her throat and spit bloody phlegm onto the ground before she could answer, "I am."

"Can you walk, or shall I carry you? I do not mind. I only wish to make this transition as easy for you as possible," said the God of Death.

Mari stood. She swayed a little, but sitting on the log and drinking mug after mug of water had allowed her to gather her strength. "I can walk, my Lord."

"Excellent, excellent. I am pleased your body holds such strength," said Death. "Would you walk beside Me? Perhaps take My arm?"

Mari nodded. Then she forced herself to place her trembling hand on the God's furred arm. She looked up at Him. "I cannot walk fast, my Lord."

Death patted her hand kindly. "I understand. I understand. I shall match My steps to yours. This way, My Moon Woman Mari." Death pointed toward an edge of the clearing.

Slowly, Mari began to walk. She tried not to lean too heavily on the God's arm. It disgusted her to touch Him, but it felt as if the earth pitched and rolled under her feet, and she had to cling to Him to remain upright.

The God covered her hand with His massive one and gently guided her from the clearing. Walking beside them, the white doe kept pace. They moved slowly as Death chatted with Mari amiably.

"I wish you and I had known one another longer," said Death. "It saddens Me that all you know of Me is through what the Storyteller has passed along to you, or what Dove has told you of Me. I believe had you and I traveled together you would have understood Me better than either of them did . . ." He paused and added softly, "They think Me cruel. I do not want you to think Me cruel."

Mari looked up at the God. Even through her fever haze she understood Him. He was one of those people who commanded enough power to behave in whatever way they so desired—even if their desires hurt others—and was only saddened by His actions when He was held accountable for them. *How could the Great Earth Goddess love Him?* But Mari realized she didn't need to understand the hearts of the gods. All she need do was complete her destiny and save her people.

"My Lord, You are going to cure me, are You not?" Mari asked Him.

"I truly am," said the God.

"Then how could I think You cruel?"

Death stopped and touched her cheek gently. "Thank you, Moon Woman Mari."

When they began walking again, the God placed one of His hands under her arm so that He could support her better. Death talked of His vision for the plain—how He would make it a mighty, unconquerable nation, not understanding that it had been both for generations and would remain so long after He was gone.

When they came to the edge of the tree line, Death stopped again. He spoke softly to Mari as she stared in horror at the scene He'd set. In the cleared area in front of the tall, impenetrable gates of the Valley of Vapors Death's men had driven a thick, cross-shaped stake firmly into the ground. Ropes to bind her had been thrown over the stake. Beside it was a wide, flat rock on which the sharpened tripod dagger rested.

All around them, just within the tree line, was Death's army. The multitudes of Milks stood silent and unspeaking, staring at something beyond this world. The mutated Skin Stealers were there as well, scratching and muttering to themselves. The mutated Hunters and Warriors, with Thaddeus leading them, waited in rows just outside the forest, but out of range of bowshot. And, finally, their miserable Companions huddled together in a pack behind them at the edge of the tree line, in view of the changing men, but as far away from them as possible.

Mari wanted more than almost anything not to enter the cleared area, not to be tied to that stake and used as a vessel to bring forth a goddess. But *almost* was the key. What Mari wanted *more* than to save her own life was to ensure a life for those she loved, free of the monster who stood at her side. Mari shivered.

"Do not be afraid. I will not cause you unnecessary pain. What happens here will show the Wind Riders that it is not simply futile to struggle against Me, but it is acting against the will of their own goddess." He patted her hand again. "I shall be gentle with you. I shall take great care with you."

Mari met His gaze and was surprised to see true remorse in His eyes. "You seem sorry to cure me."

He sighed. "It is only that the cure will drastically change you, and I find that I wish we had more time." His heavy brows lifted. "Do we have more time, Moon Woman Mari? Tell me yes and you and I will walk away to return later—perhaps in several days."

Mari coughed and shivered as a wave of chills caused her teeth to chatter. "M-my Lord, I do not have several days. I do not believe I even have one more day."

Death nodded slowly, sadly, and said, "I agree. I feel you are close to your end, and I am eager to reconcile with My Goddess. But I also would like to spend more time with you."

Though Mari knew exactly what He meant, she said, "I am confused, my Lord."

"I know, my Moon Woman Mari, but all shall be clear soon. Come, let us cure your suffering."

But before Death could walk to the stake Mari spoke quickly. "My Lord, might I sit for a moment and have a drink of water? I—I feel as if I may lose consciousness."

Death frowned. "You must remain conscious, if only for a little while longer." He looked around and then guided her to a nearby fallen log. The doe remained close beside them. "Dog-man!" Death bellowed, and Thaddeus raced to Him on all fours. "My Moon Woman Mari needs more water to strengthen her for the cure. Fetch it for her. Now."

Thaddeus gave her a disgusted look and then rushed away.

Death patted her back. "Sit. Rest. Then drink. We shall proceed after you have refreshed yourself."

"Th-thank You, my Lord." Mari sat on the log and closed her eyes as if she rested. Instead, she remembered the dream the Great Earth Mother had sent her. *She knew I would need them!* Mari used the last of her strength to quest with her mind—to follow the connection that had been hers since Rigel had Chosen her as his Companion.

First she found her Shepherd. *Rigel! My sweet boy!*

Instantly, she was filled with warmth and strength from her Companion. Her chills ended and her mind cleared.

Then Mari really got to work.

Drawing on Rigel's strength, Mari continued to quest. Next she found Laru. She felt his fear and worry for her. *Laru, stay with me! I need you!* Then she searched farther and connected with Anjo.

Moon Woman, we have been worried for you. The mare's articulate voice sounded clearly in her mind.

I am doing the work of the Great Mother Mare. Stay with me, Anjo! I need you!

Still attached to Rigel, Laru, and Anjo, Mari searched for one last connection and found the mighty golden stallion, protector of Herd Magenti. *Mari! Dove is worried for you.*

I am sorry to worry her and the rest of our people, but I am about the work of the Great Goddess. I need your help. Will the four of you help me?

YES! The answer from the four Companions echoed in her mind.

Then hear me well. The Great Goddess of Life, our Earth Mother, the Mother Mare, has guided me to where I am today. Death is going to publicly call forth the Goddess in my body. When He does so, if He also allows the Goddess to embrace Him She will remove Him from our world and force Him to sleep in Her arms again—and you will all be saved.

Rigel's grief-filled whine drifted through their connection.

As my sweet boy already knows, that will mean my soul's tether to my body will be broken and I will be no more. Nik will know this, too, as will River and Dove. Anjo, Tulpar, Laru and Rigel, you must stop Nik and River and everyone else from interfering. If they do, my sacrifice will be for nothing and Death will rule these plains.

Tulpar's deep voice filled her mind. *That cannot happen.*

It will happen if Death does not call forth the Goddess into my body today. Will you help me?

YES! The answer rang true and clear in Mari's mind.

Thank you. Be there for Nik. I'm sorry that you will all have to watch me—

"Drink, my Moon Woman Mari," Death interrupted her as He thrust another mug of water into her hands.

Mari blinked up at Him and then drained the mug. She sat up straighter and brushed her hair back from her clammy face.

"I think I am ready now," she told Him.

Death held out His hand and Mari took it, allowing Him to help her to her feet and then wrap her hand around His arm. Slowly, with the white doe beside them, she and the God walked into the cleared area to the waiting stake.

When they arrived, Death smiled at her. "Moon Woman Mari, forgive Me for this slight unpleasantness, but I must bind you. It will make what happens next easier."

Mari could only nod. She kept her eyes downcast, unable to look at the walled city.

Death led her to stand against the stake, facing the entrance to the Valley of Vapors. At first He blocked her view of it, and for that she was momentarily grateful. He tied her securely around the waist to the stake, though not uncomfortably. Then, gently, He tore first one sleeve and then the other from her tunic, exposing the angry, oozing sores that covered her flesh.

"I am sorry that these cause you pain," He told her as He carefully lifted one arm and tied it to the cross stake, and then the other. "But your pain will end quickly. I give you My word on that."

Mari said nothing. She stood, tied to the cross, as Death finally moved to the side to take the tripod knife from the big, flat stone. He turned to the doe and began cutting strips of her living flesh from her delicate flanks. The doe did not run. She did not cry out. She did not move. She only stood still and silent, like an exquisite marble statue that bled scarlet.

Mari could not watch. Instead, her gaze finally went to the wall. She felt a jolt of shock. The wall was lined with people. They were packed, shoulder to shoulder, silently watching. She found River and Dove quickly as they were astride Anjo and Tulpar. Anjo's coat gleamed like moonlight and Tulpar shined like the summer sun. Their beauty lifted Mari's heart.

Beside them was Nik. Even from a distance Mari could see that tears flowed down his face. Next to him, with their front paws on the wall, were

Rigel and Laru. Mari almost couldn't look at her Companion, but when she did Rigel sent her a wave of warmth and love that she clung to.

Lining the wall on either side of Dove and River, Nik, Laru, and Rigel were her people—her family. Sora and O'Bryan were there, as were Davis and Claudia. Davis held little blond Cammyman in his arms. Antreas and Danita stood silent watch, too, with Bast peering over the edge of the wall, as well as sweet Jenna and Isabel—and every member of the Pack, along with the Herdmembers.

Anjo's voice rang in her mind. *We will not interfere. We will watch. We will witness. We will wait, and we will forever honor your sacrifice, brave Moon Woman Mari.*

Mari was filled with gratitude for them. Through happy tears she stared at them, memorizing each beloved face and drawing strength from their silent witness.

When Death began packing the doe's bloody flesh into her wounds, Mari was surprised at the instant relief it gave her. Reluctantly, she looked to her right at the beautiful, gentle doe.

The creature had fallen to the ground. She lay on her side. Her belly was a raw scarlet slash against the white of her coat, and her sides heaved as she struggled to breathe. Her gaze met Mari's. In the doe's eyes Mari saw no recrimination, no fear, no pain, and when the doe breathed her last breath, her body wavered and then disappeared into the earth as if she had been a mirage.

Death followed Mari's gaze and nodded His massive head. "She was a gift from our goddess. The doe has returned to Her."

"I am glad." Mari's voice was a whisper.

"Now, Moon Woman Mari, what comes next will be the most unpleasant part of this, but the pain will be brief," Death said. "Are you ready?"

Mari's gaze lifted to the wall and her family again. "Yes. I am ready."

Her breath hitched as the God sliced the inside of her forearms, from her wrists up to where He had packed the doe's flesh into the sores in the creases of her arms.

Death had been right. The pain was brief. Her blood felt cool against her fever-flushed skin, and as it pumped from her body a sound drifted to her. It came from the Valley of Vapors and swelled on the wind. Mari blinked, trying to think through the fog that shrouded her mind, and then she could not hide her smile.

From the wall her people had begun to stomp their feet in a heartbeat rhythm. It swelled around her, matching the beating of her laboring heart, and seemed to lift her with it.

"Why do you smile, Moon Woman Mari?" Death asked.

Mari was beyond lying. She did not look at the God. That monster would not be her last sight. She said, "They are my heartbeat. They are everything."

"I do not—"

"Sssh!" Mari hissed at the God, though she did not take her gaze from the wall—from Rigel and Nik and Laru, Sora and little Chloe, Danita and Jenna, Davis and Cammy, O'Bryan, River, and Dove. "This moment is not yours. It is mine. It is the Goddess's. It is ours."

Then Mari closed herself to the God of Death. It did not matter that He spoke beside her—that He prattled on and on about *His* Moon Woman Mari and the brilliant future He planned. He was inconsequential. All Mari heard was the beating of her heart echoed through her family.

As the blood continued to pump from her body and Mari grew weaker and weaker, the echoing heartbeat from the wall slowed. Then the God's words did penetrate Mari's consciousness as He spread wide His massive arms and invoked.

"Come, My love! Come, My world! Come, My Goddess! Into this willing, worthy vessel I command that You awaken, *awaken, AWAKEN!*"

Mari heard the rhythmic heartbeat from the wall abruptly end as her vision narrowed and grayed.

Then she felt the first touch of the Great Goddess. She slid within Mari's skin, and suddenly Mari understood so much!

The Goddess of Life wasn't vengeful. She did not pick one person's death over another's. She loved all of Her children so much that She had irrevocably gifted them with free will, which meant some of them chose poorly—like Thaddeus and his followers. And some chose wisely—like Sora and Nik, River and Dove, and the rest of the people Mari loved.

But as her vision continued to fade, Mari began to panic. She gasped for air and tried to struggle against her bonds.

Do not fear, brave Mari. Just release. All will be well. I give you My oath and My blessing.

Mari blinked, still attempting to cling to consciousness, to life. Death moved into the space in front of her, blocking her view of the wall and her family. As Mari looked at Death through eyes already claimed by the Goddess, the image of the mutated monster shifted and was replaced by a tall, strong man who carried the beauty the release of death can be in His face, in His body, in His soul. It was just beyond Mari's ability to truly understand, but she saw that the God of Death wasn't horrible—not when He was tempered by the Goddess of Life.

Then Mari felt a wrenching within her, and her spirit lifted from her body so that she hovered above it, staring down at a scene that astounded her.

Her bloody body had slumped so that only the ropes that bound her to the stake held her up. Death lifted the tripod dagger and sliced through the ropes, gently guiding her fall to the ground. Mari's body lay there, crumpled and battered, while Death watched and waited.

Then her body twitched. Trembled. Shook. Her head lifted and she opened her eyes, which were no longer Moon Woman gray, but the black of a fertile field.

"Beloved?" Like her eyes, Mari's voice was utterly changed. It was deeper, stronger, and filled with a magickal beauty that was indescribable.

"Is it truly You, My love, My own?" Death asked.

Mari's body stood. She shook off the ropes that clung to Her bloody flesh and then lifted Her chin and gazed around. "The waking world! You were correct, beloved. It is remarkable. I have, indeed, slumbered too long." She stretched mightily and drew in a deep breath. The Goddess laughed joyously. Then Her gaze returned to the God of Death, and Her expression turned intimate, seductive. "It has also been too long, *far* too long, since I have felt Your touch." Slowly, seductively, Her hands traced a path over Her breasts, down Her waist, to the juncture between Her thighs, where She touched Herself intimately before the Goddess of Life opened Her arms to Her beloved. "Must you force me to wait an eternity?"

"Never, My love! We have waited long enough!"

Then the God of Death stepped into Her embrace and lifted the Goddess of Life into His arms. Their lips met, and They drank each other in; ravenous and eager, His hands pressed Her close to Him.

Slowly, languidly, the Goddess of Life wrapped Her arms tightly around the God's wide shoulders.

The God of Death went very still. At first Mari did not understand what was happening; then she realized Death was trying to release the Goddess. He struggled to break their kiss and their embrace, but it was as if the Goddess of Life had turned to living lava. She melted into Him.

Death's struggle became erratic. He stumbled around the stake, trying to rip the Goddess away from Him. From the tree line, the strangest of the mutated men—led by the boar creature Death had called Iron Fist—began to surge toward their god, weapons raised, but the Warriors on the wall sent arrows flying into them. Iron Fist was the first to fall, with an arrow through his forehead. The rest of the mutants backed out of range quickly.

Thaddeus and his men held just out of crossbow range and waited silently with the ghostly Milks.

As the Goddess's body wrapped, cocoon-like, even more securely around the God, He ripped his lips from Hers and bellowed.

"No! Do not do this!"

"Oh, beloved, You knew I could not allow You to destroy that which I created," said the Goddess.

"Stop! We will not destroy it! We will remake it!" Death shouted as He continued to struggle against Her.

"That is not possible, for death does not create life, just as hate does not forge love. My beloved, You seem to have forgotten that the only force in this world stronger than death is also something I created—love." The goddess inhabiting Mari's body began to glow. "And with that power I command that You return to the womb of the earth to slumber in My arms for eternity."

The earth before the bloody stake shuddered and slowly began to open. As Death roared and struggled, the Goddess continued to dissolve into Him. They sank into the swallowing earth as if a giant consumed them.

The Goddess's voice lifted to Mari's spirit. "Remember, brave Mari, the only force in this world that is stronger than death—stronger even than life—is love."

Just before the earth closed around them, Mari's body was spewed from the rip, as if the giant had spit it out. It lay lifeless, bruised, and bloody. The strips of the doe's flesh had disappeared, along with all signs of the skin-sloughing sickness. Mari stared down at her body, wishing it would breathe—wishing she could return within it. She concentrated on it, searching for a tether to guide her back, but her mind was foggy and she felt increasingly disoriented.

There was complete stillness, and then the grinding of rock on rock rang from the Valley of Vapors. Mari was feeling more and more dizzy—more and more confused. She turned from staring at her body to the wall in time to see horses and their Riders pouring from the now-opened entrance as the chilling war cry of Herd Magenti pierced the silence.

From the tree line Thaddeus shouted, "Kill them! Kill them all and we will rule their city without the tyranny of Death!" The mutants and the Milks roared their own challenge as they raised their weapons and rushed from the forest to meet the Wind Riders.

Mari looked from one group to the other and felt nothing except weariness. Her spirit drifted down to rest beside her body. She curled on her side, closed her eyes, and waited for what would happen to her next.

Mama? Where are you?

CHAPTER 38

What they did was Dove's idea. It came to her over the course of that strange morning and she realized the Goddess of Life had planned for it to be this way all along.

Because of Sora's help, Mari's absence hadn't been noticed that night. Much longer after sunrise than was his usual wake-up time, Nik left their pallet with Laru. Yawning, he joined Dove and River at the big campfire that burned cheerily in front of their building. Sora was there, too, with Rigel curled beside her appearing to sleep, and little Chloe nestled against him. Laru padded to Rigel, sniffed him, and then lay down beside his son.

"Have you seen Mari?" Nik asked. "I did not notice when she joined me in bed last night." He smiled wryly. "I'd forgotten how taxing building those lifts can be. She must have left our bed very early, and I am concerned. Yesterday she didn't seem to be feeling well."

"She went to soak in the pools," said Sora without meeting his gaze. "Rigel was waterlogged from last night's soak, so she told him to stay away and rest here with Chloe and me."

That was when Dove began to realize something was wrong. It was completely unlike Mari to send Rigel away. Dove focused her senses on the young Shepherd. Rigel seemed to be sleeping, but she could feel that he was not. She could feel the sadness that was so thick within him that it spilled from his body in waves.

Dove opened her mouth to question Sora further, but her Goddess-given intuition silenced her. She *knew* she must say nothing—and so Dove remained silent. She listened and considered, and as she did the Seer thought back, remembering the vision dreams sent by the Great Earth Mother to her, to Ralina, to River, and most especially to Mari.

"Well, I'll go to the baths and see how she's doing," said Nik.

"Break your fast first," said Sora quickly. "I checked on her not long ago."

Dove heard the lie in Sora's voice.

"I am hungry," said Nik. "I'll eat first. Do you think I should take Mari something to eat to the baths?"

"No. She said her stomach was still upset," said Sora.

Another lie, thought Dove. She reached out with her connection to her stallion. *Tulpar, have you seen Mari today?*

No, my Dove. Shall I find her for you?

Yes. Look at the baths first.

River squeezed Dove's hand, leaned close, and whispered, "What is it? You feel far from me."

"I am not completely sure yet, but something is amiss. I will let you know when I understand more fully," Dove murmured to her lover. River squeezed her hand again in acknowledgment.

Nik seemed in a lazy mood. He ate slowly. O'Bryan joined Sora and he and Nik began a long, complex conversation about a second type of lift they could build. The two men thought the new lift might even be able to hold a horse, should the need arise to send a Rider pair from the city during the siege.

My Dove, Mari is not at the baths. Bard and Ralina were there and said they have not seen her. Shall I search for her, or shall I seek Rigel?

Rigel is here, but Mari is not. Do not ask him, but do quickly search the valley for Mari—though I do not believe she is still within our walls.

That is very bad news, my Dove.

Yes, it could be.

Dove grew more and more restless as the morning lengthened toward midday. She had just decided that it was time to speak her fears to River when she felt the change in Rigel.

"Rigel?" Nik's voice was filled with concern. Then almost immediately he said, "Laru? What has happened? Is it Mari? Is she—"

The sound of hooves pounding on the stone road interrupted Nik.

"Oh, Great Mother Mare, no!" River stood, and Dove also got to her feet as Anjo and Tulpar raced to them.

My Dove! Mari has gone to Death!

Tell me everything. Dove sent the thought to her stallion.

The golden horse slid to a halt before her and knelt so that Dove could mount him, and by doing so see through his eyes. As Tulpar explained what Mari had done, Anjo filled in River and Dove watched her lover's face go pale. Nik dropped to his knees beside Laru. Rigel had stopped pretending to sleep and was whining softly, constantly, as he pressed against Sora and Laru and Nik. Little Chloe licked the tears from his face and then nuzzled him, trying to comfort the big Shepherd.

"She infected and sacrificed herself," said River.

Nik looked wildly up at River. "We have to save her! We have to go out there and get her!" He turned his gaze to Sora. "You can heal the skin sloughing sickness. You can make her well again."

Rigel whined pitifully.

Sora shook her head slowly and wiped tears from her cheeks. "No. Mari is doing the will of the Goddess."

"You knew," Dove said.

Sora looked up at her. "Yes. I helped her leave the city last night."

"Why?!" The word exploded from Nik. "How could you let her go to her death?"

"My choice was to help my best friend go to her death to save us all, or try to stop her and act against the Great Earth Mother. I had to honor the Great Earth Mother, just as Mari did," said Sora.

"But I was going to do it," said River. "I was ready to do it."

"The Great Goddess chose Mari instead," said Dove.

"No! We have to save her!" Nik insisted.

"Nik," said Dove. "Listen to your Companion."

"We have to save her!" Nik repeated.

"Nikolas, Son of Sol, Sun Priest to the Pack, you must listen to your Companion!" Dove's voice was filled with authority.

Laru sat and pressed his face against Nik's chest as his Companion sobbed and repeated, "No, no, no, no, no."

A sentry called from the front wall, "River! There is movement in the woods. Death's men are dragging a post into the cleared area before us."

Nik stood and shouted, "Do you see Mari? Do you see the Moon Woman?"

"No, just the mutant men," replied the sentry.

Nik turned to River. "This has something to do with Mari. Death is going to make a spectacle of her."

"Yes, I am sure you are right." River's response was swift and decisive. "Tulpar, Dove, gather the Herd. Have all Riders arm themselves and go to the wall."

Nik's gaze flew to her. "We rescue Mari?"

River's voice was almost unbearably sad. "We cannot, Nik. You know that. But we can wait for what will come, bear witness to her bravery, and ready ourselves to overrun Death's army should the Goddess of Life succeed and force Death to sleep once more."

"I cannot lose her." Nik cried brokenly as Rigel whined.

"You may not have to," Dove said. Everyone turned to her. "I believe I know what the Great Goddess intends, and if I am correct we have a small chance to save our Mari."

"Anything!" Nik said. "I will do anything to save her."

"Then you must ready yourself for what will come, and you must not attempt to interfere with what the Goddess, and Mari, have put into motion," said Dove.

"I said I will do anything to save her. I meant it," said Nik.

"Even if it means watching her die?" Dove asked.

Nik nodded shakily. "Anything."

"Good. Then here is what the Goddess of Life has whispered to my heart. It is our only chance at saving Mari. Listen carefully." As the Herd and the Pack rushed to the wall, Dove explained her plan to them.

Nik felt Mari's absence like he was missing a limb—or rather something more valuable: His heart. His soul. His mind. The only thing that kept him moving forward was Laru's calming presence and the knowledge that Rigel was barely holding on and he needed their support.

He climbed the wide ramp with River and Anjo, Dove and Tulpar, and the rest of the Pack and Riders. They all knew Dove's plan. Tulpar and Anjo had spread word of what they intended to the other horses of the Herd. Laru notified the canines, who also shared the knowledge with the Pack.

The valley was of one mind, which had Nik feeling almost hopeful—until Death left the tree line with Mari at His side. The way she looked broke Nik. He swayed from a rush of fear and panic.

"Steady, Cuz." O'Bryan's hand rested warm and solid on Nik's shoulder. "Be strong for her. We must all be strong for her."

Next to O'Bryan, Sora added, "Remember Dove's plan. Believe it will work."

Nik nodded shakily. His hands gripped the rock wall so hard that his knuckles whitened and his palms bled. He was crying soundlessly. Unashamed, Nik let the tears wash down his face.

Death bound Mari to the cross-shaped stake. When her gaze lifted to the wall, Nik could see the resignation in her face. He also saw her lips tilt up as her eyes swept the wall and she took in the presence of her people—of *all* of her people silently, somberly paying respect to her.

It was terrible to watch Death fillet the flesh from the beautiful white doe. Nik heard Ralina, who was at the wall somewhere to his right, sob as the God hacked into the doe's flesh. When the exquisite creature drew her last breath and then disappeared into the earth, hope stirred within Nik.

The Goddess of Life sent the doe. That was a fact. It was how Ralina had escaped Death. Didn't the doe's presence prove that Mari was following the will of the Goddess? And Dove had insisted that she believed the Goddess did not intend for Mari to truly die.

Please, Great Earth Mother. Please allow us to save Mari. Please keep her spirit here, in this realm, until we can get to her.

When Death slit Mari's forearms, Nik had to turn his head and vomit over the side of the wall.

"Hold on, Nik," Dove said from astride Tulpar. "It will not be much longer. Now, Tulpar!"

Tulpar began to stomp his hoof against the wall in the rhythm of a beating heart. Anjo joined him, and soon every Herdmember, every horse, every Packmember—canines, Lynxes, and a single Bobcat—tapped out the heartbeat against the wall so that the sound of it swelled from the valley to surround Mari.

When Tulpar's hoofbeat changed and slowed, Nik wanted to bolt back down the wide ramp and rush out to the cleared field and get Mari out of there.

"It is almost time, Nik," said Dove.

"Now," Nik ground the word between his teeth. "Let us leave the wall and ready ourselves *now.*"

"And warn Death something is amiss?" River said. "No, Nik. We must wait until the Goddess manifests. Only She can defeat the God of Death. If we act too soon, Mari's sacrifice will be for nothing."

"Nik, this is the only chance we will get," added Dove. "I know Death. He will not be fooled twice. Hold on, Nik—for Mari. For Rigel. For Laru and O'Bryan, Sora and River, and all of us. Hold on."

Nik nodded tightly. He stared down at the love of his life. The God of Death spread His arms wide and shouted for the Goddess to awaken. Mari's head bobbed weakly as the heartbeat rhythm that echoed around them slowed, slowed, and finally stopped.

Mari's head lolled. There was no sound in the valley. It was as if when Mari's heart stopped the world had been silenced.

Death cut the ropes from her body and gently placed her on the bloody ground. Then, with the rest of them, Death waited.

When Nik didn't think he could stand there one moment longer, Mari's body shivered spasmodically, and when she lifted her head to look lovingly up at the God of Death, Nik knew Mari was no longer present within her body. He watched breathlessly as Mari's body got to her feet. Death stood before her, blocking much of Nik's view of Mari, but he did see her open her arms to the God—and the valley held its breath as the God of Death stepped into the embrace of the newly awakened Goddess of Life.

When the Goddess wrapped Her arms securely around Death and began to somehow melt into Him, there was a stirring in the men who stood in the clearing, just out of bowshot range. The movement pulled Nik's attention from the struggling god and his breath hitched in shock.

They had become horrible, twisted things—not man, not animal. Led by a creature who appeared to be a monstrous, manlike boar, they descended on Death and She who had been Mari.

"Nik! Do not let them reach Death!" River said.

With one smooth motion, Nik pulled his crossbow from where it rested strapped across his back. He notched and let fly the first arrow, which ended the boar creature's life. His followers turned and raced for the edge of the forest as arrows chased after them.

Death continued to struggle against the Goddess. He lurched around the stake, ripping up the bloody earth with His enormous cloven hooves as He roared His rage impotently to the sky. When the ground opened and began to swallow the couple, Nik thought his heart would physically break, but just before the ground closed over them Mari's body was spewed from it to fall lifeless on the ground.

"Now!" River shouted. "Roll away the boulder! Get to Mari!"

Nik paused only long enough to let Anjo and Tulpar charge down the ramp past him, but he followed close behind with Laru and Rigel running with him. O'Bryan was there, too, and suddenly so were Wilkes and Davis, Sheena and Claudia, Jaxom, and the rest of the Pack. With Nik they stood impatiently aside to allow the Riders to race out the narrow opening as Dove had instructed.

"Hurry!" Nik shouted restlessly as he could see Thaddeus and the mutated ex-Tribesmen descending on the Rider teams galloping out to form a circle around Mari's body. "Hurry!" he repeated as more Riders rushed through the opening to create a tunnel for them of shields and throwing spears.

"Go, Nik! Go!" River called from just outside the entrance to the valley.

Nik ran through the narrow opening. With Laru and Rigel beside him, he raced across the field while the Wind Riders held back the monsters the men he'd grown up with had become—the men who had once lived with him in the sky.

When he reached Mari, he slid to a stop beside her. Slipping in the blood that covered the ground around the stake, he pulled her limp body into his arms.

"Mari! Mari! Stay with us! Stay with me!" He felt her face, which was colorless and cool. She was not breathing. He felt for a pulse in her neck, and found nothing. Nik looked up from his love to Rigel. "Please try. Please. You can do it, Rigel. I believe in you." Nik gently placed Mari flat on the ground and stepped back, allowing the canines to surround her.

Rigel went to Mari and lay beside her so that his head was in her lap. On the other side of Mari's still body, Laru also lay down, draping his head across her body, too.

And then more and more Companions crowded around Mari. Bast and Mihos were there, joined by the strange creature called Rufus. Cammy and Mariah were there, as well as all of their chubby pups and one plump white wolverine. The little Terrier Fala pressed her muzzle against Mari's shoulder. Following their mother's lead, Chloe, Dash, Khan, Kit, and Cleo nuzzled Mari's head as they licked her gently. Nik was jostled as more Companions flooded through the tunnel of Wind Riders, and he realized that *every* canine in the Pack was there, surrounding Mari. While a battle raged outside their barrier of Wind Riders and members of the Pack who steadily fired crossbows into the throng of bestial men swarming around them, Nik stared at Mari, and prayed fervently to the Goddess of Life, *Please don't take her from us. Please.*

It was painful for Mari to watch Nik rush to her, sobbing and calling for her to stay with him. She wanted to return to her crumpled body, but the longer she was detached from it, the harder it was for her to remember *why* she wanted to return.

Then Nik stood and stepped away from her, and Mari actually felt relieved. She did not want Nik to suffer. She had already lifted from the ground and was hovering above her body. The sounds of the battle raging around them seemed so distant. Mari only wanted to drift away to her mother. Where was her mama? Mari vaguely remembered Leda was supposed to be there.

But Mama is dead. Oh. Yes. She stared down at her body. *I am dead, too.*

Then Rigel lay beside her, putting his wide, intelligent head across her lap, and Mari felt a distinct tug on what was left of the slender, frayed tether that bound her to this life.

Stay.

The single word reverberated within Mari's mind. She knew it came from Rigel—her sweet boy—her precious pup who was all grown-up now. She could feel his sorrow. It was molasses thick and sticky. Anger stirred within her as a memory washed through her spirit.

The Goddess promised my sweet boy would not suffer. He suffers.

Then stay! The two words came from Rigel. Mari also remembered how difficult it was for Rigel to be articulate.

He is trying very hard, she thought.

Laru joined his son. He, too, lay with Mari, warming her cold body with his heat. *Stay, Mari.*

More and more Companions rushed inside the circle of protection to join the two beloved canines. They pressed against her still, cold body, warming it as they reached out to her spirit, calling to her, beseeching her, reminding her of the love that waited right there for her.

Stay, Mari! I love you! Cammyman's voice echoed in her mind as the little blond Terrier pressed close to her body. He looked directly up at her spirit and huffed encouragingly.

Stay with us, Mari! Fala sent the words to her, and each of her pups joined in. *Stay! We need you, Mari! We love you!*

It will break Danita's heart if you leave us! Bast lay across her feet, purring fiercely.

Stay! Stay! Stay! echoed from Cammy and Mariah's pups—too young to truly have voices of their own, yet still they called to her.

Stay! My O'Bryan loves you! came the cheeky little voice that belonged to the only wolverine in their world who was being raised by canines and humans.

Mari's spirit stopped drifting away and began to lower toward her body, which was barely visible as, puppy-like, Companions pressed against her, curled up on her, and sent waves of love to her.

We love you, too, Mari! Anjo's voice joined the chorus of canines and felines—and it was as if the mare loosed an equine dam.

Tulpar called to her, *Mari! You must stay!* And then there was a cacophony of voices filling Mari with their love and hope and with life.

Stay, Mari!

We do not want you to go!

Please stay!

Mari, you are loved!

As equine voices joined with canine and feline, the frayed tether that had been releasing Mari's spirit began to repair itself.

Memories flooded back to Mari.

She remembered Rigel Choosing her.

She remembered becoming friends with Sora.

She remembered falling in love with Nik.

She remembered becoming a true Moon Woman to her people.

Mari remembered how very much she loved her life.

There was a terrible wrenching deep in her gut and suddenly Mari was struggling to breathe. Panicking, Mari gasped and reached out. Her hand sank into the thick fur of Rigel's neck, and her Companion surged to his feet, barking joyously and licking her face. The other canines joined him in lifting their muzzles to the sky as Nik—her beloved Nik—dropped to his knees and, sobbing with happiness, pulled her into his arms.

CHAPTER 39

Mari lives! Those two glorious words rang through River's mind as Anjo blazed the good news.

River shouted over the sounds of battle, "Anjo! Tell Tulpar the stallions need to push back the army so Nik can get Mari within the city walls!" River loosed another throwing spear, which skewered one of the men who had become more canine than human.

My River, the stallions cannot hold them. We must retreat back inside the walls. The undead things are joining the battle. They ride the bison. We cannot stand against all of them. Anjo spoke urgently within her Rider's mind.

River looked around them frantically. Her mare was right. The things Ralina had called Milks had mounted the bison bulls and were racing from the forest in a dark, powerful line that descended upon them. Fear fluttered in her stomach. There were so many of them!

"Join the circle around Mari," she told Anjo. "We'll get her inside and then regroup. We should be able to shoot them from the walls. Retreat! Tell Tulpar to retreat!"

But even as she spoke the words to her mare, River could see that it would be impossible for them to retreat within the city as quickly as they needed to. The narrow entrance that worked so well to keep them safe had become a death sentence. Only one horse and Rider team could go through that entrance at a time—and there were *hundreds* of Wind Rider teams battling the mutant army outside the safety of those walls.

"Now! Anjo!" Panic began to build within River. "They need to retreat now!"

They try, my River, but they will not get through the entrance quickly enough.

Echo galloped up to River and Anjo. "The mares must stand and fight. We cannot retreat fast enough. They will pick us off as we struggle through the entrance."

River nodded and hurled another throwing spear at a dog-man. "Anjo, rally the mares. We join the stallions. We must defeat the Milks."

We shall, my River. Mares, come to me! We stand with the stallions!

All around River mares raced to join her. April and Deinos, Cali and Vixen, Skye and Scout, even Morgana and her ancient Ramoth as well as the entire Mare Council rallied to Anjo's call.

But River didn't see how they would hold their line. There were just too many Milks. The bison had almost reached the mutant men, and when they joined their ranks River knew that they would eventually cut down or plow over everyone who could not escape back within the walls.

River's mind raced. Should she order her Riders to flee? They could outrun the bison and separate into the mountains to make their way back to the city later. But what if their return was cut off?

My River, look at the creatures on the bison.

Anjo's voice shook River out of her near panic, and she gazed out at the line of bison that had just reached the mutant men. At first she didn't understand what she was seeing and then she gasped in shock.

The Milks were killing the mutants!

"Join them!" River shouted. "Help the things on the bison kill the mutants!"

Their line raced forward, sandwiching the mutants between the Wind Riders and the Milks.

The mutants began to fall. They fought fiercely, more animal than human, tearing with teeth and raking claws across the flanks of horses and bison alike—but they did not have numbers on their side. One by one, they died roaring and growling, screaming and chattering—during their final breaths their humanity was completely lost.

It was over quickly. Every mutant was dead or lay dying as Riders wove between bison, putting a humane end to them—one they did not deserve, and yet River was glad her people chose to do the right thing.

River turned in her saddle and looked back at the center of the cleared area where Death had staked Mari, and where the Goddess of Life had taken Him back with Her to the womb of the earth.

The riders and Pack members were helping their wounded. She saw Sora there, and then felt a jolt of surprise when she recognized Mari. She was moving slowly but had joined Sora in the tending of the wounded. Rigel was by her side—as were Laru and Nik, who held his crossbow, eternally ready to protect his mate. The rest of the Companions who had joined together to re-tether Mari's spirit to her body had returned to their people, but whenever Mari passed nearby one of them the canine or feline—or even equine—paused to greet her happily.

The Great Goddess, the Mother Mare, healed our Mari as She left her body, Anjo said.

"I'm so glad Dove was right. I'm so glad Mari was saved," said River.

Then, as if River had conjured her lover, Tulpar galloped up with Dove astride. The young Seer's body was spattered with blood and gore, though she held no weapon. Her only weapons had been Tulpar's hooves and teeth. He would never have allowed any danger to get past him to his Companion.

"River, please come with me. I ask that you witness what happens next with the Milks," said Dove.

River nodded and Anjo trotted beside Tulpar to stand with him and his Rider before the crowd of Milks, which were still astride the bison.

"I felt your call." Dove's voice carried across the silent crowd of white-eyed reanimated corpses.

One of the Milks nudged its bison so that he strode from their ranks to stand before Dove and River.

"Have we saved the Chosen One of the Goddess of Life?" The Milk's voice was eerie, as if it spoke to Dove from underwater.

"You have," said Dove. "Is there something we can do for you in return?"

The man nodded stiffly. *"Yes, accept our act as atonement for our apathy that, so many generations ago, allowed Death to awaken and end our world.*

*We have been waiting since then for the chance to finally be free to rest. Do
you accept our atonement? Will you free us?"*

Dove's voice was filled with compassion. "I do accept your act as atonement for your past mistakes, and if it is in my power, I declare your spirits
free."

For a moment the Milk's eyes cleared of their milky film, and River looked
into the face of a man who blazed with joy. "We are free!" he shouted.

"We are free!" the men behind him cried.

And then every one of their bodies fell from the bison on which it sat
and from those lifeless, decomposing corpses lifted spectral forms, shining like sunrays breaking through storm clouds. With a sound like the
rustling of wind through the tall prairie grasses, the spirits swirled around
the clearing before they disappeared.

The bison snorted and shook themselves as if they had just awakened
from a disturbing dream. As one, they turned and charged back into the
forest.

"Let us go care for our people, my love," said Dove.

"Always," said River.

Thaddeus remained perfectly still as the Riders moved among his men,
putting those who clung precariously to life out of their misery. He had
tucked himself under Wilson's dead body, glad that the blood that flowed
from the Hunter had washed over Thaddeus's face, further obscuring his
features. *Odysseus, we cannot be recognized.*

When the Riders turned away, he crawled quickly, silently, through
the bodies to the tree line, where he staggered back to their empty camp.
Thaddeus dropped to his knees before one of the rain catcher barrels.
First he drank thirstily and then he splashed water over his face and body
as he decided what he should do next.

"We will go south, Odysseus, and winter at one of the Wind Riders' abandoned campsites until spring. When the pass reopens, we will
enter the mountains again and retrace that terrible journey Death so
stupidly took us on. We will go home to the Tribe of the Trees. I know
how to cure the sloughing sickness. There must still be some Tribesmen
alive. They will, of course, be eager for leadership. We will have our
own Tribe yet, Odysseus! . . ." When Thaddeus paused in his mono-

logue to drink from the barrel again, he heard something that had his ears pricking.

Slowly, he moved away from the barrel as he peered around him at the silent camp. The God's campfire still burned, though the flames were low and sputtering, but still they caught the eyes of the canines who watched Thaddeus from the shadows.

Thaddeus felt fear shiver down his twisted spine as every canine who had been bonded to a mutated Tribesman approached him. They padded around Thaddeus as they growled menacingly and tightened their circle.

Thaddeus stood. He attempted to straighten fully—to stand like a man—but the change within him had gone too far, though even with a bent spine he stood taller than any of the canines. He glared at them. "Why are you still living? Your Companions are dead. You should have followed them!"

The canines, Terriers and Shepherds, continued to growl softly as they crept ever closer to him.

Panic skittered down his spine to lodge in his gut. He made a shooing motion with his hand and silently cursed the fact that he had left his crossbow on the killing field. "Go on! Follow your Companions in death or just go! You are nothing to me and I am nothing to you."

"Oh, but you are wrong, Thaddeus. And though it is far from the first time you have been wrong, this *will* be the last time."

Thaddeus whirled around to face the Rider with the sickeningly familiar voice and scent. He sneered at her. "I see you, traitorous bitch."

Ralina shook her head. She held a crossbow loosely in the crook of her arm. From astride a huge black stallion she looked down at him. Her Companion, Bear, stood alert beside the horse. He, too, growled menacingly at Thaddeus.

"Let me be very clear before you die," Ralina said. "You are the only traitor left alive this day. You betrayed your Companion and caused his death. You betrayed your Tribe and caused their death. You betrayed the Hunters and Warriors who were foolish enough to follow you and caused their deaths. You are a shallow, selfish, evil little man . . ." She paused then and snorted. "Though you aren't even truly a man anymore. Why could you have not been satisfied with what you had?"

Thaddeus bared his teeth and hurled his answer at her. "Because I was entitled to more!"

Ralina sighed. "No, you were not, but that is something men like you will never understand. You should have been put out of your misery years ago." Her gaze went from Thaddeus to the canines who encircled him, still growling. "Do not do this. It will taint your spirits forever. You have already survived so, so much. Leave him to me and choose to begin your lives anew without the poison this violence will bring you. We will welcome you to our Pack, our Herd. You will have Companions again who will love and care for you as you deserve."

The canines stared at Ralina. As one, they stopped growling and sat on their haunches, watching her closely.

"What now, you bitch?" Thaddeus spit hatred at Ralina. "Will you drive me before you to the Wind Riders so that they can pass judgment on me—*me* who should be ruling this world!"

"No," Ralina said. "I am going to kill you." She lifted her crossbow and fired.

The arrow embedded itself in his throat. Clawing at his neck, Thaddeus fell to the ground and gasped for air as blood filled his mouth. His eyesight began to gray and then blacken. And then through the encroaching darkness Thaddeus saw his Odysseus! The little Terrier padded toward him. Thaddeus tried to call out to him—tried to reach out to him—but the canine stopped at the ring of Terriers and Shepherds who silently watched as life slipped from him. Odysseus sat beside the other Companionless canines and stared at Thaddeus.

Come to me, my Odysseus! Thaddeus's mind screamed the words at his Companion.

Odysseus met his gaze. *I have not been your Odysseus for a very, very long time.*

Thaddeus's face contorted into an expression of disbelief. The dog-man's last thought as he stared at his lost Companion and exhaled his final breath was, *I have been wrong?*

Mari felt good. Really good! That shocked her, but apparently not as much as it shocked her family and friends, because as she moved across the battlefield, triaging the wounded and dying with Sora and the Herd's healers, Griffin and Mikayla, people continually asked her if she was sure she was okay, and shouldn't she be resting.

Nik, who like Rigel would not leave her side, had begun to answer for her.

"She is well. The Great Goddess's touch healed her."

Mari smiled to herself. *The Great Goddess's touch also almost killed me.* But "almost" was the most important word in that sentence, and Mari was more than content. She was ecstatic. *I am alive!* Since the Goddess had awakened briefly in the nursery, Mari had believed she would never have children. She would never grow old with Nik. She would not see her Pack thrive on the Wind Rider Plains. Now that she was free of that nightmare, Mari felt as if the whole world sparkled with possibility.

They hadn't lost one Wind Rider or Pack member. Yes, there were injuries. Many injuries. And anyone bitten or scratched by the mutant men had probably been infected with the skin-sloughing disease, but Mari knew she and Sora could Wash that from their people and rid this beautiful land of that horrible pestilence. She shivered as she remembered the pain and despair that came with the illness. *Never again will it poison our world.*

"Are you okay? Should you rest?" Nik touched her arm gently.

She smiled at her mate. "I am perfectly well. Just remembering."

Nik pulled her into his arms. "I wish I could take the memory of the past day away from you, but I'm pretty sure Ralina is going to be telling ballads about *Magnificent Mari* for years to come."

"Oh, Goddess, no! Is she really calling me Magnificent Mari?"

"You can ask her for yourself." Nik gestured with his chin. "Here she comes."

Mari turned in his arms to see Ralina astride Bard, who trotted from the forest into the clearing. "What's that following her?"

Mari felt the shock jolt through his body before he answered her in a voice filled with awe, "Those are the Companions of the Tribesmen who followed Thaddeus."

"But, they're all dead, aren't they?" Mari asked.

"They are." Nik took her hand. "Come with me, please. I may need you to speak with them."

"Of course!"

Mari and Nik hurried to meet Ralina and the canines who padded behind Bard and Bear. As the unusual group made their way through the dead bodies of the mutants to the center of the clearing, they drew the attention of the Riders and Pack members. Those who were able joined with Mari and Nik.

Bard halted when they reached the center of the field—not far from Mari's bloody stake—but the canines did not halt. Instead, they scattered, as if each had a special mission to complete.

One blond Terrier Mari recognized right away as Spud, the Terrier who had kept Rigel's secret, trotted just past Mari to where Dawn was standing beside Echo as she spoke with River. The Terrier reached Dawn and pressed his face against the front of her leg while he whined softly.

Instantly, Dawn crouched and took the canine's face between her hands. "Oh, Spud, yes, of course I will accept you! Gladly! Joyously! Echo and I will be yours!" Then the retired Lead Mare Rider scooped up the little Terrier in her arms and laughed as he licked her face.

"Bloody beetle balls, Spud just Chose Dawn!" Nik said.

"Nik, look!" Mari pointed. Scores of canines spread out among the Herd and Pack. Every time one of the canines stopped, he or she Chose a new Companion until the battleground became a celebration of life as joy chased away the last of the ghosts of the dead.

Nik put his arm around Mari and she leaned into him. "I do not think I have ever been so happy." His voice broke as tears washed his cheeks.

"I think we will have a lot more joy to come," said Mari. She turned in his arms and stepped fully into his embrace.

"Whatever is to come, we will be together. Always and forever, my beautiful Moon Woman. I will have your back always and forever," said Nik.

As the canines howled in celebration of the new Companions and the horses neighed with them, Mari kissed Nik.

Against her closed eyes, for just a moment, Mari reconnected with the Goddess of Life. She could even see the Goddess, deep within the womb of the earth, resting in the arms of the beautiful God of Death.

The Goddess's words, spoken in Leda's familiar voice, drifted through her mind. *I knew the girl would survive, for the only other force in the world stronger than life or death is love. Isn't that right, beloved?*

Death touched her face gently. *It is, indeed, My love.* Their lips met and the God of Death willingly sank into Her embrace as they began to dream anew.

EPILOGUE

It's coming along really well." Sora sat on a sun-bleached log that rested along the sandy bank of Pawhuska Creek and gazed up at the big nests Nik, O'Bryan, Wilkes, Davis, and a large group of Herd carpenters were almost finished building on the ridge overlooking the crystal creek. "But I'm still not sure about living up there in the trees." Sora shivered delicately. "Being so far aboveground just doesn't seem right."

Mari laughed. "You should've seen the nests the Tribe of the Trees built in their tall pines. They had to be at least fifty feet above the forest floor."

"No thank you." Sora shivered again and little Chloe jumped up on the log and licked her Companion's face. "I'm fine, sweet girl, but I am going to work on convincing O'Bryan to stay in our cozy little burrow." Sora jerked her chin at the rocky ridge below the trees where the Earth Walkers, with the help of Herdmembers, had expanded the caves that had formed naturally there.

"You may change your mind this summer," said Mari as she tickled Rigel's ears. "River says it gets pretty hot here, and there is always a nice breeze up there." She pointed at the trees.

Sora fluttered her fingers at the clear creek. "It's nice here by the water, too, and I am not in danger of falling to my death."

467

Mari grinned. "I think you're exaggerating. You know O'Bryan would never put you in any danger."

"Sure, unless it's *imagined* danger, which is what he calls my fear of heights." Then she turned to face Mari. "Hey, what was it you wanted to talk with me about? Surely O'Bryan hasn't put you up to trying to convince me to live like a bird?"

"No, it's nothing like that. I want to share—" Mari's words broke off as she burped loudly and then grimaced, gagged, and rushed a few feet away to vomit into the sand and rocks. "Ugh." Mari spit in disgust and covered what had been her breakfast with sand. "I really hate doing that. I have to rinse out my mouth."

Sora went with Mari to the creek and watched silently as her friend bent, scooped a handful of water, and rinsed out her mouth.

"Are you sick?" Sora asked her.

"No, not at all." Mari stood and wiped her mouth with her sleeve and motioned for them to return to sitting on the log before she said, "I'm pregnant. That's what I wanted to tell you."

Sora stared at her for several long breaths before she laughed joyously and told her best friend, "As am I!"

"What? Truthfully?"

"Truthfully!" Sora assured her. "Does Nik know yet?"

"No, I'm going to tell him today, but something made me want to tell you first, and now I know what that something was." Mari's face glowed with contentment. "Our daughters are going to grow up together."

"Best friends," Sora said.

"Best friends," Mari agreed. "Does O'Bryan know yet?"

Sora's smile was radiant. "No. I'm going to tell him today, but something made me want to tell you first."

The friends looped their arms together. "This is magick," said Mari.

"Absolutely," agreed Sora.

A whirlwind of sound swirled around them, making Mari and Sora laugh together as they watched eight fat kittens sprint along the bank of the creek. They were being chased by several of Mariah and Cammy's half-grown puppies, who barked riotously with pretend aggression. Behind the noisy group, little Cammyman raced after them, huffing and yapping.

"Cammy is such a little father," said Mari. "You see Bast and Rufus are nowhere to be seen."

"Well, sure, because they know Cammy won't let those kittens—or the puppies—get in too much trouble." Mari motioned to the far bank of the creek where weanling horses were grazing on tender clover. "I cannot wait until it is time for the Choosing. It's going to be so interesting. I really hope some of the younger members of the Pack are Chosen."

"I hear Jaxom is going to be presented as a Candidate for a yearling," said Sora. "I do hope he gets picked."

Mari smiled. "April would like that."

Sora raised a brow. "Really? The two of them?"

Mari nodded. "Definitely. Deinos told me."

The whirlwind of kittens and puppies changed direction and ran straight at Mari and Sora, jumping over the log on either side of them as the two Moon Women laughed. Bringing up the rear, Cammy paused at the log long enough to greet them before he raced off after the pack of young ones.

Sora snorted another laugh. "I think even Cammy will be thrilled when those kittens start choosing their Companions."

"I wish they'd hurry," said Mari.

Sora shrugged. "I wish so, too, but Antreas says they won't choose until they're a lot older."

"That's not what Bast says. She thinks they'll start Choosing soon," said Mari.

Sora met her gaze. "Are you still talking with all the Companion animals?"

Mari nodded. "Not all at once, but yes. I think I always will. Talking with them keeps me tethered."

Sora scooped Chloe off the log and hugged her close. "I can understand that."

Beside Mari, Rigel barked in agreement, and Mari kissed the top of his head.

"Sora! There you are!" O'Bryan ran up to them. He was cradling Cubby in his arms. The wolverine kit had finally shed his baby fur and was now a beautiful deep brown with white accents around his face and chest and down his back. O'Bryan's kind face was flushed with happiness. "I have the best news in the world to tell you!"

Sora looked up at him and his Cubby and smiled. "Really? The *best* news in the world? This I have to hear."

"Me too," said Mari.

O'Bryan lifted the young wolverine as if he was a trophy. "Cubby spoke to me! I can hear him!"

Sora reached out and took Cubby from O'Bryan and kissed him on his little black nose. "That *is* wonderful news." Then she and Mari shared a look before Sora added, "I also have some news that is pretty wonderful."

"Really? I can't wait to hear it." O'Bryan grinned.

"I'll leave you two to talk. I need to find Nik and share news of my own." Mari winked at Sora, who returned her wink.

She stood and with Rigel wagging happily beside her Mari headed to the ridge to find Nik and tell him what she considered to be the best news in the world, and as she did Mari imagined the future, filled with joy and family and laughter, spreading out before her, sparkling like Wind Rider crystals.

ACKNOWLEDGMENTS

Thank you to my team at Macmillan for producing another gorgeous book—most especially the art department! You have outdone yourselves.

A giant thank-you to my awesome agent, Rebecca Scherer, for not giving up on this book.

I love the gorgeous chapter illustrations completed by the very talented Sabine Stangenberg. Thank you, Sabine!

Again, I appreciate the passion and loyalty of my readers. This book is from my heart to yours.